EVERYTHING
must
change

EVERYTHING must change

GRAHAME DAVIES

seren

Seren is the book imprint of
Poetry Wales Press Ltd
57 Nolton Street, Bridgend, CF31 3AE, Wales
www.seren-books.com

ISBN 978-1-85411-451-8

A CIP record for this title is available from
the British Library.

This book is a work of fiction. The characters
and incidents portrayed are the work of the author's
imagination. Any other resemblance to actual persons,
living or dead, is entirely coincidental.

Cover image: Musée Rodin, Paris
Photograph by Matt Thomas

Everything Must Change is a translation and extension by the author of
Rhaid y Bopeth Newid, published by Gomer, 2004.

The publisher works with the financial assistance
of the Welsh Books Council.

Printed in Plantin by Creative Print and Design, Wales

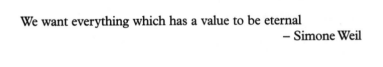

We want everything which has a value to be eternal
                                                    – Simone Weil

The Soldier

The road through Neufchateau was not beautiful. But, to the young soldier marching with his company through the village this morning in the shade of the poplar trees, beautiful was how it seemed. He had never expected to see this road, or any road, again.

The hot air was full of the dust scuffed up by the soldiers' boots. It was late August, and the third summer of the Great War was nearing its end. Neufchateau was so close to the front that the villagers paid no particular attention to another group of servicemen returning from Verdun. At least these had managed to return, which was more than could be said for hundreds of thousands of others the French generals had thrown into the crucible of that ruined city on the Meuse.

The soldier detached himself from the column. Standing at the roadside as the rest of the company marched past, he pulled a piece of paper from his uniform pocket, and checked the address written on it. Yes, this was the right place. He looked up at the house across the way. It was large and double-fronted, with a wrought-iron veranda overlooking the main road. The soldier went up the worn wooden steps and rang the bell.

The noise of the marching company made it difficult to hear if the bell had rung. As he waited for an answer, he turned to watch the unit march past. They would be spending their two days' leave in town. But he had received permission to spend the time at this address.

Turning back to the door, he could see, through the patterned glass, two figures approaching down the hallway. The door opened, and the soldier was greeted by a dark-haired couple in early middle age, the husband wore a smart grey suit, and had a well-trimmed little moustache; the woman too was immaculately dressed, and had an air of poise and self-possession. They welcomed him in, smiling. The door closed behind him, shutting out the sound of the company tramping on by.

In the hallway, the soldier looked around at the spotless furniture. The floor tiles gleamed under his dusty boots. This was a much more prosperous home than he was used to entering. He had almost forgotten that things could be so cared-for. He instantly felt uncomfortably untidy and unclean. But his host, taking his guest's kitbag from him and leaning it against the hall stand, was keen to put him at his ease.

'M'sieur,' he said. 'Permit me to introduce the family Weil.'

There was a hint of something foreign in his accent. What was it exactly? The young soldier was a long way from his home in the far south of the Languedoc, and he had come across many different types of Frenchman by now, not to mention the colonial troops with their strangely accented French, but still he could not begin to guess exactly where his host's accent belonged.

At the entrance to the living room, two young children were watching him silently; a boy of around ten, alert and bright-looking, and a thin girl of perhaps seven, her pale face shadowed by a cloud of dark hair. Behind them, through the patio doors, was a sunlit garden. His host was speaking.

'I am Doctor Bernard Weil,' said the householder, with mock solemnity. 'Physician in the army of France, although just for today, as you see, my country is managing without my humble services. This is my wife, Madame Selma Weil, officer commanding the home front in all matters – except medical matters!'

He and his wife exchanged glances at what was clearly some long-running family joke.

'And these are your "godparents",' he indicated the children. 'André, the genius of the family, and Simone, the little dreamer.'

The soldier thought the girl looked slightly abashed at the descriptions. But he wasn't sure. Probably she was just shy at meeting this uniformed stranger. Dr Weil was continuing, more formally and more seriously now.

'You will already know the children from their letters and their gifts.'

The soldier nodded, smiling at the children.

Dr Weil went on: 'Well, we are honoured to have your company. Please, consider this now your home.'

The soldier thanked him. He and Simone exchanged a shy smile.

●○●

Jayne

'Meinwen, please. Just a touch of make-up.'

Jayne hated this routine. Every time Meinwen came in for studio interviews – which was often – she had to cajole and coax her to put on a bit of powder. Jayne thought Meinwen's reluctance was something about hating pretence. Whatever it was, it was a blasted nuisance.

'Just a spot, Meinwen, come on.'

Jayne was a pro. No one was going on *Wales on Wednesday* with an unhealthy shine on their face. She had made up princes and presidents, filmstars and ex-jailbirds. If some of them were occasionally reluctant, there was always a key that would persuade them. Flattery almost always worked. But some, like Meinwen, sitting unsmiling in the green room, needed more subtlety than that. Meinwen cared no more about her physical appearance then she did about the lives of the stars in the copy of *Marie Claire* which was lying unread on the coffee table in front of her. For her, there was only the cause. The cause, thought Jayne.

She squatted alongside Meinwen and lowered her voice to a comradely confidentiality.

'Meinwen,' she said, 'If you looked your best, it might actually help the campaign. You don't want people to dismiss the message for the sake of a touch of foundation.'

Meinwen looked at her properly for the first time, searching Jayne's eyes for the kindred spark of belief. Jayne found the candour of the dark, serious gaze as unnerving as that of a child's, but she forced herself to hold it, and tried to project a look of significance into her own eyes, hoping it would show through her new tinted contacts. After long seconds, she saw Meinwen complete her own version of retinal scanning, and

9

accept Jayne as unquestioningly as a computer given the right password. With inner relief, she saw Meinwen nod.

She motioned Meinwen through into the make-up room chair, reached for her compact, and touched the clear, pale cheeks with beige chemicals. Cheekbones to die for, she thought. But surely, just a touch too prominent? And those candid, appraising eyes, didn't they draw some of their depth from the faint shadow beneath them? The girl was clearly too thin for her own good. But since when did Meinwen think of her own good? Women's rights, child slavery, fair trade, nuclear disarmament, asylum seekers, 'Stop the War'... What hadn't she campaigned for? And the language of course, always the precious, threatened Welsh language, the issue she and her fellow guests would be discussing tonight, the issue which provided the constant foundation to Meinwen's rainbow palette of causes.

How long had she been campaigning? Jayne had been in this job for 15 years, and she could remember Meinwen from then. Her straight black hair in that same shapeless boyish cut, the same fits-where-it-touches sweater, the same ugly hiking shoes. Yes, the very same shoes, she was sure. The girl hadn't an ounce of dress sense. But she was no girl really, now, was she? How old was she? She looked about 25, but she must be pushing forty. In the days when she had led parties of students daubing English-only roadsigns with green paint, the English-language newspapers had dubbed her 'The Green Goddess'. The Welsh-language newspapers, for once with less alliterative instinct, but greater accuracy, had called her '*Y Forwyn Werdd*', 'The Green Virgin'. The name had stuck. Very apt, too, thought Jayne, as she put the last touches of make-up on the immaculate cheeks of the expressionless image before her.

The Soldier

A little later that day, uniform brushed, boots polished, hands washed and hair combed, the soldier sat at dinner with the family. He tried not to stare as the maid brought the food to the table. Never in all his life had he been waited on.

In the distance could be heard faintly the heavy artillery of the battle around Verdun, many miles to the north. For months, the Germans had been pressing on that vulnerable salient with the declared intention of bleeding the French army white. The colossal casualty figures among the soldier's fellow-defenders seemed to be proving the German strategy right.

'So. Will Verdun still stand without you there?' Dr Weil asked.

'It will stand, Doctor. We'll never let it fall. Not after so much sacrifice.'

Dr Weil nodded, quietly, allowing his guest the opportunity to continue. He did so.

'Do you know? When we went into the line, we were fifty boys, from the same town. Now there are only...'

He checked himself, glancing at the children around the table.

'Please. Continue,' said Dr Weil. 'We don't hide these things from the children. It was our choice that the family should stay together even though we're so close to the front. Madame Weil takes them to my hospital several times a week to visit the wounded.'

'Several times a *week*?'

The soldier had visited a military hospital once, to see a wounded comrade. Once. He'd vowed that only if wounded himself would he ever go to one of those places again. And he hoped he'd be killed rather than end up like some of the wretches he'd seen there. Several times a week?

Dr Weil did not seem surprised at his guest's alarm; he spoke quietly and matter-of-factly: 'Well, there are so many new admissions, and many of the patients don't... stay very long. So if we don't call fairly regularly, some of the patients would never get a visit at all.'

'We take them presents, M'sieur. Fruit and cakes.' It was Simone, speaking for the first time.

'Yes,' said Dr Weil, turning to her. 'The men like those, my angel, don't they?'

He turned back to the soldier. 'We just hope,' he said, 'that because the children will know about suffering, they will appreciate love.'

The soldier nodded. Front-line chaplains sometimes spoke like that. Now he came to think of it, there was more than a little of the pastor about this urbane army medic. They must be a religious family, he thought; devout lay Catholics like the family of Thérèse of Lisieux, whose story he had been told time and again by the nuns in the orphanage where he was raised. He'd have to watch his tongue.

He sought for a safer topic.

'How long are you on leave for, yourself, Doctor?' he asked.

Dr Weil looked a little uncomfortable. The children exchanged knowing looks.

'Well, I'm not actually on leave,' he said, rather hesitantly.

The soldier was puzzled. If Dr Weil was on active service, how could he be enjoying all the comforts of a normal domestic life? He was sure that wasn't the usual practice. Perhaps he had received special permission. Perhaps there were different rules for doctors.

'I didn't know soldiers, even officers, could live with their families,' he asked, with genuine curiosity.

'Ah... yes, that's quite true,' said Dr Weil, shifting a little in his seat. 'Yes, quite true. In fact, the regulations specifically state that they can't. So, I am... how can I put it...? I am, technically, a visitor here tonight, like yourself.'

The soldier absorbed this for a moment, then nodded his understanding. His host clearly had his own unique attitude to military discipline.

'Of course,' Dr Weil continued. 'I do have lodgings of my own nearby, and I do stay there. Occasionally.'

'He means when his chief officer is visiting,' said Simone happily. Clearly, the family all enjoyed this shared intrigue.

'I'm sure I can rely on your understanding and your discretion in this matter, M'sieur?' the doctor said.

'Of course.'

The soldier was about to try another subject of conversation. But the maid had set the last dish on the table. The meal was ready.

'Now! The food!' said Dr Weil.

The soldier, thinking this an indication they were to say grace, crossed himself and bowed his head. There was silence. Then more silence. After a moment or two, Madame Weil gave a slight cough. The soldier opened his eyes a crack, then looked around him, discomfited.

Madame Weil smiled. Her eyes were filled with a genuine concern. 'I'm so sorry. I should have told you. We're Jewish. I didn't mean to embarrass you.'

Dr Weil leant slightly towards him across the table and said, with mock confidentiality: 'You didn't want ham anyway, did you?'

They all laughed, more with relief than at the weak joke.

'My wife and I are both of Jewish background,' Dr Weil went on, as he passed the beef round. 'But we don't practice any religion as a family, Jewish or Christian. We're all freethinkers.'

'And they're all quite mad.' It was the maid who spoke, bringing an extra bottle of wine. She was smiling. 'Don't take any notice of their crazy ideas, M'sieur,' she said to the soldier.

'Marie and I have some interesting debates,' laughed Dr Weil. 'We disagree about almost everything. She's a devout Catholic, and a conservative, and I'm an atheist and a radical.'

'Radical? You can fetch your own wine then,' said Marie with a wink at the soldier as she left.

Dr Weil smiled. He raised his voice so Marie could still hear.

'Ah, perhaps I'd better postpone the revolution until after dinner.'

Marie's voice came back.

'No, Doctor, you should have the courage of your convictions!'

Laughing, Dr Weil turned back to the table.

'Now. *Bon appetit!*'

●○●

Jayne

Useless to ask Meinwen to smarten up her clothes. Getting the make-up on was a major victory in itself. At least those horrid shoes would be out of sight under the desk on this set.

Who else was on tonight? Jayne looked back into the green room, where two other figures were now seated. They were both regulars. There was Sir Anthony Thomas, AM. He was absorbed peacefully in the crossword and didn't notice her. It was the *Daily Telegraph* crossword, of course, as befitted the Conservative group leader in the National Assembly for Wales. The 'Group Captain' the press called him, playfully, thanks to his years in the Royal Air Force. Then there was John Sayle, the newspaper columnist. While Sir Anthony had natural repose, Sayle seemed to have inherent agitation; he was shuffling through the papers and magazines on the coffee table, scanning and discarding. He finally selected one newspaper and sat back. As he did so, he saw Jayne looking in his direction, and, noticing Meinwen leaving the chair in front of the mirror, he threw down his paper and stepped quickly over to the make-up room.

'*Esgusodwch fi*,' murmured Meinwen, trying to slip out by him as unobtrusively as possible.

'No – excusio me!' parodied Sayle, stepping aside ostentatiously to let her through. She passed him without thanks, her dark eyes downcast.

'Bloody hell, Jayne,' Sayle said, as he dropped into the make-up chair. 'I've just been giving evidence at the Assembly. I had to wear some sodding translation headphones. I felt like the bloody Mekon.'

'Like the what?' asked Jayne.

'The Mekon.'

Jayne shook her head.

'Haven't you ever heard of Dan Dare – Pilot of the Future?' Sayle's voice was becoming testy.

'Sorry, Mr Sayle, I haven't.'

He muttered something under his breath. Then, with forced patience, he explained: 'The Mekon was an alien. In a comic strip. Dan Dare's enemy. He was green. And he wore headphones.'

'I see.'

'Never mind. You're probably too young to remember.'

He made it sound as if this was Jayne's fault.

Jayne patted the powder into the deep lines on Sayle's face. How old was he, then? He must be in his mid-fifties, but looked older.

'You'll have to have an interpreter to talk to Meinwen soon, Jayney', Sayle said, loud enough to be sure his tobacco-deepened voice could be heard in the green room. 'The Welsh Language Board won't like people like us making her speak the hated Saxon tongue.'

Couldn't he keep still? He seemed to be perpetually scanning for an audience, or for something to comment on. Jayne was having difficulty getting the powder on evenly. And, fair play, she thought, noticing the sheen of perspiration near his thinning hairline, Sayle needed it a sight more than the others did.

But she was almost done. She stood back for a moment to check. Sayle took this as a sign she had finished, and stood up, pulling the cape from his neck and pushing it into her hand. For a moment, she thought of asking him to sit down again, but he was already on his way out.

'Thanks, love,' he said. 'I'll make way for Wing Commander Flak now.'

'Ready for take off,' he called to Sir Anthony as he went back through to the green room.

Meinwen

Meinwen was sitting there silently. Disdaining the magazines, and lost in thought, she was looking down at her shoes. She loved those shoes. Her parents had bought them for her when she graduated, about eighteen years ago. They had thought she would be going backpacking after finishing college. The shoes had cost her parents a fortune even then. They were the best that the hiking shop – in a mountainous area with a lot of hiking shops – could offer. 'They'll last you a lifetime, *cariad*," her father had said to her proudly, as she tried them on for the first time. Well, it was a bit early for a final judgement on that, she thought now, but after nearly two decades it looked like Dad might well be proved right.

Meinwen had never worn the shoes for backpacking. But they had come with her on nocturnal missions to remove offending roadsigns. They had marched on demonstrations. Their soles had been kicked by frustrated policemen during sit-down protests. They had had their laces removed in police stations when Meinwen was taken to the cells, to be solemnly handed back to her again when she was bailed. Likewise, they had been kept in prison lockers with the rest of her own clothes for weeks, sometimes months. They were scuffed but still sound. She loved the memories they evoked, she loved the way that in a city studio like this, they showed that she belonged in the country, and most of all, she loved them because they reminded her of her parents' love for her: costly, tough and, through everything, scratched, stained and battered, but never broken.

Sayle sat down familiarly next to Meinwen, who ignored him, still looking down.

'Cheer up, love,' he said. 'It might never happen.'

Then he laughed.

'Except, of course, in your case, it will!'

The Soldier

The main course was over, and the soldier had quickly found himself at ease with the Weil family. They had listened with real interest to his experiences in the front line. Madame Weil seemed to have inexhaustible – although slightly exhausting – curiosity about his circumstances, and those of his friends, while the Doctor seemed to have an equally endless supply of stories and anecdotes; many of them, to the soldier's surprise, the kind of Jewish joke he would not have expected a Jew to tell.

Marie brought in the dessert: a bowl of simple mixed fruits. Madame Weil ladled the mixture into the individual bowls.

'They're from our own orchard here,' she said. 'That was one of the reasons we rented this house. We were so lucky to find it. Bernard has had to move around so much with the war. We hope we'll be able to stay here for a long while.'

'I'll tell the Ministry how important these fruits are for the war effort,' said Dr Weil. 'Then they'll be sure to keep me here.'

'And I'll tell my company that we have one more reason to hold the line at Verdun,' the soldier smiled.

The family passed round the sugar bowl, and each of them sprinkled a small amount on their dessert. The soldier followed suit, then turned to Simone at his side.

'Shall I put some on for you too?' he asked.

Simone looked up at him.

'Do they let you have sugar at the front, M'sieur?'

'Well, no. Not as a ration. We manage to get some sometimes, though.'

He was about to move the spoon towards her, when she said.

'Well, I'm afraid I can't have any then. But thank you very much for offering, M'sieur.'

The soldier, his spoonful of sugar suspended, looked over at Simone's parents.

'Simone has refused to eat sweet things for more than a year,' her father explained. 'She says if it's not in the soldiers' rations, then she can't eat it herself.'

'I see...' said the soldier. He replaced the spoon in the bowl, and passed it across to André with a touch of apprehension. But the boy accepted it happily and sprinkled a liberal amount on his stewed apples.

'Don't worry, M'sieur,' André said. 'My sister's mad.'

●○●

Jayne

Last one for tonight, thought Jayne, as Sir Anthony walked in, smiling, folding his *Telegraph* as he came.

'Good evening, Jayne.'

'Good evening, Sir Anthony.'

Straight from Central Casting: that was how one of her colleagues had described Sir Anthony. It was easy for her to see why. He was an old-school Tory, not only an ex-military man but a landowner too.

She had met him first about ten years previously when he had just left the airforce and entered public life during the final years of the last Conservative government. She recalled how angry the opposition parties had been then when he had been given the chairmanship of a big quango. She remembered how coolly he had dealt with the whole thing when he came on programmes like this to answer angry complaints of favouritism.

At the time, it had only been for English-language programmes like tonight's that he had come into studio. But since being elected to the National Assembly in 1999, he had started taking part in Welsh-language programmes too: first pre-records, then, as his fluency grew, live shows. Apparently, he had learned Welsh as a child on his parents' farm in north Wales, and had brushed it up once he realised it would be a political asset.

'Now, Jayne,' he said pleasantly as he sat down. 'If I remember rightly, your daughter was sitting her GCSEs when I saw you last. How did she get on?'

'Five A Stars, four As and a B.'

'Excellent! You must be very pleased.'

'Chuffed to bits,' said Jayne. Sir Anthony always made it sound as if he had a real interest in her. Perhaps he did.

She dabbed the sponge across his forehead, and he closed his eyes. He was an attractive man, there was no doubt about that, thought Jayne. Her eyes flicked to his ring finger. Empty. She tried to think what she had heard about his marital status. Yes, she remembered: his wife had died, comparatively young. Cancer or something. No children. He could only be about fifty at the most.

He opened his eyes again. Jayne resumed the safe theme of education.

'I can't help thinking these exams must be getting easier, though,' she said. 'I struggled to get eight passes.'

'Ah, Jayne. That was under the Tories. We didn't believe in making things too easy, you know!'

Jayne smiled. She had finished her powdering. Scarcely necessary in Sir Anthony's case. However hot the lights, however fierce the debate, he never seemed to look anything other than cool. She looked at the clock. Ten minutes to airtime.

Bernard Weil

After dinner, Simone silently took the soldier's hand and took him out into the garden where the evening sun was still bright. Dr and Madame Weil watched from the patio. The soldier would have only this one night with them before he had to rejoin his unit.

Simone and André had been writing to the soldier for many months, after making contact with him through a charity which put young soldiers with no families in touch with volunteer 'godparents' on the home front. But this was their first meeting. For Simone, as intense as any young St Thérèse, the soldier had become the focus of her passionate concern. The rumble and rumour and uncertainty of the war, which had formed the background to her childhood ever since she could remember, had simplified itself into a focus on one imperilled individual. This evening, she and the soldier had become friends.

Dr Weil could see that from the moment Simone had declined his offer of sugar, the soldier had adored her. Simone's conscience certainly seemed unusually developed for a child of her age, he thought; much more so than could be explained even by her liberal upbringing. The previous year, when her aunt had given her a magnificent chocolate Easter egg, she had simply said 'I don't like luxury'. She had sent the egg to her 'godson' at the front. Inordinately alive to the hardships and sorrows of others, Simone had the ability to evoke the most protective tenderness in everyone – in everyone, that is, who didn't find her insufferable, as he knew some, like her aunt, did. It was clear, however, that the soldier fell into the former category. Now, child and soldier walked hand-in-hand under the trees in the hazy evening sunshine.

Dr Weil thought about those hands: one pair which was used to handling guns and bayonets, and the other which had never held anything more dangerous than a fountain pen, and even that with some discomfort. Simone was a delicate child, and her hands were disproportionately small and slightly misshapen. Not that this prevented her from writing, endlessly, precociously: stories, poems, theories, and, of course, letters to her soldier.

Simone and the young man sat on a garden bench in the orchard, deep in talk. The trees cast a deep shade at their feet, where the first fallen apples lay unnoticed, their skins still perfect, as yet untouched by insect or worm.

Dr Weil put his arms around his wife and held her close. In the distance, the guns were a low thunder.

Jonathan Rees

Over the years, the studio format of *Wales on Wednesday* had become a familiar ritual to Jonathan Rees. For a 'one-plus-three' like tonight's, he would do a brief piece to camera outlining the topic, and would then walk over and seat himself among the panellists. A question to each in turn; a minute or so to answer, and with half a dozen questions, a half-hour was soon filled. Occasionally, if he was lucky, the panellists would strike sparks off one another, and there would be a bit of unscripted verbal sparring. Tonight was a fair bet for that, he thought, with Sayle and Meinwen on the bill. How long was there to airtime? Five minutes. He pondered the likely dynamics of tonight's guests. They were a good mix.

Meinwen, now sitting there impassive behind the desk, would represent the radical leading edge of the Welsh-speaking community, always pushing for further rights and concessions. No one could better exemplify the tireless, bloodless, Gandhian activism which, over the years, had forced one institution after another to capitulate. Thanks to people like her, official bilingualism was now enshrined in law, and Welsh-medium schools had sprung up all over Wales.

And not before time, Rees thought. He recalled his own membership of *Y Mudiad*, 'The Movement', as the group styled itself. It had been brief, a long time ago, and on paper only, but it had been sincere. True, his acceptance to Oxford had diverted him permanently into respectability. But although he felt his lifestyle, bank balance, clothes and accent every year to be further from the activists' world, his heart was really still with campaigners like Meinwen.

On set tonight, he'd be careful to address her formally as 'Meinwen Jones'. But she was simply 'Meinwen' to everyone else in Wales. Or rather, his journalistic objectivity forced him to correct himself, she was 'Meinwen' to everyone who spoke Welsh – maybe one in every five – and to a smaller penumbra of others who could not speak the 'language of heaven' but who followed its affairs. However, Rees thought, the sad fact was that the rest of the population knew her not at all, by any name; and they cared no more about the struggle which was for her a matter of life or death than they did about the struggle of some obscure tribal activist defending his Amazonian habitat. In fact, he reflected, the majority of them probably cared a good deal less.

Sayle meanwhile, currently fidgeting with his radio-mic, was the self-appointed spokesman of that majority – the 'vast' majority Sayle would call it; in his newspaper column, he never seemed to allow that noun out except when escorted by that reassuring adjective. He had become all the more vociferous, and all the more inventively eloquent, now that a century of decline in the numbers of Welsh speakers had finally been reversed. That the perilous slide to extinction had been stopped was thanks in part to the efforts of people like Meinwen. But, Rees thought with some satisfaction, it was also thanks to people like himself who spoke the language to their children and who sent them to Welsh-medium schools.

For all his antipathy to the language, Sayle had not attacked the schools, sensing, Rees knew, that they had the active, or at least tacit, support of the majority – the 'vast' majority even – of English speakers. But on another point he was relentlessly critical – the Welsh-speaking areas of the north and west, whose defenders he routinely pilloried as racists, an accusation Rees suspected that Sayle knew perfectly well was unfair, although irresistibly effective. Rees remembered with irritation how Sayle invariably spoke of those areas as places where Welsh was 'still' spoken – the word 'still' was attached by him unfailingly to the practice of speaking Welsh, like a mark on a tree due for felling.

Time and again, Rees had seen Sayle justify his views by deftly deploying the rhetoric of social hardship as though he himself was fresh from the coalface or a hunger march. In fact, he knew, Sayle's father had been a librarian, and Sayle himself had lived in a comfortable Cardiff suburb for the last quarter of a century. But this seemed to have done nothing to reduce the ferocity of Sayle's loyalty to the socialist valleys of his youth, a pristine vision he would not allow any more recent acquaintance with those communities to pollute. God, couldn't he leave that radio-mic alone? Two minutes to air.

As for the third panellist, Sir Anthony, he wouldn't lose his cool, that much was certain. Rees remembered interviewing him over that quango row. Sir Anthony hadn't turned a single silver hair, although even his best friends would have found it hard to deny he'd profited from shameless cronyism. After a few years in the post, though, even his worst enemies would have found it hard to deny he'd done the job well. He had a talent for command: chairing, delegating, deciding; he seemed to find it easy. Even though he'd lost the quango job when Labour got in and established the National Assembly, he had quickly readjusted, quietly revising his previous opposition to devolution, getting himself elected, and now leading the Assembly's minority of Tories with his customary assurance. He had a calm confidence which Rees suspected emanated not from some changeless conviction, but from the faultless, endlessly readjusting inner compass of expedience.

Yes, they were a pretty good balance, those three. Pretty evenly matched. Rees practised his link for the last time. The gallery talkback in his earpiece told him to prepare for the titles. The signature music began. The red camera light was on, and the autocue words were ready to roll. The floor manager, his fingers splayed open next to the lens, started counting him in. Three, two, one. On the air.

●○●

Selma Weil

A few days later, Simone and her mother drew up outside the military hospital in their taxi. The building had not been designed as a hospital; it was a large chateau which had been pressed into service as the ruinous casualty rate of the French army had filled all the country's hospitals to overflowing.

The mother and daughter got out of their taxi, carefully unloading two large bags of parcels each. They crossed into the cool of the entrance hall, and into the familiar reality of the hospital smell: antiseptic, fresh bandages, sweat. The familiar sounds too: echoing voices, hurried footsteps, rustling starched uniforms, slamming doors in corridors. These things were as much a part of Simone's upbringing as traffic noise, birdsong, or the smell of mown hay were to other children. She and her mother went upstairs to the new arrivals' ward.

The white paint on the door was scratched and dented where the constant traffic of stretchers had bumped against it. It opened onto what had once been a ballroom, but which was now a world of pain. No human being in any of the beds was whole. There were amputees, men with their heads swathed in bandages. A nurse walked past carrying a bowl of bloodied clothes. As she walked in, Madame Weil forced an expression of bright efficiency; Simone, for her part, became more silent, more attentive, her dark eyes absorbing everything. Mother and daughter took their parcels from bed to bed.

Madame Weil adopted a matter-of-fact and reassuring manner, as if it was the most natural thing in the world that she should meet these young men in these circumstances. She was tireless, unshockable, and able to be charming even here. She began with the nearest bed. The soldier looked at her dully.

'Good morning, M'sieur! We thought we would bring you a few small comforts.'

The soldier made no reply, and did not move his arms to accept the gift. Madame Weil placed the parcel on the bed clothes. Her other hand rested lightly on the soldier's upper arm.

'I am sorry to see you have suffered, M'sieur,' she said. 'But I am glad you are being so well cared for. I would like to thank you for what you and your comrades have done for France, and for children like my young daughter here.'

Still the soldier did not speak. But he turned his eyes towards Simone, who looked back at him, silently.

Madame Weil held the contact for a few moments more. Then she said quietly, 'Be well'. It was somewhere between a wish, a prayer and a command. She moved on.

And so on, from bed to bed. Each time, similar words. And each time she spoke them, they sounded as sincere as the last. They were.

Simone said nothing. She simply handed her mother the parcels from her bag. Madame Weil stopped to talk to one of the casualties, whose eyes were bandaged up. Freed from the necessity to make eye-contact as she talked, she glanced over at Simone, who was looking at the soldier in the next bed. His one pyjama sleeve was empty; the other hand was a ball of bandages. The tips of three fingers poked through. She saw Simone's hand straying, apparently involuntarily, to the bandaged limb, wanting to comfort through touch. Normally, Simone detested human contact. She had been taught the dangers of germs, and this seemed to have developed into a worrying revulsion against kissing and touching: a condition Simone called 'my disgustingness'. She recalled one occasion when a family friend had kissed her hand, and to his dismay she had burst into tears and run away to wash it. Sometimes, she even refused to touch things which had been handled by other people.

Now, though, it seemed her compassion was stronger than her repulsion; her hand moved towards the blackened fingers of the injured soldier. He looked at her through his pain, shook his head gently and moved his hand away.

Jonathan Rees

'Good evening, and welcome to *Wales on Wednesday*. We're entering dangerous territory tonight – the sometimes bitter dispute over the future of the Welsh language. I'm going to risk getting caught in the crossfire as I host a debate between three of the leading protagonists in that discussion.

'In recent months,' he went on, 'My guests have all involved themselves in the arguments over the survival of those communities in Wales where Welsh is the majority language. No one would deny that those areas are experiencing large-scale in-migration, mainly from England. No one doubts that local people find it difficult to buy houses there because of the result-ant high prices, and that they have to move away. No one doubts this is dangerous for the future of the language. The question is, what, if anything, can be done about it.'

He took his seat and introduced the guests in turn. Then each was given a few minutes to put their case.

Sir Anthony went first: 'Well, I think it has to be clear that the Welsh language is a vital and ancient part of British culture,' he said. 'My party has no problem in giving its fullest support to its survival and its development. After all, it was we who created the Welsh Fourth Channel in 1982, who introduced the Welsh Language Act in 1993 and who made Welsh compulsory in schools up to age 16. But, this question of a Property Act – that's more complicated. We'd really have to be cautious about intervening in the free market to that extent.

'The Movement is proposing that houses shouldn't be offered on the market until local people have had the first chance to buy them, and that the price should be pegged to local incomes. I believe that's not only unfair and unworkable, but that it could never get political support. The key to this question isn't through restricting people's rights to move where they wish, but through the economy. If we can strengthen the economy in these areas, raise the income levels, then local people will be able to compete in the housing market on equal terms.'

Then it was Meinwen's turn. Rees knew how grudging in reality had been the Tories' concessions to the language, and how many campaigners, Meinwen among them, had needed to be jailed before those policies for which Sir Anthony was now blithely claiming credit had finally been conceded. But those were old battles; Meinwen wasted no time on grudges, merely drove headlong for the next concession, in this case, affordable housing.

'It's all very well to say that,' she said, 'but you know very well that the main employers in those areas are tourism and agriculture, and both of them are notoriously badly-paid. It's simply a fantasy to say that somehow the economy can be improved. How exactly? How can you hope for local people on poor incomes to compete with someone who's sold their house in London and who can move to Ceredigion or Gwynedd with a huge sum of capital?'

Rees watched, impassive. In the corner of his eye, he saw Sayle lean forward, impatient to get involved. He could wait a bit longer. Meinwen was continuing.

'If you look at Denmark, they have a property law preventing their houses being bought up by Germans. So does Poland, for the same reason – because their economy isn't as strong as Germany's. Laws like this are normal throughout Europe. It's Britain that's the exception. By refusing to have such a law here, you're letting the last communities on earth where Welsh is spoken be exposed to the full force of the uncontrolled market. Which means that Welsh is going to be wiped out as a community language just so some rich people can escape the cities and enjoy a nicer view. A Property Act is a question of simple natural justice...'

'Simple natural racism.' Sayle hadn't even waited for his cue. He spoke with dismissive authority, as if the collective impatience of a nation was impelling every word. Years of conducting the public soliloquy of a newspaper column had given him the apparent conviction that his views were shared by all but fools, whom he did not suffer gladly.

'Let's be clear,' he went on, 'this Property Act business is just a front for your childish hatred of all things English, for your primitive rejection of cultural diversity, for your backward-looking, fascistic, bigoted mindset which is bent on forcing the Welsh language down everyone else's throats.

'There is no place, no place at all, in a civilised democracy, for the kind of ethnic cleansing you're proposing. We all know the results of this kind of thinking – we've seen it in Nazi Germany, in Kosovo, in Rwanda, in Darfur. Drive out the hated minority, leave the land free for you and your cronies to exploit. The privileged, exclusive, Welsh-speaking elite that you represent are the greatest threat to modern Wales, and you must not be allowed to succeed.'

As the camera turned towards Meinwen, Jonathan noticed Sayle allowing her to see a hint of a satisfied smile, hoping it would needle her to lose her cool. An accusation of racism was the new smart weapon in Welsh politics: it never missed, caused no collateral damage, and those who fired it got to feel good about themselves into the bargain. The ethnic cleansing line was absurd, of course. But he knew that the sheer pungency of those comparisons would compel many viewers into unthinking sympathy for Sayle's viewpoint.

He turned to Meinwen for her response. He did not think she would fall into Sayle's trap of becoming angry; she had long ago learned to keep her temper in situations like this. But she was certainly on the back foot now.

'That's outrageous, and you know it,' she said to Sayle. 'Those comparisons are absurd. No one's ever been killed in the name of Welsh nationalism.'

'Yet,' interjected Sayle.

'Never. Our campaigns have always been non-violent.'

'You're forgetting the Free Wales Army.'

'No I'm not. I'm not saying I agreed with them, but they never targeted people. They sabotaged some economic sites and some public buildings. Empty public buildings. I suppose you're happy to support the British Empire, which killed and enslaved... '

But Sayle was ready for her attempt at a counter-offensive.

'Oh, I thought the British Empire abolished slavery... '

'Eventually. Belatedly. But I don't hear you condemning English imperial world-domination... '

'Ancient history. Let's stick with the present day. Your movement is promoting an exclusive, sinister, racist agenda... '

'No we're not. We're talking about help for socially marginalised and economically disadvantaged communities.'

Sayle leaned forward, impatient for the *coup de grâce*. His look conveyed mingled pity and contempt.

'More help for the privileged, you mean,' he said. 'For an elite self-serving clique which wants to run Wales for its own benefit and shut everyone else out. You can try to dress up your cultural fascism in the language of disadvantage if you like, but the people of Wales won't be fooled. They know racist and fascist bigots when they see them.'

If Jonathan Rees could have allowed himself, he would have winced. He knew the bulk of the Welsh-speaking population lived in communities which were among the poorest in Europe, let alone in Wales. He knew that Sayle must know that too. And so did Meinwen. Why on earth didn't she make the point herself?

Could he venture to put that matter straight without appearing partial? Maybe. He began to search for suitably balanced wording. But the voice in his earpiece was warning him – thirty seconds to the end titles. It was too late now. He turned to the autocue, thanked his guests, and delivered his closing 'only time will tell' piece to camera. The end credits ran. The show was over.

The studio lights came up, revealing the dust and gaffer tape on the floor below the shining set. Rees unclipped his radio-mic, and saw Sayle do the same.

'I enjoyed that,' Sayle laughed, speaking to the room in general.

'What you said was disgraceful,' Meinwen said quietly. 'You're just saying lies.'

Sayle's smile became a sneer.

'"Saying lies?" Bloody hell, you're a great advert for bilingualism, aren't you? "Saying lies!" It's "telling lies" girl. If you had your way we'd all be talking like bloody cavemen.'

Meinwen closed her eyes with frustration, then continued, choosing her words more carefully.

'You're dishonest. You're just trying to make Welsh speakers sound like an elite so you can attack them and make it look as if you're doing everyone a favour.'

Sayle laughed again. '"Dishonest" – that's better. You're learning, slowly. But let me tell you something, girl: I *am* doing everyone a favour. And less of the accusations of dishonesty, please. Didn't anyone ever tell you "All's fair in love and politics"? Mind you, I don't suppose you'd know much about either, would you?'

He winked at her and walked off.

Jonathan Rees watched him go, then came over to Meinwen. He was in a quandary.

He longed for the endorsement of comradeship from someone whose principles he admired as much as he did hers, but how could he convey personal sympathy and professional impartiality at the same time? He decided he'd use neutral wording, and hoped his look and tone of voice would convey his genuine fellow-feeling without providing traceable forensic evidence of his personal convictions.

'Thank you for your contribution, Meinwen,' he said, trying to load the stock phrase with more weight of significance than it had ever been designed to carry.

But Meinwen had used up her supply of words for the evening. She didn't even meet Rees' eyes as she handed her radio-mic to the technician and left the studio without another word. Rees hid his disappointment as he walked slowly after her towards the make-up room.

When he got there, Meinwen was at the washbasin, cleaning the foundation from her face as impatiently as if it was dirt. She valued integrity of appearance almost as much as integrity of motive. It was only in sheer naked honesty that she was prepared to meet the world. Her clear, scrubbed face looked back at her.

●○●

Simone

The garden of the Weils' house in Neufchateau was filled with the shouts of the children. Autumn had come, and Simone and André were play-fighting in the piles of leaves. Simone, laughing, looked up as she heard the door bell ring. Always inquisitive, she left her brother, brushed the leaves off her white dress and stepped across the lawn and up the stairs to the patio. Perhaps it was a neighbour come to ask for free medical advice. Her father's generosity made him a magnet for all kinds of callers, deserving and otherwise. He rarely turned anyone away. Her mother pretended to be exasperated with him, but secretly, Simone knew, she was proud.

Down the hallway she saw her mother and father talking to the visitor. It was the postman. He was giving them something. A telegram. She saw her mother look at it for a moment, then put her hand to her mouth. As her parents closed the door and turned, she could read the news in their faces. She turned and ran into the garden.

She sat on the bench, alone, her body shaking, her tears dropping among the rotting apples and the fallen leaves.

●○●

Dewi

Dewi Wiliams was waiting for Meinwen in the foyer of the television studios. That night's output was playing on a bank of television screens on one side of the reception area. Outside, a late spring storm was scattering cold rain on the tall glass walls.

In his teeshirt with the Movement's logo, and with his ripped combat trousers and battered trainers, Dewi looked out of place among the business suits and designer casuals of the media types who were coming and going on clacking heels across the glassy lobby. But that was fine. The last thing Dewi wanted was to look as if he belonged in a place like this, a capsule insulated from the problems of the world outside. He pitied these sleek wage slaves with their empty, fat-free, purpose-free existence. He ran his fingers through his thick brown hair to make it just a little more unruly.

He had watched the programme on the bank of televisions, and had been pained by the way Meinwen had been outmanoeuvred by Sayle. A few minutes after the show came off air, he saw Sayle come out into reception, looking very pleased with himself.

'There you are, darling,' Sayle said to the young woman on reception as he slapped his visitor's pass on the glass counter. 'See the programme, did you?' He motioned with his head towards the televisions.

'Sorry sir, I've been busy on the phone.'

'Oh, you missed a treat, you did, girl. Missed a treat.' He looked around the lobby in search of a more appreciative audience. But there was only Dewi, who was pretending to be interested in the publicity leaflets on the glass-topped table in front of him. Sayle turned back to the receptionist.

'Get me a taxi, love. Thanks.' He spoke with his customary assumption of assured, easy intimacy.

'Certainly sir. What name shall I tell them?'

Sayle coughed. Dewi smiled, and, out of the corner of his eye, Sayle saw his amusement. Sayle lowered his voice as he turned back to the receptionist to give her the information she needed.

'Hale?' Dewi heard the receptionist ask.

Sayle's voice was suddenly audible again.

'No! "Sayle"! Like "*For* Sale". "John Bloody Sayle!"'.'

The receptionist was dialling the number as Meinwen came through reception.

Dewi got up quickly and went to greet her, but they did not embrace or kiss. He knew from long experience that she hated to be touched, even by her closest and oldest friend, which he was.

'Well done, Meinwen,' he said, making sure his upbeat tone would carry to Sayle, who was standing at the reception counter. If Sayle couldn't understand the actual words, he hoped the manner of their delivery would convey confidence and satisfaction. 'You really got the arguments over well,' he continued.

Meinwen didn't reply. Her look told him she knew it was a lie, although a kind one. Then her glance softened.

'Thank you,' she said.

She handed her visitor's name tag to the receptionist. Dewi did the same with his, noting mentally, as he did so, that his surname had once again been given the incorrect anglicised spelling. Never mind. That was the least of their troubles.

'Come on,' he said. 'Let's go to Clwb Ifor. I've got a taxi waiting.'

They both hated taxi rides in Cardiff. Often, just the fact that they were picking up a fare from a place with a high number of Welsh speakers, or taking them to a destination associated with the language, was enough to set the cabbies off on a rant against 'north Walians' taking over the city, using the language to talk about people behind their backs, being rude, being ignorant. While not a visible minority, Welsh speakers were nonetheless an audible minority, and this was enough, sometimes, to draw hostility from people who seemed to get their opinions straight from Sayle's column. And Dewi was sure they had both had enough of Sayle for one night. For a lifetime. But they couldn't walk tonight, in this weather. He saw Meinwen nod her assent.

'OK', she said, 'But can you just take me to the flat, please? I don't feel like Clwb Ifor.'

'Of course.'

Dewi could never refuse Meinwen anything. He suppressed his disappointment at not having a night out with her. If they weren't actually partners, he and Meinwen were certainly a kind of partnership, and he enjoyed the illusory feeling of being a couple which he experienced on those rare occasions when Meinwen permitted herself, for a few hours, to set politics aside.

There had been few enough hours like that in the nearly two decades they had known one another. Since they had met in college they had been fellow campaigners, wedded, not to one another, nor to anyone else, but to the cause. Dewi, however, for all his readiness to risk arrest and jail, lacked Meinwen's readiness to face trial by camera. Her preparedness to undergo that public inquisition time and again only increased the admiration and the protectiveness he felt for her. For both of them, the political struggle had long taken the place of family and work. They lived from protest to protest, each new campaign absorbing the energy and hope their contemporaries put into their careers. The vulnerable, fragile language, so in need of protection and nurturing, was their surrogate child. But a disabled child, one that would always need their care.

In all this, Meinwen was Dewi's touchstone of reality. She never flinched, never lost faith, never gave up. He thought of her as he'd known her in college. She didn't look a day older now. Sometimes he thought that if she changed, he'd lose his own direction, like a compass if the North Pole suddenly lost its magnetism. But even that was more likely than Meinwen shifting her ground. Like all compasses, it was the pull and power of the north that controlled her, and Dewi was drawn along with her, willingly.

It was raining more heavily than ever as they left reception. Meinwen didn't seem to notice the weather, but, as they walked down the stairs to the taxi rank, Dewi held his jacket over her head all the same.

Mademoiselle Sapy

The classroom in the *Lycée Fénelon* was silent apart from the scratching of the children's pencils, and the faint noise of the Paris traffic outside the high windows. Normal life had returned to the capital now that the war was over.

Mademoiselle Sapy, who was in charge of this class of ten and eleven-year-olds, had a few minutes' quiet, as her pupils were absorbed in a drawing class, their heads down, their pencils busy. All except one of them, her most enigmatic pupil, Simone Weil, who had joined the class when her parents had moved back to Paris after the war. She was sitting with her head in her hands.

She knew Simone dreaded the drawing class. With her misshapen hands, she found the work almost impossible and she hated the sense of inadequacy that it gave her. She excelled at anything academic – writing, mathematics, French, Latin, Greek, or history – but anything requiring manual dexterity was a torment to her. She had been asked to compose a picture with the title 'What I did at the weekend'. After a few minutes of scratching away at the paper, she had clearly given up.

Mademoiselle Sapy came over to Simone's desk. Simone's parents had told her of the difficulty Simone had with drawing, so she was keen to encourage her. Standing behind the child, she looked down at the picture. It was not a thing of beauty, that was for certain. What was it? A crowd of people with banners. A church parade, perhaps? Some kind of patronal festival? But no, Simone's parents weren't religious, so it couldn't be that. There hadn't been some kind of celebration in the city during the weekend, had there?

'Well done, Simone. A parade, yes?'

'Yes, Mademoiselle,' Simone took her head out of her hands.

'In the park?'

'No, Mademoiselle. In the street.'

'I see. And those people, are they musicians?'

'No, Mademoiselle. Those are the Bolsheviks.'

'The Bolsheviks?!'

'Yes, they always march in front. That's the red flag there. But I haven't coloured it in yet.'

'But Simone,' said Mademoiselle Sapy gently. 'This is supposed to be a picture of what you did at the weekend...'

'It is, Mademoiselle. We marched for ages. And we sang the *Internationale*.'

'What? Your parents took you on a political demonstration?'

'No, Mademoiselle. They didn't know. But I saw the march outside and I went to join in. I was right at the front!'

'And what did your parents say when they found out you'd been marching with communists?'

'Well, they said I should have told them before going. But I'm not a communist, anyway, Mademoiselle. I'm a Bolshevik.'

'I see,' said Mademoiselle Sapy. She looked again at the picture. Sure enough, there at the front was one figure smaller than the others, a fragile grey outline, with the dark mass of the Parisian proletariate behind.

●○●

Meinwen

The taxi made its way down the tree-lined Victorian length of Cathedral Road, heading for the student district on the east side of Cardiff. Although the broadcasting company had offered to pay for a hotel, Meinwen had opted instead to take a flat fee and to stay with a friend in the Cathays area. That would allow her to keep the overnight expenses – a useful contribution to her always precarious finances.

The taxi smelt of air freshener, vinyl and stale tobacco. A talk show was playing on the radio: some caller was trying to make a point about drug control, while the presenter repeatedly simplified the contributor's statements to the point of absurdity and threw them back at him as challenges, trying to anger him. It made the programme Meinwen had just taken part in sound like a Socratic dialogue. After less than a minute of it, she felt exhausted and defiled. She took her attention away and looked out of the window.

Through the rain, Meinwen noticed a faded Movement campaign poster on a wall. *'Os yw'r Gymraeg i fyw, rhaid i bopeth newid!'* 'If Welsh is to live, everything must change!' Everything. Just everything, that's all. It was either touchingly brave or blindingly naive, depending on how you looked at it. Tonight, it was the naiveté she felt. When it had been a matter of forms, signs and education, they'd faced simple establishment intransigence which needed simple tactics to confront. And they'd succeeded to a degree that would have seemed inconceivable thirty years previously. But those external successes had masked an inner malaise: the heartlands were being pushed into what could be terminal decline; out-migration of young Welsh speakers turning from a trickle to a flood, in-migration of English people turning from a few drops to a deluge.

The taxi passed the Cayo Arms, recently renamed, daringly, after the former Free Wales Army leader, Cayo Evans. Poor old Cayo, thought Meinwen. Despite Sayle's accusations earlier in the evening, Cayo had been more of a danger to himself than to anyone else. And a pub was only too appropriate as his memorial.

The taxi passed scores of other premises named after places and people which had nothing to do with Wales: St Kilda, Holme Lea, The Lincoln Hotel. Meinwen habitually scanned the written evidence of her environment for signs of change, growth or decline in the language's fortunes. Every street was a fever chart of her sick nation.

Renaming was one of the most galling aspects of the 'coloni- sation,' as the Movement called the influx to the heartlands. True, some of the incomers – 'the righteous gentiles' one campaigner called them – rose to the challenge, learned the language, went native. But too many chose to pretend the indigenous culture didn't exist, and wasted no time in changing the ancient names of their newly-acquired farms and smallhold- ings to suit their English country garden dreams.

Meinwen thought of the region where she had been brought up. Incomers were already the majority in many of the more scenic parts; the remaining Welsh speakers being regarded by many of them as surly old rustics somehow still impertinently hanging around. That was if they knew of the natives at all, as the incomers largely kept to their own circles, which were steadily growing, making interaction with the dwindling number of natives less and less necessary.

Stalin could hardly have displaced a population so thor- oughly, Meinwen thought bitterly. It was the biggest assimilation process of any minority in Europe since the second world war. And all done with unimpeachable legality: its weapons the chequebook, the Pickfords van, and the hardwood windows that every incomer seemed to install as a badge of their house's changed ownership. *You've Been Framed*, but without the laughs, and no one to step in and say no, it's all a joke.

Over Cardiff bridge, past the Animal Wall, past the entrance to Womanby Street, where clubbers would be hurrying out of the rain on their way to Clwb Ifor Bach, the Welsh-language nightclub where Dewi had planned for them to go tonight if Meinwen had felt up to it. If the interview had gone better perhaps she would have agreed. But it was the cause, not a missed night out, that most occupied Meinwen's thoughts as she sat silently beside Dewi, looking out of the taxi window at the drenched city.

The rainwater fed the swollen river Taff over which they had just passed; it pooled on the corner near the Angel Hotel, more than the drains could cope with, flowing up over the pavements, spreading the debris of the city's gutters ever wider. The rising waters brought the image of Cwm Tryweryn to Meinwen's mind like a recurring dream. She had not been born when Tryweryn was seized, its people evicted, their homes and chapel demolished and the valley flooded to provide water for England, but she had absorbed the black-and-white image of the desecrated community into herself, and felt the loss and exile like a personal pain.

Tonight, Meinwen knew it was the waters of mobile global capital that were threatening her world. The slogan 'Everything must change' was meant to challenge that. Just now, though, she thought it sounded forlorn and pathetic. Everything was changing, that much was certain. But changing the wrong way. Her world was a sandcastle facing a rising tide.

●○●

Simone

The lecture theatre at the *Lycée Henri IV* in Paris was full, and there was an air of concentrated attention in the high-windowed room. Simone was listening intently to the introductory lecture from her class tutor, a diffident-looking middle-aged man with a moustache and spectacles, who was formally dressed in a dark three-piece suit.

'You are privileged,' he was saying. 'You are the absolute academic elite of France. Destined to lead.'

The tutor's name was Emile Chartier, but he was better known to Simone, as to the rest of France, by his one-word alias, 'Alain'. Simone and her fellow students found him all the more intriguing for his retiring nature and his unusual record in the Great War: at the age of forty-six, disdaining the officer's rank he could have claimed, he had enlisted as a common soldier, sharing, as a matter of principle, the working classes' dangers and deprivations. His experiences in the trenches had given him the respect of ensuing generations and had bought indulgence for his eccentricities; they had also left him with a permanent limp, which was apparent now as he paced slowly in front of this new class.

'You have outstanding gifts,' he was saying. 'You therefore, have outstanding responsibilities. You have the chance to use those talents, and to use the facilities of the *Lycée*, for good, not for gain.

'And this,' he went on, 'this is the best school in France. Here I know what it is like to hold genius in my hands. But I won't extort it from you. I won't cajole it through soliciting confidences and confessions. You must not mistake instruction for affection. You are here to learn.

'You are young. Your minds are full of questions. In some cases, they may be full of doubts about your ability, about your future, about your worth when you compare yourself with the great minds we will be studying.'

Simone felt he was speaking directly to her. She had always felt in the shadow of her brother André. When she thought of his abilities she almost despaired. He was a true mathematical genius; at the age of twelve, he could perform post-doctoral algebra problems, and he had gone to university while only sixteen. Simone was tormented by the feeling that she was falling behind. Two years earlier, when she was fourteen, she had been tortured by the sense of her own inadequacy compared to André, and had considered suicide. Only her longing for finding the truth had sustained her. She felt an overwhelming desire to experience reality, beauty and goodness wholeheartedly, whatever the result. That desire had pulled her through.

'You are not damned,' Alain was saying. 'Or wretched, or

useless, or cowardly. I am telling you because I know, and you – you are just badly informed.'

This was what Simone had been desperate to hear. Alain's words seemed to have been directed especially at strengthening her own fragile self-worth. She felt the excitement of new possibilities and new powers within her.

●○●

Meinwen

The taxi carrying Meinwen and Dewi swung round the corner past the lights of Queen Street, and the statue of Aneurin Bevan, poised in perpetual debate with an invisible audience. The so-Welsh name, the so-British politics. And yet, Meinwen tried to remember, what had he once said in defence of the Welsh language? 'It will not die. We will not let it.' Meinwen wished she had quoted that to Sayle tonight. An *esprit d'escalier*. Or *esprit de taxi* in this case.

The French phrase reminded her of Simone Weil. Would she have been lost for words in that debate tonight? Scarcely.

Meinwen found that Simone meant more and more to her as time went on, and as the global nature of her own struggle became more apparent. Every unjust system would be defeated in the end. Simone had understood that. She had spent her life unswervingly in the effort to change the world; the patron saint of every radical activist. It was her example that always spurred Meinwen on to work harder, to sacrifice more. Change would come. It would.

But it would have to come soon. Otherwise there'd be no Welsh-speaking communities left to save; one more irreplaceable cultural ecosystem would be extinguished, the one which had created her, loved her, given her a sense of belonging, and without which her life would lose all meaning. The words of her earliest memories, the words of the poetry she loved, the words which had named the fields, the rivers and the hills among which she was raised, and which bound all those things and more together in one living, intimate web of belonging, they would become silent forever. The culture which had taken thousands of years to create looked set to be eradicated in less than a decade, levelled like a rainforest whose trees fall in moments to the chainsaw while the world looks away, the millennia-old trunks being processed into cheap garden furniture and – of course – hardwood windows. Someone's fast buck; someone's bargain; someone else's end of the world.

Some creatures were doomed when their habitat was destroyed. Meinwen felt the same. She could not survive in a world without Welsh; at least, even if she could, she didn't want to. But that world seemed to her an increasingly likely prospect. She was hiding her growing hopelessness from Dewi, but she couldn't hide it from herself. She felt a crushing burden of personal responsibility. Was she doing enough? What was she prepared to do to save her world? Tonight's experience in the studio had convinced her that she had to do more. They had to find a new way forward. But which way? Outside the taxi, there was only one road to be seen, leading away into the night.

Alain

Alain was accustomed to teaching the cream of the country's young people. The *Lycée's* main aim was to prepare students for the entrance examinations for the *École Normale Supérieure*, the best college in France, where the next generation of university teachers was trained. It accepted only the very brightest students. He was used to having the sharpest young minds of France under his care; but even so, he knew that this new class of 1925 contained some remarkable talents. He was glad to see they were giving a respectful hearing to his introductory address.

He was speaking now about the challenges they would face in post-war Europe; the rebuilding of shattered societies, the finding of new ideals suitable for the modern world – a world changed beyond all recognition, lacking in social, political and religious certainty – in which they now found themselves.

They seemed content to listen. All except one young man in the row behind Simone. He put his hand up slowly. He had a sardonic smile.

Alain stopped. 'Yes, M'sieur...?'

'Jean Reynard,' the young man said. He glanced around him to confirm that he had, as he clearly hoped, attracted everyone's eyes.

Alain, familiar with generations of hubristic young people, knew he had deep resources of patience and experience on which to draw, so he simply waited without expression for whatever was coming. Better to let the boy get it out of his system.

'M'sieur Alain, you are talking about how we should behave in the modern world.' Reynard said. 'But is it true that you won't have a telephone, that you won't fly in an aeroplane, that you won't even use a typewriter?'

He looked round quickly at his neighbours, seeking approval, although it was clear he would be content, if necessary, simply with their attention.

Alain listened carefully. He would not gratify the questioner by becoming angry.

'Yes,' he replied calmly. 'Yes, I do suspect the modern world. I do suspect the machine age. It is not a simple matter. Some of these machines bring freedom from drudgery. Good. Others deprive people of work, or make them servants of some industrial monster – impersonal parts of a giant production process. Are you sure, M'sieur, that turning individuals into a mass is a good thing? There's more to life than making more things, making more money.'

Most of the students, clearly considering the debate closed, were looking at Reynard, expecting him to sit down. He did not. He was enjoying himself too much.

'It's not a question of money,' he said. 'It's a question of power.'

'Your meaning, M'sieur...?'

'Mankind is becoming a mass, like it or not. Haven't you heard of Nietzsche?'

'I have come across his work, M'sieur. He is particularly popular with clever young adolescent boys.'

Reynard ignored the irony, and continued; his speech had more than a touch of the manifesto about it. It was not uncommon for these students to be involved with politics at an early age.

'Nietzsche showed that the will to power is what drives the world. You said yourself how the old structures of society have broken down – people crowding into cities, working in mass production, being told what to think by newspapers.'

Alain looked down, waiting for Reynard to finish. He did not.

'You might not like it, but it's a fact. France has to harness the power of the masses, or else we'll be at the mercy of other nations who will. Look at what's happening in Russia. We have to be ready to meet the communist threat on its own terms: discipline, order, ruthlessness. That's the only way we'll keep our greatness. If we followed your way, we'd be slaves.'

'Better a slave than a fascist!'

Alain looked up, surprised. The dark-haired girl in front of Reynard had turned on him. She was one of only three girls in the class. What was her name? He tried to recall. Something German-sounding. Yes. Weil.

Reynard looked surprised too. He had clearly not expected any of the students to speak, much less one of the girls.

The girl went on, her quiet voice insistent and intense: 'Power. Prestige. Do you really think that's greatness? Choosing sacrifice, like M'sieur Alain. That's greatness.'

Reynard held his hands up in a mock defensive gesture as if to say he would not argue with someone so agitated. He resumed his sardonic smile, and sat down.

Alain looked on, impassive. This class of 1925 was going to be one to remember.

●○●

Dewi

The taxi arrived at the house in Cathays where Dewi and Meinwen would be spending the night. As the passengers had scarcely spoken during the brief journey, there had been no opportunity for the driver to express any opinion on their being Welsh speakers. Which was a relief to Dewi, as he didn't want Meinwen to have to go through any more grief tonight. He hated to see her being misunderstood and maligned. He stepped out and held the door open for her.

As the taxi pulled away, they turned to the house. It was a terraced property with a door opening straight out onto the pavement. Litter, spilt from the black bin bags, was plastered to the cracked, wet paving slabs. They stood in the pouring rain as Dewi rang the rusted doorbell. It seemed to make no sound.

Probably not working, although it was difficult to tell with the sound of the rain and the traffic swishing by outside. Dewi looked for a knocker on the letter box. Broken. He rapped his knuckles on the frosted glass.

With his other hand he held his jacket over his and Meinwen's heads. He felt the slight pressure of her thin body as she was forced to lean closer to take advantage of the shelter. He glanced down at where Meinwen's head, her black hair glossy with the rain, was almost, but not quite, resting on his shoulder. It was with a touch of disappointment that he saw through the frosted glass a door being opened at the end of the corridor, and the shape of their host, Arfon, come down the hallway to open up for them.

Simone

As the students left the lecture, Simone found Reynard waiting for her in the corridor. He greeted her with cold politeness.

'Mademoiselle, a word, if I may.'

Simone looked expectant, anticipating a renunciation or at least an apology. But Reynard lowered his voice and spoke with hatred.

'You stinking Jews are the curse of this country.'

'What?!'

'You're nothing but a bunch of rootless, grasping parasites living off the Christian nations. Lining your own pockets...'

'Now look – my family aren't wealthy. They saved to send me here...'

'You'll pay for it. We'll make you pay.'

'What are you talking about? Pay for what?'

'For nearly losing us the war – conspiring with our enemies to make money out of the arms trade.

'Arms trade? My father's a doctor...'

'Weil? What kind of name is that? German, isn't it?'

'Now, wait a minute. My father served...'

'My father *died*,' said Reynard. 'And you talk to me of sacrifice. You may fool Alain by sucking up to him and his stupid, backward ideas. But you won't get the choice of sacrifice when we're in power. You'll suffer, like it or not.'

'You're threatening me...'

'I'm promising you. I want you to know what's coming to you.'

Simone forced herself to look composed. The anti-semitic attack was new to her, but all the more hurtful for that. She was trying to think of a reply when a broad figure stepped between her and Reynard. It was Pierre Letellier, another of her classmates.

'Hold on, Reynard,' he said steadily. 'Let's not start a pogrom just yet. Not over losing an argument. Leave the young lady be.'

By now, the scene had attracted several onlookers, among them Yvette Bertillon, one of the other girls in the class. Anger rose in Reynard's eyes and for a moment, he sized up Pierre, but it seemed he realised he had met his match, and he turned away, giving Simone a look of contempt. She and Pierre watched him go.

'*Au revoir* Christian France,' he said. 'Give me the Jews any day!' He turned to Simone. 'Or, begging your pardon, the Jewesses, of course. I...'

'Forgive me M'sieur,' interrupted Simone. 'I would prefer not to be categorised by my racial heritage, either by an enemy or a friend. My family are atheists, and we had no Jewish upbringing. I consider myself as belonging to the Catholic and humanist cultural traditions of France, like all French people, nothing more or less than that.'

'Oh... yes... yes, of course. My apologies.' He quickly regained his composure.

'I admire your courage, Mademoiselle. It seems to me that we share much the same political outlook. May I ask – would you care to have a drink with me this evening? We could...'

Simone looked at him simply.

'No,' she said.

●○●

John Sayle

Early the following morning, Sayle arrived at his newspaper's offices in Cardiff Bay. He fished in his pocket for his identity card, with its passport photograph of a slightly younger version of himself. He found it and pressed the plastic against the security panel on the wall. With a confirmatory electronic beep, the glass doors opened, then, as he stepped inside, swished closed behind him with a slight click as the electro-magnetic lock shut out the outside world. He never failed to get a faint tingle of pleasure when the doors opened obediently at his touch. You're accepted, they seemed to say. You're an insider.

Sitting at his desk a few minutes later, Sayle was typing an email to a friend. He liked to come in to work early, as it showed the staff who were younger than him – which was nearly all of them – that he still had more stamina, more commitment, more sheer bloody professionalism than they did. God, he was using typewriters before most of this lot had been born. They wouldn't even know what a typewriter was. They thought nothing existed unless they could find it on the internet; he used to have to get his information the hard way – door-knocking, conversations in pubs, clubs, street corners. Real journalism. He told himself that none of them, for all their fancy-sounding media studies degrees, could rival his knowledge of Wales, gained from a lifetime on weekly and daily papers. He was the star columnist, and he damn well deserved to be. What's more, these days, he got to be on television quite regularly. He loved being on television.

Today, he was still enjoying the afterglow of his performance on *Wales on Wednesday*, and he wanted to view the programme at his leisure. But, never the most technically-minded person, he hadn't set his video recorder properly, and had recorded a repeat of *Sex in the City* instead. He'd enjoyed watching that, admittedly, but he was damned annoyed that the recorder had let him down, and he did want to see his own show, particularly as the debate had gone so well for him. However, email was one technology he felt he had mastered, and now he was messaging his friend Dewi Williams, the archivist at the Welsh Broadcasting Records Centre, to ask for a VHS copy. The Centre recorded all programmes from Wales for posterity, and Dewi was an old Labour Party mate of his who wouldn't mind doing him a favour. Sayle finished the note and typed the word 'Dewi' in the address field. The computer, recognising the only Dewi in Sayle's electronic address book, obediently filled in the remainder of the address. Sayle pressed 'Send'.

He cursored to his inbox. Among the usual spam, viagra offers and invitations to send his bank details to high-ranking

West African government officials, there was a message entitled "Wales on Wednesday". He opened it. Congratulations on the show, he hoped. No. Criticism from a language campaigner. Bugger. Someone with one of those names which looked like it belonged in a genealogy of medieval princes. Something ap something-or-other. What did the message say? The usual stuff: they weren't racists... they were just trying to preserve the last refuges of an indigenous culture... just like Native Americans trying to keep their way of life... he was guilty of a grotesque misuse of the terminology of racism... language was an acquirable skill not a racial characteristic. And so on. The usual claptrap – or *ap*-trap, in this case. He stopped reading, pressed 'Reply' and wrote: 'Kindly refrain from sending me your paranoid ravings. If you wish to debate this subject, I suggest you contact Sohail Mohammed at the Commission for Racial Equality. They know all about racists like you.' He pressed 'Send' again.

He sat back. Their sheer naiveté made it easy. Why were they so bloody clueless? Maybe it was because they were products of communities whose methods of thought and behaviour sometimes seemed years behind those of the rest of the country, communities whose members didn't realise that the terms which served for their own defensive internal discussions sounded crude and primitive to a wider audience. Pitiful, if you allowed yourself to think about it. They were just like some kind of sect, their closed cohesiveness providing both the key to their endurance and the barrier to their wider appeal.

They thought the tactics of abject defenceless protest which had worked in the sixties and seventies were still a magic formula. It reminded him of what he'd read about the Holy Ghost Army in Uganda. They believed that, if they anointed themselves with ground-nut oil, they could advance unarmed against the bullets of the government troops. Needless to say, their revolt, although spirited, had been short-lived. What would the Welsh-language lobby anoint themselves with? Laverbread, perhaps. No – wait – green paint, of course. For all that they wanted to survive, they seemed to lack the necessary ruthlessness. Think of the Aztecs. They fought only to take prisoners, while the Spanish conquistadores fought to kill. The Aztecs wouldn't change their tactics, and so they lost the continent. Silly sods.

He'd enjoy viewing that programme again. He thought back over this latest victory for his forensic rhetoric, savouring it. The activists weren't racists in the true sense, of course; he knew that. But their single-issue fanaticism was still holding Wales back, preoccupying public forums which should be dealing with issues like health, schools and the economy. And God help the country if this linguistic Taliban ever came to power. If accusations of racism were what it took to get this issue off the scene, then so be it. It served the greater good; what's more, he prided himself, he was one of the few people brave enough to speak out against the politically-correct madness that allowed this lobby such influence.

God, they annoyed him. He damn well hated their self-righteousness, the implicit assumption, whatever they said to the contrary, that they were the real Welsh, that people like himself were some kind of mongrels. He wouldn't have these woollybacks making him feel like a second-class citizen in his own country. They thought their Wales was the only one – some humourless, inbred, slate-grey redoubt in north west Gwynedd; they had no idea of the warmth and value of communities like the ones where he'd grown up, with their belonging, their socialism, their shared wit. God, that Meinwen didn't look as if she'd laughed in twenty years. When he'd been growing up, Welsh wasn't taught in the local schools, nor seen on signs or official forms. And they were perfectly happy; they didn't have any public identity crisis; they didn't have to mouth some alien shibboleth in order to be accepted. If they were aware of the language at all, the valley people had thought of it as something belonging to the past; perhaps spoken by a grandparent, and kept from the children like a contagion the inoculation of modernity had rendered moribund, like diphtheria or polio. But now it was back, like some retro malaise, and it was his job to stop the reinfection spreading. He knew the value of the real Wales: it was epitomised by the Valleys of his youth, and he'd defend it against all comers.

Just for a moment, he felt a pang of sympathy for Meinwen. It must be bloody lonely living in a state of perpetual opposition to the rest of society, devoting your energies to a doomed cause, spending your life imprisoned in the personal ghetto of your mind. She wouldn't be a bad-looking girl either if she smartened herself up. What a bloody wasted life.

But then the anger returned. It was up to her if she wanted to throw her life away. But she had no right to insist that everyone else follow her. He wished he could shut the mouths of Meinwen and her kind for good. What he needed was not just name-calling. He needed something clinching: a real, unmistakeable, scandalous exposé that would disgrace her and her group permanently. But he knew that the Movement gave him little hope of that: paradoxically, their delinquency was transparently public, while their virtues were modestly concealed. Awkward sods. Why couldn't they be like everyone else? But some day he'd find their real weak spot.

Meanwhile, there was still name-calling, and that was working pretty well. His mind returned to that comparison with the Taliban; there were possibilities there; he could be as inventive as any Welsh speaker addicted to wordplay. Yes. He'd got it. The 'Taffyban'. That would do for his next column. The 'Dai-atollahs'; that would do as well. 'Ap Qaeda'. Perfect. He smiled at his own ingenuity. No time like the present. He opened a new document file and started typing.

Yvette

The flames of the fire were the only light in Simone's college room, which was bare even by student standards. A table, a candle, two chairs. And books everywhere. She had spread her papers out on the floor on all sides.

Simone and Yvette sat beside the fire. Yvette had a playful smile as she tried to draw her classmate out to talk. She was fascinated by this strange girl, with her unnerving candour and her eccentric dress – she wore boy's clothes and seemed to repress all signs of her own femininity, cramming her beautiful cloud of dark hair down under a black beret.

Simone seemed to be full of contrasts. Her eyes behind her round glasses were keen and interrogative, but the slightly intimidating effect was offset by the gentle half smile which was her face's natural cast. Her political radicalism, meanwhile, was inflexible and rigorous to the point of absurdity. Yvette recalled that on one occasion, when the vice-principal had suggested that the boys and girls be kept separate in the classes, she had put up ironic home-made notices saying 'Men's Section' and 'Women's Section'. When the vice-principal had tried to remove them, she had physically grappled with him. And yet there was her ready compassion for the poor. Earlier that day, when a group of the students had been discussing the current famine in China, Yvette had been struck by Simone's unwonted silence and had looked across at her to see tears rolling unchecked down her face. But it was her asexuality which intrigued Yvette tonight.

'Well, you must have plenty of admirers if you can turn down a man like Pierre Letellier,' Yvette ventured, with a cautious attempt at teasing.

Simone looked up from where she was gazing into the flames, but didn't answer.

'I'd have said yes straight away,' Yvette went on. 'And he's your type. He's from the country. His father was a labourer and an author. He was telling me.'

Simone looked into the fire again. She spoke quietly.

'It's not permissible for me.'

Yvette just looked at her questioningly. She could sense Simone was not as inhuman as she appeared. Most of her class-mates, unable to see beyond the forbidding intellect and bizarre clothes, dismissed her as a crank. But, even on brief acquaintance, Yvette sensed that the more you got to know Simone, the more her personality revealed new layers of tenderness and consideration. Practically-minded, Yvette longed to steer her friend into a form of behaviour where her rare qualities could best be displayed. If she was attracted to Pierre, as Yvette was sure she was, then why was her frankness – so disconcertingly evident when discussing matters of principle – so lacking when applied to her own natural desires?

'It's not that I don't want to, Yvette,' Simone was saying. 'It's just... I don't feel I can allow myself to love. At least, not until I've done what I have to do.'

'Your life's work?' Yvette could hear the involuntary note of scepticism in her own voice.

'I don't know. But I just know I can't be happy when there's so much suffering, so much injustice in the world.'

She lowered her eyes and went on.

'When I was a very little girl, my mother told me a story. Golden Mary and Tar Mary. A step-mother sends her step-daughter into the forest. She sees a house with two doors. One's labelled "Tar Door", the other "Golden Door". She thinks: "The tar door's good enough for me" and opens it. And she's covered with a shower of gold. She goes home, her step-mother sees the gold and so she sends her own daughter to the house. She goes in through the Golden Door, and comes home covered in tar.'

Yvette smiled uncomfortably, not sure if this was a joke or not.

Simone looked up at her with something close to an appeal in her eyes. 'Do you understand?' she said.

Yvette made no reply. She looked at where the fire was consuming the coal, devouring it steadily to a grey ash.

Meinwen

Meinwen was woken by the sound of a door slamming. She looked up at the bare lightbulb on the artexed ceiling, the familiar sight above her prison bed. Her body felt instantly cold as she took in the prospect of more months inside. She steeled herself to face the day, as she had to every morning in prison. She could cope with the deprivation of liberty – as Waldo Williams had said, it was possible to find a *'neuadd fawr rhwng cyfyng furiau,'* a 'great hall between narrow walls': her inner vision of justice was expansive enough for her spirit to find freedom despite any external confinement. She could cope with the bad food: it could be avoided by simply eating very little, something she found comparatively easy. She could cope with the physical discomfort: every bruise from the workshop or scratch from the kitchen was, to her, an honourable scar. As for the social stigma of jail, for her, there simply was no stigma. Rather the contrary: imprisonment was the greatest honour an activist could attain. A cartoon from the Movement's heyday had shown a middle-aged woman walking down the road with her nose in the air, and wearing a supercilious smile, while two bystanders commented: 'Look at her, giving herself airs. Just because her daughter's been in jail.'

But it was the enforced intimacy of prison that she detested: the sight, smell, and worst of all, the sound of other women, all day, every day. Their endless inane chatter. While Meinwen's mind roamed inner vistas of liberty, most of her fellow prisoners' minds appeared to be narrower than the cells which confined them, their thoughts running in well-worn grooves of envy, malice, self-pity and deceit, visiting and revisiting the same few exhausted sources of anger, self-justification or complaint. 'So I sacked my barrister. I sacked him, I did. I said: "If you can't tell them what I want you to tell them, then I'll sack you." And I did. I sacked him, the bastard. Sacked him I did.' In their monologues of injustice, their pitiless condemnation of those they considered worse than them – which was everyone – their endless probing for weakness or frailty among every person they encountered, they were at once more immoral and more moralistic by far than the society which had incarcerated them. She pitied them, more from a sense of duty than from real compassion; she tried to be charitable and to understand why they were the way they were, but she found the endless verbal assault close to intolerable. She would have to try to numb her emotions against it. It was the only way not to be infected by the words, like bitten-down fingernails, clawing at her mind for attention, approval, and respect.

Then she remembered. She was in the house in Cathays, not in jail. Relief warmed her, and she pulled the thin, borrowed duvet of her friend's spare room more tightly around her. She had the room to herself. There was no one to bawl at her to get up; no cellmate to insist that she agree with her latest conspiracy theory, or even worse, her *old* conspiracy theory; no canteen full of shouts, sweat and nauseating cooking smells. She wouldn't even have the discomfort of making conversation over breakfast. That slamming door was Arfon leaving for work. That meant there would only be Dewi in the house, and with him she felt no discomfort with either conversation or silence. He was the only person with whom she felt like that.

It was a while since they had been alone together under the same roof. It had happened a few times at Yr Hafan, the house she and Dewi and three other activists had once shared in the hills above Porthmadog. It had been on one of those occasions, when their other housemates had been away, and they had shared a bottle of cheap wine and some fresh bread, that Dewi had asked her if she would go out with him. She thought back over the occasion now.

It had come like a physical shock, and she had felt the pleasant tingle of the wine in her body stopping as if a switch had been clicked off. As she made no attempts to make herself attractive, and gave no signals of availability, never for a moment had she considered that he – that anyone – could have thought of her in that way. A comrade, yes. But something more than that? What was he thinking of? There was nothing more than being a comrade. Anything else was less. The whole thing would have been a distraction from their purpose, from 'the cause'. Not wanting to hurt his feelings, she had promised to think it over. And she had. And when the other housemates, Gethin, Arianhrod and Bedwyr, had come back, she had even discussed it with them and asked for their views to make sure she was making the right decision. They had all looked shocked too. Gethin and Arianhrod had said they could not get involved, while Bedwyr had simply said that he doubted whether Dewi made quite such a priority of the cause as Meinwen. That had been enough for her. Later that day, she gave Dewi her decision. Later that week, he moved out. Since then, he had rented a flat in the town itself. He said it was more convenient.
She had considered the matter closed then. And Dewi, though soon resuming their comradeship, had never spoken of it again. But she had often thought of that conversation. And just now, for the first time, the thought occurred to her that perhaps the reason her housemates had looked so shocked was not because Dewi had asked her out, as she had always thought, but because she had asked them about such an intimate matter at all. And could Bedwyr's comment really have meant not that Dewi wasn't committed enough to the cause to be worthy of her, but that Dewi actually had his priorities right in putting love before the cause? Her mind fixed on those hitherto unconsidered possibilities and held them for a few moments, motionless and uncertain. Then the pulse of her familiar priorities returned. No, whatever they may have meant, the cause was still the most important thing. But now, for the first time, she realised the mortification Dewi must have felt when she shared that conversation with their friends, and she felt a swell of sympathy for

him. Right decision, Meinwen, she thought. But wrong method. Very wrong method. Poor Dewi. She really was very fond of him, although she could not allow herself to think of him as anything other than a friend. He must be truly dedicated to the cause to have stayed friends with her despite the way she had treated him, she thought.

She pushed the duvet aside, swung her pale legs out of the bed and stood up. The threadbare carpet felt gritty under her feet. Housework was not Arfon's strong point. She put on her unlaced boots to walk across the landing to the bathroom. She looked for the cord for the light switch. It was knotted and filthy, so she reached up as high as she could to find a comparatively clean part to pull. Then she closed the door behind her.

Dewi was already sitting at the blue formica kitchen table drinking his coffee when Meinwen came downstairs.

'Coffee?' he asked her.

Meinwen nodded, and made the effort to smile. This morning, she was conscious how much she took him for granted, and she wanted, somehow, to show how much she appreciated him. But, she thought, why should the smile have been so difficult to give? It made her realise how little effort she usually made with him. Dewi deserved better than that from her. She sat down at the table, while he busied himself with the kettle.

'Did you sleep well?' she asked.

'Not bad. Arfon woke me up going to work, though. I didn't realise teachers started work so early.'

'They don't. It's just that the school's up in the top end of the Rhondda. It's the best part of an hour's drive away.'

'Of course.'

'But he'd sooner make the drive so he can live in Cardiff rather than up there. Better nightlife.'

'I suppose so.'

He put the coffee down in front of her.

'Thank you.' The smile again. It came a little easier this time.

'Toast?'

'No thanks.'

'Cereal? Look: Shredded Wheat. Frosties.'

'No thanks.'

Dewi did not push the matter.

'What shall we do today, Dewi?' Meinwen was trying to think of something Dewi would like to do to pass the free morning they had ahead of them before they caught their bus back up to north Wales. Something that would give him pleasure. She wanted to see him enjoy himself. In fact, she thought she would get pleasure herself from that. But while her feelings could anticipate the emotional content of the occasion, her imagination had failed her on the detail, and she was hoping Dewi would help her out.

'Well,' he said. 'I was just looking at this here.'

He indicated the morning newspaper in front of him. Of course, thought Meinwen, there's probably an item about some event that's going on: an art exhibition maybe, even a film matinée. They showed films in the morning, didn't they? Perhaps they could even take a later bus back.

'What is it?' she asked, leaning a little closer.

'This,' said Dewi.

He turned the paper towards her. It was a news item previewing an event taking place at the Senedd in Cardiff that morning. The article said that 'the Welsh scholar, former National Librarian, and activist, Professor Emeritus Andreas Mallwyd Price', was due to give evidence at the Languages of Wales Committee, which was gathering material for a major report. Mallwyd, who had taught both Meinwen and Dewi in Aberystwyth, was the mentor and grey eminence of the language movement; the two jail terms he had served for language protests in the 1980s had been catalytic events in the campaign, making him a legend, at least among the activists. 'See,' said Dewi. 'I think we should go and give him a bit of moral support, don't you?'

Meinwen hesitated for a moment. Art gallery, matinée, or Assembly committee. Of course, there could be only one decision.

Simone

The following day, Simone was walking across the college quadrangle to the library. She loved the architecture of the *Lycée*. The building, a former convent with many later additions, was a mixture of medieval and baroque. The whole complex reflected the style of a convent, with one narrow, guarded, exterior door, opening onto an enclosed square with a few trees and low box hedges. There was something comforting about the sense of enclosure, although – she thought as she passed a group of male students standing under one of the autumn-bare beeches in the square – enclosure had its negative aspects too.

'There she is,' said one of them, loud enough for her to hear. 'The Martian. All brain and eyes!'

The Martians, taken from H.G. Wells' novel *The War of the Worlds*, were the current insult to be used on anyone whose intellectual powers seemed to have developed beyond their physical or social abilities. Simone seemed made for the jibe.

'You should read something besides science fiction,' Simone retorted, holding her books closer to her chest as she walked past.

'No. She's not a Martian,' said another boy to her back, assuming an air of mock piety: 'She's an archangel, judging us all from on high!'

'She's intolerable,' said a third, sourly.

Simone was almost at the library, when the last jibe reached her.

'She's the categorical imperative – in a skirt!'

The boys all laughed.

'Well, at least he's read Kant, not just childish novels,' thought Simone as she passed into the cool quiet of the library.

Silence, muffled footsteps, the shine of the tiled floor, the fragrance of centuries of learning in the leather-bound volumes on the gleaming dark wooden shelves on every side, the light reflected from the white-stuccoed vaulted roof. Sanctuary.

Meinwen

The committee had been sitting for half an hour when Meinwen and Dewi arrived. They had been delayed by the airport-style security at the Senedd's main entrance, where their appearance had aroused the suspicions of the guards. Now,

duly cleared and wearing their plastic '*Ymwelydd*/Visitor'
badges, they slipped into the committee room quietly, and
found two of the many empty seats in the public gallery.

They could recognise a few familiar activists in the front
rows, a few journalists on the press benches, the translators
murmuring inside their soundproofed chamber. And the politicians, of course: most of them placemen, and women, of the
majority party, with a few opposition representatives. All the
members of the Languages of Wales Committee looked bored
beyond the ability of any language to express.

Meinwen wondered why the activists even bothered trying
to make their case in a forum like this. No one expected the
committee to produce anything substantial. Even its name
betrayed its inherent inertia. It had originally been entitled the
'Welsh Language Committee', but after an outcry from some
Labour members who decided that title was 'exclusive' and
'divisive', it had been renamed 'The Languages of Wales
Committee'. The plural was clearly intended to put Welsh in its
place. You want cultural diversity? You can have it. And you can
fight it out with English, Urdu, Punjabi and British Sign
Language. For the committee organisers, it was a case of safety
in numbers. For Meinwen, she was certain that if they had
thought they could have got away with it, they would have
included Morse Code and Cockney Rhyming Slang in the
committee's remit too. Why had she bothered to come? But
even as she asked herself, she looked at the diminutive figure of
Professor Mallwyd Price, already well into giving his evidence,
and she knew the answer: it was because of people like
Mallwyd, and all that they stood for.

She remembered her first tutorial with Mallwyd during her
initial year in Aberystwyth. She had prepared an extensive treatment on rural imagery in the poetry of R.Williams Parry, and
was anxious to make a good impression. But two hours later –
her session having run to twice its allotted period – it was she
who had been impressed, and in a way that was to change her
life. They hadn't discussed Williams Parry at all. But they
discussed everything else: her home community, which Mallwyd
seemed to know at least as well as she did; her parents, whom
Mallwyd also knew well, and her ideas, with which Mallwyd
seemed to be more familiar than she was herself. But it was not

simply his knowledge; sheer information would have been impressive but not affecting. It was more than that. It was the love. He loved the same places, people, writers and ideas that she did, and, unlike her, he could give reasons why they were loveable, why they were unique and precious. It was as if she had shown him a childhood collection of shells, stones and ephemeral keepsakes, and he had taken them, examined them, polished them, and handed them back to her as jewels. He transformed her personal, unformed, visceral loyalty into a rational universal principle which she could defend against all attacks, a belief by which she could live and for which she could die.

Mallwyd had seemed to understand all the half-formed notions that her 18-year-old mind was trying to assess and prioritise. Career, friends, family, community, the cause; they all seemed to have a claim on her; the future had seemed to be like one of those confusing corridors in the university with many identical doors, and a different world behind each one. But by the time Meinwen had stepped out of Mallwyd's chaotic, book-littered office, she knew which door she was going to take. It was the door to freedom – but, as the saying had it, that door led through the prison gate.

Alain

As she walked down the hallway towards the library, Simone almost bumped into Alain.

'*Bonjour, Mademoiselle.*'

Alain never called the students by their first names.

'Oh, *bonjour M'sieur.* I was just on my way to do some more revision for tomorrow.'

'You'll be fine tomorrow,' he said, and motioned her to accompany him. They walked slowly along the hall towards the library, which opened out into tier after tier of books.

'Now, while we're talking, I want to say something to you,' said Alain. 'If you do well in your examination – and you will – you must remember the responsibilities that go with being a professional academic...'

'No,' said Simone.

Alain stopped. He looked at her. She was a strange creature. 'I don't want comfort,' she said.

He knew of Simone's ideals and her austere lifestyle: the monastic cloak she wore, her bare feet in sandals even in the coldest winter. These practices, and the asceticism which motivated them, seemed to be propelling her towards the margins of life. He hated to think of those resplendent intellectual gifts being squandered on the petty leftist politics and sterile factional in-fighting which were already absorbing too much of her time. He was hoping to channel that idealism into a more productive course.

'It's not comfort,' he said. 'It's strenuous. It's demanding, the life of the mind.' He thought for a moment, trying to frame his argument in a way her singular conscience would find palatable. 'And if you don't do it for yourself, do it for others.'

They had reached the end of the hallway where the bookshelves began. He lowered his voice as they approached the study area. They had stopped at an alcove. As she listened to Alain, Simone idly took down a volume from the shelf. It was a life of St John of the Cross. She opened it, as her teacher continued.

'Think of those you could help, Simone,' said Alain, breaking with his rule and using her first name in order to impress upon her the seriousness of what he was saying. 'Think of the good you could do as a professor. You have a strength of mind that's very rare, and you'll succeed brilliantly if you don't go wandering off down obscure paths.'

That was what he had wanted to tell her. Normally, he held himself aloof from his students, wary of his own power to mould their minds to his own, respectful of their need to make their own mistakes. He was making a rare exception in seeking a *tête-à-tête* with her, and had only done so because he judged her intellectual powers, and the strength of her personality, to be robust enough to deal with his intervention on something like equal terms. How would she respond?

Simone looked thoughtful but did not answer. Alain looked at her more closely. She didn't look up. He looked closer again. Yes, he was right. She was absorbed in the book. She had forgotten he was there. So much for his attempt to ignore his own advice and solicit a confidence. He smiled to himself, and left her to her

strange, self-directed studies. He walked off towards the entrance.
Simone did not even glance up as he went.

Meinwen

Meinwen had finished her college years with a first in Welsh,
and her other tutors had urged her to go on and study for a
Masters, then a PhD. She was one of the brightest students they
had ever taught, they told her. But the cause had been everything for her. She had turned them down. Her parents, who
loved her and supported her activism wholeheartedly, had taken
a long while to accept a daughter who lived, not for a career,
home and children, but for a political campaign. They had been
dismayed at her choice. Mallwyd, however, had been delighted.
Now, twenty years on, Mallwyd was still striving for that cause.
Jailed by the courts who thought him a misguided zealot, patro-
nised by the academic establishment which regarded him as an
amiable crank, and reviled by the opponents of the language
movement who considered him an irresponsible demagogue, he
had nonetheless retained his goodwill, and was sustained
through all disappointments by his political convictions and his
religious faith which were blended into a single stainless alloy.
For politicised Welsh speakers, the single name 'Mallwyd' was a
byword for integrity.
But Meinwen wondered how many of the other people in the
committee room knew of him. The single nationalist AM, yes.
But the Labour ones? The Lib Dems and Tories? Half of them
had moved to Wales long after Mallwyd's heyday. For Mallwyd,
Welsh history began sometime before the Roman invasion. For
most of this lot, it began sometime after Labour's General
Election victory in 1997. If Sir Anthony Thomas had been on
the committee it would have been something, thought
Meinwen; he might be a Tory, but at least he knew his Wales.
Mallwyd was talking about how the committee had the responsibility for ensuring the continued future of Welsh. Meinwen
smiled to hear him addressing the committee as 'we', as if they
were engaged in some shared enterprise. She knew the first

person plural was no mere rhetorical device. Mallwyd assumed everyone shared his views, and that, at worst, all that needed to happen was for their latent agreement to be awakened. Neither were his biblical cadences just a trick of oratory. Mallwyd assumed everyone shared the Christianity which, in the family and community in which he had been raised, had been as essential as the air they breathed, and as unquestioned. The language of Bishop Morgan's 1588 translation of the Bible permeated his speech, like camphor in a wardrobe, preserving and adding a cloying pungency. It must be the devil of a job for the translators to cope with though, thought Meinwen.

Meinwen knew that she gave little enough attention to her own appearance, but just now, as she looked at the committee chair-woman, Gloria Milde, she wished Mallwyd had given just a little more attention to his own grooming, if only for today. Even under the translation headphones the monolingual Milde was obliged to wear, her highlighted, feather-cut hair was sleek and immaculate. For his part, Mallwyd, though unencumbered by headphones, looked as if his hair had not been combed in a year. Milde's jacket, blouse and skirt were tailored and flattering, while still managing to look smart and businesslike. But as Meinwen's eyes flicked back and forth between the chairwoman and the witness, she noticed with a wince that Mallwyd's trousers were too short, that one shoelace was untied and that he had a large ink stain on the top pocket of his wide-lapelled jacket.

Alain

As Alain reached the hallway, he was met by Martin Blanc, the Principal of the *Lycée*. As always, his superior seemed in a hurry.

'Ah, Alain!' said Blanc. 'I see you've had an audience with the Red Virgin.' He indicated Simone, who was still leaning against the shelf, lost in her study of the Spanish mystic. 'I hope she wasn't too hard on you?'

Alain smiled: 'Oh, it wasn't like that.' He looked back at his pupil. 'I know she can be off-putting, but she really has an extraordinary mind. Utterly original talents. But she has no idea how to employ them for the best.'

'A female Lenin, perhaps, do you think?' said the principal. 'My God! Do you know what she did to me? You know she roams the corridors here all the time trying to get people to sign petitions for the unemployed, for the oppressed workers, and God knows what?'

Alain nodded.

Well, a couple of weeks ago, she asked me for a donation for the unemployed. So I gave her twenty francs – no less – but I asked her to tell no one. Understandable enough. And the next thing, I found she'd put a note on the noticeboard saying: 'Follow the example of your Principal. Give anonymously to the unemployment fund!'

'I had heard something about it, yes,' Alain answered with a cautious smile.

Blanc laughed despite himself: 'God help us if she ever got real power. Imagine her as our first woman prime minister!'

Alain looked thoughtful: 'Well, I think Reynard and his *Action Française* might have something to say about that. But you can be certain of one thing: if once that young woman finds her vocation, she could do something quite outstanding. But what exactly, I don't know. She certainly doesn't know herself.'

They looked over at Simone's dark figure. She was still reading.

Gloria Milde

Professor Price's sartorial lapses had not been lost on Gloria Milde. They had decided her opinion of his contribution even before his translated words had started coming through the headphones. So it was only with half an ear that she listened to the speech of the odd little man in front of her.

He was talking about the enlightenment in Wales in the eighteenth century. 'Was that like Buddhism?' Milde thought idly. She liked the idea of Buddhism. It sounded much more reasonable and inclusive than Christianity; and, as far as any of her social circle had any religious views, it seemed to be meditation and becoming enlightened that they discussed over the red wine. The idea that anyone would propose Christianity as a serious set of beliefs in such a situation, or indeed in any situation, was inconceivable to her. She didn't think she had ever met anyone who believed in it.

Milde was thinking that this job had turned out rather well for her. She had hoped for advancement when she had come to Wales in 2001, attracted from her position as a public relations executive in London by the Welsh Labour Party's policy of all-women constituency shortlists. But she hadn't expected to be made a chair quite so quickly. She found the languages committee deadly dull, but she hadn't wanted to refuse the appointment, as she was hoping she would be given something more interesting in due course. Some of the contributors managed to get really worked up about the subject, though. The current witness for one. He was on to the nineteenth century now, and some 'Welsh Knot' or something. And something about 'blue books'. Welsh pornography, she thought. Now that was an idea. Mind you, he looked like he was probably into that kind of thing.

Some letter-writers to the *Western Mail* had suggested that Milde knew nothing about Welsh, and that she had no policy of her own on the matter. She hadn't bothered to reply. If it had been in the *Guardian*, it might have mattered, but nobody bothered with the *Western Mail*. The critics were wrong anyway; while all this stuff about blue books and whatnot was going on, she had worked out what would actually be a far-reaching and influential policy. She had concluded that if there was a Welsh Language Board, then there could jolly well be an English Language Board as well, which would make sure that the English language wasn't oppressed or disadvantaged or whatever. It wouldn't even cost any more money, as her plan was to divide the budget currently given to the Welsh Language Board equally between Welsh and English. And because English was a world language, there'd be a need for fact-finding trips abroad. She smiled at the thought. The witness had reached the twentieth century now. She thought she had better tune into him, if only for a while.

He was saying that after years of quiet labour, this was finally his chance to present a long-cherished project. Concerned that mastery of Welsh was eroding from generation to generation and that the traditional engines of transmission, the home and the chapel, were failing, he had conceived a simple, practical plan to keep a critical mass of expertise within the language community. Students with a gift for language would be talent-spotted at secondary school and given special tuition, a mentor, weekend schools and a virtual guarantee of a university job if they undertook a demanding syllabus of linguistic training. They would be the future arbiters and sustainers of the language's standards. What the tradition could no longer do unaided, this would accomplish simply, effectively, sustainably and even cheaply. And it would all be sweetened with small but worthwhile extra incentive payments.

He was building up to his peroration. He was quoting names which Milde thought sounded like a list of rugby players: O.M. Edwards, Waldo Williams, D.J. Williams, Gwynfor Evans... She had been offered tickets for the rugger game that weekend. Oh, no, they didn't call it 'rugger' did they? Rugby. Whatever; it was a good place to make contacts. She began thinking who she was likely to meet. The little man was still droning on.

'We have it in our power to bring this to pass in our day,' he was saying. 'Where there is no vision, the people perish. We can prevent that fate from coming upon them.'

Milde noticed that her fellow-panellists' eyes remained downcast. Pens doodled, but faces retained their 'Workshop on Listening Skills' composure. It had been a long morning. Milde's mind began to wander again. How long was it until lunch? The cafeteria in this new building wasn't at all bad. She wondered what would be on the menu.

'Friends, we can accomplish this great thing, this act for which future generations will be forever in our debt. Friends, we can bring to pass the creation of...'

There was a long pause.

'... the creation of... The Guild of Home Spun Cloth!'

Another longer pause. Much longer. Recalled from her reverie, Milde looked up in alarm. The little man was looking at her with an air of expectancy. Clearly, she was supposed to give some sort of response.

'The... what?' she asked.

'The Guild of Home Spun Cloth,' the man repeated, and then pronounced the name in English for extra emphasis, the gears of his accent grinding as he did so.

There was a murmur from the public gallery. Milde thought she heard the words 'Oh my God'.

'The Guild of Home Spun Cloth...' she repeated tentatively. She was reluctant to admit that she didn't have a clue what this witness was talking about. And now she wished she'd paid more attention during his presentation, instead of musing on Buddhism and her future career. He was clearly expecting her to say something, but why were they suddenly talking about rural crafts? What had she missed? She looked to Mallwyd in a silent appeal for explanation.

It looked as if he thought she had simply repeated the words 'The Guild of Home Spun Cloth' with relish and appreciation. He was merely nodding his agreement and looking back at her with what looked horribly like quiet confidence.

Finally one of the other panellists came to the rescue, asking cautiously: 'Why... "The Guild of Home Spun Cloth," Professor Price?'

The witness came alive again.

'To remind them of their roots,' he explained. 'If these young people are going to form the vanguard of the salvation of Wales, we wouldn't want them to forget the farms and villages from which they've sprung, the toiling generations of folk who have passed on to them the incomparable riches of our language. This name will keep them humble, keep them close to the earth and to the civilisation founded by the Carpenter of Nazareth. It will bring them back to their trees.'

Milde felt a slight frisson of alarm. Back to the trees? Was this some kind of survivalist thing? Suddenly it wasn't funny any more. It was time this witness got back to whatever parallel universe he came from. Or back to his trees. She might not have listened to much that he'd said, but she now felt confident in closing him off.

'Mr Price, we thank you for your valuable and... er... original contribution,' she said. 'I'm afraid it's now time for lunch. We'll resume afterwards with evidence from the Black Women's Empowerment Initiative.'

●○●

Selma Weil

Madame Weil and Simone were sitting at the breakfast table of their home in Paris when they heard the clatter of the letterbox. Simone banged down her coffee cup and ran to the door. Madame Weil was just getting up from the table when she heard her daughter shout from the hallway.

'My results!'

Madame Weil waited as Simone came slowly down the hall, reading the letter to herself as she walked.

'Well?' said Madame Weil.

'Third,' said Simone, expressionless, her eyes downcast.

Then she looked up, laughing: 'Third... in the whole of France!'

'So. Third.' Madame Weil was suddenly pensive.

Simone's smile vanished, replaced by instant fury.

'What have I got to do?' she shouted, brandishing the paper. 'What would be good enough for you, Mother?'

'Simone, I'm sorry. I didn't mean...'

Simone's voice was bitter. 'I'm sorry I'm not a boy, Mother. I'm sorry I'm not brilliant like André. I'm sorry I'm not beautiful. Or good. I'm sorry... Third in the whole of France was the best I could do...'

She crumpled the paper in her hand and threw it away. Hot tears were bowling down her cheeks. Madame Weil approached her, and embraced her.

'Simone, Simone. I'm sorry. It's my fault. It's just that I always expect you to do so well, my darling girl. You know I love you.'

Simone continued to cry, but silently. Her mother held her.

Meinwen

'"Back to basics." I should have said "back to basics",' the young translator was speaking to Mallwyd in the Assembly's concourse afterwards. She put her hand to her forehead in frustration at herself. 'I'm sorry. It's just that there were so many quotations and idioms, I couldn't think of what corresponded to *"dod â nhw at eu coed".'*

Meinwen listened. She and the activists had gathered around Mallwyd, as the rest of the committee members and officials filed past them on the way to the cafeteria. Instinctively, the campaigners felt they should shield Mallwyd from the amused and curious looks he was attracting from some of those who had been present in the session. Such was the magnetism of his integrity among those, such as the translator, who carried within them the answering metal of commitment to the cause, that it could draw forth, as now, the most painful honesty.

Mallwyd was entirely unaware of the effect he had on his followers, a fact which only served to make its influence greater. Now, he seemed bemused at the translator's confession.

'Don't worry, my dear girl!' he said reassuringly. 'I'm sure you did a wonderful job. I'm sure the literal translation would get the meaning across perfectly well. They're intelligent people after all.'

The translator looked unconvinced, but nodded, unhappily.

Meinwen felt her fellow campaigners' indignation at those rootless blow-ins on the committee who had belittled Mallwyd. Even so, as the campaigners kept up a pretence at conversation, none of them could look directly at Mallwyd. Meinwen stole a glance at the great man of letters as he shuffled his papers back into his battered briefcase; he wrote all his work in longhand, believing typewriters an example of soulless mechanisation. He seemed calm and unruffled despite everything. Thank God, she thought: he doesn't realise what a débâcle that was. He thinks he's put his case successfully. What was the point of letting him know otherwise? Everything must change, maybe, but let poor Mallwyd stay the way he was.

He finished putting his papers away, and looked up, straight at Meinwen, seeing her for the first time. His face broke into a delighted smile. Leaving his briefcase on the floor, he took both her hands in his.

'Meinwen, *cariad*, how lovely to see you! Thank you so much for coming.'

'You know me, Mallwyd, I live for pleasure. Just try to keep me away.'

'Bless you.' He looked at her approvingly for a moment longer. Then his voice turned suddenly serious: 'Now, as you're here, come with me. I've been wanting to talk to you. I saw you on television last night...'

'Oh dear. I'm sorry. I wish I'd done a better job.'

'What do you mean? You were marvellous. I couldn't have done it better myself.'

That was less of a compliment than Mallwyd intended, Meinwen thought.

Her former mentor was still speaking.

'You did tremendously well. But it's not your TV skills that I want to talk to you about.'

He took her arm and began walking towards the exit, forgetting his briefcase, which was on the floor behind him. Meinwen looked back and saw Dewi, who picked up the briefcase and set off slowly after them with a wry smile, keeping his distance so that she and Mallwyd could talk. They passed through security and down the broad slate steps on the way to the pizza restaurant nearby.

'I'm worried about you, Meinwen,' said Mallwyd, his voice lowered confidentially.

'Why?'

'Can I tell you honestly?'

'Since when were you anything but honest, Mallwyd? Of course you can.'

'You're doing too much, and you're being too hard on yourself.'

'How much is too much? I'm not doing half enough. None of us are. Except you.'

He stopped and turned to her.

'Look at you. Meinwen. No one else will tell you this, but I'll tell you. You're starving yourself. Even I can see it. I saw it on television last night, and I can see it now. When did you last have a square meal?'

'Mallwyd...' Meinwen turned away from him.

'Dewi wouldn't tell you this, Meinwen.' Mallwyd looked behind him, but Dewi was out of earshot, talking with some of the other activists. 'And do you know why he won't tell you? Because he loves you, and he doesn't want to lose you. But he will lose you if you carry on. We'll all lose you.'

Meinwen wanted to get the conversation back onto the safer ground of politics.

'But, Mallwyd, it was you who always said the cause was worth devoting your life to.'

His hold on her arm slackened slightly, and he resumed their walk to the restaurant.

'I did always say that. I still do say it. But you have to be alive to devote your life, Meinwen. I didn't mean don't bother living. I meant live your life for the cause. That's a different thing altogether. It's a joy. It's a privilege. I thank God every day that I have a cause worth living for.'

'But we're not winning.'

'It doesn't matter. We're fighting. We're living. We can't be responsible for the outcome, only for our own actions. We can't assume we're failing. We don't know. We might just as well assume we're winning. It's a sight happier way to live. How old are you now...?'

'Mallwyd... please.'

He stopped again. They were at the entrance to the restaurant. He sighed, and abandoned his cross-examination; his voice moved from the confidential to the conversational.

'You're going to have lunch with me,' he said. 'It's my treat. I won't take no for an answer.'

Meinwen looked past him into the restaurant. She saw the stainless steel basins full of pale, glistening chips, the sagging discs of pizza, the trays of wizened brown sausages. Her gorge rose. She felt trapped. Alarm gripped her.

'I can't, Mallwyd. I really can't. We've got to catch a bus to north Wales. If I stay, we'll miss it.'

'Meinwen...' Mallwyd's voice was sceptical, like a parent listening to a child's artless falsehood. Meinwen was looking around for Dewi. She caught his eye.

'Dewi, we've got to go, haven't we? The bus.'

Dewi looked at his watch, and looked back at her, puzzled. He seemed about to disagree. But then he saw the mute appeal, almost a command, in her eyes, so he said, uncomfortably: 'Oh yes, of course, the bus. We can't miss that.'

'I'm sorry, Mallwyd,' said Meinwen.

'So am I, *cariad*,' he said.

Dewi

Mallwyd cupped the side of Meinwen's face in his hand gently for a moment, in farewell, then turned to Dewi, who was handing him his briefcase.

'Dewi, lad. Thank you! Where would I be without you?'

'I could ask you the same thing, Mallwyd. No, I know the answer. We'd probably have jobs and mortgages and children by now. And no criminal records. Thanks for saving us from that!'

Mallwyd looked over at Meinwen, who had already moved away from them towards the exit to the building. He gave Dewi a knowing glance.

'I'd better let you go. You've got a bus to catch, haven't you?'

'Yes – in about an hour and a half.'

'Better be off quickly then,' Mallwyd smiled. 'The station's a good twenty minutes walk away.'

'Oh. Is it that much?'

Mallwyd looked over towards Meinwen again, and his face became pensive. Then he said quietly: 'Look after her, Dewi.'

Dewi simply nodded. Then he turned away to follow Meinwen, who was already walking away from the shadow of the restaurant and out into the early afternoon sun. Behind her was the sunlit expanse of Cardiff Bay, and beyond that, to the south, the open sea and the world. But Meinwen had her face set away, heading north.

Simone

Madame Weil put the brush through Simone's curls one more time, and checked her appearance in the fitting room mirror.

'He called again last night, Simone,' she said.

'Who?'

'You know very well who – Pierre Letellier. He asked if you'd be at the graduation ball.'

'He knows I will.'

'He said you're welcome to come to his parents' farm again this summer. Do you think you'll go? You enjoyed it there last year didn't you? It will be lovely at harvest time.'

'It wasn't "lovely at harvest time", Mother. Not for the workers. You make it sound as if I was sight-seeing. I was working. Ten hours a day, until my back ached and my head was swimming.'

'Yes, dear. And then came back to your studies at the *École Normale Supérieure*, all the more virtuous for the callouses on your little white hands.'

Simone sighed her exasperation. She felt her mother's fingers tugging lightly at her hair, shaping her, moulding her into acceptability, into conformity. She turned round. 'Mother. Do I have to dress up? It feels so false. It's not me. It's not right.'

Madame Weil turned her firmly towards the mirror again, and continued putting the finishing touches to her hair. Released from its normal confinement under the old black beret which Simone customarily wore, it now fell in long rich curls around her shoulders. Her fingers teased it into a perfect frame for Simone's delicate pale features. The glasses Simone wore for her short sight only seemed to increase the size of her dark and serious eyes.

'Simone, we have to accept the role life has assigned us,' Madame Weil said. 'You enjoy a *Normalienne* education – you wear the *Normalienne* clothes. You can't have the advantages and the freedom. It's not ostentation to conform. It would be ostentation *not* to. Now let me look at you.'

Simone stood up. Normally she wore a shabby dark cloak over a man's black jacket, and a long black skirt or trousers. Now, in the finest white gown that Madame Herbeaux's boutique could offer, she was transformed. She could not suppress a faint smile as she regarded herself in the mirror.

Meinwen

The bus journey from south Wales had taken hours. Dewi had got off at Porthmadog to go to his flat, but Meinwen had travelled on to Colwyn Bay, where her parents lived. It had been a couple of weeks since she had visited them, and she thought she may as well combine two journeys. She could catch the bus back to Porthmadog the following day.

Meinwen could drive, but she didn't have a car, and there

was something about bus travel that she liked. Perhaps it was because so much of her life involved trying to invigorate the inert and trying to make progress against society's currents, so that when she travelled by bus it was a relief, for once, to surrender to the flow, and leave the direction of her life to someone else. Also, the bus was the most cost-effective way for her to travel. But, by God, it wasn't time-effective. How could Wales ever be a nation when you could cross the Atlantic by plane in less time than it took to travel from Cardiff to north Wales by bus?

Now the coach was finally pulling into Colwyn Bay. She could see the sea shining in the gaps between the redbrick Victorian buildings. Meinwen's parents had retired to Colwyn Bay some years ago, seeking, no doubt, like many of the English retirees who also chose to spend their later years in Welsh resorts, the happy memories of holidays in younger days.

During Meinwen's childhood holidays there, Colwyn Bay had been one of the more genteel of the north Wales coastal resorts. It was where you went if you couldn't afford the upmarket Victorian ambience of Llandudno but considered yourself too good for chip-strewn, raucous Rhyl. But when she went there now, she was appalled. Many of the fine old redbrick hotels had been turned into bed-and-breakfast hostels, filled with shifts of what Meinwen was tempted to dismiss as displaced jobless scousers. But she conscientiously corrected her instinctive assumptions – they might well be displaced jobless Welsh people, unable to afford accommodation anywhere else; the Merseyside accent had spread so far along the north Wales coast by now that it was no longer a demarcation between incomer and native.

Now, as the bus approached the town centre, Meinwen, on an impulse, decided to get off the bus a couple of stops early, and visit Eirias Park. She wanted to stretch her legs after the journey. If she arrived straight at her parents she would probably fall asleep right away. A walk would wake her up a bit. It was in Eirias Park that Meinwen had spent day after day of her childhood holidays, and where, if she could have had her way as a child, she would have spent every day of her life. As the bus pulled away, she walked in through the park's wrought-iron gates.

With the decline in the town's fortunes, most of the park's

attractions now seemed to have vanished. The kiosk shops were gone, so was the little half-timbered amusement arcade; the pitch-and-putt was now overgrown, the outlines of tees and greens hidden and softened like those of ancient earthworks. The boating lake was a weed-choked swamp and, as Meinwen passed the veranda of the shuttered boathouse, three youths, sitting there smoking, looked up at her, with pinched faces and eyes darting from under their hoodies. She thought they looked like water rats with clothes on. The whole park seemed so much smaller than she remembered it. She walked on to the town centre.

Colwyn Bay had previously opened out onto the curving sea front. But for the last fifteen years it had been separated from the water by the A55 dual carriageway; the road which had put north west Wales within commuting distance of Manchester and Liverpool. Severed from the sea by four lanes of pounding traffic, the town's fortunes had dived, and the shops where Meinwen used to browse as a child had closed, to be replaced by charity enterprises, everything-for-a-pound outlets and building societies. She was sorry she had taken the detour.

She remembered the Kwik Eat café, which used to be in this street. In the 1970s, when burger-joints were a novelty, the thick spongy vinyl menus and the shiny formica tables of the Kwik Eat had seemed the height of chic. She used to beg her parents to be taken there. It was a highpoint of any holiday in Colwyn Bay. The café tables offered not only bottles of tomato ketchup and brown sauce, but also a condiment previously unknown to Meinwen – Worcestershire sauce. She remembered the difficulty she had in pronouncing the name, and her pride when she had memorised the slogan on the bottle: 'Made to the recipe of a gentleman in the county'. What would the Kwik Eat be now, she thought, as she walked down the street where it had used to stand. A hairdressers'? No, an estate agents' probably. They were the only businesses which seemed to thrive, the housing stock of north Wales, thanks to the A55, having become a price-less cash crop. She wondered if she would even be able to remember which building the Kwik Eat had occupied. The memory could often play strange tricks.

Then she stopped. The Kwik Eat was still there, unchanged. Its stylised smiling chef symbol the same. Its menu, too. It was still in business. Better than that. It seemed to be full of customers. She pushed open the smeared glass door, and stepped three decades back over the threshold. The room was thick with cigarette smoke. Almost everyone in the café seemed to be smoking. No, correct that, *everyone* in the café was smoking. She found a free table in the rear of the room, ordered a cup of tea and, for old time's sake, her favourite omelette and chips. If she had a meal now, even if she didn't eat all of it, she would have an excuse to refuse the dinner her mother would otherwise insist on putting before her later on. And she'd avoid yet another row about food. As she waited for the order to arrive, she looked around her.

It was late afternoon, and most of the customers seemed to be teenage schoolchildren. Fags, flirting and f-words. Next to her table, an elderly man and a middle-aged woman, his daughter, perhaps, were chatting in accents she guessed were those of Kirby or Skelmersdale or somewhere on Merseyside. Meinwen looked around her, trying to recall familiar features. She looked up at the ceiling, Now that was something she'd forgotten. How on earth could she have failed to remember it? Perhaps it had been blotted out like a traumatic memory. From the centre of the room a kind of angular white plastic tree sprouted about seven feet high, spreading its shiny branches across the stained polystyrene tiles of the ceiling. From its pale limbs hung giant orange and brown lanterns the size of small dustbins. The place should have a preservation order put on it. It was a time capsule of genuine unchanged seventies decor; ugly beyond description, but heroically ugly, defying all the changing tides of taste and style.

As she waited for the food, the wonderment that Meinwen had initially felt at finding herself back in her own past was beginning to fade, to be replaced by a faint nausea. She tried to push the feeling away. She wanted comfort, a sojourn in the untroubled past. She didn't want to feel that physical repulsion here of all places. Sometimes she wished she had an appetite like she'd had as a child; an appetite like those of the people working their way through light-brown mounds of pies, pasties, chips and peas on the nearby tables. But, despite herself, she couldn't fight down the feeling of disgust. Here it was a combination of the cigarette smoke, the body odour of the man on the next table, the chemical reek of industrial-strength air freshener from the nearby toilets, and the knowledge that the carpet under her feet was compacted with squashed food. When her meal finally arrived, it was all she could do to drink the tea.

'Eh, love, that'll get cold if you don't eat it.' It was the elderly man on the next table. His daughter, if that's what she was, had just left.

'Oh, I'm not hungry all of a sudden,' said Meinwen. 'I'm sorry. I shouldn't waste it really.'

He recognised the tell-tale signs in her accent.

'*O ble chi'n dod 'te?*' he asked. 'Where do you come from then?' It was the traditional greeting of Welsh speakers every-where. Profession, interests, qualifications, social standing counted for little to them. All that mattered was people's community of origin. The geographical establisher was the preface to a benign interrogation that would continue until the interlocutor had found at least one contact, however tenuous, in common: a mutual friend, a schoolteacher, councillor, chapel minister. Once that link had been established, they could relax.

Meinwen was surprised that this man's English should sound so scouse, but his Welsh be so good. She thought about his question for a moment. Where could she say she was from? She had been brought up in Caernarfon, but her parents now lived here in Colwyn Bay, while she herself lived in Porthmadog. She decided to take the shortest route to satisfying his curiosity. It would make the conversation briefer.

'Well, I live in Porthmadog, but I'm here visiting my parents. They live up in Bryn Eirias.'

'Bryn Eirias. Nice houses there,' he smiled knowingly. 'Must be worth a tidy bit.'

'Well I don't think they're planning to sell. They're retired. My father was the headteacher of Ysgol Glan y Môr. Idwal Jones.'

Her interrogator computed this information for a moment.

'Idwal Jones from Blaenau?'

'That's right.'

'Used to live in Caernarfon?' This with a note of triumph.

'Yes.'

He sat back satisfied with his detective skills. It was Meinwen's turn now. Politeness demanded it. She sighed inwardly and asked.

'So are you from Colwyn Bay?'

'No, I've retired here too. I'm from Mold.'

No more clues. He wasn't making it easy for her.

'I see.' She ran through her mental address book. 'Do you know Rhydderch Williams, the minister of Bethel?'

The old man's face brightened.

'Rhydderch! Yes, I should say so. Know him well. Would never darken the doors of his chapel, mind.' He said this with a warning note as if Meinwen was about to suggest that he attend a prayer meeting there. He pondered for a moment what was clearly some ancient grievance, then said, 'but Rhydderch himself, great bloke. Have a pint with you anytime.'

Their mutual credentials established, Meinwen's store of smalltalk was running dangerously low. She was trying to think of what to say next when the old man saved her the trouble. He pointed to her plate.

'You really don't want that?'

'No. I've just got no appetite. I'm sorry.' Then she realised suddenly, and belatedly, the point of the man's question, and added: 'Do you want it?'

'Well, only if you don't.'

Meinwen shook her head and passed the plate across.

'It would be a shame to waste it,' she said.

The old man was already tackling the chips as Meinwen excused herself, paid her bill and left.

From the street, she looked back at the Kwik Eat. In the background, she could hear the traffic on the coast road. The noise had even drowned out the sound of the sea. But through all the changes, the Kwik Eat had remained the same. She should have felt reassured that this one formica oasis had withstood the challenge of the decades that had thundered past like the juggernauts on the dual carriageway. But she didn't. She felt somehow cheated. It seemed to have been preserved by inertia not by love. Maybe change wasn't always such a bad thing. She turned away and walked on to her parents' house.

Selma Weil

That evening, at the graduation reception in the grand hall of the *Normale*, Dr and Madame Weil were talking with the parents of some of the other students. The almost universal topic was their children's prospects, which were – such was the *Normale's* reputation – unfailingly good. In the background, over the hubbub of voices, the master of ceremonies could be heard announcing the arrival of each new guest.

Pierre Letellier approached the group. He had a natural physical grace which the evening wear only accentuated. While many of the other young men, even the wealthy ones, looked uncomfortable in their formal clothes, he, the labourer's son, seemed entirely self-possessed. Madame Weil turned towards him with her warmest smile.

'Pierre, how lovely to see you.'

'Madame Weil, Dr Weil,' Pierre nodded his respects.

'Congratulations on your results, Pierre,' said Madame Weil. 'I heard you did very well.'

'Thank you. But Simone did even better, didn't she?'

'Well, she worked hard. I'll say that for her. And what are your plans now? Lecturing?'

'No, Madame. Politics. I have the offer of a place on the *Worker's Voice*.'

'Ah, yes. The *Worker's Voice*. Simone sometimes brings that home. So I assume material advancement is not a consideration for you, either, Pierre?'

She knew Pierre well enough to know her irony would not be thought unkind.

'No Madame, only the advancement of the working people.' Then, as if conscious how cold that sounded, he said, in a more personal tone: 'You know my father died last year?'

Madame Weil nodded, closing her eyes for a moment in sympathy.

'Well, when that happened, I made up my mind that I would do all I could to help people like him, people who didn't have the advantages of education or privilege.'

'That's very commendable, Pierre. I'm sure your father would have been very proud.'

'I hope so, Madame Weil.' Then, changing the subject, he looked around him: 'Is Simone here?'

'She should be here any minute,' answered Madame Weil. 'She wanted a little longer to get ready. We came on by cab. Our servant's bringing Simone. I'm sorry she's delayed. But,' she smiled at Pierre: 'She's been making an extra effort for tonight.'

As she spoke, she heard the master of ceremonies announce 'Mademoiselle Simone Weil.' She, her husband and Pierre turned to look towards the entrance hall. Through the crowd, they could not see Simone, but they heard a sudden murmur of comment and laughter.

The press of men in evening dress and women in ball gowns parted as Simone approached. The murmur continued, increasing in volume. Now, the Weils and Pierre could see Simone properly.

She was wearing a dark and shapeless man's jacket, a white shirt, and trousers. Her hair was scraped back and crammed untidily under her everyday beret.

Madame Weil and her husband had their eyes fixed on Simone, scarcely believing what they were seeing. Madame Weil heard Pierre murmur his farewell and saw him take advantage of the movement Simone's entrance had caused in the crowd to move quietly aside.

Simone came up to her parents, smiling candidly. A circle had grown around them. Some of the other guests were looking amused, others annoyed, and some were clearly passing ill-intentioned comments. Simone, seemingly oblivious of the sensation she had caused, greeted her parents affectionately. Madame Weil, although inwardly mortified more than she had ever dreamed possible, had mastered her initial shock and was not going to allow herself to be abashed in this company. She could hide her horror when visiting the wounded, her sorrow when comforting the dying. She could hide her embarrassment now. She kissed Simone warmly, and spoke loudly enough for the nearby guests to hear.

'Yes, darling, you were right about the dress. It's so boring to conform, isn't it?'

Dr Weil stepped over, took both Simone's hands and looked into her eyes, as though he wanted to appreciate her beauty to the full.

'Simone,' he said. Then, looking down at her clothes, and back at her, amused, he said more quietly: 'Or should I say, "Simon"?'

Simone smiled back artlessly. 'Oh, I'm more comfortable like this. I didn't want to make a show of myself.'

It was the only comment she was to make on the matter. She looked around her, searching the crowd, then turned to her mother.

'Didn't I see Pierre with you?' she asked.

'Er... yes,' said Madame Weil. 'Yes, he was here for a few moments. But he must have been called away. I'm sure he'll be back.'

Simone looked round the room, ineffectually.

Madame Weil's sharper eyes had already seen Pierre on the balcony talking with some friends. He was close enough to see her, surely. After all, she was prominent enough, at the centre of the room, in dark isolation among the colourful ball gowns. But he did not look in her direction.

●○●

Meinwen

Every time Meinwen visited her parents' home, her mother's conversation would circle around the same subject, like a hungry seagull eyeing a picnic. The life events of Meinwen's school and college contemporaries usually provided the starting point.

'Anwen has had another baby. It's her third.'

'Who?'

'Anwen Roberts. Well, Anwen Davies she used to be. You'll remember her from school. Married Emrys Roberts' boy, Rheinallt.'

'Rheinallt with the spots?'

'That was twenty years ago. He's Rheinallt with the big house and the people carrier now.'

'Sounds like he'll need it, with all those children. They'll probably be sick all over it.'

'... and a steady job with the health authority...'

'Good, well he'll be able to ask their advice about... whooping cough or whatever it is babies get.'

'And Judith Evans and Mark Preece have got married as well.'

'I thought they were married already. They've got children, haven't they? They've been together for ages.'

'Yes, well. They were... you know...'

'Living together, Mam.'

'Yes. But her dress was beautiful, and their daughters were the bridesmaids. Her mother was showing me the pictures.

Beautiful. They had the wedding in St Deiniol's.'

'St Deiniol's? Since when have they been churchgoers?'

'They're not, really. Well, Judith's grandmother used to go. Sometimes. At Christmas. But St Deiniol's gives a lovely background for the pictures.'

'Well, I'm very glad for them. I just hope they didn't have to tell too many lies to the vicar.'

It was coming now.

'Do you... still see much of that Dewi?'

Dewi's name was always prefaced with 'that'. Even after nearly twenty years, the indeterminate nature of his relationship with Meinwen meant that her mother used this little verbal prophylactic to keep him outside the circle of acceptance.

'I see him every week, Mam. Every day sometimes.'

'But he's not... sharing with you any more.'

'No, Mam. You know he's not. He moved out five years ago, and he hasn't started "sharing" with me again since you last asked me. He lives in Porthmadog, OK? By himself. And I live in Yr Hafan. By *my*self.'

'I was only asking...' offended now.

Meinwen sighed. The interrogation was over. Until next time.

Bernard Weil

'A schoolteacher?' Madame Weil almost shouted. 'In some dismal little town in the middle of nowhere? Simone, with results like yours you could be a professor like your brother.'

'No. I want to teach,' Simone said. 'I want to help the poor. Don't you understand?'

Dr Weil sat on the sofa, saying nothing. He flicked through the pages of a book, unseeing. Experience taught him that it would be better to wait until some of the heat had gone out of the dispute before he intervened.

'Throwing away your education. Your future. Alain – Alain, the man you hero-worship...'

'I don't hero-worship him. Alain himself says hero-worship is stupid. A person has to make his own decisions, rationally, honestly...'

'Whatever. Alain himself told me you have the most brilliant mind he's ever encountered. A schoolteacher! Why can't you be something I can be proud of?'

A note of self-pity had entered Madame Weil's voice. Dr Weil, sensing the mood had moved from outright stormy anger to mere blustery regret, decided it was time to speak.

'She wants to help the poor, Selma. Of that, I am proud. She doesn't care for possessions, or for position. Of that, I am proud.'

Madame Weil drew a deep breath, and looked down. No one spoke for a minute or so. Then Madame Weil opened her arms to Simone and a moment later, they were embracing.

'I will help you pack,' whispered Madame Weil.

Simone smiled her thanks, and left the room. Dr Weil motioned his wife to sit down beside him. He spoke now not in French, the language they used with their children, but in their native Alsace German.

'It will pass. It's just a phase,' he said. 'She's young. After she's got this out of her system she'll settle down. We used to be like that, remember? Young anarchists wanting to change the world. The world doesn't change – people change. Anarchists turn into bourgeois radicals. A few more demonstrations, a few more political meetings, it'll be over. She'll meet a nice boy and settle down.'

Madame Weil nodded.

'A nice gentile boy,' Dr Weil added mischievously. Although prepared to own his Jewishness when necessary, he was not religious, and felt little concern for the continuance of the Jewish race. Rather, recalling the Dreyfus affair, he felt the immense pressure in France for Jews to assimilate for their own good, as the ultimate escape from persecution. His comment was only half joking. He knew that his wife, too, would not wish on her daughter the history of persecution, pogrom and flight which had driven her own family from Eastern Europe.

'Yes,' said Madame Weil, 'a nice gentile boy.'

Meinwen

Meinwen reached the top of Bryn Aur. It was quite a climb from Porthmadog. There in front of her, outlined against the mountains of Eryri, was the angular shape of the hilltop chapel, Hermon, and next to it, the attendant manse, Yr Hafan, a gaunt, unadorned, square building in heavy stone. Grey. Forbidding. Home.

For the last fifteen years Meinwen had lived here. Not that she owned it. Meinwen owned virtually nothing. Dewi had teased her about this, telling her that in medieval times there had been a lively and sometimes acrimonious debate in the Catholic church as to whether Jesus had owned his own clothes. He said that if any similar conclave ever sat to consider the case of Meinwen Jones, they might find it equally challenging.

Meinwen felt the same distaste towards money as she did towards food: it was necessary sometimes, but was generally best avoided, certainly in all but the most meagre amounts. She gave away most of the little income that came her way: to the Movement, to Third World charities, to children's hospices, to beggars on the street, even if they looked better-dressed or better fed than she did. In material terms she gave 'no thought to the morrow', and yet she was clothed and fed like one of God's own sparrows.

●○●

Yvette

Yvette Bertillon made her way through the narrow streets towards the address Simone had sent her. Although, as a communist activist, she was accustomed to visiting working-class areas, she felt uncomfortable here, where there were no familiar faces, and where a lone woman, not in working clothes, looked out of place.

Eventually, she found the tenement block, checked the number, and ventured inside. There was a reek of urine from the communal toilet at the back of the stairwell, and a stench of garbage from the cans piled by the door. A dirty child of about three years old squinted at her from one of the open doors. Yvette ascended the stairs. She was about to put her hand on the banister, when she thought better of it, and walked up without touching it. On each landing was the same smell of urine. Reaching the top floor, Yvette knocked hesitantly at the door of one of the flats.

It was snatched open by Simone. She smiled with pleasure as she greeted Yvette and stood back to let her come in. They didn't embrace. Yvette had long learned that embracing wasn't something Simone did unless she absolutely had to. Apparently, it was a family thing. Her mother, so Simone had told her, was morbidly afraid of microbes and had even forbidden anyone from outside the family to kiss the children. Simone seemed to have taken this concern to heart, and now even avoided all physical contact with everyone except her parents and brother. More than once Yvette had noticed her putting the sleeve of her coat over her hand before opening a door. How she could live in a district like this when she was so abnormally fastidious was beyond her.

Yvette stepped inside. The room was almost completely bare. Just a table, a sink, one chair and no bed. Although it was November, there was no fire. But there were books, of course. Hundreds of them. Yvette doubted if it was possible to live on books alone, but Simone seemed to be giving it a good try.

'Are you moving out, then?' she asked Simone.

'No. Why do you ask?'

'The room, it's almost empty.'

'Oh, that. Well, I have everything I need.'

'But where do you sleep?'

'There.' She indicated a rolled-up blanket on the floor.

Yvette was just starting to take in the kind of life Simone was living. Compared to her college rooms, which had been spartan enough, this was positively masochistic. She looked at the few provisions on the table. A dark loaf, a bottle of milk, a small piece of butter and two eggs. It was plain fare, that was the best that could be said for it.

'The dish of the day?'

'The dish of the week.'

Yvette could not conceal her concern. Simone hastened to reassure her.

'Oh, it's plenty! You see – this is all an unemployed worker could afford. I'm here trying to understand the sufferings of the poor. I can hardly do it on a bourgeois diet. I've worked it all out to the centime. This is all you can afford if you're unemployed, so it's all I can allow myself. Half a kilo of butter. Three eggs. One loaf. And milk from M'sieur Bloom – watered down I'm afraid.' She held up the bottle of thin liquid ruefully.

Yvette was not reassured. There was something dangerous about Simone's eccentricities; something positively unhealthy. Simone had always given generously to the poor, but she seemed to be living on less than the poorest unemployed labourer. What possible purpose could that serve? Not really comprehending, Yvette nonetheless nodded as if she understood. Simone clearly thought her explanation left room for no further questions. She was serene. The fewer externals she had, the happier she seemed to be.

'But I wouldn't expect a guest to make do on this,' Simone continued, putting on her cloak from where it hung on a peg behind the door. 'Wait for half an hour, and I'll go the shop and get us some better bread, and some wine. And a nice bit of cheese. Make yourself at home.'

She hurried off down the stairs.

At home, thought Yvette. Not much chance of that. She looked out of the window. Although the area was squalid, there really was a splendid view from here. If you looked across the rooftops to where the river was shining, you could almost forget the hunger and the filth below. She sat at Simone's table, and looked across the mess of material on the rough wooden surface: half-finished essays, socialist magazines of all kinds, some of them containing articles by Simone; she was a prodigious and prolific writer. There were posters and handbills for a clamour of different, sometimes contradictory, progressive causes: ones calling for strikes against the government, help for refugees in China, for the Left in France to unite against capitalism, for workers to take over their own industries, for the French to get out of Indo-China. She looked at the row of books: *Das Kapital*, of course. Trotsky's speeches. So far, so Simone. But then Yvette noticed less familiar books: the *Koran*, the *Upanishads*, the *Bhagavad Gita*, the *New Testament*. Among these, Yvette found one loose sheaf in Simone's distinctive small manuscript; she picked it up and started to read.

'He came into my room and said "Poor creature: you understand nothing; you know nothing. Come with me and I will teach you things which you have not suspected." I followed him. He took me to a church. It was new and ugly. He led me up towards the altar and he said "Kneel down". I replied "I am not baptised". He said: "Fall down to your knees before this place, in love, as though it were the place where the truth lies." I obeyed him.

'Then he led me out and made me climb up to a garret. Through the open window the whole city could be seen spread out below. The garret was empty, except there were a table and two chairs. He asked me to sit.

'We were by ourselves. It was no longer winter; it was not yet spring. The branches of the trees lay bare, without buds, in the cold air full of sunshine.

'The daylight would come, shine out in beauty, and fade; then the moon and the stars would come in through the window. And then once again the dawn would come.

'From time to time he would become silent, take some bread from a cupboard, and we would share it. It really had the taste of bread. I have never found that taste again. He would pour some wine out for us both – wine which had the taste of the sun and of the soil on which this city has been built.

'At other times we would both stretch out on the garret floor, I would be enfolded by sweet sleep. Then I would wake and drink in the sunlight.

'Although he had promised to teach me, he did not do so. We simply talked about all sorts of subjects, in a desultory kind of way, like old friends do.

'Then one day he said: "Now go". I fell down in front of him. I grasped his knees, I begged him not to drive me away. But he cast me out on the stairs. I went down with my heart in pieces. Then I realised that I had no idea where this house could be found.

'I have never again tried to find it. He had come for me by mistake. My place is not there in that garret. It can be in any place – a prison cell, a middle-class drawing room, a railway waiting room – anywhere, except there in that garret.

'Sometimes, fearfully and sorrowfully, I cannot help trying to repeat to myself some of what he said to me. But I can't know if I am remembering it rightly? He is not here to tell me.

'I know well that he does not love me. How could he? And yet, deep down inside me, something, a tiny atom of myself, cannot help thinking, with fear and trembling, that perhaps, in spite of everything, he does love me.'

Yvette heard Simone's footsteps on the stairs. She wasn't moving very quickly. She had never been the most athletic of people. There was time for Yvette to hide the memoir if she wanted to. But she did not want to.

Simone came in and put the cheese, bread and wine on the table. She was breathless from the climb. She came over to where Yvette was sitting at the table.

'Who is he, then?' asked Yvette.

'Who?'

'Him.' She indicated the paper in her hand.

Simone took the paper, thoughtful, but not at all angry.

'I don't know,' she said. She turned to look out of the window. Yvette followed her gaze. The sun was going down.

'I don't know,' she repeated, 'but I'm looking for him.'

She looked out to where the city was spread out below them. She continued, more quietly: 'And, I think, he's looking for me'.

The last of the evening light was turning the windows of the tenement opposite to gold. For a few moments, the slum was beautiful.

Meinwen

Meinwen opened the door to Yr Hafan and went inside, picking up from the dusty hall floor the post which had accumulated during her few days' absence. She went through to the kitchen and put the kettle on. As she waited for it to boil, she looked around her at the house where she had spent most of her adult life. It occurred to her that this remote manse embodied almost exactly a century of history.

The date on the gable was 1905, the year of the great religious revival which was the high water mark of Christianity in Wales, a time when the zeal of Welsh nonconformity had moved working people to sacrifice their scarce pennies to build chapels and their accompanying manses wherever their fellow mortals had settled. By the time the revival had peaked, even the bare forehead of Bryn Aur had been given its angular grey diadem.

The decline from there had been swift. The great war had harvested the converts in their thousands and left the faith in their homeland as little more than a haggard aftermath. Throughout the century, the chapels had been closing steadily, as the graph of religious observance in Wales moved ever closer to zero.

The ebb had reached Yr Hafan in the 1960s, when the population of the high hills, and their commitment to religion, had dwindled so that a full-time minister could no longer be maintained. Hermon chapel itself remained open, served now by one exhausted minister whose cure of souls included no fewer than nine separate places of worship, each with only a handful of members, but Yr Hafan had been sold off to a chapel member. Twenty years later he had left it in his will to the Movement. Rather than sell it, the Movement had kept it as a kind of safe house in Gwynedd. It was about as safe as any house was in Gwynedd these days, where homes were sold to incomers almost before their previous owners were cold in their graves. Scarcely a house became available but it went to someone cashing in on the housing boom in London or Birmingham or God knows where else. Many estate agents no longer even bothered advertising locally, as they could sell the houses by a single phone call to colleagues across the border who had waiting lists of buyers looking for a rural retreat and just itching to try out the new Provençal peasant-style decor schemes from *Country Living*. Yr Hafan must be worth about five times more than any local first-time buyer could scrape together on the depressed local wage.

Yr Hafan now felt like a monument to a vanished world, Meinwen thought. Even the years it had belonged to the Movement felt like they were in a different age. From the beginning of Meinwen's time there, in the late eighties, Yr Hafan had been the home to five activists. The Crew they called themselves. They didn't need a proper name, as they weren't really an official group. It was just that, living together as they did, they naturally became a kind of movement within the Movement; the full-time activists, living only on their commitment and their state benefit. The fact that the house was rent-free made it all a lot easier.

Meinwen thought of those days as a kind of golden age. She and the others had held all things in common. They pooled their benefit money, and any donations that came their way. They lived frugally. Yet, had they not all been ardent republicans, one could say their lifestyle was princely in its independence. Yr Hafan was Protest Central for any visiting campaigner. South African anti-apartheid activists stayed there, and when Nelson Mandela walked free from jail, the Crew felt they had helped turn the key that released him. The odd wandering Breton came too, with guitar, gutturals and *Gaulois*; Irish republicans stayed there, amused by the tame domesticity of the Movement's revolution; they thought of the Welsh as Celts who had been house-trained. Yr Hafan was a kind of YMCA for revolutionaries. And about as secret. Even some of the police who regularly made the trek up to Yr Hafan to question the occupants in the wake of some latest daubing or sign-removing became almost part of the family. The local sergeant had his own mug there for his tea. It had a picture of Mr Plod from the Noddy books.

The cup was still there, on a rack with the others. For the sake of the memory, Meinwen pulled it down from the rack now to make herself some tea. As she poured the boiling water, she reflected that it was a while since the police had visited her; in fact, it was a while since anyone had visited her, apart from Dewi, and her father.

It had been different once. In the heyday of Yr Hafan, the four other activists who lived there permanently had become Meinwen's family. Closer than family, really, she thought. She shared not just her worldly goods with them, but her whole life. She lived as if she were part of a federation; one cell in a body. Loyalty for Meinwen meant total loyalty. She would make no major decision unless the Crew endorsed it first. That was why she had referred the decision on going out with Dewi to them. She assumed their loyalty was no less absolute, and she was utterly, unswervingly loyal to the Crew, even now, when, for various reasons, they had all, except her, left Yr Hafan and gone their separate ways.

Bedwyr Roberts' family had farmed in the Vale of Clwyd since before records began. Bedwyr himself, with his stubbly red hair and swinging gait, could hardly have looked more like a farm boy if he'd tried. But he saw no future on the land, and, leaving the farm to his younger brother, he had made a career out of activism. In all his clashes with police and courts, he retained an independence of spirit that made their censures and sanctions appear like mere annoyances, like horseflies swished away by the tail of an unbroken young stallion. That same independence had stood him in good stead when he eventually left to start his own business distributing European grants.

Since then, there had been plenty of criticism about how much money Bedwyr spent on offices, cars and secretaries, and how little actually reached the communities for which it was intended. But he ignored it all with the same effortless disdain with which he had defied the police. Every business needed administration, he said. And the Mercedes was the best car for getting around in rural Wales. You needed something with plenty of acceleration to get past the bloody English holiday-makers in their caravans. Every hour saved on the road was more time he could spend attracting grants to the communities of Gwynedd. And if he wasn't doing this job, who would be? Some carpetbagger who wouldn't make sure, like he had, that all his secretarial staff were Welsh speakers. Meinwen sometimes saw him on TV talking about some new initiative which had just received financial help. Sometimes he was answering more diffi-cult questions about why particular ventures had not borne fruit despite substantial grants. The initiatives always had good Welsh names. He always had ready answers.

Arianrhod Môn had been the star of Yr Hafan. Blonde, beau-tiful, photogenic; it had been her picture that almost always appeared in the press whenever there were public demonstrations or arrests. Meinwen's darker looks and boyish hairstyle simply never attracted the lenses to the same degree. Meinwen was happy with that; she was not in the protest business for the publicity, and she would never allow herself to think of herself as an object of attraction to others. Neither would Arianrhod, of course, she knew. But no one blamed her when, after so many television appearances as the face of the Movement, she had finally accepted a job as a children's television presenter, eventually getting her own arts show for adults. She still kept in touch with Meinwen, though, and a card arrived for her at Yr Hafan each Christmas. For a couple of years they were the Movement's own crudely-produced fundraising cards. Then they'd become more tasteful artistic ones; the Adoration of the Magi, that kind of thing. But they were still charity ones, fair play.

Then there was Gethin ap Dafydd, despite his name, the only one not a native of Wales. In fact, he was an Englishman born and bred. His real name was Keith Davidson, but that had changed not long after he arrived in Bangor to study history. Enchanted by his encounter with the language whose existence he had not even suspected when he filled in his UCCA form, he had learned Welsh and had become, in due course, one of the Movement's most effective activists; a vital bridge between the native Welsh speakers and those who could not speak the language or who were learning. He never got his degree, but he acquired a record of convictions that put most native Welsh speakers to shame.

Meinwen had missed him when he left Yr Hafan. His humour was different, more whimsical than that of the natives; kinder. That same passionate commitment that had made him such a firebrand activist had meant that when he fell for a young Irish republican girl who had stayed at Yr Hafan, he pursued her with the same single-minded intensity. He'd moved to Derry, begun living with her, and after a couple of years was approaching fluency in Irish when she left him for a newly-elected Sinn Féin councillor. Gethin came back to Wales, but not to Yr Hafan, and not to activism. He was now a press officer and translator for a local authority in the Valleys, and his humour was now as rare as any levity in the council documents he translated day after day.

And finally, Dewi. Gentle-mannered and rather naive, he lacked Bedwyr's self-confidence, Arianrhod's presence and Gethin's one-time wit. He was one of the most pathologically law-abiding people Meinwen had ever met. For the others, laws were made to be broken. For Dewi they were only to be transgressed as a last resort after long consideration and only after his conscience had been satisfied that the infraction was necessary. He wouldn't even park on a double yellow line when they were out painting roadsigns in the town centre. Every act of civil disobedience was a crisis for him. And yet he'd done it. He'd carried on being arrested and coming back for more. In fact, Meinwen thought, as he was still a full-time activist, he'd stayed the course much better than had Bedwyr, or Arianrhod or Gethin for that matter. But he hadn't stayed at Yr Hafan. In fact he'd been the first of them to leave. That was five years ago. But he and Meinwen still had an instinctive, intuitive understanding of the way each other thought. They were old comrades; jailings and court appearances their life milestones; policies, statistics and projects their shared smalltalk. Compatible and companionable, they could talk about anything with the elisions that can only come through long friendship. Except there was one subject which neither of them ever mentioned.

●○●

Yvette

'No. It's not an either-or,' the communist delegate said. 'It's not a question of either keeping our purity as communists or uniting with other groups against fascism. If we don't have pure communism we can't defeat fascism...'

Yvette stood at the back of the shabby room in the Workers' Hall with Simone. The room was crowded, and filled with the smoke and noise of the political meeting. On the platform at one end were half a dozen delegates, all wearing red star lapel badges – understated, but in the world of left-wing politics in 1930s France, enough to ensure respect, if not fear. Pierre Letellier was among them. Despite the heat of the debate, he looked cool and assured.

'Why not let us have a free vote on it, then?' a heckler shouted. 'Why are there no non-communists on the platform...?'

At the side of the hall, two heavy-set men were watching. They too had the red star badges. One of the men pointed out the heckler to his companion, and said something to him. The second man nodded and set off in the direction of the heckler, who was still shouting.

'And what about Trotsky, Serge, Riazanov and the others? Persecuted! Exiled! Is that what you want in France too? We've had our Terror. We don't need to import another one...'

The heavy-set man pushed closer to the challenger through the crowd.

Yvette and Simone watched. For years, the politics of the Left had absorbed them. Meetings like this were their nights on the town. Smoke, sweat and slogans were the background to their social life.

They scanned the platform, where Pierre was waiting his chance to speak. From his elevated position, he must be able to see them clearly. Certainly, he could hardly miss Simone. While always desiring to efface her own personality and to be absorbed into the life of the proletariat, Simone nonetheless seemed to have the knack – accidental or otherwise – of making herself conspicuous in any company. Yvette remembered her dark-suited appearance among the bright ball gowns on their graduation night. She had told Yvette afterwards that she had simply done it to avoid dressing up. In reality, she could hardly have created more of a sensation if she had walked in stark naked.

Tonight, among the dark suits and working clothes, she was wearing a long red cape. Yvette supposed it was intended to indicate solidarity with the workers. But it made her look like a visiting actress. Poor Simone, the more she tried to blend in, the more she stood out. She thought of one recent protest march in which they had both taken part. In high spirits, Simone had bought each of her group of working men an ornate clay pipe from a street vendor. She didn't realise that they saw a pipe as a sign of effeminacy. They had accepted the gifts politely before hiding them in their pockets out of sight. Now, Yvette looked back at the platform, and could see that Pierre's eyes had noticed Simone. Yvette turned to her friend.

'There!' said Yvette. 'I told you he likes you.'

Simone was watching the platform, seemingly not hearing.

'He respects you, Simone. He likes you.'

Yvette looked half-teasingly, half-seriously at Simone, who by this time had registered a slight smile, but kept her eyes fixed on the platform. The heckler had stopped shouting now, although there was some kind of a commotion in that part of the hall. The communist leader was speaking again.

'See, if you'd only let me fix you up,' Yvette continued. 'A little lipstick. A little rouge. It's red after all, Simone – it's politically acceptable. It will go with your cape. Then something besides these mannish clothes...'

Simone smiled back without answering, and looked again at the platform, still smiling to herself. The speaker was in full flow.

'How else can we fight the capitalists except with iron determination, with the organisation the Soviet Union has given us? Unless the other workers' groups accept communist leadership, we'll all be defeated, we'll all become a prey to the fascist monster which is growing in Europe...'

Some of the listeners shook their heads, but, seeing the

communist heavies ranged in pairs around the hall, were clearly hesitant about speaking. Yvette and Simone could see that the man who had earlier heckled the speaker was now being confronted by one of the heavies, who had his fist raised in front of his face. Simone's smile vanished.

On the platform, the first speaker had finished. Pierre stood up.

'My friends,' he said. 'Our comrade is right. But it's not just about organisation. It's not just about discipline. It's also about vision. Yes, we need Moscow's organisation. We need Moscow's discipline. But most of all, we need Moscow's vision. Where else in this world has socialism been established? Where else has oppression and tyranny been overthrown? It is only the Soviet Union which can show us how we can establish a workers' state here.'

As he continued, Simone began waving her hand, trying to get his attention. Yvette saw Pierre register her gesture, and, perhaps hoping to get some support from the floor, invite her to speak. He stopped, looked encouragingly at Simone, and said: 'Yes, sister.'

'Thank you,' Simone's voice was high and clear. 'But you're wrong, comrade.'

Pierre looked shocked. Heads in the audience turned towards Simone. The heavies craned their necks to see who was speaking. Simone continued.

'The Soviet Union is not a workers' state. Workers there are just slaves to new masters.' She raised her voice even more, addressing the room at large: 'What are we fighting for? What is it we all want? We're not just fighting fascism or capitalism. We're fighting for liberty. Freedom from all forms of oppression, and that includes oppression carried out in the name of socialism.'

Pierre glanced uncomfortably at his comrades on the platform, as Simone carried on.

'Liberty for the workers and the poor, and liberty for the human spirit. You can't create liberty through oppression. That's what Moscow wants us to do. It can't work. You can only secure liberty with weapons of freedom, and there has to be freedom to disagree, to dissent...'

'Viper!' A communist in the audience shouted angrily at Simone.

'Puppet!' she shouted back, 'Moscow's puppet!'

Another hard-faced older communist on the platform stepped to the front of the stage. Pierre sat down helplessly. With the help of the microphone, the older communist's voice drowned Simone's.

'Silence! Silence!' he shouted at Simone. 'Be quiet, comrade! Be quiet!

'There's no place for selfish soul-searching here. We have a war to fight.' He looked around at the audience. 'A vote! All those in favour of all the workers' groups represented here tonight coming under communist direction?'

All the delegates on the platform raised their hands. So did most of the audience. Some of those who did not raise their hands looked uneasy, glancing across at the heavies.

'All those against?'

Twenty or so hands were raised, Simone's among them.

'Thank you, comrades,' said the communist. 'A unanimous decision.'

'No it's not!' Simone shouted. 'No it's not!'

But the meeting had broken up. People were arguing, some were pushing for the doors. In the crowd, Pierre and Simone came face to face.

'I'm sorry, Pierre, but I had to speak up for what I believe. And you were wrong.'

Pierre's voice was cold. 'I was wrong. I was wrong in letting you speak, Simone. Without order and discipline, our movement will be nothing. Unless we have power, all your ideals will mean nothing. Fascism's not the only enemy. There's the bourgeoisie, the capitalists – and worst of all, traitors of the Left. Goodbye.'

He walked away. Simone looked dismayed. Yvette, at her side, was pained, but not surprised. She turned to watch Pierre, where he now stood, engaged in conversation with some admiring friends of both sexes.

She put her arm around Simone's thin shoulders. She knew Simone abhorred contact, but if ever there was an occasion for the warm gesture, it was now.

Simone stiffened as Yvette's arm touched her. She shook her head. Yvette could see tears behind the thick lenses. Then Simone had pulled herself away without a word and was gone with the crowd leaving the hall. Yvette watched as her friend's scarlet cloak was quickly lost in the shoving dark coats of the workers.

Yvette looked over towards Pierre and his group. His friends were laughing at some remark of his. Simone didn't know a good thing when she saw it, Yvette thought. Well, that was Simone's problem, not hers.

She walked over to join Pierre.

●○●

Meinwen

Meinwen listened to the wind rattling the windows of Yr Hafan. However proactive she and the Crew may have been politically, house maintenance had not been one of their main priorities, and some of the window frames needed replacing. At 1,500 feet above sea level, the house was the prey of the wind which seemed to want to leave nothing on the high hills except grass and stones. If the house was ever sold to incomers, it would get its new window frames within a couple of weeks. It was the first thing they always did. You could tell where the native Welsh still lived by the peeling paint around the glass panes. The houses with the tasteful hardwood features plundered from some diminishing rainforest, those would be where the colonists had settled. Well they wouldn't get Yr Hafan, and Meinwen was determined it would keep its scabby window frames just to annoy them.

But it was draughty. Yr Hafan had no central heating, and even in summer like this, it was still cold in the evening. Meinwen thought of lighting a fire. When the Crew had lived here, the fire had seemed to burn constantly. But then the upstairs rooms had been used as well, and they had kept the interior doors open to allow the heat to circulate. Now that Meinwen was here alone, the rooms upstairs, with the exception of Meinwen's own bedroom, were closed up, and she only lit the fire if she had visitors. Left to herself, she could not get rid of the feeling that a fire was a luxury. The money she spent on coal could have gone to the cause, to Shelter Cymru, to the Urdd's relief project in Calcutta. She wrapped her overcoat around her and settled herself in the big armchair in front of where the fire would be, if she had felt it permissible to light one.

It was teatime. The most natural thing to do now would be to make something to eat. But Meinwen did not feel like it. For years, she had never really enjoyed food much, and she rarely felt like eating these days. It left her feeling bloated and guilty. Anyway, there was virtually nothing in the house to eat. She kicked off her shoes and tucked her feet under her to keep them warm.

There was something agreeable about the cold, though, she thought. The fact that you could feel it, that you could hear the wind roaring outside, it made you appreciate your comfort all the more. It felt a bit like the eternal Welsh experience: sheltering from external threat, cultivating an inner warmth against a coldly hostile world. It was not such a bad state. It kept you awake, that was for sure. Perhaps the soul needed an external inclemency in order to prove itself.

Sometimes her mother would ask her if she wasn't afraid, living up in the hills by herself. True, there was only the empty bulk of Hermon Chapel next door and its mute congregation of headstones in the overgrown graveyard for company, but Meinwen wasn't lonely. She loved the solitude. It was like wine to her. Or no, wine was too indulgent a simile; it was like pure mountain spring water when thirsty; to come back from the conflict and the compromise of the town to this unpolluted, windswept silence. Not even the proximity of the burial ground made her uneasy. The faithful departed of this mountain chapel were, for her, part of a continuum, a community of shared values and common culture stretching back to the undiscoverable but certain past, and forward to a future, albeit an increasingly uncertain one.

She remembered when she was a child of nine or maybe ten years old. Always fond of wandering by herself through the district where she lived, she had found herself one afternoon in the long grass and shoulder-high thistles of a graveyard much like Hermon's. Even then, in the early nineteen seventies, chapels were closing and being abandoned.

Alone, among the groves of nettles, which were almost as tall as she was, she had tried to decipher the names from the eroded, snail-trailed, moss-covered headstones. *'Er serchus gof...'* In loving memory. The loving she understood; didn't all families love one another? What she could not understand was the shortness of the memory. Some of these graves were less than a hundred years old. Her grandparents could have known these people. And yet, here were their resting places untended and forgotten. She felt more than saddened. She felt outrage at the sheer unfairness of it. Just like her own parents and family, these were loving, beloved people – the stones said so. How could they be neglected now? How had this been allowed to happen? She would tell her parents about it. They would understand. They would have a campaign. The graveyard would be cleared and mown like their own front lawn, and every name, every last carved letter of memory and loss would be scraped clean and preserved, as they deserved to be, forever.

Back home, at the kitchen table that teatime, she tried to tell her parents. They listened with half an ear, while looking past her at intervals to the black-and-white television in the living room at the news of the latest killings in Ulster, and the latest threat of something called 'industrial action' in Britain.

'Can we, Dadi?'

'Can we what, *cariad*?'

'Oh, you haven't been listening! Clean them. The graves. You can't see the names any more. It isn't fair.'

Idwal Jones put down his knife and fork and gave Meinwen his full attention. She looked at him with an appeal for help in her dark, troubled eyes.

'Can we do something, Dadi? Please.'

But as she looked at him, she realised this request wasn't as simple as a homework question or a broken toy. She could read an answering distress in his own eyes as he searched for the words to answer her.

'Meinwen, *fach*. No, it isn't fair. But... there are some things you just can't do anything about.'

She looked down at her plate. The food seemed suddenly distasteful to her, an unpardonable indulgence while those people were lying there, their names fading a little more with every rainstorm, the short-lived memorials of their lives sinking further and further every year beneath an impassive sea of grass.

'You can't fight time, my angel,' her father was saying.

She wasn't angry with him. She loved him for the tenderness and sorrow in his voice. But that just made her feel more keenly the injustice of the fact that anything so precious should be lost. How could her love for anything be worthy of the name if it consented to destruction, if it didn't resist oblivion with every effort at its command? Anything else would be a betrayal of that love itself. She swore to herself that, whatever else happened, she would never betray what she loved.

She felt her mother kiss her softly on the top of her head as she took the unfinished meal away from in front of her. In the living room, the television newsreader's voice continued, recording a litany of untimely deaths in a medium even less durable than the carved letters on the weathered stones.

Alain

Alain read the letter with amusement, but not incredulity. The local branch of the teachers' trade union in Haute-Loire was asking him to sign a letter to the Ministry of Education, appealing to them not to dismiss Mademoiselle Simone Weil from her teaching post in Le Puy, the small town where she had been working for the past few months.

It appeared that, when finding that the only provision for the unemployed in Le Puy was for the men to break stones in the town square for a few francs a day, Simone had organised the stonebreakers into a group and marched them into a town council meeting, where she demanded better pay and conditions.

The mayor and councillors had refused to consider the demands, as the item was not on the agenda, and the next day Simone had been called before the school inspectors who had demanded she cease her political activities. It seemed they were at least as shocked by the fact that a member of the middle classes had been seen consorting with the unemployed as they were concerned at her politics. She had asked them politely for a precise ruling as to under exactly what conditions each category of the teaching profession could associate with different social classes. They had been nonplussed.

She had then returned to the fray, getting the workers' demands put on the agenda of the next council meeting, and again bringing her group of stonebreakers to the chamber. When their demands were refused, the men went on strike, picketing the town square and holding a protest meeting outside the mayor's house. Eventually, the council had acceded to most of their demands, but Simone was still under threat of dismissal.

Alain smiled to himself as he began to draft his letter of support. Who but Simone could start a strike among the unemployed?

Meinwen

For a while the Crew had tried to be self-sufficient at Yr Hafan. It was part of the ideal of a radical alternative to Britishness: consolidate the communities of the Welsh-speaking areas; detach yourself from the capitalist system, opt out of it; make your own livelihood, your own values. But none of them had been farmers, except Bedwyr, and he knew better than to try to make a living from the thin soil so high up the slopes of Cwm Aur.

The experiment had lasted until the first winter. From then on they had got their supplies from the Spar shop in the village. Meinwen consoled herself that buying food rather than trying to grow it was a lot less time-consuming, and it left her more time for the cause. And they were supporting a local business, too. However, in recent years, that argument had weakened, as the shop had been taken over by English incomers, like almost every other retail outlet in the area. After that, for a while, Meinwen had found some comfort in the fact that at least they employed some locals to work the tills. Then that changed too, as the owner's brother and his family, attracted by reports of cheap housing, low crime and great views, had also moved out to Gwynedd, and were soon providing the entire shop staff. Chain migration they called it. Then Meinwen was reduced to telling herself that at least locals used the shop, making it a valuable community resource; until that argument was soured for her by the knowledge that the new owners wouldn't let people put up Welsh-language posters there any more, on the grounds that they couldn't understand them. Now Meinwen bought her few essentials and her ever-diminishing list of groceries at Tesco's in town; she hated supporting the chain store whose outlets seemed to be fastening on the outskirts of every community like lethal parasites, but at least the signs there were bilingual.

As for farming the high hills, the Welsh couldn't seem to get out of it fast enough, gratefully leaving the hilltop smallholdings to city-fleeing downsizers and moving themselves to the easier life of the towns, from where their offspring were duly decanted to the cities.

Meinwen still felt as though The Crew had yielded to the pressures of the age, that somehow, they had shirked the opportunity to challenge capitalism in the most fundamental way. And if they couldn't change capitalism, what real hope was there for their way of life?

But she had to hope. To hope against all the evidence. It was what her movement lived by: the expectation of the coming day when nationalism would sweep the country and when the old language would once again be enthroned at the heart of Welsh life. In Meinwen's mental republic, only the language was accorded anything so royal as a throne.

Monsieur Clerc

"'Before the demonstration, there was a meeting at the Labour exchange. Mlle Weil, red virgin of the tribe of Levi, bearer of the Muscovite gospels, indoctrinated the wretches whom she has led into error and folly.'"

Monsieur Clerc, the headmaster, settled his glasses on his nose, straightened out his copy of *Le Mémorial*, and resumed his quotation from the article: "'Then, after organising them in ranks, and taking the red flag in her own hands, she led them to the mayor's house. He had the good fortune to be serenaded in the musical part of the programme, which comprised the *Internationale*. This, of course, shows the true nature of this movement; for it is perfectly obvious to all that it is nothing but a political movement – communist, to be precise.'"

Simone watched composedly as he read the article to the end. Her headmaster looked up at her.

'Your race doesn't interest me...'

'It doesn't interest me either, I can assure you,' said Simone.

'Your race doesn't interest me,' he repeated, forcing himself to sound patient. 'What does concern me is your politics. You are employed by the state, to teach what the state wants to be taught. You're not employed to bring the teaching profession into disrepute with these communist antics.'

'They weren't communists,' she answered, evenly. 'They were anarcho-syndicalists. You're simply using the word "communist" to dismiss all radicalism *per se*. It's just an excuse to defend the status quo and stigmatise people like myself by associating us with fanaticism, oppression and mass murder.'

'Mademoiselle, I have not asked for a lesson in politics...'

Simone ignored him and continued.

'There's a fundamental difference between anarcho-syndicalism and communism. I don't agree with communism because of the excessively strong role it accords to the state. Anarcho-syndicalism, on the other hand, is more grass-roots, groups of workers in particular professions, labourers, factory workers – even teachers. You see...'

'These communist antics, Mademoiselle Weil! However you dress it up. These communist speeches, meetings. I'm told you were seen in the square, shaking hands with an unemployed labourer! I'm told you've gone, unaccompanied, to cafés where workers meet! It can't go on. Do it again, and I'll be forced to let you go.'

'I've always considered dismissal the crowning of my career.'

The headmaster regretted having moved so quickly to threatening dismissal. When he had rehearsed this conversation, he had planned for it to be much calmer, more adult. But then, Simone had hardly made it easy for him. He spoke more softly: 'Mademoiselle Weil. You are a young woman of uncommon gifts, of extraordinary academic ability. Your students adore you. Please, curb your political activities. For the sake of the school. For the sake of the students. For your own sake. I will need your promise, Mademoiselle Weil.'

Simone made no reply.

Simone

Later that day, Simone left the tree-lined school campus. As she reached the gate, she stepped aside to let two automobiles pass. They belonged to parents on their way to collect their children, and, no doubt, to show off the fact that they could afford automobiles.

Her walk took her into an area where the streets narrowed, with no room for trees or automobiles, even if the residents could have afforded them, which was inconceivable. Some of them might work in a car factory, but that was the closest they would ever get to this new symbol of affluence. A few doors ahead of her, as she walked, a woman was sweeping rubbish, potato peelings, and loose newspaper pages, from the pavement into the gutter. Simone looked at the newspaper headline as she passed. It was telling of the latest success of Adolf Hitler's Nazi group which was trying to win power in Germany. It was depressing news.

Simone had entertained high hopes of the German leftist groups and trade unions; they had seemed so much better organised then their French counterparts, with whom she had become increasingly disillusioned. But they seemed to have been outmanoeuvred by this little Austrian demagogue with his paranoid beliefs which he seemed to have the uncanny ability to communicate to others. Increasingly, it was not in the workers' organisations that she felt herself putting her hopes, but in the workers themselves. Surely they would stand up against this beastly hate-mongering?

She reached her tenement block, and climbed the seven flights of stairs to her top-floor flat. Once inside, after regaining her breath, she poured herself a small glass of cheap wine from a half-full bottle on the table, took a yellow *Normale* notebook from her bag and sat on the floor next to the window, where she could make use of the early evening light. She began to write.

'Physical labour is a specific contact with the world's beauty, and in its best moments it can be a contact so full that there is nothing to compare with it. The artist, the student, the philosopher and the contemplative should really admire the world and break through the membrane of unreality which conceals it... but more often than not they cannot. It is only he whose every limb is aching, worn out by the effort of a day of labour... it is only he who bears the reality of the universe like a thorn in his flesh. If he can look and love, then it is the Real that he loves.

'No earthly finality separates the workers from God. It is only they who are in that position. All other circumstances imply that there are special aims which make a screen between man and perfect goodness. For the workers, however, there is no such screen. They have nothing superfluous which they have to strip away from themselves.

'The poor have an immense privilege. But they scarcely ever realise the fact. No one ever tells them. They have too much work, not enough money, not enough real culture. It would only take a small change to open for them the door to a treasure.

'Manual work. It is time entering into the body. Through work, man makes himself into matter, in the same way Christ does through the Eucharist.

'Joys which come with fatigue: tangible joys, eating, resting, the pleasures of Sunday... but not money. No poetry about the people is real if fatigue does not have part in it, and the hunger and thirst which come from fatigue.'

Monsieur Clerc

The next day, Simone was back in the headmaster's study again. But this time, at her own request.

'I'm sorry, M'sieur Clerc. I can't give you my promise,' she said. 'I will finish my lessons until the end of the term, so you can make arrangements for my replacement, and then I'll leave.'

The headmaster nodded. He knew it was no use trying to argue.

'Where will you go, Mademoiselle Weil?' there was a note of respect in his voice. 'Can I be any assistance to you?'

'Perhaps,' said Simone. 'What do you know about motor cars?'

'Motor cars? Well, I drive a Renault... I...'

'No, not driving them, M'sieur Clerc – making them!' Simone laughed as if it were strange of him to have thought she meant anything else. 'I want to work in a car factory, and I was wondering if you could suggest one.'

'Well... Renault!' He was laughing too, now, despite himself, the conversation having taken one of those bizarre turns which so often happened with Simone. 'Their factory's just outside Paris. I've seen it on the newsreels, the latest mass-production techniques. The division of labour, the employment of women. It's the biggest car factory in Europe.'

'Fine. That sounds just the place.'

'But why? With your gifts.'

Simone looked around at the book-lined room, which seemed to be the symbol of all she was renouncing, as she answered.

'I have to. I keep thinking of those people, our fellow Frenchmen, our fellow human beings, who are being crushed by industry, while we live our comfortable lives. It seems to me that the people who do the crushing don't feel anything. It's only those who are being crushed who feel what's happening. Unless you've put yourself on the side of the oppressed, to feel with them, you can't understand.'

Through the open window, the rooftops of the district where Simone lived were just visible through the campus trees.

'One of my friends – she's a worker, and the daughter of workers – told me once how she felt when she saw a factory at night, with all its lights blazing. She said it was a place of beauty, real beauty, where you come into contact with the real, material world through physical labour.'

The headmaster thought of the newsreels he had seen of the Renault factory. It looked efficient, and busy. But beautiful? No.

'I've had a fortunate life,' Simone was saying. 'This comfort, these academic discussions – this isn't really living. Out there, with the workers, that's the real world.'

She had no more to say. Neither did Monsieur Clerc. Through the open window could be heard the wind in the trees, the cries of children in the yard outside, and, gradually drowning these, an increasingly frequent sound, that of an accelerating motor car.

Meinwen

Meinwen heard the sound of a car coming up the hill towards yr Hafan. As the road was a dead-end, this could only mean it was a visitor for her. Meinwen hoped it was Dewi. She enjoyed her own company and felt little need to socialise. But it was different with Dewi. With him, it wasn't so much socialising. She needed his company like she needed almost nothing else. No one understood her like he did. But she didn't want him to know that. It would be too... distracting. She went to the window and looked out.

It wasn't Dewi. It was her father. She dismissed her disappointment and allowed it to be replaced by affection as she saw the old man's car pull up into the parking bay outside the house, and watched him climb slowly out of it. A little more slowly each time, Meinwen thought. She walked down the gravel path and went to greet him.

'How are you, *cariad bach*?' His face brightened as he embraced her. He was suddenly not an old man any more. He was not to know it, but he and his wife were the only people whom Meinwen allowed to embrace her. The habit was older than the defensive fastidiousness that had grown in her over the years and which made her avoid even the most perfunctory handshakes with other people. But the habit of her father's embrace, and the endearments he used for her, had never changed.

'I'm fine, Dadi. It's good to see you. What brings you here?'

'Oh, it's not far really. Less than an hour. I came through Beddgelert for a change, and over through Llanfrothen. It's a lovely run. I brought you these.'

He reached into the back seat of the car and brought out a pile of books. Second-hand ones by the look of them. As a retired head teacher, he never tired of adding to his, or his daughter's, library. He handed them to Meinwen, who struggled to keep the pile steady in her arms. He reached back into the car and brought out a supermarket carrier bag, but did not explain what was in it.

'You'd better come inside, Dadi,' Meinwen laughed. He took her arm as they walked up the path to Yr Hafan.

Simone

The academic term ended, Simone presented herself for work at six in the morning at the Renault factory. It was a giant structure covering a whole kilometre-long island on the river Seine. Over ten thousand people worked there. Simone had long used the term 'The Great Beast' to describe the complex of power, politics, greed and mechanisation which seemed to be increasingly dominating the world. Now, as she queued in the rain waiting for the foreman to select the casual labour, she felt as if she was truly entering the belly of that beast. She could hear the thump and rattle of the presses in the machine shop behind the rough concrete wall.

She had called here twice before, joining the queue of women waiting to be hired. On both occasions she had been turned down without explanation. But on those unsuccessful visits, she had noticed that the foreman was selecting only the most attractive and smartly turned-out women. So, this time, although it went against all her principles, she had asked Yvette to help her apply some makeup. After all, it was for the sake of the cause. Now she waited, rouged, lipsticked and impatient, as the foreman, a man in his fifties, accompanied by a clerk, walked down the line as if he was at a cattle show. He stopped next to Simone; there was an unpleasant roguishness in his eye.

'Have you got any experience?' he asked her. The *double entendre* was obvious even to Simone. But she too could use ambiguity.

'Not here,' she replied. 'Not yet, anyway.'

She looked at him steadily.

'Very well,' he said, with a short laugh. 'We'll sort you out.'

She was in.

'Thank you. What work have you got for me?' Simone used the intimate *'tu'* form. We're all workers here, she thought.

'You can help the women on the presses,' the foreman replied, pointedly addressing her as *'vous'*. 'They'll show you what to do. Go with Thomas. I'll call later on to see how you're shaping up.'

Thomas, the clerk, who had watched the exchange silently, motioned Simone through the office door and into the factory compound. In the background, the sound of the presses grew louder.

Once inside the building, Simone found the sudden heat unbearable, and she removed her top coat. Wearing just her white blouse, she felt more comfortable. As Thomas guided her through the aisles of machines in that giant, girdered, cacophonous space, she tried to smile at her brown-overalled future colleagues as she passed. She could not understand why they all stopped to stare at her as she did so. Perhaps it was just the surprise of seeing a new face.

The heat, noise and movement were almost overwhelming. Simone turned to her impassive guide and smiled.

'I feel a bit like Dante with Virgil!' she said.

'Pardon?'

'You know, being guided through the Inferno.'

'No.'

Simone believed many workers concealed rich intellectual

lives beneath their tough exteriors. Perhaps Thomas hadn't heard her properly in all this noise.

'You know, *La Divina Commedia*.'

Thomas made no reply. Perhaps he only knew of it in French translation. She tried again. *'The Divine Comedy...'*

Thomas simply shook his head.

'You won't find much comedy here,' he said.

He stopped walking. They had reached the end of the aisle, and Thomas left Simone with an older woman who was busy feeding metal components into a mechanical press, where they were punched and folded. Her hands moved expertly, turning the metal this way and that until it was the required shape. The woman scarcely paused in her task as she explained Simone's duties to her.

'Right,' She held up a finished metal component. 'We have to make a hundred of these an hour. That's where you'll find the unfinished ones,' she indicated a bucket on the floor. 'As you see me take one off the machine and put it in that bucket,' indicating another bucket on the bench, 'have another one ready for me from that one.'

Simone nodded seriously as if the woman had explained an obscure point of philosophy.

'Don't keep me waiting for the fresh one,' the woman went on. 'Don't let that bucket get empty – you can get more from the store at the end – and don't...' she allowed herself a slight smile and a slightly softer tone, 'don't wear a white blouse to work'.

Simone looked down at her dress, realising for the first time how she stood out. Then she rolled up her sleeves carefully, picked up a metal shape from the bucket, and stood ready to serve, a handmaiden to the great beast of industry.

Idwal Jones

'I don't have any milk for the tea, I'm afraid, Dadi,' said Meinwen from the kitchen as she prepared the kettle and cups. 'I haven't had time to go to the shop.'

'Don't worry, *cariad*. Black is fine for me,' he lied. 'Better for my cholesterol, too.'

Idwal Jones sat down and put the carrier bag on the floor next to the settee. He looked around him at the living room. The ancient, heavy furniture, the blistered, scuffed paintwork, the threadbare carpet, the dusty hearth, the pile of old newspapers serving as a kind of newsprint coffee table, the posters for decade-old fundraising gigs for the Movement, the photocopied picture of that French woman philosopher Meinwen admired so much.

Meinwen didn't seem to have a woman's touch for homemaking. She didn't seem to have a man's touch for DIY either. The living-room door was missing a handle on one side, as it had been on all his previous visits. One of the window panes was cracked right across. He wished he could bring his toolbox and spend a week fixing the place up. Or a couple of weeks, more like. But he knew Meinwen would never let him. That would be far too passive a relationship for her. Her independence, which he had nurtured and admired, would never stoop to accepting charity for her own comfort. He knew what she would say if he offered: if he wanted to do DIY for nothing, he could volunteer to help the shelter for victims of domestic violence in Blaenau Ffestiniog, or the home for asylum seekers in Penmaenmawr. Yes, he could do that, he thought. No doubt the battered women and the asylum seekers could do with some help. But they weren't his daughter. And Meinwen was. He heard the sound of cups in the kitchen, and looked up as Meinwen came in, smiling, with the milkless tea.

She put the cups down on the table, pushing aside a copy of the Movement's magazine to do so.

'So, what are these then?' she said, turning to the pile on the settee between them.

He would bring her books from time to time. Books – their shared passion since her earliest childhood – were the only gifts she was usually willing to accept. They both knew that the gifts were simply an excuse for a visit, a fiction in which they were both happy to acquiesce.

'I got them in a second-hand bookshop in Llandrillo-yn-Rhos,' he said. 'They'd just taken delivery of a whole batch of Welsh books, from a house clearance. There were some real classics there.'

'There were,' Meinwen agreed, looking at the volume she

had taken from the top of the pile. It was a pristine copy of T. Gwynn Jones' *Manion*. She looked at the flyleaf. It was a limited edition from 1932. There was a signature too. She looked up.

'V.R. Williams?' she said in surprise.

'The very same.'

Meinwen picked up a second volume and turned to the flyleaf. The same signature. V.R. Williams. Certainly one of the greatest poets of twentieth century Wales. He had died a few months earlier, in his late eighties. She looked at her father for an explanation.

'It's his library,' he said sadly. 'The shop had the whole lot of it.'

'But... you'd have thought this would have been given to the National Library. Look, this one's got his own annotations in it.'

'They nearly all have. Some of them have got press cuttings and articles which he'd put in them as well.'

'So what were they doing in the second-hand shop? Do his family know about it?'

'It's his family who gave them to the shop,' Mr Jones said. 'Didn't have room for them, his son said, according to the shopkeeper. Or the inclination to keep them, obviously. He didn't even bother sorting through them for the valuable ones. He just took the whole lot away in black bags. The shopkeeper gave them £50 for the lot and told him he was doing him a favour, "cos this Welsh stuff's really hard to shift".'

Meinwen closed her eyes, pained. That one first edition itself wouldn't be worth much less than £50 to anyone who knew its provenance. She looked at Williams' annotations. *'Ond gweler Platon,'* said the note by the side of one poem, 'But see Plato.'

'I bought as many as I could,' her father was saying. 'Just to give them a home, really. The shopkeeper didn't know how much they were worth himself, so I managed to get the best of them. I couldn't bear to think of them going to someone who wouldn't understand them or appreciate them.'

'No, of course.'

'I knew V.R.' her father continued. 'It would have broken his heart to think of these being thrown away.'

'I'm sure it would. Son not much interested in literature, then?'

'Not interested in Wales, or the language or anything to do with it, from what V.R. told me. He's lived in England most of his life. Stayed there after college. He's a lawyer in London. A wealthy one. That's probably why he didn't think of trying to get any money for the books.'

'All the same, you'd have thought he'd have wanted them for sentimental value. Family pride.'

'I don't think there was much of that. "Too much pudding choked the dog," the son said, apparently. V.R.'s grandchildren haven't got a word of Welsh. So the books wouldn't be much use to them.'

He looked at Meinwen with a sad smile.

'Never mind, Dadi,' said Meinwen, putting her head on his shoulder. 'I'll have your books after you! And I'll look after them.'

He put his arm around her.

'Well, that won't be for a while, I hope,' he smiled. He knew Meinwen would indeed value what he passed on to her, as she always had. But whether there would ever be any grandchildren for her to pass those values on to in her turn, was, of course, another question altogether.

Simone

'What do you think of mass-production?'

It was Simone's second day at the factory, and she was busy handing the components to her fellow worker, whose name was Claudine. Simone got no reply to her question. The work went on, punching and folding the metal into the shape the process required. Simone wondered what the component was used for. Claudine had said she didn't know.

'What about the Taylorisation of industry? Do you feel your work would be more rewarding if you had more of a say in the design process?' Simone tried to make the question as casual as possible. She didn't want to be a nuisance, but she really did need to find out how the workers felt.

Claudine looked mystified. Simone had only been with her for a day and already her patience seemed exhausted. Simone could not understand why. She thought Claudine would have wanted to help articulate the workers' cause.

'What about the class struggle? Surely...'

Claudine lost her temper. Stopping work, she slammed the component down on the workbench.

'Look, isn't this enough of a struggle?' she said. 'Getting up at five every morning to come here. Working eight hours with hardly a break. Getting home so tired you can't think about eating let alone about the "class struggle" or whatever you call it. You can go running back to your parents whenever you want. You try living on fifty francs a week, Do you know what that buys you? Half a kilo of butter. One loaf. A bit of cheese if you're lucky. And watered-down milk from that thieving Jew who keeps the shop.' Simone winced. 'When you've faced that kind of struggle, talk to us of the class struggle.'

Simone said nothing further, and reached to the bucket for the next piece of metal.

●○●

Meinwen

Meinwen walked back to the car with her father. They embraced. She stood at the gate to wave until the car had passed down Bryn Aur and out of sight towards Porthmadog. It was late afternoon, and the sun had declined towards the hills above the estuary, turning the water to a dazzling white gold. This was truly a beautiful place. The shimmering of the estuary melted into the ocean and the horizon in one infinity of light. No wonder the old Celts had thought that the land of eternal youth lay away to the west. No wonder some of them had sailed away to find it.

Meinwen felt the first faint chill of evening. She tucked her hands in the sleeves of her sweater and walked back to the house. It would be good to have a proper look through the books her father had brought her from the library of poor old V.R. Williams.

She sat on the settee in the place where her father had been sitting, and picked up the first volume. Another first edition: *Buchedd Garmon*, 'The Life of St Germanus', by Saunders Lewis. This book, which had first appeared when Lewis was in jail for the Penyberth protest in 1936, would be worth something too. But its cultural value far outweighed its monetary worth. Like many nationalists, Meinwen knew the great speech from that drama by heart: 'A vineyard given to my care is my country of Wales, to be passed on to my children, and my children's children, an eternal inheritance...' But not tonight, she thought. Not more struggle and sacrifice, rhetoric and resistance. Just for once, she could do with a night off. Was there anything lighter among these volumes? She looked down their spines. Yes – T. Gwynn Jones' *Caniadau*, his *Songs*: 'The Passing of Arthur', 'Madog', and stories of other journeyers to the Celtic Otherworld away to the west. That was more like it. She could do with some escapism. She could dream of that journey to the west, to be absorbed by the welcoming light beyond the world. She leant forward to put *Buchedd Garmon* on the table. As she did so, she noticed her father's supermarket bag on the floor next to the settee. He'd forgotten it. She picked it up, put it on her lap and looked inside. A fresh loaf of sliced bread; farmhouse butter and cheese, all local of course; orange juice, and a ginger cake. It was when she saw the ginger cake that she realised. That was always her favourite as a child. Her father hadn't forgotten the bag at all. He'd left it behind deliberately, filled with what he remembered as her favourite things; concerned, as she knew he was, that she wasn't eating enough, but knowing she wouldn't accept a handout. Meinwen hugged the bag on her lap. Little though her appetite was, she would take care to eat these things over the following days, for the sake of the love they represented. She looked out of the window to where the sun was setting over the hills. She smiled. She didn't need to escape to the west to find the welcoming light.

Simone

Simone was learning to use the pressing machine herself. It was difficult and dangerous; many times she had set it wrongly and it had needed to be re-set by another worker, usually impatient at the time wasted by her clumsiness. But gradually, she was learning how to do it for herself, although her productivity was not even approaching that which her foreman had asked for. She turned the metal under the punch for it to be moulded and bent to its new shape. Her existence had narrowed to this oil-stained bench, to the thumping, insatiable machine she had to feed, and to the merciless timetable she had to obey. Her head pounded. Her imagination was shut down, her dreams were postponed, her willpower was focused only on the one repetitive, impossible task.

Yet still, this was what she wanted. In the *Lycée* and the *Normale*, a world of choices were open to her, bewildering her and daunting her with the fateful responsibility of choosing the one right path, the one correct transaction in which to spend the single precious centime of her existence. Here, she had dropped beneath that fate, had submerged herself in a world where there were no choices. The factory workers had their lives decided for them at birth, by class, by economic status, by geography. They would never have to agonise over how their talents should best be employed. This slavery was perfect freedom. But as Simone fitted another metal component on the bench, and let the machine press the hard metal into conformity, she was aware of one thought, far off, like a distant voice drowned by the factory noise. She did not want to be aware of it. But even as she concentrated harder on her task, her hands moving the bent metal more urgently, she knew what that voice would say if she did listen to it: You have chosen this.

Meinwen

The Anglesey Show was in full swing as Dewi parked his car alongside the mud-spattered four-by-fours in the field which served as a parking ground. He and Meinwen joined the trail of people stepping over the tussocks and cowpats on their way to the little concrete booth which was the showground entrance. Once they were inside, Dewi and Meinwen fished a few hand-fuls of leaflets from their shoulder bags and split up to distribute them. They each carried a clipboard for their petition; they needed to get their campaign for a Property Act onto the public agenda, and every signature helped.

To hand out leaflets, it was best to move against the flow of people. From that familiar perspective, Meinwen watched the succession of faces move past her. As she did so, for a moment she wondered what it would feel like to be them, going with the flow of society, not against it; simply attending the show for fun, not duty. It was hard to imagine. She had never been there except on Movement business.

Meinwen and Dewi belonged to the Movement's middle generation. Its founders, like Mallwyd, the young radicals of the 1960s, were now elderly. But Meinwen's generation had grown up with the Movement; it had shaped their lives, providing a system of values and an alternative community to set against the insolent individualism of the Tory rule which had begun when Meinwen was thirteen, and had ended only when she was in her thirties. For most of her life, she had known nothing other than a lifestyle based on local resistance to remote misrule.

But, she reflected, as she handed out the leaflets, things had changed. The Assembly wasn't remote in the same way as London rule had been. Cardiff might be a long way from north west Wales, but the Assembly was elected by the people of Wales, and wasn't as blatantly illegitimate as the succession of London-run Welsh Office regimes had been. As such, the battle lines were no longer so clearly drawn.

She knew that some said the Movement's youngest genera-tion, those who had grown up under the Assembly's new dispensation, were more sophisticated, shrewdly drawing their terminology and tactics from the anti-globalisation movement rather than what they saw as the exhausted emotional grand-standing of the past. While Meinwen was glad the Movement could still attract and inspire radicalised youth, she was not entirely convinced of its increasing new direction. Sophisticated was all very well. But effective was what mattered. She felt that she and Dewi now represented the Movement's core values, and she had yet to be convinced that anything better could replace their tried and trusted methods.

After an hour, their leaflets gone, and several dozen more signatures added to their petition, they met by arrangement at the HSBC tent for a break. They chose it, not because either of them were customers of the Pacific Rim financial giant, but because it offered free tea and biscuits. They sipped from their polystyrene cups while watching people a few yards away paying £1 a time for the same beverage from a catering stand.

They felt a little glimmer of self-satisfaction.

'Why do they do it, do you think?' asked Meinwen.

'Do what?'

'Give us free tea and biscuits.'

'Custom, isn't it? Brand loyalty.'

'Yes, but it's not like we're even customers. Do they really think people are going to open bank accounts with them because they had a free custard cream in Anglesey Show?'

'Damn,' said Dewi. 'You're right. This lot would be in trouble if their bosses in Shanghai found out.' He attempted what he hoped was a Shanghai accent: '"What this? This expenditure item from HSBC UK – twenty box of Rover Biscuits for Anglesey Show. Please to explain."'

Meinwen laughed. Dewi was one of the few people who could make her laugh these days.

She looked idly at the people around them. On the next table was a young mother with a toddler of perhaps eighteen months. A full-faced, placid-looking child. Meinwen smiled at her. The child smiled back, two dimples slowly appearing in her fat cheeks.

The mother was talking with a friend. She carried a bag of marshmallows the size of a sofa cushion, obviously bought from one of the sweet stalls around the ground. She wasn't eating them herself, but every time her daughter came near, she absent-mindedly pushed another marshmallow into the child's mouth.

Meinwen watched with mounting unease. The child wasn't even asking for the marshmallows. It was just that whenever she approached to get her mother's attention, the mother stuffed another sweet in her mouth to shut her up. Already the bag was nearly a third empty. Clearly, she would keep on stuffing the little one until every marshmallow had gone.

Meinwen felt indignation mixed with real physical nausea. She put down her own custard cream, uneaten.

Then, catching sight of someone walking past the tent, she sat up suddenly.

'Look,' she said. 'There's Bedwyr.'

It was indeed Bedwyr Roberts, formerly of the Crew. Bedwyr was an exact contemporary of Dewi and Meinwen. But while they had extended their student lifestyle for nearly two decades, Bedwyr had entered middle age with what Meinwen could only regard as relish. He filled his sharp suit; his skin was tanned to the same colour as the fake walnut inserts on the dashboard of his Mercedes. Gone was the swinging gait of the farmboy. Every step he took now seemed pre-meditated. His complete self-possession, the absence of any shyness, made him the centre of any gathering.

Meinwen saw him look in their direction. Behind his sunglasses, it was hard to tell if he had actually seen them. She saw him hesitate for a moment, then walk over towards them, removing his sunglasses and squeezing a smile into his eyes. He put the delicate frames of his glasses into his top pocket; the sun glinted off his cufflinks as he did so.

'How's the cause, friends?'

Meinwen noticed Bedwyr's eyes flick round the tent momentarily, like a radar sweep. It only took a second. Failing to detect anyone more significant, they returned to Dewi and Meinwen.

'Fine, Bedwyr,' said Dewi. 'Looks like you're doing OK too. You're not showing any animals, I take it.' He glanced at Bedwyr's spotless polished shoes; not even the dust of the showground seemed to stick to them.

'No,' said Bedwyr. 'I'm promoting *Cymunedol*.'

'What's that, now?'

'It's a new venture to develop enterprise units in rural areas. We've got some major players in the international market lined up.'

'Aren't there plenty of rural enterprise groups already?' said Dewi. 'There are more of them than there are farmers, these days. You could have a show for them: Best Grant-Distributor in Breed; Supreme Champion Business Advisor. You'd look great with a rosette.'

Bedwyr kept a politic smile while he thought quickly: 'It would spoil the suit, Dewi *bach*,' he said. Then he returned to the subject of business: 'Well, this enterprise agency is different. It's going to be a platform for the delivery of a high-quality production facility for our client-base in the multi-media industry.'

'Wow. I see. And who's paying? No, let me guess – Europe.'

'Yes. Objective One,' said Bedwyr. 'At least, they're providing the start-up capital, and the initial staff costs.'

'And your consultancy fee.'

'And my consultancy fee. A labourer's worthy of his hire, as the good book says. But once we start drawing down contracts we'll be completely self-sufficient.'

Meinwen could not help but admire Bedwyr's cheek. Dewi was clearly planning to needle him just a little more.

'Multi-media? Since when have you been into that. You couldn't even work the video in Yr Hafan.'

'Ah, well, you can learn. I've picked up a working knowledge of HTML, Java, Flash. Let me give you my ULR.' He reached into his pocket and brought out a little aluminium business card case.

'URL,' Bedwyr didn't notice Dewi's murmured correction as he handed him the card with *Cymunedol's* internet address and his own email address. Dewi really *did* know about computers, and was a regular contributor to the Movement's online campaigns.

'Yes, the office is in Penygroes,' Bedwyr went on. 'And there are two staff in place already.'

The only two staff the project would ever generate, Meinwen thought. Bedwyr knew as little about business or attracting clients as he did about computers. But he knew how to say the right things, pull the political strings and release the grants. At that, he was a master. Those two staff would be there as long as the start-up money lasted, writing business plans for the Assembly and progress reports for Brussels. Then when the money dried up, Bedwyr would have them out of the door and the '*Ar Osod* / To Let' sign up on the building before you could say 'Objective One'. But two Welsh speakers would have had a decent wage for a couple of years. Better than nothing. And Bedwyr, of course, would have an even bigger car.

'Will you sign our petition, Bedwyr?' Meinwen spoke for the first time.

'What is it this time? Vegetarian Women for Peace?'

It was a cautious witticism, delivered with a wary, lop-sided smile. It gave the impression of roguish good fellowship without taking the risk of offence. Everything that Bedwyr said these days seemed designed for a wider audience than those he was talking to. Once, his unconcern about people's opinion of him meant he could be refreshingly direct. Now, that unconcern seemed to have contracted to a core of careerist shamelessness, protected by outer defences of perpetual vigilance. Wherever he was, he now behaved and spoke as if the cameras were on him all the time. Even his *bonhomie* felt monitored.

Meinwen explained the purpose of the petition. Bedwyr nodded and signed, looking suddenly businesslike. He handed the pen back to Meinwen with an air of finality, as if, through the addition of his name, the success of the campaign were now assured. He looked at his watch. It was chunky, silver with gold details. Were those diamonds on the face? Meinwen wasn't sure. She didn't know anything about jewellery. Then the watch had disappeared behind the cuff again.

'I've got to go,' said Bedwyr. 'I've got some clients waiting. Good luck.'

The sunglasses were back on. They watched him go.

Dewi looked at the business card. 'bedwyr clwyd', it said, all in lower case.

Bernard Weil

'So, did you make any friends at this factory?'

Dr and Madame Weil and their daughter were sitting by the fire in their house in Paris. The firelight played on the polished leather and the brass buttons of the chairs. Simone stared into the flames.

'Slaves don't have friends,' she said.

This was going to be a long night, Dr Weil thought, as he listened to the conversation.

'But the evenings – you must have been able to go to the play. Or perhaps... perhaps a dance or two, at the local workers' hall, eh?'

'Some people can't even walk, Mother, let alone dance.'

'Simone,' Dr Weil rarely contradicted his daughter, knowing that it was almost always counter-productive. But the way she was talking was worrying him. It was all very well researching the conditions of working class people in order to be able to help them; it even made sense to live like them for a while for the purposes of understanding their situation; but it was something else altogether to seriously try to be truly absorbed in their world, sacrificing the benefits of one's own existence in the process. What possible purpose could that serve?

'You think only you understand the suffering of the world,

Simone,' he said. 'Do you think *I* don't? I've seen *real* suffering. Not suffering as a self-imposed penance to purify your precious conscience.'

Simone looked away. He went on.

'Suffering that *wasn't* chosen, suffering that people didn't want. Soldiers; legless, blind. Gas victims coughing their lungs up. Grown men crying for their mothers as they died.'

Madame Weil closed her eyes, remembering.

'Young boys cursing God for their agony. Week after week, little children dying before their time. Tuberculosis, diphtheria. Do you think you're helping them by starving yourself, or taking a job an unemployed worker could do?'

Simone was silent for a minute or so.

'No,' she said quietly. 'I'm not helping. I want to help, but I don't know how. I don't want to be just a commentator. I want to feel their pain so I can help them to see that there can be hope, even in the worst suffering. When you experience the most extreme affliction, when God seems furthest away, that's really when you're nearest to him.'

At the mention of God, Simone's parents exchanged an involuntary glance of surprise. Simone, still looking down, did not notice.

'He can't be present with us. Not in this world. But in the worst suffering, he can be almost perfectly absent. That's the only possible way we can experience perfection on earth.'

Now it was the parents' turn to be silent. Simone continued to look into the fire, lost in thought.

'Perfection...' said Doctor Weil tentatively. Certainly he and his wife had always wanted the best for their children, always wanted them to fulfil the great potential they knew they had. They had encouraged them, yes, pushed them sometimes even, to achieve the highest possible success. But perfection? That was never part of the plan.

But Simone's reverie was over. She looked up, suddenly conversational, and changing the subject.

'I'm going to Germany. For three weeks. *The Worker's Voice* wants me to do an article on the state of the Left under the Hitler regime.'

From mystification to concern to alarm in the course of a few minutes' conversation. Talking with Simone was never dull, Doctor Weil thought. His wife's voice grew resigned.

'So. Germany. Under Hitler. And you a Jew. And an anarchist. And these are *friends* of yours on this newspaper?'

Simone smiled at the irony. 'Yes. Anyway, I'm going next week. I have to try to meet with one of the Trotskyist leaders. He's been living in Berlin for a while, and my friends haven't heard from him from some time. They're worried about him.'

'A secret mission at last, Simone,' said her mother.

'I know,' she replied, trying not to sound too pleased.

'And may we ask who is this Trotskyist that you're prepared to go to such lengths for? Or is it top-secret?'

'Well, I suppose I can tell you. If you promise not to tell anyone.'

'Of course.'

'It's Léon Sédov himself.'

'Trotsky's son?'

'Yes,' said Simone. It was clear she was proud of the association, although she was trying not to show it. However, Dr Weil knew that, for once, they were in a position to surprise her.

'Well,' said her mother. 'That's what I call a coincidence. Now, if you can find him, you'll be able to give him news of his father.'

'What do you mean? How can I do that? I've never even met Trotsky.'

'Not yet, you haven't,' said Madame Weil. 'But if you'd care to have dinner with us tomorrow night, you'll have the pleasure of his company. I'm sure he'll be glad to hear you're going in search of the young "crown prince".' She looked knowingly at Dr Weil.

'Trotsky? Here?' said Simone.

Her parents enjoyed her amazement.

'Why not here?' said Dr Weil, with a casual air, as if a visit from an exiled revolutionary was an everyday occurrence. 'He can't go back to the Soviet Union, can he? Not with a price on his head. He has to stay somewhere. And tomorrow he's staying here.'

'But how did he come to hear of you?'

'It was Pierre Letellier,' said Madame Weil. 'He called at your father's surgery yesterday. Trotsky has had to leave his other accommodation in a hurry, and they needed somewhere for him. Pierre said he didn't agree with Trotksy's views, but he didn't want to see him assassinated either. He's asked us to give him shelter until they can find somewhere safer.'

'Will... will Pierre be here tomorrow too,' asked Simone as

casually as she could. But there was more than a flicker of interest in her eyes.

'He won't, Simone. I'm sorry,' said her mother, with sympathy. 'He said he's being watched and he couldn't afford to come here. It would draw too much attention.'

'Oh. I see. I thought perhaps...'

Dr Weil was still pleased at having, on this rare occasion, shocked Simone.

'Pierre came to the surgery because it looks as if he's just another patient,' he said. 'It doesn't arouse suspicion. Then if he has any message, I can pass it on discreetly. In this case, I prescribed a night in our house, and a three-course dinner.'

He was enjoying this belated return to the conspiracies of his anarchist youth, in those brief years before the demands of a career and a family had channelled him into less radical ways.

'You see, Simone,' he went on, 'you think your mother and I are such reactionaries. You think we don't have a social conscience? When you see M'sieur Trotsky tomorrow, remember it's bourgeois gradualists like us who are giving him shelter.'

Simone brightened. 'Of course. You're not gradualists, anyway. I consider you true comrades. You're just less... impatient than some of us.'

●○●

Meinwen

Driving back to Yr Hafan that night, Dewi and Meinwen found the road up Bryn Aur blocked by a caravan which had become wedged on a narrow bend. The driver of the car towing the van was arguing with a tired-looking John Evans, the farmer of Ty'n Mynydd, who was trying to get his tractor past to his farm entrance. It looked like this was going to take some time to clear. Dewi reversed back down the lane. There was another route to Yr Hafan. It was more roundabout, but it would probably be quicker than waiting for the blockage to be removed.

They had taken this road before, but not for about a year. As they dropped down into the little gorge behind Bryn Aur, just before the steep climb up, they saw the familiar outline of

Dan y Pistyll Farm. But as they approached they saw that the old sign which had advertised *'Gwely a Brecwast'* was gone. Now there was a bright new sign with a yellow and red African tribal design. Dewi stopped the car. It was Dan y Pistyll, all right. At least, it used to be Dan y Pistyll, and Meinwen couldn't think of it as anything else. But now, the sign said, it was called 'Hakuna Matata', and it had been turned into a series of holiday 'theme chalets'.

Dewi and Meinwen looked through into the farmyard. Once it had been stained with manure, and old farm implements had been rusting in the corners. Now it was spotless, the windows hardwood, the stonework repointed, the yard concrete-washed. All the outbuildings had been turned into holiday chalets, all named after Disney themes. The farm's new name was taken from the film *The Lion King*, and Meinwen knew from watching the video with her friends' children that *Hakuna Matata* was Swahili for 'No Worries'. The old coachhouse of the farm was now called 'Pocahontas' Lodge'; the laundry was 'Ariel's Cavern', and the stables were 'Woody's Toybox'. Woody was the cowboy doll from *Toy Story*. If the Disney Corporation ever found out how their intellectual property was being ripped off here in Snowdonia they wouldn't be happy, Meinwen thought. But the new owners of the former Dan y Pistyll had calculated, probably rightly, that they were too far away to be found out. They probably just thought *'Hakuna Matata'* about the whole thing, anyway. However, if Dan y Pistyll's purchasers had no worries, they had just added one more anxiety to Meinwen's already overflowing collection of troubles.

Dewi started the car again and drove on. Neither of them said anything until they reached Yr Hafan. Dewi switched off the engine. Meinwen made no motion to get out. Her eyes were closed.

'I can't take this any more, Dewi,' she said. 'We're just wasting our time with these petitions. Nobody's taking any notice. Do you think Gethin could get us in to see Haydn Davies?'

Since he returned from Ireland, Gethin had worked for the local authority in which Haydn Davies, the Assembly First Minister, had his constituency. Gethin had no personal pull with Davies, as far as they knew. In fact, for some years, Gethin had been so withdrawn that he would have had little personal pull with anyone. But, it occurred to Meinwen now, he was one of Davies' constituents, and constituents had a right to see their Assembly Members.

Dewi thought for a moment.

'It's worth a try,' he said.

●○●

Selma Weil

Madame Weil heard a car draw up outside their house. She went to the window in time to see two men getting out of the black sedan. Both carried revolvers openly in their hands, and looked ready for trouble. They were followed by an older man with a goatee beard, Léon Trotsky; he was wearing a heavy overcoat and dark hat. One guard knocked at the door of the house, as Trotsky, head bowed, ascended the steps. Madame Weil went to the door to let him in.

'M'sieur Trotsky, we are honoured...' she began.

Trotsky ignored her and walked straight in. The first body-guard followed him.

'Where is Comrade Trotsky's room?' he said, the Russian accent heavy upon his French. Trotsky stood at the foot of the stairs with his back to them, removing his coat. Madame Weil spoke to the bodyguard.

'First of all, where are your manners, comrade?'

Madame Weil's fluent Russian startled the bodyguard almost more than her challenge. Trotsky looked round, surprised, and amused at his guard's discomfiture.

'My apologies, Madame Weil,' he said, in Russian. 'Many months of this underground life have made some of us forget our social niceties.'

He looked sternly at the bodyguard. '"Where is Comrade Trotsky's room, *if you please*?"'

'If you please, Madame,' the bodyguard said stiffly.

'This way,' said Madame Weil sweetly, harmony restored. She led the guard towards the stairs. 'Comrade Trotsky, please go through. You will find Dr Weil and my daughter in the drawing room.'

She led the bodyguard upstairs. He carried Trotsky's bags.

Trotsky's two secretaries, who had been waiting at the door, each with a large briefcase, followed them up.

'Permanent revolution is the only way. When the revolution comes in the West it will repeat the essential features of the Revolution in Russia. It will come first from the populace, and the political organisations must be prepared to give direction to the impulses of the people...'

'More vegetables, M'sieur Trotsky?' asked Madame Weil, offering the bowl.

Trotsky helped himself without acknowledging her. He continued: 'The irresistible drive of the people, like the Bolsheviks in the revolution, will carry the process along...'

Madame Weil was prepared to challenge most people over the social graces, but faced with Trotsky's flow of argument, and knowing that he had suffered so much for his principles, she was reduced for once to something approaching awe. Dr Weil and his daughter simply listened. Dr Weil eating absent-mindedly, Simone, her mother noticed, once more having left her food untouched.

'The processes of history will inevitably force the result of the overthrow of capitalism...'

By the window, one of Trotsky's guards sat in an armchair, eating cold food from a plate with one hand. His other hand held a revolver. As he ate, he watched the dark street outside.

In the drawing room, after dinner, Simone's parents retired briefly to the kitchen to prepare some drinks, leaving their daughter and Trotsky alone, apart from the ever-present bodyguard. The politician occupied the armchair, while Simone sat on the floor. The attitude was one of master and disciple, a relation with which Trotsky was clearly comfortable. Unlike his dinner table conversation, this was now a personal talk. Through the open door between the two rooms, Madame Weil could hear the conversation continue.

'I'm sorry I had to condemn your statements in that pamphlet I wrote,' Trotsky said. 'But your point of view was too individualistic.'

'If I remember, you said I was guilty of "vulgar liberalism", "cheap anarchist exaltation" and "the most reactionary petty-bourgeois prejudices".'

'Did I? Yes, well, you seem to have despaired over what you call the unfortunate experiences of the working people in the Soviet Union, and you've simply retreated to a position where you seek to defend your own personality against the world. When you are older...'

'So, how old will I be when Russia's truly a workers' state?'

'It is a workers' state. But Russia found itself cut off. It was isolated. History moves slowly. If you have to fight the enemy you need an army.'

'Using the same weapons, and the same methods, as the capitalists? All the Russian workers are doing is putting up with the Soviet government because they prefer it to having the capitalists in power again.'

'You don't understand. The Revolution has brought about a great deal for the workers – and for women and children. Now, if we consider that production will progress...'

'Progress? The fact of it is that you and Lenin have simply done what the big capitalists did when capitalism was still "progressive" – and you've crushed thousands of human lives into the bargain!'

In the kitchen, Dr and Madame Weil listened anxiously to the unexpected turn the conversation had taken. They should have known better than to leave her alone with him, Madame Weil thought. Trotsky's voice was raised now.

'You are completely reactionary...!'

Simone was still calm, but insistent.

'Well, what have you got to say to young people who are just being brainwashed?'

'Brainwashed?! Why must you question everything? Running a country isn't what you imagine it to be. We're not like the gods on Mount Olympus! If you feel like that, why are you bothering to put us up? Are you the Salvation Army or something?!'

'Well at least the Salvation Army try to do something for people's spirits too.'

'Yes, give them religion, the promise of some distant heaven. The opiate of the people.'

'And what do you give them? The promise of some distant victory of the proletariat? Revolution is your opiate.'

There were footsteps in the drawing room. The Weils composed themselves and entered the room, just as Trotsky was opening the door into the hallway, his bodyguard behind him.

'What's wrong with that girl?' he shouted.

He left the room and they heard him stamping his way upstairs.

●○●

Meinwen

Gethin ap Dafydd was wearing a suit. Meinwen hardly recognised him when she and Dewi met him in the Assembly lobby. In the days of Yr Hafan, he would no more have worn a suit than he would have voted Conservative. In those days, he was almost never seen without a sloganed teeshirt. Space on his clothing had been allocated to different campaigns as carefully as advertising space on a Premiership football strip, although not as lucratively. But his experience in Ireland had changed him. He didn't vote Conservative, it wasn't that bad, but the fire of his humour and optimism that had brightened Yr Hafan seemed to have gone out. Once a catalyst, he was now quiescent, overweight and middle-aged before his time. They had needed to prod him with several phone calls to get him to set up this meeting with Haydn Davies. But he'd done it eventually, using his original name of Keith Davidson to avoid arousing suspicion, and claiming to want to deliver a petition on behalf of a community group, whose name he managed not to specify. After all, Meinwen had reasoned, their appeal was a petition of a kind, and the Movement was a community group, of a kind. They had expected to be referred to one of Haydn Davies' regular surgeries in his constituency, but were told that, as Mr Davies was due to miss the next surgery due to a foreign trip, he would see them – briefly – at the Assembly itself. They were now in the waiting area outside the First Minister's office.

Meinwen and Dewi waited while Gethin made the arrangements with one of Davies' secretaries.

Meinwen rarely heard Gethin speak English. Listening to him now, with his broad Manchester accent, she felt the same faint surprise she always did when he spoke his native language. She had to force herself to remember he was an Englishman.

Gethin finished his conversation. The secretary went into Davies' office, and Gethin came to join the other two as they sat down on the two sofas in the anteroom. He sighed.

'I'm not sure there's much point to this, you know,' he said.

'Well, we've got to try, haven't we?' said Dewi. 'Go straight to the fountainhead. This is the guy who makes the policies after all.'

'Yes, but he hasn't done much – anything – to rein in the anti-Welsh faction, has he? I don't think he's interested. I mean, good luck to you, but I just don't want you to be disappointed.'

'We're used to disappointments, Geth,' Meinwen said. 'One more won't make any difference.'

She stopped herself from saying anything further. She knew that Gethin had suffered one disappointment too many. That's what happens when you mix love and politics, she thought.

'I suppose not,' Gethin began again. 'But you're swimming against the tide, you know. It's not just house prices that are the problem. Young people don't want to live in the country any more. Not in Wales or anywhere. They want to live in the city. It's happening all over the world. In Spain they're advertising for people to emigrate there from South America because their villages are dying. There was an article in *The Telegraph*...'

'*The Telegraph*? Since when did you read *The Telegraph*...?'

'I have to read it. I'm a press officer, remember? Well, anyway, they've got the same problem in Spain. And there are tens of thousands of abandoned villages in Russia. It's happening in the USA too. Has been for years. And it's starting to happen all over the developing world. There's nothing we can do about it.'

'Some young people still want to live in their home communities, Geth,' said Meinwen firmly. 'We need to give them a chance.' She didn't want to argue with her old friend, but this fatalism was the last thing they needed just now.

'Yes. That's true,' said Gethin. He didn't seem to have the rancour necessary for an argument. It was more as if he was thinking out loud. But the sheer objective detachment of his views made them all the more unsettling. He went on: 'But this drift from the country is a global thing, that's all I'm saying. The only difference in Wales is that some people want to move in to the country as well, and I'm not sure that's so terrible. It's better than having ghost towns, which is what we'd have otherwise.'

Meinwen could see the logic, but her feelings impelled a different reaction: what she saw happening in her home area day by day, their transformation into a new England, felt to her far worse than seeing those communities become ghost towns. Better to be a ghost than be reincarnated as something entirely antithetical. Conscience forced her to acknowledge that this feeling contained a large amount of an inherited antipathy she felt to the incomers as representatives of English domination; but this was an attitude perilously close to prejudice, and one she knew she couldn't allow herself to entertain, so she compelled herself to say something conciliatory.

'I'm not saying incomers are bad, Geth. Some of my best friends are incomers.' She smiled at him. 'I just wish they were all like you, that's all.'

'Give it time, Meinwen, perhaps they will be. Look at the Valleys. People were moving there from England in their hundreds of thousands a century ago, for the industry. Lots of people thought it was the end for Wales. But now the descendants of those incomers are as Welsh as they come. And loads of them are learning Welsh and sending their kids to Welsh school.'

Meinwen was having to revise her opinion of Gethin. His abandonment of activism may have been spurred by disenchantment, but, as they discussed politics now for the first time for years, she found that his disillusion seemed to have healed into a kind of wary optimism, although a passive one. She recalled that his subject in college had been history. Perhaps that's what came of taking the long view. She hoped he was right, but with so much at stake she didn't feel it was permissible for her to take the perilous course of trust.

'OK,' she said. 'But just in case, let's try and give history a bit of a helping hand, shall we?'

Gethin just nodded. They looked down at the table between them. It was strewn with a collection of pamphlets detailing the Assembly's achievements in various fields; health, education, community development.

For something to do while waiting, they flicked through the leaflets. Automatically, they scanned each document for any reference to the Welsh language, their one measure of a policy's relevance. They had found none by the time the door to the First Minister's office opened.

Haydn Davies

It was Haydn Davies himself. He carefully avoided the body language of power. He opened his own doors, greeted his own guests, and, when he invited them into his office and motioned them to sit down, he did not sit behind his desk, but on the same soft chairs, ranged around the coffee table, as the rest of them. Just before he had let them in, his secretary had come in to warn him that there were three visitors instead of the expected one, and that one of them was a language activist she recognised from television. So he had already guessed this meeting wouldn't be about potholes in the roads of his constituency. He decided to play it by ear. He didn't want to appear petulant or inaccessible. So when he had opened the door and seen Meinwen, he hadn't shown any surprise. Their paths hadn't crossed before, but he knew her by reputation, and he thought it would be politic to let her know that. A little bit of *Cymraeg* was in order, he felt.

'*Te neu goffi?*'.

The visitors looked at one another, coming to a quick consensus. Teas all round. Davies' secretary appeared in the doorway again.

'Four teas, please, Catrin,' he said in English. 'And make sure Meinwen's is fairly-traded. None of that exploitative stuff, now.'

He looked at Meinwen with a guarded half smile to see whether she had caught this. She met his eyes, but with no flicker of answering humour; she had clearly decided she wasn't going to be charmed. Seeing his attempt to establish a rapport rebuffed, Davies became businesslike.

'Now, forgive me, but I'm learning Welsh,' he said. 'I think it would probably be better if we spoke in English. What can I do for you?'

Gethin began by explaining why they were there, and that, although Meinwen and Dewi were not constituents, he had taken the liberty of bringing them along to help put the case.

Davies nodded, keeping his counsel as he waited to see how the meeting developed. He knew he had every right to feel considerable annoyance that they had secured this meeting under false pretences, but he didn't let a scrap of that irritation show. It scarcely ever paid to indulge one's own feelings. Don't give anything away. Don't let them know what you're thinking. The best result was what was needed, not a personal victory. He let the annoyance fall away, and gave his uninvited guests his full attention.

After Gethin's brief introduction, it was Meinwen's turn. He had often seen her on television, but this was the first time they had met. He was struck by how slight she was; almost fragile. He turned his mind to her words. She was explaining how a culture of priceless value was in danger of being expunged just so rich people could have the pick of the housing market. History would never forgive any of them if they stayed silent while this process was happening, if they did nothing to arrest it. They'd tried democratic means: they'd lobbied, they'd held protest rallies, they'd picketed, they'd leafleted, they'd marched. Still the housing stock was being snatched from the reach of local people, still the young people were having to leave their home areas, still the lifestyle migrants were replacing them, changing the character of Wales house by house, farm by farm.

As he listened to Meinwen running through the arguments, Davies sipped his tea. Despite his earlier teasing, this really was fairly-traded tea, and that was because he had insisted on using fair-trade goods in his office for years as a matter of principle. He and Meinwen shared many ideals, he thought. Although he knew she was not much younger than he was, she reminded him of a much younger version of himself. He remembered his own career as a campaigner helping the miners during the 1984 strike, opposing nuclear weapons and standing up for the unemployed during the bitter Thatcher years. He knew something about the vilification of which these three were complaining too. He had never been a communist or a Trotskyist, but that hadn't stopped the right-wing press pillorying him as such week after week as he and his fellow socialists tried to stand against the mayhem which Thatcherism had unleashed upon working-class communities. That was before he traded the megaphone for the manifesto, deciding that he could have more influence inside the system than shouting from the margins. He had changed, that was certain. His tactics, vocabulary and appearance were all very different. But he was confident that he still had the same aim – justice.

Meinwen was continuing. House prices, capital-rich incomers, economically-disadvantaged locals, inequities, iniquities, uncontrolled market forces, basic human rights. Yes, he could see the point. Beyond the crude nationalistic assumptions there was a simple basic principle of fairness here – of access to the housing market – which could be readily detached from the language issue. People in his own constituency couldn't afford houses these days. People were commuting to Cardiff and even to Bristol from the Heads of the Valleys. Perhaps there would be a way of creating an all-Wales policy which would protect people's right to live in their own communities. If such a policy were created for the whole country, then it could meet these language campaigners' aims without it looking as if the language were being given preferential treatment. Not rocket science. If they put the words 'sustainable' and 'community' in enough times, it would pass. With a policy of that kind, he could withstand the anti-Welsh-language rednecks in his own party, and get the job done. If everyone just played the game, it would be fine. He continued to listen.

Justice, rights, communities, belonging. He glanced at the clock on the wall behind his visitors. They had another five minutes, he thought. The death of a nation, the judgement of posterity. Time to wrap this up. He put his cup down and leaned forward. He nodded as Meinwen took the cue to draw her argument to a close.

'So what do you want me to do?' he said. He made it sound as if they had only to name the policy and he would command it into being. His visitors clearly knew better than that.

'A Property Act, Mr Davies,' said Dewi. 'While there's still time.'

Haydn Davies knew of the Movement's campaign, but he had never given it any consideration, largely because of who was promoting it. Now, forced to find a response, he thought quickly. He wouldn't argue the detail. As a former rugby player, he knew that, under pressure, it was safer to kick for touch.

That would buy him time for the policy he was considering formulating, and he wouldn't lose face by looking as if he had been forced to give in to pressure from campaigners. His party had either created, or inherited, a range of policies to promote the language on the institutional and educational levels, and many of his party, himself included, felt a general support for that principle; he was now beginning to warm to the idea of being seen as the preserver of the language in the community sense as well.

His mind began calculating the process and how it could be presented. The language would be taken from the hands of the politicised campaigners, for whom its continuance was an ethnic survival project, and would be given to all the people of Wales as a skill, regardless of their heritage. It would be all the safer for that. It would be depoliticised, mainstreamed, normalised. His mind ran on. If he could do that, then perhaps the Labour party could steal the clothes, and even the seats, of the nationalists in their strongholds. Perhaps indeed.

He felt sudden annoyance with himself, frustrated at how readily and instinctively his mind mutated altruism into advantage. There had been a time when idealism and self-interest were strangers within him; now they were inseparable companions. In the painful, compromised complexities of his life in office, there were times he longed for the simple dualities of the wilderness where Meinwen and her kind still lived.

'Let me think about it,' he said, putting a note of seriousness into his deep voice.

The tactic worked better than he had expected. It killed the conversation completely. The visitors exchanged glances. No one could think of anything to say. Job done, thought Davies. He sat back again and relaxed.

'So are you just down for the nightlife?' he turned to Meinwen and Dewi. 'Or have you got people to lobby, signs to paint? I think you'll be a bit disappointed here, you know – all our signage is bilingual.' The smile was mischievous again.

'We're not painting signs just now,' said Meinwen, unsmiling. 'We managed to win that battle. But if there's no movement on a Property Act, we'll have to take direct action again. And we won't stop until we get justice.'

The ball was back in play, then. But Haydn Davies wasn't

playing any more. Meinwen used the 'we' as if she could summon up twelve legions of activists at a word. He'd seen enough news reports to know that, even when their members were jailed, the Movement's protests now scarcely merited a few paragraphs in the newspaper or a fifteen-second item on television. Those tactics only worked when they coincided with the *zeitgeist*, when there was support in the country at large. But things had moved on. Roadsigns were one thing; no one really lost out if they were made bilingual. But the property market? They might as well try to tell people what clothes they should wear or what kind of cars they should drive or what names they could call their children. Even if Meinwen did have an army, she wouldn't win that campaign; he knew it. He looked at her quizzically, as if to say 'Who are you kidding?' Meinwen remained impassive. She really does think she's got twelve legions, Davies realised. However, he thought he'd give her another chance to bring this conversation back within the bounds of consensual *realpolitik*, so that they could regain the compromise he felt was within reach. This time it was not mirth, but manoeuvre, that consciously kept the mischievous half smile on his face while he said:

'You're not threatening me, now, are you, love...?'

'Not you personally, no,' said Meinwen. 'The system you represent.'

If that was meant to be conciliatory, Davies thought, she was badly mistaken. His half smile disappeared. He'd thought to call her bluff, but he could see it wasn't even a bluff, but a settled belief. He was the enemy, and to her and her blinkered zealots he always would be. He was wasting his time. The visceral annoyance which he had ignored welled back up, instantly displacing the fragile compromise his mind had constructed.

'Thanks for the advance warning,' he said. 'But let me think about what you said first, OK.'

When he had offered to think about it earlier in the conversation, he had actually planned to do so. After Meinwen's threat, however, he had no such intention. Even as he decided this, he could feel the expedience within him deftly take anger, not altruism as its new partner, and begin tracing new patterns, very different to the previous ones, but just as coherent and every bit as convincing. If preserving Welsh-speaking communities meant producing more generations of resentful, self-right-eous, ghettoised confrontation-addicts like these, they could forget it. His government was funding Welsh-medium education and measures to promote Welsh within public institutions, and they'd continue to do that. But that would have to be the extent of it. Why should he channel the energies of his party into preserving communities whose values were so openly hostile to his own? He stood up and opened the door.

'Thanks for coming,' he said to them in Welsh as he showed them out. Then in English: 'Be careful – it's a jungle out there.'

●○●

Simone

The official examined Simone's travel documents closely. He took his time. She knew it was one of the pleasures of the job for this kind of man that they could make people wait as long as they wanted. As he turned the pages, Simone had time to look around her at the Hauptbahnhof, Berlin's main railway station. There seemed to be uniforms everywhere: railway staff, police, soldiers, Hitler Jugend. And propaganda posters on every available space. Some of them depicted communists as sickle-wielding ape-like subhumans; others showed Jews as sneering top-hatted capitalists.

The official looked up from the papers at Simone. As her mother had warned her before she left, in her red beret, black cloak and round glasses, she could not have looked more like an anarchist agitator if she tried. Her name too, was a sure clue to her Jewish identity. But they were not arresting French citizens – not even Jewish ones – yet, so she felt no real alarm, only a deep distaste.

'Your race?' the official asked casually, as if he were inquiring about her journey origin.

'My nationality, do you mean?' Simone replied. 'My nationality is French.'

She looked up coolly at the Nazi, as if challenging him to identify her as Jewish. He shrugged, handed back her cards and let her go.

Simone passed through the barrier, found the taxi rank and, in German, asked the first driver if the cab was available. It was. As the driver got out to open the back door, Simone opened the front passenger door herself and got in. She thought it more comradely to ride in the front seat. She smiled at the driver. He stiffened.

'Where to, Fraulein?' he said, looking straight ahead.

'The offices of the *Worker's Voice of Germany*, please.'

The driver looked across at her, alarmed. She smiled encouragingly.

'It's in Albrechtstrasse,' she said.

Cursing under his breath, the driver pulled away.

'Herr Driver,' Simone began, conversationally, 'Perhaps you can tell me, how do working people like yourself feel about Hitler?'

'I'm not political, Fraulein.'

'No, but you're German, you must have an opinion about what's happening here.'

'I'm just a taxi driver, Fraulein... I don't need opinions.' He shifted uncomfortably.

They were silent for a minute or so, while Simone tried to think of a more fruitful line of inquiry. The taxi came to a stop at a junction; on the corner outside were a group of Hitler Jugend selling newspapers.

'But all this!' Simone indicated the uniforms in the street outside. 'You must have some opinion on it!'

'Very well, yes,' he said, finally opening up. 'I have an opinion. Three years ago, I had no job. All my savings had gone with the inflation. We didn't know what we'd eat from one day to the next. Now, as you see, I have work. I also have a new flat. We have a holiday every year at a workers' resort.'

Simone was happy that they had dialogue at last.

'But your ideals, as a working man. Surely Nazism can't satisfy them?'

'Fraulein, if you'd lived through the war, the inflation and the chaos in Germany, you'd realise. A job, a home, a holiday. Those *are* ideals.'

He turned a corner into Albrechtstrasse, and stopped the car.

'You will understand, of course, if I let you off a block away. It wouldn't be... wise... for me to be seen taking you there. Everyone's watching everyone else these days. And to be going to a socialist newspaper, with somebody of your...'

'Of my... what?'

'Of your... background.'

'My background is France, Herr Driver. The Christian, Hellenic, Catholic tradition is my tradition. No anti-semitic law can alter that.'

She got out of the taxi, and counted out the exact fare.

'You will understand, of course, Herr Driver. For me to tip you would be patronising.'

He drove off quickly without a thank you or a goodbye. Simone crossed the street to the offices of the newspaper. As she approached, she could see it was boarded up, both the windows and the main door. There was a new notice pasted onto the boards, saying that the premises had been confiscated as a result of criminal activities. Simone was at a loss what to do. She looked to see if there was a side door. There was not.

She looked around her. On the opposite side of the street was a café with pavement tables. One man there seemed to be watching her intently. Feeling uncomfortable, she turned back to contemplate the front of the newspaper offices again. After a few moments, she heard footsteps crossing the street behind her, moving in her direction.

'Mademoiselle Weil?'

She turned round, startled. It was the man from the café.

'Yes.'

'Léon Sédov. Columnist, until yesterday, of the *Worker's Voice of Germany*.'

●○●

Meinwen

After their meeting with Haydn Davies, Dewi, Meinwen and Gethin pushed their way out through the revolving doors of Crickhowell House into the street outside. They were in a subdued mood, and Gethin quickly took his leave, saying he wanted to get back for a council meeting that afternoon.

Just to the left of them was the slate, steel and glass structure of the new Senedd, Wales' first elected democratic forum for six hundred years. At one time, they would have regarded this with hope and pride as the tangible result of their support for devolution. They had believed devolution would ensure

Wales' recognition as a nation and would bring democratic, accountable government. It had. That very accountability was now the unexpected problem: the Welsh government was answerable to an electorate of whom only a fifth spoke Welsh, and of whom even a smaller proportion were nationalists. It had been easier to pressurise the unelected Tory Secretaries of State who had governed Wales for a decade and a half; they were afraid of antagonising restless natives in the unfamiliar territory which was in their temporary, but total control. But getting concessions from the Assembly was an uphill struggle by comparison. Broad-based, established for the long term, it could not be pushed or chivvied. Dewi and Meinwen passed the building with scarcely a second glance, and walked up through Butetown towards the city centre.

This was the area once known as Tiger Bay. But now, the remnants of the traditional multi-racial community, Yemenis, Somalis, West Indians, which had given the area its exotic reputation, were corralled into a couple of enclaves in the centre of the district. On every side, blocks of bland new apartments were being thrown up as fast as the developers could build them, to serve the booming demand for waterside dwellings around the expanding precincts of Welsh government. If devolution had not brought a new dawn for the language activists, it had certainly brought one for the property developers.

As she passed the new developments, Meinwen gave them her habitual textual appraisal. None of the blocks had Welsh names. None of them even had Cardiff names. The closest any of them came to a sense of place was an insipid nautical theme which some of them affected: Chandler's Rise; Maritime Gate; Leeward Bank. None of the developers wanted to scare off potential buyers by giving the blocks a name the purchasers might not be able to pronounce. In price terms, none of them were remotely within reach of the average incomes of the indigenous population, who were being squeezed out, family by family, to areas of cheaper housing miles from their home patch, their culture diffusing with them. Black and brown faces appeared ever more frequently on the promotional literature for the Bay area, even as the community to which the owners of those faces belonged was itself gradually being dispersed. It was a striking parallel with the Movement's own concerns, and possibly a politically useful one. But Meinwen felt too depressed to follow the thought through. Lost in her own concerns, she walked with Dewi past the Alice Street mosque and the Yemeni community centre, past the Somali mosque, past the church of St Mary the Virgin, and past the Greek Orthodox church, without reflecting on the future of the communities those places of worship were built to serve, and around which a ring of redbrick and aluminium-detailed real estate was closing like a trap.

●○●

Simone

'A columnist until yesterday? What happened yesterday?' asked Simone.

She and Sédov had taken a seat at the café opposite the closed offices.

'The Nazis closed the paper down,' said Sédov. 'They confiscated the presses and the typewriters, and they burned the newsprint and the backnumbers; all for the "criminal" activity of challenging the Nazi party. And they've sealed the building, as you see. I knew you were coming this morning, so I waited here.'

Simone looked back at the offices, a powerhouse of the German Left shut down literally overnight. The day after its demise, people were passing the gagged and blindfolded building without a second glance.

'So what do you do now? Continue the struggle underground?'

He shook his head, 'The struggle's over in Germany. The Nazis are taking control of everything. The press, the economy, the armed forces. And the propaganda in the cinemas: my God, you wouldn't believe it.'

'Do the people believe it.'

'Most of them seem to, yes.'

'But when I came to Germany before, I thought the working class here was the best-organised I'd seen anywhere. I thought it was the best hope in Europe for the proletariat.'

'So did I. That's why I came here. But we were both wrong, weren't we? Have you noticed any agitation since you've been here?'

'Well, I've not been here very long, but no. Lots of Nazi propaganda activity, but no opposition. It all seems very calm.'

'That's just the thing. It's apathy. The Left in this country's in pieces. The different groups hate one another more than they do the Nazis. I'm convinced there's no prospect of organised resistance here. I'm planning to go to France.'

'Ah, well I can give you some news of France. I met your father in Paris a couple of weeks ago.'

'Did you? How is he?'

'He's well. Well enough to quarrel with me.'

He laughed, then thought for a moment.

'Oh, yes, about that pamphlet, was it? I heard about that article. Don't worry; he quarrels with everyone. I hope you stood up to him.'

Simone nodded.

'But he's safe?' Sédov asked, serious now.

'Yes, he was staying with my parents. Just for one night. Then they were going to find him a safer place still.'

'I'm glad. It will be good to see him again,' he said. He looked thoughtful for a moment; then he laughed again. 'So you had a quarrel with him?! I'm sorry you didn't have a better introduction. He's not as hard as he seems, you know.'

'That's not the impression I got.'

'No, I'm sure. But, here, let me tell you one thing he did since he's been in Paris. It will appeal to you. Do you know Maria Skobtsova?'

'I'm afraid not.'

'Well, perhaps you haven't moved in the same circles. She's Russian. She works mainly with the Russian refugees in Paris. There are thousands of them. She runs a kind of refuge for them in rue de Lourmel. Feeds them, clothes them, sorts out their papers.'

'I see.'

'Well, she's quite a character. She's an Orthodox nun now. But before that, she was a revolutionary, and she was one of my father's comrades in the early days of Bolshevism.'

'She sounds quite a woman.'

'She is. She worked with my father until 1917, but then she disagreed with the way he was using the Red Guards to put down the opposition to the revolution.'

'Lots of people disagreed with that.'

'Yes, well Maria went further. She joined a plot to assassinate him.'

'I see,' Simone was intrigued.

'The plot didn't get very far, and when it failed, Maria left Russia and ended up in France. Then she joined the church, and started running this hostel. That's where I met her – through the Russian emigré connection.'

He smiled to himself and went on.

'Well, when my father heard she was in Paris, he actually called on her in person. You've probably noticed he likes giving advice, well he advised her to leave France and go to America because he thought, the way things are going in Europe, she'd be persecuted if she stayed, because of her political beliefs.'

'What did she do?'

'She just thanked him and said the poor needed her in Paris, and that she'd be staying there. So then my father asked if he could do anything for her, in memory of the past. And she just gave him this smile and said, "Well, our poor coal merchant hasn't been paid for months". So my father asked for the address, and he went straight there and paid the whole bill.'

'That was a kind act.'

'Wasn't it? Do you know what Maria said when she heard about it? She said God would forgive my father all his crimes – for the sake of the Lourmel coal bill!'

He laughed at the memory. Some heads turned on the nearby tables. Sédov lowered his voice again, recalled from the redeemed enmities of the past to the unresolved dangers of the present.

'Will you do me a favour?' he asked Simone.

'I'd be glad to.'

'It's dangerous.'

'Then I'd be even more glad to.'

'I need to get some documents out of Germany. I've got a file. It's got the addresses of all the Trotskyists in every major city in Germany. It's essential for our organisation. There's no way I could bring it out myself. But they won't search you, as a French citizen. Will you take it for me?'

'Of course.'

'Thank you. It won't be safe for any of us in this country soon.' He looked across at the boarded-up offices. 'But I wonder how safe we'll be in France even. I don't think Hitler will stop at Germany. It's like some beast has been unleashed.'

Dewi

The Little Connoisseur was a Cardiff institution. Tiny and cramped, with red plastic seats and plastic tablecloths, it nonetheless lived up to its advertising slogan, 'The Home of Home Cooking', by serving traditional comfort food. For its patrons, it was nostalgia on a plate. For the members of the Movement, in the pre-devolution days before Welsh-themed restaurants cafés and bars became *de rigeur*, it was also the nearest they could get to supporting a local Welsh café in Cardiff. On the wall there was a huge poster of Shirley Bassey from the 1970s, in a long flowing orange dress, and under it the words 'Cardiff's Own'. Crucially, this little restaurant had the added attraction of being cheap. Many a campaign had been planned there over sausage and mash, ham with parsley sauce, or bread and butter pudding. The Movement members felt that by frequenting it, they were authentic Cardiffians, residents of their capital, habitués of its public places, sharing its secrets and backstreets like any native. What most native Cardiffians would have made of their conspiratorial Welsh conversations, they preferred not to think.

Going there today was really a sentimental journey for Dewi and Meinwen. Dewi hoped the years of shared memories would connect with Meinwen, who was reduced to more than her usual quietness by the meeting with Haydn Davies. He hoped it would bring her back to an earlier version of herself; one who could laugh. And eat.

'The roast beef and Yorkshire pudding for me,' he said. 'What about you?'

'I'll just have a cup of tea.'

'Come on, Meinwen. They've got your favourite – omelette and chips.' He detected an uncomfortable coaxing tone to his voice, as though he were talking to a reluctant child. As he realised this, he was struck for the first time by just how worried he really was about Meinwen's eating. When had he last seen her eat anything? He couldn't remember.

'Come on – my treat.' The coaxing intonation was there again.

'Really, Dewi, I'm not hungry.' The tone was final. He recognised Meinwen's determination. She could no more be persuaded to eat than she could be persuaded to leave a sit-down protest.

Dewi closed his eyes and nodded as if to say he understood. He placed his order, and reached over to the paper rack for a copy of the city's morning newspaper.

Every time he read this paper, he was struck afresh by the way it amplified the discord of the community's life. Its articles seemed to be a distillation of discontent: the views of the intolerant and the ignorant of the city filtered of any lingering nuance and subtlety and then simplified into the most inflammatory form; every annoyance a 'fury', every disagreement a 'war'.

He flicked through it with the well-practised speed of an internet search engine. News about Westminster cabinet reshuffles he ignored; a hospital closure in the eastern valleys, sad, but no; an earthquake in Turkey, desperate, but no; the latest European Commission scandal, intriguing, but no. The two words he was looking for were 'Welsh' and 'language', preferably together. He found them. In John Sayle's column. It was entitled 'Ban the Taffyban'.

'Why has Wales failed to emulate the Celtic Tiger economy of Ireland?,' he read. 'Why are Welsh companies not multinational forces like their Irish counterparts? Are the Welsh less enterprising, less intelligent than their cousins across the Irish Sea? God forbid. If you want the answer, you need only look at the main difference between the two countries. Ireland has quietly allowed its language to die. It's recognised the futility of trying to compete with the global power of English, and it's harnessed its fortunes to those of the English-speaking world, leaving Gaelic as the province of a few Aran-sweatered romantics. Result? Prosperity.

'But in Wales, so much of our public policy, and so much of our scarce finance, is taken up with propping up the Welsh language, that it's sapping the nation of the drive and energy we need to compete and succeed. People like Wales' own female Taliban, Meinwen Jones, would be happy to keep us living in a folk museum. And it's the disproportionate influence that fanatics like her exercise in the corridors of power that stifles the healthy creativity that would allow Wales to prosper. They're the virus in the body politic. Next time you hear that someone is out of work, you know who to blame.'

As he read it, Dewi decided he wouldn't show the article to Meinwen. But his very absorption had betrayed to her the fact that he had found something of interest. And interest meant interest in only one subject.

'What does it say?'

'You don't want to know.'

'Maybe not. Show me.'

She read it. They both knew to the decimal point how much money was spent directly on supporting the Welsh language each year: a few millions – less than the cost of a new Apache helicopter, and a drop in the ocean of the billions the government spent in Wales on health, education, roads and industry. From long experience, they knew that people who cared not a scrap about any other item of government expenditure suddenly became piously concerned for the public purse when it came to spending on the Welsh language, always singling it out as the one thing that was too costly, wasteful and unnecessary. Railing at the expense of supporting the language was a tired argument, but it was enough to satisfy minds who only wanted something which sounded like a reason on which to hang their prejudice. They had even heard the environmental argument used against them before now – printing things bilingually was apparently destroying the rainforest. The people making that complaint were apparently not concerned about the effect of pornographic magazines, trashy novels or junk mail on the rainforest, only the effect of Welsh-language forms, which were, Dewi could only assume, uniquely destructive. Even Sayle's jibe about their excessive influence in the corridors of power was an old chestnut, and after the brush-off they had received from Haydn Davies that morning, it was risible. But Meinwen didn't even give a bitter laugh. Dewi watched her face. She didn't even get angry. He could see she'd taken the article in. What worried him was that she didn't let anything out.

●○●

Simone

'The Great Beast. A phrase from the book of Revelation. What precisely St John the Divine was referring to, imprisoned and persecuted as he was, we cannot be certain.'

Simone paced slowly back and fore as she addressed her class. This was only a small provincial French town, and the students had initially found her open-ended, discursive method of teaching unfamiliar. There had even been some complaints from the parents to begin with. But the unease had quietened down after a few weeks, when the children had said they looked forward to her lessons more than anyone else's. That had been gratifying. They were an attentive class, that was for sure, Simone thought. She loved teaching them.

'But we do know of the Great Beast of oppression, of tyranny in our lives. Nazi Germany. Totalitarianism of the Right. But also... totalitarianism of the Left. Soviet Russia. Anything which enslaves, which oppresses, which excludes. The Catholic church when it declares heretics anathema, the Jewish religion when it calls down the curses of God on its enemies, the Roman Empire which created a desert, as Tacitus said, and called it peace.

'And other empires – France,' she gestured at a map on the wall, where large areas of Africa, Asia and the South Seas were marked in blue. 'To the populations in Indo China and the Pacific *we* are the Great Beast, destroying their cultures and forcing our own in their place. Our *gendarmes* are enforcing unjust laws, our teachers are rapping the knuckles of children for speaking their native language. We drill little black and brown children to say their ancestors were the Gauls and that they had fair hair and blue eyes! We must oppose this beast in every way, in other countries, in our own country, and in our own hearts.'

One of the students had her hand up. Simone stopped talking and invited her question.

'What about the Civil War in Spain, Mademoiselle? Who's the beast there?'

'The fascists. Franco's forces.' Simone didn't even have to think before answering. 'The matter's clear. The republicans, the socialists, are the legitimate, elected government of Spain, and the nationalists, the fascists, the army and the church have risen in rebellion against them in pursuit of reactionary aims, to keep power in the hands of the rich. Yes, that's where the beast can be seen most clearly in our day, in all his naked aggression and all his lust for power.'

'But Mademoiselle, if that's where the beast is, and if that's where he's is at his worst, shouldn't we be opposing him there?'

Simone stopped pacing. She turned slowly and looked at the girl who had asked her the question. Simone felt more as if she had just been given an answer than as if she had been asked a question.

'Yes,' she said. 'I should.'

The next day, Simone went to see her headmaster. She handed him a letter and waited as he read it. He did so, nodded, and looked up at her.

'Thank you, Mademoiselle Weil. I'm grateful you've given us ample notice of your resignation. We'll be sorry to lose you. But why Spain? Surely, this is hardly the time to be taking up teaching there?'

'I'm not going there to teach, M'sieur. I'm going there to learn.'

'To learn what? Spanish?'

'To learn how to fight. The anarcho-syndicalist militia needs volunteers. I've volunteered.'

Arianrhod Môn

Arianrhod Môn had arranged to meet Dewi and Meinwen outside Rhyddid/Freedom, the new club in Womanby Street, a few doors down from Clwb Ifor Bach. The two clubs, although neighbours, and both aimed at a Welsh clientele, belonged to different generations: Clwb Ifor was studenty, with peeling posters, sticky floors and untidy piles of nightclub fliers; Rhyddid was professional, with polished hardwood furnishings, Welsh slate floors, brushed aluminium fittings and expensive contemporary paintings on the exposed brick walls.

From her taxi, Arianrhod could see Meinwen and Dewi standing outside the club. She looked at her new wristwatch, a present from her husband when they had gone for a weekend in

Venice a few weeks previously. Was she late? A few minutes. Nothing too terrible. The car stopped and she got out. Having booked the taxi on her business account, there was no awkward fumbling for the money for the fare, no waiting for the change, just a smiling 'Thank you' to the driver.

As she turned to her friends, she was suddenly conscious of how expensively she was dressed. The memory of her slopping around Yr Hafan in jeans and teeshirt seemed to belong to a different world. The clothes she was wearing now had cost more than Dewi and Meinwen spent on clothing between them in a year. She noticed Dewi, who knew nothing of fashion, nonetheless looking at her appreciatively. Meinwen, she knew, simply did not notice clothes at all.

Arianrhod embraced Dewi. 'Sorry I'm late, *cariad*.' She kissed him on both cheeks.

'Twice?' he teased her.

Arianrhod laughed. 'It's usually three times. I'm going easy on you.' She turned to Meinwen, and took a half step towards her. But Meinwen stood with her arms folded in front of her, a barrier to any physical contact. Arianrhod hesitated, and decided instead to try to convey her affection by the warmth in her voice. 'Meinwen, how *are* you this long time?'

'I'm well, Ari. Thanks'

Meinwen was clearly here on business, not pleasure, Arianrhod thought. As she motioned her guests to the door, she cast a quick glance over Meinwen's clothes. She recognised them from of old. That sweater; its elbows and cuffs a bit more frayed now than last time she saw it. And those hiking shoes. Arianrhod had people working for her who were younger than those shoes.

The polished wooden door to the club was twice the size necessary for human beings to pass through. Arianrhod drew a little card from her silver wallet, put it against a pad on the door frame, and the door clicked open. The heavy polished wood swung inwards.

'They're ready when you are, Arianrhod,' smiled the girl on reception.

'Thanks, Suzanne.'

Arianrhod took her guests up to the dining floor by lift.

'The only slate-floored lift in the world,' she said, as they were conveyed silently to the restaurant. Then, with a mock-conspiratorial air, she added: 'It makes people from Gwynedd feel at home.'

The food was glorious; the service discreet and without servility. Dewi had said he hadn't enjoyed a meal so much in ages. Ever, maybe. Arianrhod guessed that the fact that they knew she was paying – it was going to count as 'research with contacts' on her expenses claim – made it taste even better. She had enjoyed catching up with Dewi, and found him a ready audience for her carefully-positioned detached irony about life as a *cyfryngi* – or Welsh media yuppie – in the heart of the capital's artistic life. She had whispered some unrepeatable anecdotes about some of the other diners they could see around the room. Even Meinwen, who had only toyed with the starter salad, looked mildly impressed.

But only mildly. For Meinwen, what people wore, the celebrities they knew, the cars they drove, were utterly unimportant. Just as an X-ray does not differentiate between a duke or a dustman, and seeks only for the signs of health or disease, so Meinwen cared not at all whether Arianrhod was a media star or a lollipop lady. She merely watched and listened for the indicators that would show Arianrhod's wholeness, or otherwise, with respect to the one diagnosis that mattered. Meinwen had been content to listen throughout the meal; but now, it seemed, it was time for the examination.

'We need your help, Arianrhod,' she said.

'OK,' said Arianrhod, cautious now. 'How exactly.'

'We need to get a Property Act onto the agenda for the Assembly. You know how important that is.'

'Yes. But how can I help?'

'We need to make a high-profile gesture. When Dewi or I go to prison, it means nothing any more. We don't get any publicity. We're just background noise now. Nobody takes any notice. It's like we're yesterday's news.'

'Yes...' even more cautious now.

'If somebody with a higher profile were to commit a symbolic act, then we'd put the whole issue back on the agenda. But it has to be someone people recognise. Somebody who's not seen as a full-time activist, someone who's known outside Welsh-speaking Wales. Then we'd really make an impact.'

'"We" in this case meaning "me",' said Arianrhod.

'Only if you felt you could do it,' said Dewi, reasonably. He made it sound as if he was offering her a tempting but controversial film role instead of a jail sentence and a ruined media career.

Arianrhod loved Dewi and Meinwen, she really did. She admired Meinwen's incorruptible principles, and she had more than a little soft spot for gauche Dewi, with his guileless blue eyes and his untidy schoolboy hair. Meinwen must have been mad to have turned him down that time. Now, if Dewi had asked *her* to go out with him instead... but that was water under the bridge. They were clearly here on a mission. The very fact that they could ask her something so outrageous with complete sincerity was simultaneously endearing and a colossal compliment. How could she let them down gently?

'I'm not sure I'm the person for it,' she said, putting a touch of regret into her voice. 'I'm a bit too lightweight. Perhaps you should go for someone with more gravitas.'

She remembered a television programme about ten years previously, when she and Meinwen had been in a fierce disagreement about the economy with a successful Welsh industrialist. Losing patience with their amateurish critique of the economic system, and sensing that the hard sciences were not likely to be his opponents' strong point, the capitalist had gone on the offensive, asking Arianrhod suddenly: 'What did you study in college?'

'Folk Studies,' Arianrhod had snapped back, triumphantly, without turning a hair of her blonde head.

The industrialist, who had probably expected her to say 'politics' or at least 'sociology', could scarcely conceal his amazement. His surprise was almost greater than his satisfaction at having won the argument.

'*Folk* Studies...?!'

At the time, Arianrhod had thought that in that little exchange she had simply exposed how little the businessman knew about Wales, and how superior her own knowledge of the country was. But now she blushed at the memory of the discussion, which must have been witnessed by tens of thousands of people. Never again. Now she knew her limitations and played to her strengths.

'Oh, you've got plenty of gravitas,' said Meinwen encouragingly, as if Arianrhod was denying herself a choice opportunity through excessive modesty. 'Think of it. It would be another Penyberth.'

This was really turning on the pressure, Arianrhod thought. But could there really be another Penyberth? The three nationalists who had been jailed for committing the symbolic act of arson at the bombing range at Penyberth in Pen Llŷn had acted in the face of brutal government intransigence, in an attempt to force recognition of Wales as a separate nation. Seventy years on, the promoters of Welsh identity hardly faced such obvious injustices. Did Meinwen really think the current housing question bore comparison? But the Fire in Llŷn was still the twentieth century's seminal Welsh-language protest, and for members of the Movement, invoking the name 'Penyberth' was the equivalent of what using the name 'Calvary' would be to an evangelical Christian. It bypassed logic and prudence, making its appeal directly to the heart by reference to supercharged geography.

However, Arianrhod's heart had grown resistant to this particular invocation. Yes, she thought, Penyberth was heroic, and necessary in its day. But ever since then, it was as if the nationalists had been bound to the same tactics, come what may; trying to repeat the achievement again and again, as though the world had to divide up neatly into a hostile government on one side and selfless campaigners on the other. Things were a sight more complicated than that, but the activists seemed to be drawn back to the same practices, the same flickering image, over and over, like moths to a flame.

'Yes, but there were three in Penyberth,' said Arianrhod. 'I don't think I'm the equal of D.J., Saunders and Valentine rolled into one. And there's something else,' she looked each way, then leaned forward and dropped her voice to a whisper as if letting her visitors into a secret: 'It's not 1936 any more'.

She meant it to sound ironic rather than significant. It was an exit strategy from this increasingly uncomfortable conversation. If they wanted to laugh at it, they would have an easy way out of the difficult position they were all in. She didn't want to argue politics or tactics with her two old friends. Already, she was becoming painfully aware of how great a gulf had grown between them in the years since she left Yr Hafan. But

Meinwen seemed to have taken Arianrhod's comment as an invitation for further persuasion. She leaned forward, her dark eyes shining with conviction.

'We've got to keep fighting,' she urged.

Arianrhod realised there was no point giving Meinwen discreet ways out of an embarrassing situation. She just needed to be honest.

'The fight's over Meinwen,' she said. She indicated the room around her. On almost every table, the conversations were in Welsh. The diners looked comfortable in their expensive clothes, their designer glasses. 'Haven't you noticed? We've won.'

Meinwen sat back, as Arianrhod, with the merest glance, summoned the waiter for the bill.

The conversations around them were about holidays in Thailand, about interior design, about property investment, programme pitches, foreign business trips. On the walls, there hung expensive paintings by contemporary Welsh artists. Landscapes mainly: the yellow cottages of Pembrokeshire, the grey slate villages of Gwynedd, the black mining valleys of the south, the green mountain farms of Powys. All the places where these people no longer wanted to live. All the communities they had abandoned. All safely preserved under glass.

Simone

The sun glinted off the barrels of the rifles of Simone and her fellow militia members as they drilled in the dusty town square of Pina. She felt proud to be wearing the militia insignia of the *Confederación Nacional del Trabajo*, the main anarchist trade union in Spain. She was proud too that her column was controlled by Buenaventura Durruti, the charismatic leader of the Catalan anarchist unions. At last she felt she was living out her principles to the full.

The commands of the drill instructor were in Spanish. Therefore, as well as struggling with the unfamiliar routines of military procedures, the volunteers, a collection of several foreign nationalities and both sexes, were struggling to understand the language too. Simone could see the instructor was inwardly exasperated. Earlier in the day he had said she should never have been given so much as a popgun, let alone a deadly weapon. She would never be a soldier in a million years. In target practice earlier in the day she hadn't hit the target once. They couldn't even guess where the bullets were going. The other recruits were careful to make sure they were well behind her whenever she pressed the trigger. She couldn't even load the rifle unaided. The instructor said she was was more of a danger to her own side, or herself, than she would ever be to the fascists. She thought that he looked relieved when he finally dismissed the squad. She'd try harder. Next time would be better.

They broke up, and began talking among themselves in half a dozen different languages, the temporary cohesion of the company dividing naturally into its national components. As they began to cross the square on their way back to the barracks, they saw a party of men under guard being marched through. The volunteers stopped to watch them go past.

'Who are they?' Simone asked her instructor.

'Fascists. They probably captured them in that town our people took today. They're lucky they've been taken prisoner at all.'

The column drew nearer. Simone watched it intently. These were the first enemy soldiers she had seen since she had arrived in Spain three weeks previously.

'Wait!'

Dropping her rifle, she rushed over to the column. It halted as she approached. Simone went up to one of the prisoners, who stood with his head down.

'I thought so!' Simone said, as she looked at the dishevelled figure in front of her. 'Why, Reynard?'

Reynard looked up at her. He straightened up and wiped the sweat out of his tired eyes with his bound hands. A touch of his habitual swagger returned, although his voice was very weary.

'A Jewish communist asks me "why?".'

'I'm not a communist.' It was as if the academic arguments of their college years were continuing, albeit for much higher stakes. 'I'm here with the anarcho-syndicalist militia.'

'Oh, I see. Well, that's all right, then. So I suppose you'll be letting me go? These ropes don't exactly go with anarchy, do they?'

He lifted up his hands to show her. The cords were black with caked blood, and the flesh around them was swollen and raw. Simone grimaced at the sight, and she felt a rush of compassion.

'Reynard, let me speak to your guards. Perhaps I can do something to help you...'

Reynard could see pity in Simone's eyes.

'Don't you dare.'

'Why not? I might be able...'

Her compassion had infuriated him more than any insult could possibly have done.

'You don't understand, do you?' he said. 'I'm not a victim. I volunteered. I want to fight communism. I want to save Europe from slavery. You know what's happened in Russia. Do you want that to happen in France too?'

'It's not like that, Reynard.'

'Isn't it?' He gestured with his bound hands towards the Catholic church at the end of the square.

'Did your friends tell you what they did to the priest of that church there?'

'No.'

'He was shot. Just because he belonged to the church. Ask them. It's true.'

'I don't know...'

'Well, *I* know. I helped give him a Christian burial when we found his body. Do you know what you're involved in here? If these Reds have their way, Europe will be a dictatorship. It'll be hell on earth, and you'll have helped bring it about.'

'Reynard, be quiet! You'll get yourself into trouble.'

Reynard laughed out loud. He held up his bound and bleeding hands.

'Oh yes, of course. I wouldn't want that, now, would I?'

He put his hands down again. The sarcasm left his voice, to be replaced with conviction.

'Look,' he said, 'If I have to die, then I'll be glad to have died on the right side, which is more than you'll be able to say.'

'But you don't have to die! Just let me...'

'Don't you dare. I'll take the consequences of my actions. But you just ask yourself: are you ready to take the consequence of yours?'

The militiamen leading the column, even if he could not understand French, had now clearly realised this was just some personal quarrel, and he had had enough of it. He nudged his charges with his rifle muzzle to get them moving again. As the column shuffled off, Reynard looked back at Simone.

'Whatever happens to me, Simone, you won't win. Not with Germany on our side. And don't think of asking for mercy for me, because by God, if I ever get the chance, I won't give any to you.'

Simone watched them go. Whatever else he was, Reynard wasn't a coward. Simone's instructor joined her. He handed her the rifle she had discarded.

'A friend of yours?'

'Well... we were at the same college.'

She remembered their arguments then. There was some kind of twisted love at the root of Reynard's anger. Wasn't he, in his own way, just trying to preserve liberty just as much as she was? It was an uncomfortable thought.

But no, there was a difference. It was the hatred, the longing to punish the scapegoat, the outsider. After all, wasn't that what lay behind all fascism? The desire to wield the fasces, the whip which was the ancient symbol of Roman authority. Just now, however, it looked as if the only person who was going to suffer was Reynard himself.

'What will happen to them now?' Simone asked.

'Oh, interrogation. Execution for any who've committed atrocities, prison for the rest. If they're lucky.'

The column moved out of site beyond the church and its little stone-walled cemetery, where, Simone did not doubt, lay the body of the murdered priest.

Simone ducked involuntarily when she heard the shots. She'd heard plenty of gunfire before, but only on the target range. This was for real. But it was far off. She got up and followed her squad on towards their objective, a little bullet-marked farmhouse. Simone strained her myopic eyes to see. A couple of sacks lay outside the walls. It was only as her squad moved closer, and after she had wiped the Spanish dust from the lenses of her glasses, that she could see the sacks were really dead bodies.

The leader of the squad motioned the advance party of volunteers to investigate the farmhouse. Simone, in the rear group, watched them approach, moving in rushes from cover to cover, listening anxiously for the crack of the defenders' bullets. None came. The volunteers went into the farmhouse, and after a short while one of them appeared and gestured to the rest of them that it was safe to approach.

As they walked up, Simone saw that two bodies were those of nationalist soldiers. Clearly they had been killed when an earlier party of republicans had passed through this sector. She looked at their faces. They were both young. Younger than her, perhaps. One of them looked almost familiar. She looked more closely, searching her memory. Someone she had known from college, like Reynard? A worker encountered at some socialist meeting but since misled into fighting for the wrong side? Then it struck her. The dead fascist was the image of the soldier she and her brother had 'adopted' during the Great War, and who had been killed at Verdun.

'You!' Simone's squad leader was looking at her and the volunteer next to her. 'Wake up! get those fascists buried before they stink the place out. We're occupying this farm for the night.'

That night Simone was more than usually silent as the off-duty volunteers sat drinking coffee and smoking. A few yards away, one of the party was tending a cooking pot buried in a hole in the ground to hide the flames. He left it to simmer and rejoined the circle, sitting himself down next to Simone.

'I know how you feel,' he said to her sympathetically. 'They were very young.'

'Yes. But it's not just that,' she said. 'One of them looked... like a friend.'

A soldier the other side of Simone had overheard her.

'A friend! So long as you're only friendly with them when they're dead! I'd be friends with all fascists on those terms!'

The party laughed, with the exception of Simone.

'It doesn't need to be like that, comrade,' she said. There was more sadness than argument in her voice. 'There has to be room for brotherhood. We have to recognise the spiritual values of all human beings.'

'Spiritual values!' Another soldier this time. 'I suppose you mean those priests who've oppressed us here for God knows how long? The only values they know about are the treasures they hoarded up while they let the rest of us starve. You think you've had it bad in France? At least you haven't had the church running the country like here.'

Simone was feeling suddenly isolated. Her squad leader, who had been cleaning his rifle, spoke for the first time, to quieten the debate.

'Let me tell you about spiritual values,' he said. 'In a village south of here, early in the war, we captured a priest in a church the fascists had turned into a strongpoint. We hauled him out and started interrogating him. He told me he'd only stayed to comfort the wounded.

'So I said to him: "You're nothing more than a servant of the landowners". And do you know what he said to me? He said: "No, I'm the servant of a carpenter."'

Simone nodded. She understood: 'What then?'

'Then?' the leader said. 'Then, comrade, I executed him.' He looked at Simone steadily as he continued to speak without excitement, pride or bitterness. 'Do you think I'd let some Jesuitical casuistry put me off? Where was the church when people were dying of starvation? Where was the church when workers were imprisoned for demanding their rights? I shot him while he knelt in prayer outside his burning church. I did it with this very rifle here.

'And after that, we shot his churchwardens. They'd come up from the village, pleading for his life. And later that evening, we found two Franciscan friars hiding with families in the village. And we shot them too – the friars and the men of the houses which had sheltered them. And then we burned their houses.'

Simone had closed her eyes as if to shut out the images.

'Comrade,' she almost whispered. 'If we behave like that, all we'll have left is ruins.'

'What's that to us? Do you know what Durruti says? "We're not afraid of ruins. We've always lived in slums and holes in the wall. Don't forget: we're workers. We can also build. We built these palaces and churches and cities here in Spain and in France and everywhere. We can build them again. We're going to inherit the earth. We carry a new world here, in our hearts. That world is growing this minute."

'When we've rid this country of injustice, there'll be a time for "spiritual values". Now, if you haven't got the stomach for it...'

Simone got up, blinded with tears, and walked away from the circle, taking off her glasses to wipe them as she went.

She did not see the cooking pot until her leg plunged into it up to the knee, the boiling water forcing a gasp of agony from her.

The soldiers rushed over, and gathered round her. One of them slowly removed her boot and sock; some of the flesh came away with it as he peeled it off. He examined the severe scald, then he looked up at Simone. Her face was running with sweat from the pain.

'Well, you won't be facing any more moral dilemmas in this war, Comrade Weil,' he said.

Meinwen

Later that night, having said goodbye to Arianrhod – only one cheek kiss that time – Meinwen and Dewi walked across the city centre to a pub where they were planning to collect signatures.

When it had first opened a hundred years ago, the pub had been called The Forge, a title which, so a heritage plaque near the door informed them, commemorated the real but now-vanished forge which had stood there since medieval times. If the establishment had ever flourished as The Forge, it certainly had not done so for the past few decades; it had merely ticked over with a trade composed mainly of old men and guests from the nearby street of bed-and-breakfasts who fancied a pint or two, but who did not fancy the walk into town. Dewi and Meinwen had gone there during that period once, while visiting a friend who lived nearby. Now, they could hardly believe the way the place had changed.

It had been bought by a west Wales entrepreneur called Dan Jones, who had moved to Cardiff, quickly becoming a leading figure in the capital's Welsh social life. He had renamed the pub Yr Arglwydd Rhys, 'The Lord Rhys', after the ancient warlord of the area where his family had lived since the twelfth century – had lived, that is, until, in Dan Jones' generation, the lure of the town had finally done what war, persecution and famine had failed to do, and had dislodged them from their ancestral acres, albeit in return for a million in the bank. It was Dan Jones' sale of his family farm, Bro Hedd, that had financed the purchase of the pub.

As they walked through the polished doors into the warmth and clamour of the public bar, Meinwen thought regretfully about what Dan Jones had told her about Bro Hedd. The couple from London who had bought the farm had re-named it 'Rivendell'. Apparently they thought it sounded pleasingly old-fashioned, not realising, or perhaps not caring, that the name it was replacing was older than the English language itself. Meinwen's heart had turned over when Dan had told her. However, Dan, insulated no doubt by the amount of capital Bro Hedd had produced, seemed pretty philosophical. It was all in the past, he said; you had to move with the times. The name-change he had himself brought about on his new pub had been a spectacular success – it had had a galvanising effect on trade, attracting Welsh speakers from all over the east side of the city. The old regulars vanished, and any visitors from the bed-and-breakfasts who wandered in now might have asked themselves if they had strayed into a different country, as Welsh was over-whelmingly the language on every side.

While glad to hear so much Welsh spoken in Cardiff these days, Meinwen doubted whether the language had a sustainable future there. The growth in the number of Welsh speakers in the capital – more than thirty thousand of them now, a tenth of the population – was fed largely by outmigration from the heart-lands. If those heartlands ran dry, then so would the constant infusions of Welshness to the city. Would Cardiff's Welsh speak-ers then sustain the language, passing it on between the generations, teaching it to learners, maintaining its societies and schools, creating a living network within the majority culture? Maybe. Arianrhod, for her part, had said she was confident they would. Her children went to one of the many Welsh-medium primary schools in Cardiff, and she herself taught as a volunteer in a Welsh evening class. She had said Welsh was safer in the city than it could ever be if tied to a declining rural way of life.

Meinwen hoped she was right. But she wasn't going to take the risk that she might be wrong. The heartlands underwrote all other efforts to sustain the language. They had to be saved.

These drinkers in Yr Arglwydd Rhys might have turned their back on their native communities, they might have signed away their old homes. But they could still sign a petition. Meinwen and Dewi, by long practice, split up to work the room.

Meinwen had collected twelve signatures with little trouble, when she approached a group of men standing at the bar. It was only eight in the evening, but they had the air of having been drinking all day. Particularly so in the case of the group's centre of attention, the scriptwriter, Alwyn Dyfed. His status as an artist was declared by his wearing of a black fedora hat, scarcely necessary in the confines of Yr Arglwydd Rhys, but, she assumed, fulfilling some inner need for warmth.

Now in his early fifties, he was the one-time *enfant terrible* of Welsh drama. Meinwen could just recall the furore in the 70s, when his play *Coler y Diafol* 'The Devil's Collar' had come out. She had never actually seen it, but some of its scenes were legendary all the same: a minister of religion deflowering a teenage girl on the grave of the hymnwriter Ann Griffiths; the chapel's spinster organist climaxing during a rendition of 'I am coming, Lord'. By the time Meinwen had studied Dyfed's work in college, he had produced a succession of plays, all with a reference to the devil in the title, and all at some point vilifying chapel-goers. Some critics by that stage had started to call it predictable; he, however, called it a recurring motif. He seemed unaware of the law of diminishing returns: a magazine article recently had said he was working on a play called *Emynau Uffern* 'Hymns of Hell' in which the 1904 revivalist, Evan Roberts, was shown enjoying the sexual favours of a harem of female followers. Meinwen felt wearied by the recollection as she approached the author and his party.

Meinwen knew Alwyn vaguely, their paths having crossed occasionally in the crowded matrix of Welsh-speaking Cardiff. But she had known his father, the Reverend Doctor Dyfed ap Meredith, rather better. He had been a good friend of her own father through the chapel, although he was somewhat older. Dyfed ap Meredith had been jailed as a conscientious objector during the second world war and had been forcibly volunteered for medical experiments which had left his health permanently damaged. Nonetheless, he had become a leading advocate for post-war reconciliation, and in the 1950s had traced, met, and forgiven the doctor who had conducted the experiments. They had become firm friends. The book in which ap Meredith described this healing process was a minor classic of Christian spirituality, translated into two dozen languages. He had died in the late 1980s just as his son's play *Saboth Satan* 'Satan's Sabbath' was premiering. Twenty years on, in a Wales where there were many more scriptwriters than chapel ministers, Alwyn Dyfed was still trying to shock his dead father. No longer *terrible*, he was still very much the *enfant*.

'What's this, a contract?!' he asked, as Meinwen offered him the petition. His voice was louder than was necessary simply for Meinwen to hear.

'A petition, Alwyn. For the right of our communities to survive.'

'What about an author's right to survive, then? I'm starving by here, good girl. How about doing a collection for me?'

'You do pretty well, from what I've heard,' said Meinwen. Then, with a glance at Dyfed's paunch: 'And you don't look like you're starving to me.'

'You do, though,' he retorted. 'I've seen more meat on a chicken fillet. Have you got any tits under that sweater? Or have you donated them to the cause too?'

This was clearly the middle of a long day's drinking for Alwyn. But it was the start of a long night's signature-collecting for Meinwen. She didn't have time for this.

'The petition, Alwyn.'

Dyfed was enjoying his own wit too much to take any notice. Any audience in which he could appear to be an iconoclast was too much of a temptation for him.

'You look like you need some meat on your bones.' He leaned closer: 'I know – how about I give you a meat injection?'

Meinwen turned away. Alwyn laughed at her back and returned to his friends again.

Outside, she and Dewi compared notes. She had got twelve signatures. He had clocked twenty. She didn't tell him about Alwyn Dyfed. They walked on across town, heading for the Cameo Club. Soul by soul, signature by signature, the campaign went on.

●○●

Bernard Weil

'How are you feeling, Simone? A little better today?'

Dr Weil leant back against the rail of the passenger ship and looked down at his daughter, where she reclined in a deckchair against the wall of the main cabin. Simone was facing the Italian coast which was slipping by to the east of them. Her bandaged foot rested on the rail.

Simone put down her notebook book and pen, removed her sunglasses, and looked up. Dr Weil was looking at her with what he knew she would recognise as professional, as well as fatherly, concern.

'Yes, Papa, a little better today.'

'Better still when you've put on a bit more weight,' said Dr Weil. 'You need to take more nutrition. The whole idea of this holiday is for you to rest and regain your strength.'

Simone smiled, and caught his hand. 'I'll try, Papa.'

Dr Weil squeezed her hand, noting how cold it seemed despite the Mediterranean sun. Then he and Madame Weil left Simone to her book and walked on. When they were out of their daughter's earshot, they stopped again, and looked out towards Italy. They had been cruising for several days, stopping now and again for shore visits to tourist sites. Visible on the land now was the campanile of a village church, and, faintly over the sound of the ship's engines and the seagulls, they thought they could hear church bells.

'What's wrong with her, Bernard? She doesn't eat. She scarcely sleeps. Nothing but reading and working...'

Dr Weil looked out towards the village, without answering.

'It's killing me, Bernard,' she said.

He sighed. 'Whatever it is, it's beyond my arts as a physician... and as a father,' he said.

The village church could be seen more clearly now as the ship pulled in towards the coast. The church bells were indeed audible.

'I wish she could find what she's looking for,' he said. The ship was gradually changing direction towards the coast; the church grew imperceptibly nearer. Dr Weil continued: 'But when I think of what that might be, it frightens me.'

They looked back down the deck towards Simone. She was writing again. Previously, Simone had been only too ready to share her thoughts, her half-formed essays. But whatever she was writing now seemed to be something she preferred to keep to herself.

●○●

Meinwen

Meinwen got up and walked over to the uncurtained window of her bedroom at Yr Hafan. There was no need for curtains here, where no one could overlook her except the birds and the moving clouds. It was Sunday, and a beautiful Sunday too, although, on these high hills where no one came, every day had a blessed, sabbath stillness.

The community that Hermon chapel had been built to serve had long since gone; the quarryworkers when the slate supply was exhausted, the hill farmers when their children could no longer face life in the high hills. The hobby-farmers and New Agers who had come from the cities to take over the scattered farms, cottages and smallholdings in the last twenty years or so would no more have thought of attending chapel than they would have thought of joining the Flat Earth Society. In fact, the Flat Earth Society would have seemed positively sensible to some of them by comparison. The cause at Hermon struggled on; each Sunday afternoon, some elderly faithful, fewer each year, made the trip from Porthmadog up to the hillside of their childhood for an hour of quavery-voiced *hiraeth*. If she was at home on a Sunday, Meinwen liked to listen to them. She knew all the hymns they trembled their way through, and although she knew there was more of sheer habit than of faith in the persistence of Hermon's congregation, it nonetheless comforted her to think that the doors of this little tabernacle were still open, still defying the hard facts of economics, demographics and time.

Meinwen knew nonconformist culture well: the smell of varnish, polish and damp wood in chapel; the watery tea in a chilly vestry; the fuzzy-felt Sunday school bible stories. All the faded, forlorn materials, all the glorious timeless hymns of Welsh nonconformity. They were part of her. However, her attendance at chapel was now occasional at best. Usually she would go to the Sunday service when visiting her parents in Colwyn Bay, to keep them happy. It was convention rather than conviction. But still, while she now knew how shaky was the superstructure of theology built by St Paul and his followers on the life of Jesus of Nazareth, Meinwen could not help but feel a deep response to the person of this Galilean rabbi; the man from the uncouth north of Israel who overturned the tables of the corrupt southern capital's moneychangers, who challenged the leaders of society, who blessed the poor, welcomed the outcast and who finally died at the hands of the occupying imperial power. He was her prototype radical: the persecuted peacemaker. She could do without the theology, but she couldn't do without the exemplar. She was haunted by his story, and simultaneously compelled and convicted by the thought of him, perhaps especially on days like today when the stillness and silence at Yr Hafan was at its most perfect.

Simone

The sound of the bells from the church on the shore finally surfaced in Simone's consciousness. She looked up from her notebook, and gazed at the land for a few moments. At the periphery of her vision she could see her parents, some way further along the deck, leaning against the rail and looking, like her, towards the shore. She returned to her writing.

'It was when I was at Assisi that I first felt the need to kneel and pray,' she wrote. 'It felt like coming home. I fell in love with St Francis as soon as I heard his life story. I hope I can share his spirit of poverty. It can only be in poverty that God can be truly experienced.

'At the touch of the iron there must be a feeling of being cut off from God such as Christ experienced, otherwise it must be another God. "My God, my God, why hast thou forsaken me?" That is what gives us the real proof that Christianity is something divine... The creation of God's absence in a soul which has been completely emptied of self through love – that is what redemptive suffering is.'

On shore, the church bells continued to toll, but whether for wedding, for mass or for funeral, neither Simone nor her parents could say.

Dewi

On this particular Sunday, Dewi had called to visit, thereby absolving Meinwen from any residual guilt she might have felt at not being in chapel herself even though she lived next door to one. They had just finished tea: beans on toast for Dewi; just the toast for Meinwen. As it was a warm day, they were now sitting outside on a couple of battered old armchairs they had dragged from the living room. From here, they could watch the clouds pass slowly over the green and grey mountains of Eryri to the west. It was a while since they had spent a Sunday afternoon together like this. Meinwen sat back, resting her head on the cracked leather; her eyes closed as she enjoyed the late summer sunshine.

Dewi looked at her. She was wearing a plain black teeshirt. Its short sleeves showed her thin, white arms. Because of the warmth of the afternoon, Meinwen had, for once, pulled off her sweater. Her glossy straight black hair was disordered as a result, and she had not thought to rearrange it. He thought of reaching over and brushing one of the stray strands from her pale cheek. Could a twenty-year friendship allow that small tenderness? He knew the answer was no. He contented himself with looking at her. She looked like a sleeping child.

The afternoon was so still that they could hear sounds from a long way off. The cattle being taken to milking at Evan Jones' farm on the valley bottom. A motorcycle climbing the hill opposite Bryn Aur. Dewi gradually became aware of one other faint sound at the limits of his hearing.

'Where's that coming from?' he asked Meinwen.

'It's the bell at the church in Penrhyn,' she answered, without opening her eyes. 'They have a service every Sunday afternoon.'

'I'm surprised they still have enough people.'

'You know what they say: "Wherever two or three are gathered together..".'

'Yes. A bit like the Movement's meetings.'

'Well, I'm glad they're still having the services. I like listening to the bell.'

The distant metallic summons sounded a few more times. A tiny moth settled on Meinwen's hand. Her eyes still closed, she did not notice.

'Is Hermon still open?' Dewi asked, looking round at the grey bulk of the building next door. He could not recall when last he had seen a congregation there.

'Yes,' Meinwen said. She opened her eyes and looked up. The sun had gone behind a bank of cloud. 'I keep a spare key for it. Do you want to see inside?'

Meinwen

The door to Hermon creaked open, and Meinwen and Dewi stepped inside into the quiet air of polished wood, dust and trapped, forgotten sunlight. The building was in a surprisingly good state of repair. The twentieth century seemed to have left no mark on it. The lamps must be electric-powered, but the style of the ornate Victorian brass light fittings seemed more suited to gas. Dewi and Meinwen walked down the creaking varnished floorboards. The white paint of the walls was flaking, laying a deposit of tiny white wafers on the floor like manna.

The walls were largely bare, on one of them was a stained brass plaque showing a long list of chapel members killed in the First World War, and giving the place of their distant deaths: Mametz, Ypres, Amiens, Gaza. In every case, an initial followed by a Davies, Williams, Evans or Roberts, or another of the dozen or so surnames shared by everyone in the parish at that time. A much shorter list was appended, of those who had died in the Second World War: North Africa, Normandy, Burma.

Painted on the wall above the pulpit, in a flourish of gothic script, were the words *'Ewch i mewn i'w byrth Ef â diolch'*. 'Go ye into his gates with thanksgiving.' The windows were all plain glass. At this height, nothing showed through them but the sky. The chapel seemed suspended in the air, a stone vessel for the sunlight high above the earth; an attentive space for the endless silent sermons of light and cloud. It was beautiful in a spare, quiet way.

But, unless one felt the need to pray, which neither of them did, there was little to hold one's interest after a few minutes. Meinwen found herself idly opening a little cupboard below the pulpit.

Inside there were dusty piles of old booklets. She picked some up to have a closer look. Weekly Sunday school pamphlets from the early twentieth century. She was surprised at the quality of their presentation, with colour reproductions of scenes from the Bible, high-quality paper, and only the rust on the staples to show their age. She took a handful of them for curiosity's sake. Clearly no one had looked at them for generations. Dewi and Meinwen went back out into the mountain air, locking the door behind them.

Back in the garden of Yr Hafan, she and Dewi idly flicked their way through the booklets. In the pictures, Jesus was invariably blond-haired and Nordic-featured. Meinwen smiled to herself. A Jewish-looking Messiah just wouldn't have fitted with the British Empire's body-image, would it? But then, leaving aside the external appearances and reading some of the text of the pamphlets, she found herself impressed despite herself by the seriousness of their purpose. It wasn't merely that the Welsh in these throwaway periodicals was so correct and so beautifully cadenced that even today's best writers could hardly have produced its like. It was the subject matter too: stories of people who had sacrificed for their faith, leaving their homes and jobs to follow what they believed to be their divine vocations to preach, or to help the poor. Obituaries of Sunday school children who had died, victims to their age's all-too-common illnesses; the pamphlets recorded their small achievements and endeavours, their unrealised, truncated hopes.

'They really did believe in those days, didn't they?' she asked, as much to herself as to Dewi.

'I suppose so. Much good that it did them.'

Meinwen looked at these testimonies from a faith which had failed the test of time, from a world where there was a heaven and a hell, where sin, virtue and judgement were as real as sunlight, frost or fire. Although she supposed she must count herself a Christian by upbringing, she didn't agree for a moment with the black-and-white theology of these tracts. It was decades since she had first questioned whether the Christian story was really historically accurate, and she no more believed in the miracles than she believed in Santa Claus. But now, she found herself feeling a kind of envy.

'But they had something to believe in. Even if they were mistaken,' she said.

'So do we,' he answered. Meinwen knew he meant the cause to which they were both as devoted as any Victorian missionaries.

The Sunday service was over. Meinwen put the pamphlets on the table between them, and sat back. There was still some warmth in the early evening sun, and there was a faint scent of gorse on the mountain air. She closed her eyes and savoured the sacred silence of her hilltop haven.

After a minute or so, they heard a car coming up the hill. In such a remote spot, this almost certainly meant a visitor for Yr Hafan. They walked to the front of the house to see who it was.

But the vehicle, a smart new four-by-four, wasn't carrying visitors for Yr Hafan. It stopped outside the chapel gate. As it did so, the sound of the car radio could be heard for a few seconds before the engine was turned off. They were listening to *The Archers*, and loudly; the jaunty, bucolic, unmistakeable signature tune was just coming to an end. The doors of the four-by-four opened and a man and a woman in their early forties got out and walked up the chapel's gravel path, followed by two bounding, panting English setters which, released from their confinement in the vehicle, began to run around the grounds sniffing and barking.

'Pop-py! Dai-sy! Here. Good girls! *Good* girls! Yes you are!'

Already Meinwen was irritated by the woman's voice. The visitors stopped to look the building over. But not like tourists might have done. Tourists approach tentatively, examine date plaques and inscribed foundation stones. These had a more businesslike air, and within moments they were looking over the guttering and the stonework. It suddenly struck Meinwen – they were thinking of buying it.

'Hello,' she called. The inter-lingual greeting meant she did not have to commit to either language until she knew which one the visitors spoke, although she was pretty certain which one it would be. They turned to her.

'Oh, hello,' the man said, looking at her coolly with an air of faint surprise, as if she were the intruder. He had a tan; long fair hair in a ponytail; waistcoat; unmistakeably English by his

dipthonged greeting. 'Are you the keyholder?'
'No,' Meinwen lied, ignoring Dewi's quick glance. 'What do
you want?'
'We're thin-king of buy-ing it,' the woman answered. Long lank
hair, and the kind of big eyes which adults use when trying to
convince children of some doubtful fact. She spoke a little too
slowly, as if unsure whether Meinwen would understand her.
'We've been told it's com-ing on the mar-ket.'
Meinwen didn't want them to know how shocked she was. She
thought quickly. 'You must have got the wrong chapel. There
are quite a lot around.'
'No, it's def-in-ite-ly this one. We asked down in the vill-age,
and they gave us clear dir-ec-tions.'
'Well, I'm sorry I can't help you,' Meinwen said.
One of the dogs was defecating happily on the path to the
chapel. Meinwen looked at the pile of excrement, and then
looked pointedly at the woman, who either hadn't noticed what
the dog was doing, or was pretending she hadn't.
Meinwen went back to Yr Hafan, leaving the couple to their
tour of inspection.
'Good *girl*, Pop-py!' she heard as she walked away.
In the lounge of Yr Hafan, Meinwen turned to Dewi. 'It can't
be for sale. I must call Rolant Elis. It must be some kind of
mistake.'
She imagined having that pair as her next-door neighbours;
the woman calling her crapping, barking, pampered dogs
every five minutes in that patronising voice; Hermon given
over to the languid, commanding tones of Radio Four drawl-
ing through open windows. They'd have all-day boozy
barbecues with their friends, the lane full of off-road vehicles
with GB stickers, the garden full of settlers braying about their
careers, congratulating themselves for moving to the country,
boasting of the bargain house prices, and, of course,
complaining about the rude and ignorant locals. Oh God,
they'd probably put up hanging baskets as well. She couldn't
bear to think of it. Meinwen's cause had suddenly become
very personal indeed.

●○●

Reynard

Berlin had changed, Reynard thought, as the official car drove him through the streets from the station to the government district. He had last been here before the war in Spain. Now, in 1939, he could see how the skyline had altered with new buildings, including the colossal Reichs Chancellery just visible down Voss Strasse in the direction of Potsdamer Platz. It gave him a frisson of a sense of destiny as he saw the outlines of the new Europe literally taking shape in stone and concrete around him, this Prussian city on the Spree gathering its giant energies, a beacon of purpose in the fragmented, bickering continent, a bulwark of civilisation against the inhuman empire of communism beyond the endless plains to the east.

The car stopped at a large office building, decorated, as were all official buildings, with a red and white flag with the black *Hackenkreuz* at its centre. The door of the car was opened for him, and he followed his guide through into the building's lobby.

The staircase was on the same impressive scale as the rest of the building. It was clearly some kind of small palace which had been put to fresh use under the new regime. He ran his hand across the balustrade as he ascended the steps. That was the good thing about marble, he thought: it never became warm when you rested your hand upon it. Instead, resisting the influence of human contact, it stayed cool and unchanged.

The staircase brought them to a corridor lined with tall windows. At the end, the visitor was shown into an office. His guide snapped to attention and gave the Hitler salute as he presented Reynard to the uniformed official at the heavy oak desk inside. For his part, Reynard merely bowed slightly; he might be a dedicated fascist, but he was a Frenchman, not a German, and he was not in uniform, at least not today. He had no particular love for Germany, the country which his father had died fighting more than twenty years ago. But Jews and communists were his real enemy, and he saw this revitalised Germany as the best hope for destroying them.

The official behind the desk returned the guide's salute, and then, turning to the visitor, shook his hand. He spoke in French.

'Welcome, M'sieur Reynard.'

The pleasantries concluded, they were joined by the official's secretary, who took notes as Reynard and the official continued their discussion.

'So, M'sieur Reynard, just supposing Germany were in a position, at some future time, to do something to clear away the... undesirable elements in French society, you would be prepared to help?'

'With the greatest of pleasure.'

'And you would be able to advise who, and where...?'

'Oh, yes. I would indeed.'

He opened his briefcase and handed over a sheaf of papers. As he leaned across the table, the official noticed the deep scars around the visitor's wrists.

The official took the papers, scanned them and nodded approvingly.

'Very interesting, M'sieur Reynard,' he said. 'Very interesting indeed.'

●○●

Meinwen

On Monday morning, at nine o'clock sharp, Meinwen arrived at the head offices of the United Free Church of Wales, the parent denomination for Hermon. It was a large Victorian town house in Caernarfon, with flaking paint, a fading sign and an overgrown garden. Rolant Elis, the denomination's moderator, answered the door and showed her through to his office. Unlike Haydn Davies at the Assembly, Rolant Elis opened his own doors through necessity, not choice: the denomination could not afford a full-time secretary, so he had to do most of the administration work himself.

Meinwen followed him up the stairs. Rolant Elis was wearing grey shoes. Who but ministers of religion wore grey shoes, Meinwen wondered. Come to think about it, everything about old Rolant was grey: shoes, suit, shirt, tie, hair and complexion. He dressed so plainly he made the Amish look like a crew of Gangsta rappers.

He pushed the office door open. The room was piled with

papers. On the white woodchip wallpaper, a few posters promoted Christian Aid's work in the Third World. From the state of the office, it looked more as if the Third World churches could do with sending some aid in the direction of Rolant.

'I was going to tell you about Hermon,' he said, after Meinwen had explained the reason for her visit. 'But I wanted to tell the quarterly meeting first. I can only assume someone there must have let the news out when they saw the item on the advance agenda.'

'I see.'

'Yes, word's got around quickly. We've already had a lot of inquiries from people who want to buy it. The people you saw are the first ones to come up and see it, of course. But then, they don't live so far away, so it was easy for them.'

'Who are they?'

Rolant Elis ran his eye down his telephone notepad. 'Connor Meikle and Fran Skye,' he said. 'They run a healing centre in Cheshire.'

'Skye?'

'Like the island.'

'What kind of healing?'

'Oh, all kinds, I think. Alternative therapies, health foods, that kind of thing. They're looking to expand.'

'And you're going to sell Hermon to incomers just because they can pay more than the locals?'

'Well, it's not decided yet. But if we do sell it now, we won't have to pay for an advertisement and the estate agent's fees. That could save us about three thousand pounds on a property like that. That's a lot of money for a denomination like ours. It could help support another cause.' He looked unconvinced by his own statement.

Meinwen laughed out loud. 'You mean, pay the bills on another chapel for a couple of years so another half dozen old dears can use it as a social club. And then when they die off you'll sell that one to incomers too.'

Elis didn't even try to contradict her. Meinwen leaned forward. 'Rolant, you know as well as I do that this denomination is dying. In twenty years you won't have a single chapel left. For God's sake, why don't you do something different with Hermon? Sell it to local people at an affordable price. Give it –

yes, *give* it – to a housing association. It could make flats for half a dozen people. People who need homes, who want to live in their own home areas. Don't just sell it to the highest bidder.'

Rolant Elis

As she was speaking, Elis was looking down at the papers on his desk. Plans for missionary activities that would never happen. Materials for Sunday schools that had no pupils. Repair bills for chapels which had no worshippers. The last will and testament of Welsh nonconformity putting its affairs in order before vanishing discreetly from history.

'We need the money for mission…' he said.

'Mission?! Since when have you run any missions? When was the last one – 1904? All you're running is a chaplaincy for a dying community. Who do you think you're kidding? Rolant, don't do this. Don't sell Hermon.'

Elis looked around him as if searching for inspiration, or escape. Meinwen was probing his conscience like a surgeon. Without anaesthetic. And, fair play to himself, he did have a conscience on the subject of housing. When his mother had died a few years ago, he hadn't simply sold her home and pocketed the money, he'd decided to rent it out at an affordable price to a young local Welsh-speaking couple on a low income. He could still remember the satisfaction he felt.

Three months after the letting, and no rent paid, he had visited the house to inquire. Maybe the little family needed some help, he thought as he walked up the path to what had been his childhood home.

They had trashed it. Holes had been kicked in the interior doors, the toilet was broken and leaking, and the smell of urine filled the hallway, curtains were ripped, furniture cratered with cigarette burns. The couple's pre-school child, Liam, was watching *Reservoir Dogs* on the DVD player, the only appliance in the house which seemed to be undamaged. As Rolant tried to explain to the couple his concern at the state the house was in, they had shouted to Liam to turn the TV down. They shouted in English.

What thanks would he get for giving Hermon away? He'd

probably be dragged into some row in the newspapers. Anyone who tried to advertise a home for locals only was routinely pilloried in the press as a racist. John Sayle's newspaper column that morning had described Meinwen as a female Pol Pot who would 'turn the peaceful valleys of Wales into killing fields'. Nonsense, of course, but people seemed to be able to say that kind of thing these days. And legally, he couldn't give the house away in the way Meinwen wanted without the whole thing going through the national committee. There'd have to be a debate. That meant publicity. He didn't have the stomach to face the kind of vitriol he would attract in the press. And anyway, he wasn't called to be a fool with the resources of the Kingdom. Stewardship was the principle. Sound stewardship.

He looked up at Meinwen.

'I'm sorry,' was all he said.

●○●

Bernard Weil

'I never thought... twice in my lifetime,' Dr Weil felt suddenly older as he shuffled between wardrobe and suitcase, hurriedly throwing together what he needed for the journey.

The normally quiet house was filled with noise: footsteps thumping on the stairs, doors banging, voices shouting. And, constantly in the background like a commentary, the radio. They had left it on in order to hear any further news of the political situation. The capitulation of the French forces a few weeks earlier in the face of the German *blitzkrieg* had thrown the capital into chaos. Today they had heard that German forces had begun moving that morning to occupy the capital.

Some of the Weils' circle of friends were for joining the Resistance, others were for fleeing south, others were for staying in Paris and hoping for the best. The Weils, however, suddenly more conscious than ever before of their Jewish identity, were taking no chances. They were leaving for the south of the country. The radio had said that an independent French state had just been established, led by Philippe Petain, with its headquarters at Vichy. Dr Weil knew that this was only nominal independence, but even that was better than occupation. He looked around him for any essential items he may have forgotten to pack.

He put some family photographs into the case, then, conscious of the weight, quickly took them out of the metal frames. He packed the photographs and threw the frames onto the bed. One slid to the floor. There was a crack as the glass shattered. He hesitated for a moment, then decided not to waste time clearing up the broken shards. He put his medical gear into the case, packing it carefully.

In her room on the opposite side of the corridor, Simone was busy packing too. She seemed to be filling her suitcase with nothing but books.

Pierre

The radio was repeating for what seemed like the hundredth time that the German occupation forces were on their way to Paris. Pierre turned it off. He'd heard enough, and he and Yvette were almost ready to leave anyway. They had shared this small flat on the Left Bank for the last two years. But now, they were heading for what they hoped would be a safe house in the countryside outside Paris. From there, they planned to help organise resistance to the fascists. Their current address, known to the police as the home of two of the capital's most active communists, would be high on the list when the Nazis came to call.

Yvette scanned the room one more time, and snatched up a little bust of Lenin from the mantlepiece. It had been a parting gift when they had left the Soviet Union after a study tour. She held it up for Pierre to see.

'This?' she said.

He smiled and shook his head.

'This!'

He produced a revolver from under their bed and threw it into the suitcase, along with a small cardboard box of bullets. Yvette, surprised, laughed out loud.

'I bought it from one of Trotsky's bodyguards,' said Pierre. 'It's French, so we should be able to get more ammunition for it if we need it.'

'If we need it...' the revolver seemed to make the threat they faced seem all the more hard and cold.

Their packing was almost finished when there was a knock at the door.

Yvette looked at Pierre: 'Simone!' she said.

Simone had borne no ill-will when Pierre and Yvette had become lovers some years previously. Although she found their communism stiflingly illiberal – and told them so frequently – they had repaired their differences and she kept on friendly terms with them. They had met in the frantic days following the capitulation and had discussed their options; at that time, Simone had seemed to be seriously considering joining the Resistance, even if it meant collaborating with the communists. Pierre had tried to discourage her, wary that Simone's indiscretion and clumsiness would make her a lethal liability. But he knew how determined she could be once she had made up her mind. Perhaps she had decided to join them after all.

Yvette stepped quickly to the door, and pulled it open.

In the doorway stood two German soldiers in their field grey battledress, guns at the ready. Behind them was a black-uniformed Nazi official, and next to him, in civilian clothes, Jean Reynard. He looked prosperous, important, and more self-satisfied than he had ever been in his life. He nodded to the Nazi official, confirming that they had found the suspects they were looking for.

Pierre looked at his own gun sitting absurdly on top of the packed clothes a few feet away. It might as well be a few miles away for all the use it was to him. He cursed his own amateurism, and made a mental note that revolvers are made to be carried. Although he doubted he would get a second chance to put that wisdom into practice.

He and Yvette raised their arms.

Bernard Weil

'You might need some clothes too, my dear,' said Dr Weil, looking at Simone's book-filled suitcase.

'I thought it was warmer in the south,' she said, with a touch of irony.

'It's *safer* in the south, that's the important thing. I just hope we can still get through.'

Reynard

Outside Yvette and Pierre's apartment block, Reynard was study-ing a map spread out on the bonnet of his staff car. He scarcely spared his two former classmates a glance as they were pushed, at gunpoint, into the back of a waiting lorry, already half-full of people arrested in this pre-emptive raid. He wasn't going to lower himself to gloat over them. He hoped it would hurt them more to be treated with virtual indifference, as if they were only two more of the parasites that he was rounding up. He was slightly disap-pointed that, given their shared background, neither of them had tried to plead with him. He would have refused them, of course, but it would have been nice if they had begged just a little. Never mind; the sight of them joining the other frightened faces in the darkness inside the lorry was deeply satisfying to him. And there were more to come. There'd be quite a class reunion by the end of the morning. Just like old times. He looked a little more closely at his map. Yes, that was the address. He looked up, and turned to the car driver with sudden decision.

'Right,' he said, indicating a street on the map. 'There.'

They got into the car, followed by the Nazi official and the two soldiers, and sped off. Behind them, the lorry rumbled into life and roared after them.

Simone

Simone had finished packing. She looked with regret at the books she could not take with her. It was almost as if the emer-gency of their escape had forced her to decide unconsciously between the two streams of thought which had been running together through her life. Still on the shelves were the Marxists, the union theorists, the anarcho-syndicalist thinkers. In the suit-case were the *Bible*, the *Bhagavad Gita*, Plato and St John of the Cross. She was surprised at how clearly her hurried packing had revealed what had become essential to her. But as she thought about it, she had to acknowledge that, yes, this was increasingly the way her studies had been going. But she could not bear the idea of a simple dichotomy between the social and the spiritual. The wrench would do too much violence to her conscience.

She turned to her father, struck with a new inspiration.

'Do we have to leave?' she said. 'Why don't we stay here and show them we won't give in? We can give an example of how the French can suffer, how we can resist and not be broken.'

'Simone,' her father looked weary. He straightened up slowly before continuing: 'I won't have you using a national tragedy to justify more self-mortification'.

He thought for a little, then added.

'And aren't you forgetting something? As far as the Germans are concerned, we're *not* French people. We're Jews. And you know what they do to Jews.'

Simone absorbed the implications of this; if her father had been trying to find a way to make martyrdom unattractive to her, he had succeeded. If she was going to be persecuted, she wanted it to be for her support of liberty; she didn't relish it happening as a result of being lumped together indiscriminately with a racial group whose claims of exclusivity she found indefensible. This was a dilemma. From having been, a few moments ago, a hurried attempt to escape real physical danger, the crisis had suddenly become, for her, a philosophical argument.

'But we're not religious,' she said. 'I've never even been to a synagogue. I never even read the Old Testament until a couple of years ago.' She indicated the Bible where it lay in her case. 'And then I thought it was full of violence and prejudice.'

'Simone. Do you think that matters to *them*?'

Reynard

Reynard's car sped through the streets. They were much busier than usual, with people crowding to the train stations, and with vehicles laden with people's possessions clogging the roads. The crowds on the pavements were tense; every so often could be heard the sound of vehicle horns, and occasionally, too, distant gunshots. But however packed were the streets, Reynard found that the sight of the conquerers' uniforms and guns helped clear a passage for his little convoy quickly enough. People stood aside as they passed. Some were cursing; some were crying; but they all moved out of the way. He ignored them. He looked up at the street names, searching for the one he wanted.

Simone

Madame Weil hurried into the bedroom.

'Ready?' she asked.

Dr Weil took a last look round and nodded. He picked up his two heavy cases. Simone had only the one case, although it was heavy with all the volumes which she had crammed into it. She stooped to help her father.

Reynard

Reynard's car drew up outside the Weils' apartment block. Curtains twitched in nearby windows. Reynard jumped out, checked the address on the list in his hand, then with a look of satisfaction, led the Nazi official and the soldiers inside the hallway and up to the Weils' flat. He knocked. There was no answer. He knocked again. No reply. The Nazi official motioned to the two soldiers, who got ready to kick the door down. Reynard stood back. He wasn't going to be the first in line if some communist fanatic with a pistol was going to try to sell his – or her – life dearly. If Yvette and Pierre had had their wits about them, that last visit could have turned nasty. He knew Simone had received military training, and she too may have kept possession of a weapon after Spain. Even with her short sight, she might be able to hit something at such short range. He wanted to be certain it wasn't him.

The frame splintered and the door cracked open. The two soldiers clattered in, guns ready. Reynard followed them, at a cautious distance.

He looked round the hallway of the spacious bourgeois apartment. The dark wood panelling gleamed with polish. In the parlour at the end of the hallway, sunlight glinted on the gold lettering on the spines of what looked like an impressive library. Fresh flowers stood in a vase by the window. On the hallstand next to him was a man's coat of fine quality. It was all a damned sight more comfortable than the fatherless home in which he'd been brought up. He thought back to his first meeting with Simone, in the *Lycée*. He had promised her then that he would put her in her place. Now, standing in her own home with the power of life and death in his hands, it had been worth the twenty-year wait.

He could hear the soldiers moving round the other rooms; the crunch of broken glass under a boot heel. He caught sight of his own profile in the hall mirror. It seemed to observe him carefully. He looked up as one of the soldiers appeared at the other end of the corridor. The soldier shook his head.

'Gone', he said.

●○●

Meinwen

Meinwen sat in the unattended radio studio at Penrhyndeudraeth, looking at the green baize cloth of the table-top. There was nothing else to look at. There was no window, just a list of operating instructions pinned on the wall. The list was in both languages, fair play. She scanned the Welsh for mistakes, the habitual parlour-game of the campaigner, instinctively seeking the weak spots in the grammar of people whose education had been less rigorous than hers, or whose diligence was less exacting – a missed aspirate mutation, perhaps, or the gender of a part of speech changing at the end of a long sentence. There were no errors. The Corporation at least was keen to maintain its standards. She didn't know whether to feel pleased at the correctness, or disappointed that there was nothing to complain about. Praise for standards achieved was not in her repertoire of responses. Over her headphones she could hear the chatter in the studio a hundred and fifty miles away in Cardiff.

'Meinwen, can you hear me?' It was the producer.

'I can hear you.'

'Sir Anthony, can you hear me in Swansea.'

'Loud and clear,' Meinwen heard Sir Anthony's voice. He must have been used to this kind of thing in the airforce. He probably had to resist the urge to say 'Over' at the end of every sentence.

Meinwen and Sir Anthony had been invited in to discuss a new broad-based campaign which had developed in the wake of the Iraq war. The campaigners wanted all military bases in Wales to be closed, along with all recruiting offices for the armed services, and they wanted the country to be declared a 'demilitarised zone'. Several of the more junior nationalist AMs had supported it. So did a host of small nationally-minded political and religious groups, whose membership very often overlapped. Meinwen supported it too. Sir Anthony, needless to say, opposed it. They would be on air in a few seconds. She heard the presenter begin his introduction. They were on.

'Meinwen Jones,' said the presenter. 'This call for total withdrawal has been described as mere gesture politics. What do you say to that.'

'Well, first of all,' said Meinwen, 'this isn't just a gesture, but a firm policy proposal. And anyway, even if it were simply a gesture, gestures are powerful. This would send a message that British military establishments are not welcome in a democratic Wales. They're alien to the Welsh tradition of pacifism and opposition to war in all its forms. Our people have been pulled into England's imperial wars for centuries, and now they're being pulled into America's. It's not the will of the Welsh people, and it's got to stop.'

Sir Anthony

As Meinwen's voice came through the headphones, Sir Anthony thought that her predictable message, stripped down to nothing more than an insistent voice, sounded stark and isolated. Meinwen was speaking with the conviction of someone whose social circle had, for the last twenty years, been composed entirely of people who considered themselves pacifists. She did not bother to elaborate the argument. She clearly thought that the case was so watertight that it merely needed to be stated. She had the ardour of the cloister.

He understood that ardour. Better than she could ever realise. He knew from her writings – Meinwen having long treated the narrative of her life as public property – that she had undergone a teenage conversion to nationalism. What he had never made public was that he too had experienced a teenage conversion, albeit a decade or so before Meinwen, and at a slightly younger age too. In his case, he had been trying to envisage a role as an adult where he could make a difference, where he could live a life of significance, even of sacrifice. But he could find no roles that fitted his desire: religion seemed a thing of the past and had never greatly interested him; socialism held no appeal, as his comfortable background had sheltered him from any social inequality; as for nationalism, in those days, it was hardly talked about, neither in his home, where his parents' Welshness was a matter of local loyalty rather than national allegiance, nor in the public school where he had been educated. His life lacked a central conviction, and seemed empty and meaningless.

That was when he had read George Orwell's *1984*, and at a time when that novel's nightmare dystopia of totalitarian oppression was still a couple of decades distant, and when the Cold War was as icy a threat as ever. And suddenly, with a sober, certain joy, he knew he had found his reason for living: he would protect freedom, he would fight tyranny, and he would protect the way of life he knew and loved. Within days, he had visited the Royal Air Force careers office, and, a few years later, having combined cadet activities with his studies during his time in college, he had become a full-time officer, a career which had brought him duty and danger, and which he had never for a moment regretted. He knew too well that the ideals which had driven him would seem hopelessly unfashion- able and naive, and he would never display them for public consumption as Meinwen had done with her own motivations. Yet, in his own way, he too knew the ardour which was Meinwen's inner fire.

He understood Meinwen's isolation too. Politics, while the most public of callings, was also one of the most restrictive: it circumscribed your social circle, inhibited your intimacies, and subjected your every impulse and utterance to the relentless scrutiny of enemies real, potential and imagined. Under that perpetual inner and outer surveillance, spontaneity and joy shut themselves away. He sometimes thought he and Meinwen had a great deal in common: each of them was wedded to a cause; each had put the public before the private, and each had become a symbol of their respective communities. It was hard being a symbol. Lonely too. Yes, they were more alike than they could ever admit publicly. But could they admit it privately, he wondered. He tried to imagine such a conversation, and found it was surprisingly plausible, and not a little agreeable. However, what seemed entirely impossible was a meeting in which such an exchange could take place. The public gulf was just too wide.

He turned his attention back to what Meinwen was saying. Despite his sense of empathy with another soul caught in the aspic of commitment and duty, he found himself becoming more and more impatient as he listened to her. She was expounding the version of Welsh history that was believed as gospel by the people with whom Meinwen had spent her life, almost exclusively: a version where every labourite, conservative, soldier or royalist was quietly sidelined, where world statesmen like Lloyd George and Aneurin Bevan were less than dust in the scales, but where the diminutive figure of Saunders Lewis bestrode the world like a colossus. The piquant and complex mixture of the nation's real history was filtered through the narrow mesh of nonconformity, pacifism and nationalism until it was distilled into a clear, colourless, anodyne and alcohol-free liquid – an elixir which kept people like Meinwen eternally youthful and eternally hopeful for their future victory. Well, it was his duty to make sure that the victory of fantasy over reality never came about. Whatever sympathy he might have felt for Meinwen as a person was now replaced with a hard, professional enmity. He waited for his cue.

'Sir Anthony,' it was the presenter again. 'Alien. No place for them in Wales...'

Sir Anthony chose a tone of voice which suggested that he was making a complicated problem easy: 'Very simply,' he said, 'this is false history and false politics. Most Welsh people are not pacifist and never have been. It might be true that many of the most influential cultural figures in Welsh-speaking Wales are, and have been, pacifists, but that's not true of the overwhelming majority of Welsh speakers, nor of the overwhelming majority of the Welsh population as a whole.'

'What about all the Welsh people who were conscientious objectors in the last war?' interrupted Meinwen. 'There were proportionately many more of them than in England or Scotland.'

'I don't doubt it.' His tone was still measured. 'But that's hardly something to boast about, considering they refused to fight against the most diabolical regime the world has ever seen. And those proportions were still tiny compared with the people who actually served or supported the war effort. It's just that your little handful of pacifists also tended to be nationalists, and, as they were the ones committed enough to sustain Welsh-language culture, they wrote a version of history in their own image. And that's the false version of history you're blinded by. It's a version which exists only in the closed world and the closed minds of a nationalistic minority.'

Meinwen

'Now wait a minute...' Meinwen was growing uneasy. She had never heard Sir Anthony speak with quite such conviction and authority before. But he ignored her attempt to interrupt, and continued.

'You don't speak for the Welsh people, just for a self-appointed clique for whom pacifism is just a form of passive aggression against England. Every country needs to be defended. Even a completely free and independent Wales would still have a defence force...'

'No it wouldn't,' said Meinwen, finding some firm ground at last. A completely free and independent Wales was part of her eschatology, and she wouldn't accept lectures on that future state from any Tory militarist. She went on: 'If Wales decided it didn't need armed forces, it could simply do without them.'

'And why would you want to do that?' asked Sir Anthony suavely.

'To set an example to other nations. To show that violence isn't necessary.'

'What, *never* necessary?'

'Never.'

'Not even when faced with, for instance, the Nazis? Or the Soviet Union?'

'Never.'

'And how, exactly, would you have dealt with Hitler?'

'Passive resistance,' said Meinwen patiently, as if he was wilfully ignoring the obvious answer.

'Passive resistance?!' Sir Anthony's suavity gave way for a moment as he laughed out loud.

'Civil disobedience,' Meinwen explained.

'I see,' said Sir Anthony in a voice that suggested he was working hard to keep out of his voice a sarcasm that would have impaired his dignity. Habituated to his unflappable urbanity, Meinwen had never before experienced the full power of the aggressive intellect which he had kept hidden like a handgun in the inside pocket of a suit. By now she was feeling distinctly unsettled. This wasn't going to be such an easy argument to win as she'd expected. This debate had clearly touched some unsuspected source of passion in the former serviceman, and he was looking to press his attack home. She was going to have to think quickly, come up with some new approach. Before she could do so, he had changed the direction of his questioning.

'Would I be right in thinking you're a regular at the Cilmeri rallies?' he asked.

'Yes.'

'And what exactly are you commemorating there?'

Meinwen could feel the trap opening. The Cilmeri rally, held at the spot where Llywelyn ap Gruffudd, the last native prince of Wales, was killed by English forces in 1282, was a red letter day in the nationalist calendar. Every December 11, she would be there for the wreath-laying in the ruined abbey, for the songs and the speeches at the memorial menhir – the breath of the orators cloudy in the freezing air. She could guess what Sir Anthony was planning now. She decided on a counter manoeuvre.

'We're commemorating the idea of freedom,' she said.

'Fine, and how exactly did Llywelyn promote that ideal? By sit-down protests and petitions, I suppose? "Just take this quill, put your mark on this parchment, and we'll hand it in to King Edward." "I know, let's all sit down in front of this cavalry charge..."'

'That's not fair. It was a different age...'

'Was it? The weapons were different, I agree, but I'm afraid the realities of international politics are the same. Every state needs to defend itself. Civil disobedience wouldn't have got you very far with Edward the First.'

Meinwen needed to get the debate back to the safer territory of the twenty-first century: 'I thought we were talking about military bases in Wales today.'

But Sir Anthony's ambush had been too well prepared.

'You're the one who trudges through the snow each year to commemorate a medieval warlord,' he said. Then his voice became more stern, as if he had indulged a bright child for a while but it was now time for the important lesson.

'You're living a lie,' he said. 'You're campaigning to protect a nation which only exists because people like Llywelyn and Owain Glyndŵr were prepared to defend it with violence and warfare. By killing people. Large numbers of people. Painfully, messily and frequently. That's what kept Wales in existence long enough to allow it to survive into the modern age. It's what they call the lesser of two evils. Well done to them. I salute them. If I still had it, I would take my peaked cap off to them. All your hand-wringing about pacifism is just a case of making a virtue out of a necessity. It hasn't been feasible to take military action against England for 600 years, so you flatter yourself you're pacifists. Llywelyn would turn in his grave.

'And let's come a little closer to the present day. Wales is only here because hundreds of thousands of people of my father's generation gave their lives to save this country from Nazism. I take my cap off to them too. If you really want to commemorate somebody who kept your freedom, maybe you should turn up at the cenotaph in Cathays Park on Remembrance Day. You could thank them personally. But I don't think you'd do that, would you? You'd sooner live in a fantasy world of a pacifist nation which has never existed and spend your time vilifying those who have died, and who are prepared to die, to ensure that you live in a free society.'

The presenter was conscious that Sir Anthony had had more than his fair share of airtime. 'Meinwen?' he asked.

Meinwen was furious that her position had been misrepresented. Sir Anthony may be an effective debater, but to have twisted the truth like that was nothing short of satanic. By long practice, she could contain her anger. She thought of Jesus, of Gandhi, of Simone Weil, of St Francis of Assisi. Had he been a pacifist? No matter. He was kind to animals, which was the same thing. If she couldn't win on logic, she'd make sure she won the battle of the heart. She put a note of martyrdom into her voice. It came easily to her.

'You can twist things all you like,' she said, with calm simplicity. 'All I know is that I am a pacifist. I would die rather than shed blood. War is always wrong, in all circumstances, and the fact that you can argue for bloodshed just disproves your case completely. The military presence in Wales must go, and will go. And the people of Wales will agree with me.'

'The people of Wales?' responded Sir Anthony. 'You mean nationalistic Welsh speakers. A minority of a minority. That's your Wales. The other ninety per cent of the people of this country just don't count to you at all do they?'

'Sir Anthony, Meinwen: thank you both.' It was the presenter's voice. 'We're out of time.'

The interview was over. Five more minutes of airtime filled. One step closer to a free Wales. Or one step further away.

The presenter thanked them over the headphones. Sir Anthony said goodbye. Not 'over and out' as Meinwen half-hoped he would. Meinwen did not reply. She took off the headphones and left the studio.

As she closed the door behind her and stepped out into the sunlight in Penrhyndeudraeth, there was a roar overhead. Two warplanes screamed across the village, flying low, heading for RAF Valley on Anglesey. Protecting or oppressing? It seemed to depend on where you stood. Meinwen couldn't allow herself to think of them as protectors. She pushed the thought away. But Sir Anthony's words remained in her mind like vapour trails in a clear sky.

Simone

It had been a long journey from Paris. The van which the Weil family had hurriedly bought for the journey was stuffy in the hot June sunshine. They were sure they could feel the change in the climate as they headed south. Simone had been watching the changing landscape through the window; as the hours had gone by, the rolling fields had given way to terraced vineyards. They passed farmers with their horse-drawn carts laden with produce. Here, there seemed no visible sign of the catastrophe that had come upon France. Simone turned to her father.

'Are you sure we'll be welcome?'

Dr Weil did not look at her.

'We were officers together in the war,' Dr Weil looked uncomfortable. 'He promised that if ever I was in need, I should contact him. He's a man of means.'

'But I've never heard you mention him before. What was his first name?'

Dr Weil hesitated slightly before answering. 'Gustav.'

Simone thought for a moment. The name was familiar. It came to her.

'Gustav Thibon...!'

'Simone...' said Madame Weil unhappily.

'You don't know him,' said Dr Weil.

'I know his writings,' Simone said. 'Wait a minute, I can remember what one reviewer said about him – "The voice of the old Catholic order in rural France." He supported *Action Française* – you know that, do you?'

She turned away in exasperation. For once she actually felt lost for words. She looked ahead down the road as if seeking some explanation in the landscape for this act of folly. Then she swung around again.

'Does he know we're Jews?'

'Well, you know I've never advertised my Jewishness much...' her father said.

Then he stopped speaking, and she saw his expression change from unhappiness to alarm, quickly corrected to a tense impassivity. The van slowed down. There was a police roadblock. A uniformed officer, gun at the ready, flagged the van down. As it stopped, he and a civilian official walked over to the driver's door. The official spoke.

'Papers.'

Dr Weil handed them over.

'Weil,' the official said, pronouncing the word the German way. 'Not a very French name.'

Dr Weil replied diffidently, using the French pronunciation: '"Weil". My family is from Alsace.'

The official continued to study the papers, then, without looking up, he asked.

'Jewish, I take it?'

Dr Weil nodded. Madame Weil gave Simone a warning glance. There was a long pause. Then the official handed the papers back.

'Well Dr Weil,' he said, using the German pronunciation

again. 'You won't be able to practise your profession in Vichy, I'm afraid. Nor you either, Mademoiselle. Jews are banned from all professions.'

The Weils maintained their composure. None of them had ever been in this position before, but some inherited survival instinct told them not to challenge the men. They kept their eyes downcast, and said nothing. The official continued.

'Perhaps you can find work on the land. That's the official advice to everybody in your position. Do some proper work for a change.' He looked them over with visible distaste. 'All right. You can go...'

Dr Weil inched the van forward, trying to find the pace which suggested neither a guilty desire to escape nor a fear of moving away. The policeman and the officer stepped aside and the van slowly moved forward.

'... for now,' the official said.

The van moved away.

Meinwen

There was a knock at the door of Yr Hafan. Meinwen left the article she was writing and went to open up. It was Fran Skye. Her new neighbour was carrying something in a basket, and her big eyes were watchful, as though she was observing some shy animal she hoped to catch. The image of the visit of the witch to Snow White flashed through Meinwen's mind.

'A potion,' thought Meinwen. 'She's come to put a bloody spell on me.'

Fran looked at her in a wary but encouraging way as though trying to win her trust. She reached into the basket, took out a jar of some dark substance and held it out toward Meinwen, tentatively. She tried a smile: 'This-Is-For-You,' she said in her talking-to-earthlings voice.

'What is it?' said Meinwen suspiciously, as she took the jar.

'Black-berr-y jam,' said Fran. 'We made it this summ-er. We thought you'd app-rec-i-ate a gift as it's com-ing up to Samh-ain.'

'To... Sadwrn?' For a moment, Meinwen thought Fran was

trying to say the Welsh word for Saturday. No such luck.

'Samh-ain. The anc-ient Cel-tic day of the oth-er-world.'

'I see,' said Meinwen, feeling she should really try to sound as if she knew more about ancient Celtic festivals. She was damned if she was going to let this half-baked hippy teach her about anything to do with Celts. 'Of course. Thank you very much,' she said. 'You'll forgive me if I don't reciprocate just now. We usually give our gifts *after* Samhain.'

'Why's that?' said Fran, wide-eyed, ever ready for en-light-en-ment.

Meinwen adopted a confidential tone: 'Because they're cheaper in the shops then,' she said, and held Fran's gaze.

Fran nodded slowly as if appreciating the wisdom of this. Meinwen forced an accomplice's smile and closed the door.

As she went back into the living room, she looked at the jam Fran had given her. Meinwen hated waste. But there was an exception to every rule.

She threw the full jar in the rubbish bin.

Bernard Weil

The late afternoon sun was slanting through the poplars as the Weils' van crunched across the gravel of the driveway of the little chateau and came to a stop before the door. The family got out, stiff from their confinement. As they did so, the door of the chateau opened, and a tall, heavily-built, middle-aged man with short curly white hair came out towards them. Several other people, servants or family, followed a few steps behind. The man walked up to Dr Weil and embraced him.

'Bernard!'

'M'sieur Thibon,' replied Dr Weil, embarrassed by his new-found status as unemployed refugee.

'Not "M'sieur," "Gustav",' Thibon turned to Madame Weil and kissed her hand. 'So glad to meet you.'

Madame Weil gave her most gracious smile. She would be sure to use all her considerable resources of charm in order to keep this powerful protector on their side.

Thibon was still speaking.

'You'll be our honoured guests. That is where you'll be staying.' He indicated a summer house in the garden. 'It will give you some independence. We hope you'll be very happy here.'

He turned to Simone: 'And this is your charming daughter!' He lifted his hand in order to take Simone's and kiss it. But she was holding a suitcase in either hand and did not let them go. He abandoned the gesture, but his smile remained in place. He contented himself with a slight bow.

'Welcome, Mademoiselle Weil, I hope you'll find the sunny climate of our Languedoc will put a glow back into those Parisian cheeks!'

'Liberty might do so, M'sieur Thibon,' she replied, impassive. She walked past him with her bags, refusing to let the servants take them from her. She struggled into the summer house with them.

'I'm sorry, Gustav,' said Dr Weil. 'Simone is...'

'Simone is young, and principled, and I am glad to have such a guest.' He winked at Dr Weil. 'Come inside.'

Simone

Later that evening, the Weils were unpacking in the summer house. It was a two-bedroomed wooden chalet, and there was plenty of room for the few belongings they had managed to bring with them. Simone had found some shelves to hold her library. As she arranged the volumes, she spoke over her shoulder to her mother, half in jest.

'Fancy Papa having a friend in the *Action Française*!'

'He's a friend of your father from the war,' said Madame Weil, with a warning note in her voice, unusual for her.

'He's also a friend of Petain himself! A friend of those fascists who won't let us work!'

'He's a friend of conservatives, Simone. It's not the same thing.'

'Yes it is... reactionaries, landowners...'

'Well, I'm glad he's a landowner. Because he owns land and he's willing to share it with us.'

'But he's an out-and-out political conservative.'

'Yes, he's a conservative, Simone. And he's conserving *us*.'

Thibon

That night, the Weils were sitting at the table in Thibon's large but simply-furnished dining room. Servants laid out the food: bread, wine, olives, cheese, on the large wooden table. It was a bright June evening, and the declining sun was beginning to slant through the open windows. Outside, could be heard the song of birds. As the last dish was set down, Thibon looked around with satisfaction.

'Let us say grace.'

He crossed himself, and clasped his hands. There was a momentary delay before the Weils, too, bowed their heads and closed their eyes, but without crossing themselves. Before he closed his eyes, Thibon registered the omission, but showed no sign that he had done so. He said grace.

'It's strange, this war,' Thibon said, as he poured the wine, the product of his own vineyards, for Dr Weil. 'The fall of France has focused my mind as never before on the history of the Languedoc as a region...'

Simone, speaking for the first time that evening, interrupted him. 'Once, it wasn't a region, though, was it? It was a nation, with its own language and culture.'

Thibon did not reply, but he gave her a questioning look to invite her to continue. She did so.

'The Provençal civilisation was one of the jewels of the Middle Ages. And France destroyed it, in pursuit of power and uniformity. It destroyed its freedom and exterminated its culture. Completely. Now it's no more than a name and a memory.'

Thibon looked down and ran his hand around the base of his wine-glass, listening.

'French patriotism is so arbitrary,' Simone continued, getting into the stride of her argument. 'If you think about it, it's just an equation between absolute good and a particular territorial area. If you dare to question the territorial element of the equation, they call you a traitor. Take people in Provence and Brittany – and Alsace.' She looked at her father, who looked away, embarrassed. 'We expect them to forget their past and collaborate with France even though most of them have a different ethnic or linguistic heritage, but then we condemn anyone who collaborates with Germany, which only wants to do to us what we do to our own colonies. There's no logic to it.'

Thibon looked up.

'No. That's too simple,' he said. 'Even if we grant that the annexation of Languedoc was a crime, which I do not – there were reasons for it – it's still now inalienably part of France, loved and sacred as such. That's real. This land is now a warm human environment for living souls. You can't equate the destruction of this culture today with some supposed crime, centuries ago, whose pain you cannot feel.'

'I *do* feel it,' Simone said. 'I feel it like I feel the sufferings of workers in our factories, or the natives in our colonies, or the Poles under the Nazis, or the people in the occupied zone. It doesn't matter when it happened, force is always wrong, and we have to oppose it in history as well as in the present. In ourselves as well as in our enemies.'

'Simone,' Thibon said slowly. 'I must say I admire how you put forward a case even though you could be the loser for it. I'm reminded of the words of the psalm in church today: "Who is the righteous man? He that keepeth an oath, though it be to his own hindrance." Do you know it?'

Simone shook her head. 'I'm not a Catholic.'

'I know. But it's from the Old Testament. I thought you'd recognise it. As a Jew.'

He paused. Simone's parents looked at Thibon. Simone herself had fallen silent, looking uncertainly from one face to another. There was an uneasy pause. Thibon looked at Simone, as though waiting for her to say something. She looked down.

Then he laughed.

'Don't look so surprised. And don't worry. I have many faults. But I thank God that anti-semitism isn't one of them.'

Madame Weil closed her eyes in relief. But Simone, still impelled by the momentum of her argument, returned straight to the discussion.

'I hate the Old Testament. It idolises force...' she said.

'You hate the *Old* Testament?' Thibon was puzzled. 'But...'

'Yes! I find it repugnant...'

Then she hesitated and put her hand to her temple. She tried to continue.

'A tribal God destroying his enemies... Oh, oh... I'm sorry... forgive me...'

She put both hands to her head. She was clearly in pain. Her parents rushed to her side. Thibon was there in a moment.

'What's the matter? What's wrong?'

Simone was now in a state of near-collapse. Her parents helped her to the nearby settle. Refugee or no, as a medical man, Dr Weil was suddenly in charge of the situation.

'It's her head,' he said, as he checked Simone's pulse. 'She's suffered terrible headaches all her life. Migraine. Sinusitis. We don't know. We think she has them more often than she lets us know. They drain her completely. She'll need rest for days. I must get her to her room.'

He and Thibon supported Simone between them and helped her out of the dining room.

Bernard Weil

The next morning, Dr Weil opened the door to Simone's darkened bedroom. His daughter was lying motionless on the bed, with her eyes closed. Madame Weil came in behind him, carrying a breakfast tray, which she placed on the bedside table.

'How are you today, my dear?' said Madame Weil.

'Better,' said Simone. Her voice was weak. She struggled to sit up. 'I can't lie here. I must get up. There must be work to do on the farm.'

Dr Weil had been examining his daughter with his eyes.

'Simone, as your physician, I order you to stay in bed. You must rest. And you must eat. You're far too thin.'

Simone turned her head to the bedside table: fresh coffee, croissants, cheese, preserves. It may have been wartime, but the Thibon household and its guests were clearly not running short.

'I can't eat all this,' she said. 'Morally, I can't. There's rationing in the occupied zone. It would be wrong for me to eat more than they're allowed.'

Her parents looked at one another, suppressing their alarm. All her life Simone seemed to have been seeking reasons not to eat – her solidarity with the unemployed, her sympathy for the starving in China, her natural disgust at luxury. All had the arbitrary quality of having been chosen by Simone. The reasons changed, but the impulse to mortify the self was the one corrosive constant. But ominously, this latest reason seemed to have been imposed from outside, and carried a more credible moral imperative. Although, in Vichy France, they had access to as much food as they needed, and although they knew that even in the occupied zone the black market supplied the deficiencies of the rationing system, this time it would be all too easy for Simone to allow the martyr in her to take her asceticism to new extremes. But it was hopeless to argue with her. It would only make her more stubborn. Madame Weil forced a smile.

'Well, eat your rations, then. Toast and black coffee. Is that meagre enough for you?'

As they closed the door behind them, they found Thibon waiting on the landing outside. He looked with concern at the uneaten food on the tray which Madame Weil was carrying.

'How is she?'

'She's stubborn,' said Dr Weil unhappily.

'What's wrong with her?'

Madame Weil, sensing the developing *tête-a-tête*, suppressed her inquisitiveness, left the two men and went downstairs.

'I don't know what's wrong with her, Gustav,' said Dr Weil. 'She's so compassionate towards other people, but she's so hard on herself.'

He couldn't look at his friend. They moved away to the window at the end of the landing, overlooking the garden. Dr Weil continued speaking, lowering his voice so Simone could not hear.

'I love her more than life itself. If only I could help her find what she's looking for. She might stop punishing herself. She might choose to live.'

Thibon put his hand on Dr Weil's shoulder. Neither man said anything for a moment. Then Thibon asked: 'May I see her?'

'Yes. I'm sure she'd be glad to see you.'

Thibon

Thibon opened the door gently. His voice was almost a whisper.

'Simone, I'm so sorry if I upset you last night. I didn't mean to.'

'No. No. You didn't upset me,' Simone's voice was quiet. 'I have this often, discussions or no. I'm sorry to be a burden. As soon as I can I'll get up and help your people with the work.'

'Well, there's no need... But...' He tried to think of what Dr Weil had told him about Simone's desire to identify with the working classes. He should be more accommodating to her desires, however strange. 'But of course. Of course you can help. Is there anything I can get you? Anything I can do for you?'

Simone thought for a moment.

'Perhaps. You can read Greek, can't you?'

'Er... yes. Not as well as I would like, but...'

'Would you please read to me?'

'Certainly. What would you like me to read? My books are in the main house...'

'In my bag there. There's a New Testament. Would you please read me the Our Father?'

Thibon found the book, and the page, and began to read, at first haltingly, but then with more confidence. Simone closed her eyes and smiled as she listened. She nodded faintly, as he reached the Amen.

'Thank you,' she said.

'I thought you weren't a Catholic?' he said presently.

'I'm not.' Simone continued speaking meditatively, her eyes still closed. 'I say the Our Father to myself in Greek every day. But just now, I can hardly think straight to recite it. It was good to hear you read it.'

She was silent for a moment, and then continued.

'Sometimes, I feel as if the words tear my thoughts out of my body and take me somewhere outside space. Somewhere without a perspective. Infinity. Filled with silence. But it's not an absence of sound – it's something more positive than sound. Something more perfect.'

Thibon said nothing. The room was filled with silence.

Meinwen

Since they had moved into Hermon, Fran and Connor had been getting on Meinwen's nerves more and more. Meinwen would have preferred to have pretended they weren't there, but it wasn't as easy as that. In addition to Fran's visit with the blackberry jam, Connor had called round to offer to help with any maintenance work on Yr Hafan. He would do it for nothing, he said. He was good with his hands, he had a full set of tools, and he was happy to do work of that kind. Meinwen had told him curtly that she didn't need any help. He hadn't seemed as offended as she hoped he would be, and undeterred, a few weeks later, Fran had invited Meinwen to a healing evening at Hermon – now renamed 'Cloud Temple' – where a group of people would gather to learn about different methods of spiritual healing. Although she got a cold enough reception from Meinwen, Fran nonetheless left the publicity leaflet with her. The evening was free-of-charge, which was something in its favour, but the fact that the leaflet was monolingually English was enough to settle the matter for Meinwen. That pair next door could be healing lepers and raising the dead by faith, but unless they showed some respect for the Welsh language Meinwen hadn't a scrap of interest.

It had turned out that when they weren't brewing potions or performing healing ceremonies, Fran and Connor were music lovers. If you could call the didgeridoo 'music'. Connor would play it for hours on end, the vibration finding its way through the partition wall and pervading Yr Hafan every bit as much as the sound of one of the low-flying jets that used Cwm Aur for their training, but more persistent. Meinwen hated it. The peacemaking of the English was as intrusive and insensitive as their warmaking.

Meinwen thought fondly of when she used to be able to hear Hermon's congregation quavering through their hymns. Now she put cotton wool in her ears to shut out the sound of the didgeridoo. She longed for the nights when the only sound was the wind at the windows and in the chimney.

Sometimes, she tried to drown the didgeridoo by putting on records. But playing the disembodied voices of Maffia Mr Huws, Edward H. Dafis or Dafydd Iwan just seemed like an invocation of dead and powerless gods. Because when the needle stopped, Connor's didgeridoo would still be droning on.

●○●

Selma Weil

Madame Weil was pegging out the washing in the garden of the summer house, when Simone joined her. She had been allowed out of bed the previous day. She immediately started to help, passing her mother the clothes from the basket on the ground.

'So, are you feeling stronger?'

Simone laughed: 'As strong as one of Thibon's cart horses!'

She didn't look it. She was working energetically, but her mother noted how frail and pale she still was. She changed the subject.

'Do you remember a boy called Reynard in your class at the *Normale*?'

Simone hesitated slightly, then replied: 'Yes. Why?'

'Well, it's just nice to see a *Normalien* getting on, that's all.'

Simone clearly recognised the ironic tone, and knew it wasn't a good sign. She looked at her mother for further explanation. Madame Weil continued.

'I read it in the paper. He's just been appointed to a very responsible position in the Vichy government.'

'Oh, I see. What position?'

'Commissioner for Jewish Affairs.'

She looked to see Simone's response. But her daughter just shook her head and reached for another garment.

'I think we're safe here,' she said quietly.

'We might not always be safe here, Simone. Your father and I are going to ask about getting a boat out, maybe to America. Thibon has some connections. He says he'll help us, but it could take a long time.'

She left some space for Simone to indicate her own intentions. But her daughter said nothing, so she pressed on.

'What do you plan to do yourself, Simone? We won't leave here without you.'

'I don't know, Mother,' she said. 'I hate the idea of running away. The only way I would go is if it would be a way for me to join the Free French in England. Then I could do something for France.'

'Well, if we got to America, you could go to England from there, couldn't you?'

'Yes, Mother.' Simone was thoughtful, then she smiled with a playfulness rare for her: 'But you know, I wish we could stay here for ever. I think it's the ideal mode of life. You can keep house. Papa can practise medicine for free, and I can work on the land and do teaching work with the local people. And we can all grow vegetables together!'

Madame Weil smiled and continued pegging out the laundry. The spotless white cloths flapped in the breeze like signs of surrender.

●○●

Meinwen

There was a knock at the door of Yr Hafan. Meinwen left her reading and went to open the door. A man in his early thirties: blond dreadlocks, earring, clipboard.

'Hi, I'm Jamie. I'm collecting a petition against the wind-farms at Bryn Aur.' He pronounced it 'Bryn Oyer'.

'Can I ask if you'll sign it?'

'Why?' said Meinwen.

'Well, it'll destroy a pristine landscape. We think it's a gross visual intrusion in the environment.'

'Who are "we"?'

'The neighbours. Most of them have signed.' He showed Meinwen the list.

She recognised the names of all the cottages and smallhold-ings in the address column, at least, those which had still retained their names. Bryn y Briallu, Maes Meillion, Tan y Graig Ucha', Ty'n y Fawnog. But she recognised scarcely any of the householders' names, except those of Connor and Fran next door. None of them were Welsh. Not a single one. The Welsh had vanished from the high hills like April snow.

Meinwen knew about the windfarm, of course. John Evans of Ty'n Mynydd had made the application. After generations of subsistence farming on the marginal land at the top of Cwm Aur, he had seen this crop of turbines as a way of getting some essential extra income. If granted, it might keep him and his family at Ty'n Mynydd for another generation. Meinwen felt no particular affection for John Evans, who, on the few occasions they had met, had been taciturn and sour. And she hated windfarms almost as much as Jamie, who was looking at her expectantly. She thought they were hideous, and she saw little point in despoiling the landscape simply to feed more kilowatts into a society whose energy consumption was increasing rather than reducing. But John Evans was a native, and for that reason, she said. 'I'm sorry, I don't think I can sign it.'

'But what about the visual impact?' said Jamie.

'This isn't just a landscape, you know,' she replied, starting to warm to the debate. 'It's a workplace for some people.'

'Well, we don't think this is really going to help the environment.'

She had had enough. Here goes, she thought.

'What about the *cultural* environment?' she challenged.

He looked blank. 'What do you mean?'

'John Evans is a Welsh speaker. One of the last ones round here judging by your list of "neighbours". Do you want his farm to go out of business?'

At the mention of the language, Jamie's eyes lost their, 'we're all in this together' ingenuousness, and narrowed to defensive frontier bunkhouse slits. If he'd had his womenfolk with him, no doubt he'd have told them to get back in the wagon.

'Now wait a minute...' he said. But Meinwen had the initiative. She'd had this argument a thousand times. This might be the first time for Jamie. But she wasn't going to be gentle with him.

'Do you want him to have to give up, and move to town so more of you white settlers can move in? Is that what you want?'

'White settlers..?!'

'I'll tell you what. I'd rather have a hundred windfarms on Bryn Aur – that's how you pronounce it, by the way, BRYN AUR – than more of you. At least a windfarm does something useful. And...' she had the *hwyl* now; she looked at his clothes. '... it's clean.

'*Da bo' chi*,' she added, and slammed the door before he could reply.

A temporary victory. Whatever happened to the Bryn Aur windfarm application, she knew the days of people like John Evans were numbered. Some might cling on for another generation or two. But sooner or later the business would fail, the succession would falter, and Ty'n Mynydd would get its hardwood windows, its carriage lamps, its new name. An army of forces was conspiring to drive people like John Evans off their lands. It was a powerful, mobile and international surge of self-justifying and unstoppable deracination. It was difficult to define, let alone name. Globalisation was the closest anyone could get. But Meinwen knew what Simone would have called it.

As she came back into the living room of Yr Hafan, she saw the photocopied poster of Simone's face, with her enigmatic half smile. That photograph was taken in the 1940s, just when Simone was writing her great critique of the threat of modernity. In those days, the forces of globalisation were still just gathering; they hadn't yet swept across the planet like a plague. But Simone had foreseen the results.

Meinwen had just finished a series of magazine articles, which, as well as bringing her some useful income, had set out the contemporary relevance of Simone's views. The words were fresh in her mind and came back to her now: 'Uprootedness is by far the most dangerous ailment to which human societies are exposed,' Simone had said. 'For it is a self-propagating one... Whoever is uprooted himself uproots others. Whoever is rooted himself does not uproot others.'

Meinwen wished those words could be on every estate agent's window, displayed in every newspaper property supplement, and erected as hoardings alongside every road the wagon trains were traversing, on their way over Offa's Dyke, heading west.

Thibon

A few weeks later, Simone and Thibon arrived at the entrance to one of the estate's tenant farms. As the gate clanged back into place, the farmer's wife, Madame Rochelle, appeared in the doorway, wiping her hands on a towel.

'Hello, Marie!' Thibon shouted, with the official heartiness of the landlord.

'M'sieur,' she curtsied slightly, and looked with curiosity at Simone, who was wearing her red cloak despite the fact that it was now midsummer. Madame Rochelle said nothing more. Thibon realised he was going to have to handle the niceties.

'Francois is at the top field, I suppose, at this time of day,' he said. 'Very good, very good. And how's young Bernadette? Over the chicken pox I hope. Now, if it's still itching, Nathalie tells me she has some camomile lotion at the house. I'll send Jean over with it if you think it'll help.'

'Yes please, M'sieur. Thank you, M'sieur.'

Thibon and Simone were standing at the doorstep of the farmhouse. Madame Rochelle was looking with undisguised wonder at Simone, who smiled back cordially.

'Madame Rochelle,' said Thibon. 'This is Mademoiselle Weil. She and her parents are my guests. They've had to leave Paris because of the troubles. Now, Mademoiselle Weil thinks life's too comfortable at my house.'

He smiled. Simone was expressionless.

'She wants to learn about life on the land. And so, where better? I'd like you to take her in and let her live with you for a while.'

Madame Rochelle simply stared at Simone. But her visitor was impatient at being spoken for.

'Madame Rochelle,' she said frankly. 'I'm most grateful to you. I'll be no trouble. I'll be happy to sleep anywhere, and I'll share all your work. I've worked in a factory and on a farm – I'm no stranger to physical labour. Please treat me as one of your workers. I hope I'll be of use to you and that I can learn from you.'

Madame Rochelle twisted her hands in her towel, still saying nothing. Thibon took over. He turned to Madame Rochelle's teenage son who had been watching this conversation from the farmhouse doorway.

'Jacques! Take Mademoiselle Weil in and make her... make her... er... comfortable.'

Silently, Jacques took Simone in, leaving Madame Rochelle and Thibon outside. Thibon dropped his voice to speak to his tenant.

'Marie. Don't worry. Here,' He handed her several banknotes. 'This will pay for her keep. Please humour her. She has a great mind, and a good heart. And I want to help her.'

Simone

In the farmhouse kitchen that night, the family and their new guest were having dinner. In the centre of the table was a large white loaf, and some smaller brown ones; a gleaming kitchen knife, its yellow bone handle worn thin by generations of hands, lay next to the bread. The air of discomfort in the room could also have been cut with a knife.

Madame Rochelle, with instinctive deference, kept trying to serve Simone as if she were a guest. She cut a couple of slices of the white loaf, which had been prepared, against Simone's wishes, as a special gesture for a visitor and a friend of their land-lord. She offered the platter to Simone, who, ignoring it, reached out herself for a loaf of brown bread in the centre of the table. She broke a piece off.

'Mama, she hasn't washed her hands!' the scandalised voice was that of the youngest member of the Rochelle family, five-year-old Charles. His mother gave him an angry push. He started to cry.

Simone was mortified.

'I'm sorry... I thought... I didn't want to make you uncomfortable.'

Monsieur Rochelle spoke for the first time that evening: 'You will not make us uncomfortable by washing before meals, Mademoiselle.'

Next day, the weather was dry and fine, and Simone joined the rest of the estate workers and their children, stacking the hay. She raked it into piles, from which it was expertly collected and stacked by the others.

'Is it like this every year?' she asked. Her breathing felt uneven and rather laboured. 'I mean, how many hours must you spend every day doing this?'

'I don't know Mademoiselle,' said one worker of about her own age. 'I don't count them. We get the job done, and go home. Sometimes it takes less time, sometimes more, depending on the weather. Depending on how many hands we have.'

He looked dubiously at Simone's scruffy handiwork.

'Don't call me 'Mademoiselle', please! I'm here as just another worker.'

'Yes,' the worker struggled for a moment, then relapsed, 'Mademoiselle'.

Simone sighed inwardly. 'Now, what about your wages...' she continued.

The farmworkers looked embarrassed, and seemed to be concentrating more intently on their work, as Simone went on: 'How do they compare, say, with those of a shop worker down there in Saint Marcel?'

No one answered. Simone bore the silence until it was plain no one was going to say anything.

'Do you have a union here?'

The young worker looked incredulous: 'A union?'

Simone heard some of the other workers, behind her, laughing.

'No, Mademoiselle,' one of them said. 'We do have a Freemasons' lodge in town, though.'

Simone saw the workers suppressing laughter. She had no patience with sarcasm. She tried a different tack. She looked round at the children adroitly stacking the hay.

'It must be difficult for your children to get to school when the harvest is on?'

The young worker seemed relieved at what was apparently a reasonably sensible question. 'Well, it's more like it would be diffi-cult to get the harvest in if school was on. The harvest has to come in. Education can wait.'

He took the shapeless bundle of hay from Simone and stacked it with the others.

Simone rested for a moment. In the afternoon sun, the hay stacks were a rich gold. The image was strikingly similar to the paintings of the hay harvest which Van Gogh had produced when he too had come to Provence, fifty years previously, himself a fugitive, not from outer, but from inner persecution.

She thought of mentioning the visual comparison to her fellow workers. She looked around at them, as they moved between their tasks, apparently without effort, without anxiety, without thought. No, perhaps she wouldn't mention it after all. She bent again to her task, her body aching, her mind straining to gather all the scattered broken stems of her ideas into the one perfect composition.

●○●

Meinwen

A few days later, Dewi and Meinwen met up in the town. They found a seat at a café table outside on the Sgwâr. There were other more modern eating outlets on the Sgwâr; 'modern' meaning that they had cappuccino on the menu and lower-case lettering on their signage. But they had chosen 'Y Caffi' because it was a real old-fashioned establishment, still owned by a local family, and because it had a Welsh name. All her life, Meinwen had hated the idea of anything coming to an end: farms, chapels, businesses, lives, languages, anything. She felt pained by the thought of the hopes and memories represented by each enterprise being finally defeated and lost. She remembered as a child there was a small one-room shop in her street, run by an elderly lady. It had a tiny wooden counter, some home-made cakes in a glass case, a glassy wall of sweet jars, and a tiny refrigerator selling ice-creams of an obscure brand not found in larger shops. Even as a child in primary school, Meinwen had felt that the shop was so old-fashioned that its days must be numbered, and in order to postpone that day, she had tried to persuade her mystified parents to spend as much of their money there as possible, even pretending to like the insipid ice-cream it sold. And she spent as much of her own pocket money there as she could. Not because she wanted the sweets from the dusty jars – she gave most of them away – but because of the kindness and the tiredness in the old lady's face behind the worn wooden counter.

As she looked around the Sgwâr, Meinwen performed the calculation instinctive to a veteran community activist. How many of these businesses were locally-owned? Half at the most. On the corner, shopfitters were busy transforming the old bank into a new coffee shop, one of a worldwide chain called café havana, all in lower case letters, of course. Whether they were in Auckland or Anchorage, the café havana shops had identical specifications and identical stock, right down to the last unfairly-traded bean. When it opened here, Y Caffi would close within six months, as sure as there was coffee in Brazil. Gwynedd was just one more market to be colonised by global capital.

'What will you have?' asked Dewi.

Meinwen picked up Y Caffi's menu gingerly. The thick black

vinyl cover carried a score of different stains. She opened it. Inside, there were even more food smears, and crumbs of different foodstuffs jammed between the clear plastic covering and the typewritten, capital-lettered list of fare. It was as if the café was trying to display as many of its wares as possible to potential customers. Perhaps it was more modern than it looked; perhaps it had invented the world's first scratch-and-sniff menu. But if it had, it was a turn-off for this customer at least.

'I'm not hungry,' she said.

'No? Are you sure? Well, I'll have the teacake and a coffee.'

The waitress had met a friend on another table. They were deep into a catch-up conversation. 'No, I went out with him for six months, but then I dumped him...' 'So, what've you been up to, then?' Dewi tried to catch her eye, but the waitress ignored him, pretending she hadn't seen.

While he was waiting, Dewi pulled some papers from his bag, and pushed them across the crumb-strewn table to Meinwen.

'Look. It's the details of the protest march in Haverfordwest next weekend. Mei's going to drive a group down. He's got room in his car for one more if you want to come.'

Meinwen looked at the leaflets and posters. The protest had been organised in response to plans to sell a former creamery site to an American company which wanted to use it for a high-tech factory producing anti-terrorist security screening equipment. The factory would give around a hundred local people a livelihood, but only at the cost of feeding the Anglo-American military monster. Every campaigner worth his or her salt had to be there. Plenty would be coming from beyond Wales too.

Meinwen returned the leaflets to Dewi.

'I'll come,' she said.

Dewi finally managed to get the attention of the waitress. She detached herself from her conversation with visible reluctance, and took his order, unsmiling, resentful at having had to leave her friend.

Everything about Y Caffi seemed as if it was designed to make the customer's experience as disagreeable as possible. Maybe café havana would force its native rival to change its ways in order to survive. But considering that Y Caffi hadn't changed a single detail of its menu or its decor in a quarter of a century, it was hardly likely to do so now, even under the threat of closure. No, café havana would simply kill the place stone dead. Which was a pity because, however bad Y Caffi was, at least any profits it made stayed local, and its staff, however shiftless, were local, not movers from Glasgow or Amsterdam, or somewhere else, as the managers of café havana would surely be.

The waitress returned with Dewi's order and banged it unceremoniously on the table in front of him without a word, before going back to her conversation with her friend. The teacake was burnt; the coffee weak and tasteless.

●○●

Reynard

The Vichy Commissioner for Jewish Affairs was enjoying his working day. Jean Reynard had his own office, several secretaries, and a staff of twenty. A busy staff of twenty. His secretary brought in a sheaf of letters, and quickly summarised their contents for Reynard. He was a busy man; he wouldn't waste time wading through every tearful plea. A summary was fine.

'This is from a Doctor Goldberg in Marseilles,' said the secretary. 'He's asking that he be allowed an exit visa to visit his sister in Morocco.'

Reynard smiled ironically.

'I bet he does,' he said. 'The answer's "no".'

'He says she's dying.'

'Oh dear. Still no.'

The secretary began to put the letter to one side.

'But add our condolences,' Reynard added, pleasantly.

The secretary made a note and moved on to the next letter.

'This one is from a M'sieur Cohen. He requests exemption from the ban on working as a teacher. He says he is only a quarter Jewish, and was raised a Catholic. He wants to be able to support his family.'

'Of course he does. Pass the letter on to M'sieur Roger in the Employment Department. Ask him to reply, saying that M'sieur...?'

'Cohen.'

'... that M'sieur Cohen should seek employment through his local municipality as a manual worker. And make sure M'sieur

Roger checks with the municipality to find out exactly where M'sieur Cohen finds work, and exactly where he lives. And make sure that we keep a record of it.'

The secretary made a note.

'And this is from a professor of philosophy. She's expressing her... sincere gratitude for being barred from her profession...'

The secretary began to look puzzled.

'She says she is... grateful to you for giving her the chance to work on the land. Listen to this.' He quoted: '"The government has proclaimed its desire that Jews should go into production, and preferably to go to work on the land. Even though I do not consider myself a Jew, since I have never set foot in a synagogue, have been raised by free-thinking parents with no religious observances of any kind, have no feeling of attraction for the Jewish religion and no attachment to Jewish tradition, and have been nourished since my early childhood only on the Hellenic, Christian and French tradition, I have, nonetheless, obeyed."'

Reynard frowned. There was something familiar in this argument. The secretary looked at his boss warily, wondering if he wanted him to read on. Normally he didn't listen beyond a few sentences. But Reynard's absorption was obvious, so he resumed reading.

'"I am at this moment working in a grape harvest; I have picked grapes eight hours a day every day for four weeks, in the employ of a farmer in the Gard region.

'"I consider the statute concerning the Jews to be unjust and ridiculous, for how can anyone believe that someone with a degree in mathematics could harm children who study geometry simply because three of his grandparents went to a synagogue?

'"But in my own case, I would like to express my thanks to the government for having taken me out of the social category of intellectuals and for having given me the land, and, with the land, the whole of nature. Because the only ones who possess nature and the land are those who have been penetrated by it daily through the suffering of having their limbs broken by fatigue.

'"You and the other leaders of Vichy have given me an infinitely precious gift – that of poverty... and, because you have also seen fit to refuse to pay me the insurance for Jews who are forbidden to practise their professions, you have also given me a lively feeling of satisfaction at the fact that I am in no way responsible for the country's financial difficulties.

"'I do not imagine you get many letters of thanks from those who find themselves in my position. That perhaps will make the few minutes that you have spent in reading this letter worthwhile.'"

The secretary started to smile despite himself. Reynard's frown grew deeper.

'Wait!' he said. 'What's her name?'

The secretary turned the letter over to check.

'Weil', he said, pronouncing the name the German way.

'Weil!' said Reynard, using the French pronunciation. He snatched the letter and looked at it.

'Simone Weil.' He turned the letter over again. 'There's no address.' He thrust the paper back into the secretary's hands.

'Find her,' he said. 'She's on a grape farm somewhere in the Gard. We know that much.'

'But there are hundreds of them, sir.'

'I don't care. Find her.'

● ○ ●

Meinwen

Meinwen heard the car draw up outside Yr Hafan. She looked out. At the wheel of the old Ford Sierra was Mei, arriving to collect her as arranged. With him were Dewi and two other activists. Dewi got out and waved at her.

She went out of the house, closing the door behind her, and walked down to the car. It was even more battered than when last she saw it. The only thing holding it together seemed to be the stickers: Kernow; Breizh; Nuclear Energy? No Thanks; Stop the War; Not in My Name. Words like 'No', 'Not', 'Stop' and 'Never' were prominent on these fading signs of adherence, recording, as they did, a series of attempts, most of them failed, to prevent things from happening. The back of Mei's car was a social history of Welsh radicalism of the last two decades. A student could research a thesis, or at least illustrate one, simply by walking round it. Meinwen climbed into the back seat, pushing aside a yellowing copy of *An Phoblacht*.

Mei turned round towards her. He did not bother with a greeting.

'Have you seen it?' His eyes were big with meaning.

'Seen what, Mei?' replied Meinwen.

'The Article.'

'What article?'

'In the *Economist*.'

'Well... no. I don't take the *Economist*, Mei.'

'Oh,' said Mei, surprised, as if Meinwen was guilty of neglecting her duties.

'It's by Landman.' He said the name as if it was common currency, and as if mentioning it explained everything. It meant nothing to Meinwen. Whatever effect this article had had upon Mei, it had clearly left him with the impression that everyone else had also been pondering its significance as much as he had. Meinwen was used to this. Mei assumed the rest of the world shared his concerns, although they might be somewhat slower on the uptake. Mei was now clearly feeling slightly sulky that Meinwen had not immediately grasped the flow of his thought.

She could see Dewi's face in the rear-view mirror. She looked at him as if to say: 'What is he on about?'

Dewi saved her from what threatened to be a long dialogue.

'There was an article in the *Economist*,' he said. 'It said there should be controls on the property market in rural areas of Britain in order to save local communities.'

'Oh, good. I'm glad to hear it. About time too. Who's this Landman?'

Meinwen was still wondering why Mei had referred to him as if he was a household name. Dewi closed his eyes for a moment and shook his head to dismiss the question. Meinwen understood. There was no significance to the author. Probably Mei himself had never heard the name until 'The Article' came to his attention, although 'Landman' had now clearly become a major character in some internal drama of his own.

'It's the turning of the tide,' said Mei from the front seat. He spoke with deep conviction.

He's been watching *The Lord of the Rings* again, thought Meinwen. When he wasn't being cryptic, Mei settled for the portentous.

He was silent now. Dewi and Meinwen exchanged glances.

It looked like Mei had made his final utterance on the subject of 'The Article' and it was safe to change the subject.

Dewi turned round from the front seat to hand Meinwen a copy of a newspaper.

'You might want to have a look at this as well,' he said. 'It's a bit less positive, I'm afraid.'

This could only mean one thing. She began reading as Mei drove off down the hill.

It was John Sayle's column. The title said: 'The enemy in our midst'. She began reading.

'September 11th showed us the lengths to which crazed fanatics will go to destroy democracy,' she read. 'The bombs in Madrid and London did the same. Murdering the innocent and spreading terror without pity and without regret. Don't think it couldn't happen here. Wales has its own Bin Ladens, its own al Qaeda. Or perhaps that should be 'ap Qaeda'. It's the Welsh language lobby. Like al Qaeda, they can't accept the modern world. Like al Qaeda, they'd sooner destroy it than face the fact that their way of life is doomed. And like al Qaeda, they'll stop at nothing.

'Their latest target is the proposed American security equipment factory at Haverfordwest. They ignore the fact that this will bring jobs to hundreds of Welsh people. They ignore the fact that the factory is a vital part of our shield against terror and oppression. Like al Qaeda, incensed that American bases are on the holy land of Saudi Arabia, they are determined to drive these employers out. And after the Americans have gone, who will be next? Yes, the hated English, of course. And then? Well, any Welsh people not fanatical enough to insist on speaking Welsh. The front line in the battle against terror is not just in Afghanistan or in Iraq. It's right here in Wales. And it's a battle which everyone who loves freedom must make sure the Welsh-language al Qaeda never win.'

Meinwen leaned forward to return the paper to Dewi.

'Thanks Dewi. That was great,' said Meinwen. 'I feel loads better now.'

'I'm sorry. But we have to know what we're up against.'

'I know. I know,' she said quietly. She sat back and closed her eyes. 'It doesn't change anything. We still have to act. It's action that matters.'

Fully-laden, the old car was straining its engine as it struggled up the hill towards the top of the pass in the direction of Dinas Mawddwy. Mei shuffled the gears and gunned the accelerator, trying to find the revs to maintain the speed. This car had seen a lot of protests, but it didn't look as if it would see many more.

●○●

Simone

'Mechanisation. Do you think it will free the workers or enslave them?'

Simone asked the question casually. But this seemed to be richer fare than the Rochelle family were accustomed to digesting at the dinner table after a day in the fields. Monsieur Rochelle looked at his plate.

'I don't know, Mademoiselle. I couldn't say.'

Simone nodded approvingly as if he had just solved a puzzling problem for her. She was about to try another line of enquiry when the youngest boy spoke up.

'What was Paris like? Are the Germans really as cruel as they say?'

Simone was glad of a potential pupil.

'Well, I managed to get away from Paris before I had to meet too many Germans,' she said. 'But I met some in Germany before the war. And in Spain too.'

'Were you frightened? Did they try to shoot you?'

'Well, they're just men. Some are cruel, some are kind. Nazism is an evil, of course, a dreadful one, but the Germans themselves are good and bad, the same as any other people. The same as the French.'

The child looked at his parents uneasily. Simone continued, warming to her theme.

'You must remember, French people can be cruel too. And in many parts of the world, native peoples – little brown and yellow children in Indo-China or Africa or in the Pacific islands – they look on us in exactly the way we look at the Germans. The children get beaten in the schools for using their own language instead of French, and if their parents ever protested, then the French soldiers would put them in prison or shoot them.'

Monsieur Rochelle coughed. Madame Rochelle looked quickly

at the wall behind Simone, then got up from the table and went out into the kitchen, putting her apron to her face as she did so.

Simone turned to the wall behind her. She was never observant about furnishings or decorations, and she had not noticed before that on a shelf was a picture of a young man in French military uniform, with flowers placed, shrine-like, on either side. She turned back to the family, a horrified realisation starting to dawn on her.

'My eldest boy,' said Monsieur Rochelle, still looking down at his plate. 'Algeria. Two years ago.'

'I'm so sorry,' said Simone. She was wishing now she had shown more interest in the family as people rather than as proletarians. 'I'm so sorry, I didn't know.'

Meinwen

When they got to Haverfordwest, Mei parked the car, and the five of them got out to stretch their legs. The protesters were going to gather in the main street at twelve before marching to the proposed factory site, which was on the outskirts of the town. They had an hour before the protest started.

'Time for a pint!' Mei said.

They chose the pub nearest the starting point of the protest, and found many protestors had already had the same idea. The bar was full. Rainbow scarves, hand-knits, dreadlocks, body piercings. The Movement's activists looked positively demure by comparison, and their very conventionality attracted suspicious glances from some of the campaigners. They managed to find a table, and Mei went off to the bar.

Meinwen watched Mei as he went. The cacophony of voices in the pub made conversation difficult, and so, absolved of the need for small talk, she found herself thinking about Mei. He had already been a veteran Movement activist when she had joined, and his appearance – bearded and bardic, although he was no bard – had changed little since those early days. Neither had his opinions. He lived in a world of conspiracies, secrets and ever-shifting alliances and enmities among the campaigners of nationalism and the radical Left. But in recent years

Meinwen had become increasingly conscious that he had acquired a syndrome common to those who have inhabited the fringes for too long: he thought the periphery was the centre. A change of prime minister meant nothing to him, but the back-sliding of an activist in a Welsh republican movement with a handful of members was of truly cosmic significance, and worthy of endless conjecture and discussion. Perhaps in terms of Zen, or of chaos theory, he was right; perhaps the stir of a butterfly's wing really did cause a tidal wave somewhere else in the cosmos. But in terms of practical significance to Welsh politics, that was a moot point, and Mei's influence on the course of public events remained more limited than he liked to believe.

As he returned from the bar with the round, Mei overheard a discussion on the next table. Two young women in carefully dishevelled clothes were swapping stories about their experiences at the G8 summit in Edinburgh. One of the women had a strong French accent. That was enough for Mei. He leaned over towards them.

'Are you Breton?' he asked her convivially in a voice that could have been heard in Brittany itself.

The woman stopped in her conversation, gave Mei a quick appraising glance, and turned back to her friend with a curt *'Non'*.

Mei was undeterred.

'Have you BEEN to Brittany?'

She gave him the same glance, but this time she held it a little longer so that Mei could take it in. It was a clear invitation to take himself and his questions elsewhere.

'Non, I am a Parisienne.'

Meinwen felt like telling Mei to give up, or at least turn the conversation to Paris. But she knew that, for Mei, France was composed entirely of Brittany, with Paris as a vague accidental adjunct, a city occupied by people whose only purpose was to have their latent interest in Brittany and its Celtic heritage awakened by an enlightened person like himself.

'They have their own language in Brittany,' bellowed Mei, as though addressing a public meeting. 'It's like the *Welsh* language.'

'The *what*?' the Parisienne said, with evident uninterest and growing impatience.

'Welsh! The language we speak here!' He had not even bothered to disguise the pride in his voice. He looked at her

expectantly, clearly waiting for her approval, her eager sympathetic questions, her admiration of his ethnic authenticity.

He continued to wait.

Mei looked nonplussed, but then made a supreme effort at
empathy. He thought hard, then said brightly: 'Do you know
any Bretons in Paris?'

The woman did not even glance at him, and continued her
conversation with her friend. Mei rejoined his group, puzzled.

Meinwen, who had had little choice other than to overhear
the exchange, could not look directly at Mei as he came over.
As he set the drinks on the table, she let her eyes rest on the
Celtic-patterned teeshirt stretched over his protruding stomach.
She dreaded to think what opinion of Wales the Frenchwoman
had now formed. Mei was to Celts what the Black and White
Minstrels were to black people.

She picked up her half pint and took a sip. As she did so,
there was a cheer outside the pub, whistles started blowing,
drums started beating. The protest was underway.

Thibon

Thibon looked at Madame Rochelle with an air of professional
concern, as she stood before his desk in his estate office. As defer-
ential as ever, she was nonetheless determined.

'I'm sorry M'sieur, but we don't want to have Mademoiselle
Weil any more.'

Thibon forced himself to look surprised. He was not above
having some private enjoyment at Madame Rochelle's discomfiture, especially as he already knew what he was going to do. She
went on: 'She never washes before meals. She hasn't changed her
clothes since she's been with us, and always questions, questions!
What do we think of the struggling classes, education, wages, the
Great Beast, how much we can spend on food, how much on
clothing... how much...'

With an effort, Thibon retained a look of grave consideration.
He waited until his tenant had reached the end of her complaint.

'It's all right, it's all right, Marie, I understand completely,' he
said. 'Mademoiselle Weil has studied very deeply, but she doesn't

understand how we do things here. I will speak to her, I will tell her... what? I will tell her... you will be having a cousin coming to stay, and that you will need her bed. A *poor* cousin, that'll be even better. The cousin will be coming... tonight?'

Madame Rochelle looked relieved and allowed herself a slight smile.

'Thank you, M'sieur,' she said. She went out and closed the door.

When she was gone, Thibon dropped his look of concern, and smiled to himself. Simone seemed not to realise that her generous egalitarianism wasn't always appropriate. He thought back to an incident a few weeks previously. There was a young working-class girl from Lorraine, another refugee from the north passing through on her way to Marseilles; Simone thought she showed signs of having an intellectual vocation, and she thought it was her duty to help her develop it. Hour after hour, on the terrace behind their farm, Simone had lavished on the young lass her incomparable commentaries on the *Upanishads*. Scholars would have paid for the privilege of listening, but this poor girl was bored out of the few wits she had. But she was too polite, and too much in awe of Simone, to say so.

Awe was a feeling Simone seemed to inspire in many people. Certainly he felt that himself. But boredom was the last feeling he associated with her company. Once he had got past her sometimes abrasive manner, her interrogative, even invasive, candour, and her undoubted eccentricities, he had found himself entranced by the development of a soul that seemed to have direct access to the kind of spiritual truths which he himself had only read about. He treasured their talks, which sometimes went on into the small hours and left him as exhausted as though from a day's labour in the vineyard. He looked forward to having her back on his own farm, and, as he thought of the conversations still to come, he thanked God for the fate that had placed her in his path.

Meinwen

As protests went, it was pretty successful, Meinwen thought. Several hundred of them had turned out. Grey-suited pacifist chapel deacons, rugby-shirted nationalists, masked anti-globalisation activists, kaffiyehed left-wing students, dreamy-eyed wiccans, and whistle-blowing, drum-beating, samba-rhythmed crusties. She had been glad to see television cameras and press photographers recording the event.

After they reached the site of the proposed factory, they had listened to a speech from an English MP who had been prominent in his opposition to the Iraq war. Meinwen had to admit, he spoke rather well. No Welsh MPs had been prepared to address the rally. None of them, whatever their private views about the war, wanted to argue against a hundred new jobs in west Wales. In the debates leading up to the protest, others had gone so far as to say the plant was to be welcomed because it helped ensure the security of the West against terrorist attacks like those in New York, Madrid and London. It was beyond Meinwen's comprehension how any Welsh politician could support military activity on such shaky excuses; the whole project was clearly just using terrorism as a front for creating a police state. She had had to cross a few more names off her list of the politically sound. That list was growing shorter all the time.

Wales, however, had been represented from the platform by Mallwyd Price, who was speaking on behalf of the Welsh Witnesses for Peace, a group of mainly chapel-going Christian pacifists.

He had only been included on the platform as a concession to local feelings, after representations from the small Welsh contingent among the protest organisers. As a goodwill gesture, he was accorded a five-minute slot alongside the UK politicians and globetrotting anti-globalisationists.

However, as he now addressed the protest, the effect of Mallwyd's remarks on the crowd was limited because he spoke only in Welsh, meaning that only perhaps ten per cent of the audience could understand him. Which was just as well, Meinwen, thought, as Mallwyd clearly thought the entire crowd were committed Christians like himself, and he made frequent appeals to what he assumed were their shared values. The field full of atheists, agnostics, pagans, buddhists, animists and wiccans listened in polite boredom, unaware that Mallwyd had co-opted them into what he regarded as daring nonconformity and what they would have regarded as paralysing conventionality.

He had already overrun his slot and was up to ten minutes; the crowd were getting increasingly impatient. The only words most of them could understand, breaking surface every few minutes or so, were 'George W. Bush,' and even that reference was rendered confusing, as Mallwyd refused to pronounce the American president's middle initial as 'double-u', or even 'dubya', on the grounds that these were English words. Instead, he pronounced the 'w' as if it were the Welsh vowel of the same spelling, meaning that the audience heard the words 'George Ooooo Bush' interspersing the speech. These brief flashes of comparative clarity in the many-claused opacity of Mallwyd's address were not enough to keep the crowd from getting more and more restless. It was fifteen minutes now. Every time Mallwyd reached the end of a paragraph, there was an almost audible intake of breath as people willed him to stop, then, after a few seconds, an almost audible groan as he began again.

Twenty minutes now. Meinwen could see even the Welsh speakers in the crowd looking embarrassed. The small fund of goodwill which had allowed Mallwyd onto the platform was long exhausted, overspent. With this crowd, the whole culture he represented now had a negative credit rating, one debt which the privileged majority would not find it easy to drop.

Twenty five minutes. Even if they couldn't understand Mallwyd, the crowd weren't missing a huge amount, thought Meinwen. Much as she admired her former mentor's integrity, she had recently come to find his rhetorical style somewhat over-wrought, with quotations and idioms jostling one another for attention in his sentences. He seemed unable to leave any sentence unadorned. When no figure of speech or reference suggested itself for a particular sentence, he often simply inverted the syntax to make it sound more literary. His prose was like a piece of *bara brith* stuffed too full of currants and candied peel: strongly flavoured, but when you tried to do anything useful with it, like cutting a slice, it just crumbled apart. She hated to admit it, as she heard her worldview mediated through Mallwyd's anti-quated vocabulary, but she was embarrassed.

As Mallwyd continued, quoting the Welsh pacifist mystic, Waldo Williams, Meinwen looked around her. How much did she really have in common with these protestors? Many had come from England for the protest; some, like that French woman in the pub, from further afield. But many, no doubt, were living here in west Wales, part of the drift from the English cities of people seeking alternative lifestyles, and finding in west Wales the cheap housing that made their escape possible.

Capitalism's sulky runaway children. Protective of every threatened mammal, solicitous of every dwindling species of native flora, they were, paradoxically, too often dismissive and contemptuous of the ancient human culture in the midst of which they had come to live. Most would no more think of learning the Welsh language than they would of flying to the moon. She noticed a group of protesters, bored by Mallwyd's speech, handing round a joint. No, they probably thought about flying to the moon a lot more than they did about learning Welsh. Learning a language would need more long-term commitment than any of them seemed capable of. Even with all the time in the world on their hands, none of them even seemed to be able to master a musical instrument. Banging drums and blowing whistles was the extent of their expertise. Infant school children could do as much. Some chance that they'd commit to mastering another tongue. And any attempt to challenge them on this point usually resulted in them turning on the fragile native society, which they were busy supplanting, the whole arsenal of bitter accusations which they stockpiled like survival-ists to use against what they saw as threats to their freedom: 'oppression,' they called it; 'apartheid', 'fascism', 'racism'.

'Ignorant' was a favourite insult. It made the insulter seem so knowing and superior. Many incomers were often amazed and indignant to find Welsh spoken in the area where they had moved to live; they felt it to be a calculated personal affront, and they instinctively ascribed the most sinister of reasons to the behaviour of the natives, who could clearly speak English but who chose to speak another language. She recalled overhearing a couple of these settlers walking round an agricultural show in west Wales, muttering 'ignorant' to one another and shaking their heads every time they heard Welsh on the bilingual tannoy announcements. She'd turned on them: 'I suppose it's ignorant to have two languages, is it, and clever just to have one?' If one of the sheep had spoken to them the couple could not have looked more surprised. But they recovered in a moment. 'Don't be so ignorant,' one of them snapped, and they walked on.

They'd go to any lengths to save some fungus or some rare bird in west Wales, but the natives could go to hell. It was high time that the Welsh found some catchy 'ism' they could use against this merciless acid rain of accusation. 'Cambrophobia', perhaps. Or 'Anticeltism', 'Celtophobia', 'Anglo-Saxon supremacism'.

She looked at the man sitting next to her. In his mid fifties, his grey hair was in a pony tail and he wore an embroidered waistcoat. In this area, native Welshmen of his age wore battered tweed jackets and flat caps. So he was no native. And yet, he seemed to be listening to Mallwyd as if he understood him, or at least as if he was polite enough to pretend, which was better than nothing. The stranger sensed Meinwen's glance and turned and looked at her. His eyes were a bright grey, like a storm cloud caught by the sun. He didn't look as if he was in his fifties now. Although his hair was grey, his skin was fresh and unlined. Meinwen, never one to begin social conversations with strangers, looked down. As she did so, Mallwyd's voice finally stopped, and there was a weak clatter of applause, and a faint ironic cheer.

'I wonder what Waldo Williams would have thought of it,' the stranger said.

Meinwen looked up again. The man's accent was American, but he had clearly understood Mallwyd's speech. There was the hint of a smile on his lips.

'*Cymraeg dach chi?*' she asked him. 'Are you Welsh-speaking?'

'*Rwy'n gallu deall,*' he said. 'At least, I can understand most of it.'

Meinwen smiled and nodded encouragingly. It was what you did with learners.

'But I've not been in Wales for a year yet,' he continued, 'So I'm still learning, and I'm not as fluent as I'd like to be.'

Meinwen wondered briefly how this American had felt about hearing his country being vilified by speaker after speaker that afternoon, but she did not linger with the thought; after all, wasn't America to blame for almost all the evils in the world? No, it was his knowledge of Welsh which intrigued her particularly. Meinwen was impressed at his having learned at all, let alone having become so proficient in so short a time. She complimented him on his success.

'Well, I try,' he said. 'I've learned a couple of Native American languages, so after that, Welsh is not so difficult.'

'Native American languages?'

'Yeah, Navajo and Comanche. Navajo was a bit easier, as there are more materials. But with Comanche, there aren't so many speakers and there still isn't a proper dictionary.'

'How did you come to learn them?'

'Do you really want to know?' he asked with a slight smile.

'Yes.'

At the front of the crowd, a drumming group had started: the usual samba-timed, whistle-punctuated backing track to protests. The noise made it difficult to talk, so the stranger gestured to Meinwen to come with him. Mei and Dewi looked up at Meinwen and her new companion as they stood up. Meinwen pointed to her ears, grimaced and indicated that they were going to the edge of the crowd where it was quieter. Mei and Dewi nodded and returned to listening to the band. At the edge of the crowd, Meinwen and the stranger found an oak tree. The stranger sat down at the foot of it, and Meinwen joined him. With the drums as background, he began to tell her about his life with the Native Americans.

●○●

Simone

Thibon reached up, pulled one of the grapes from the vine and tasted it. Pondering the flavour, he walked on. Simone followed him.

'But how can you defend the old order?' she was saying. 'Seriously. These antiquated ways...'

'Not everyone is like you, Simone, living on willpower and charity. People need stability, family, belonging, roots. It's what makes people whole.'

'Maybe so, but are you sure you're not just creating an argument to suit your circumstances? I'm not sure you're really doing this out of any philosophical principle.'

'I've grown my principles,' he answered, pulling down another grape, and offering it to Simone. 'I didn't have to choose them. They chose me.'

Simone accepted the grape from him. As she did so, she noticed how thick and strong his fingers were, almost like a peasant's. But she had noticed too how finely he used them, particularly when handling something he loved: the grapes, the fine wines they produced, or the rare volumes in his excellent library, where he and Simone would sit, night after night, talking until the early hours, talking as she had never done with anyone, ever before.

She felt the sweet juice of the grape in her mouth. It was perfect. She savoured it for a moment before returning to the debate.

'Yes, but what I mean is, your ideas are simply a justification of your way of life. You're just an instinctive conservative.'

'Perhaps so, but it depends what you want to conserve, doesn't it? Perhaps I want to preserve freedom from your Great Beast.'

They had stopped at the edge of the vineyard, at a gate overlooking the estate. They leaned on the rough wooden rail, looking out. Beyond, in the distance was the brown dome of the Mont Ventoux; below, in the valley of the Rhône, was a white unmetalled road along which a horse-drawn cart and its attendant cloud of dust could be seen making its way down towards the town. Ranged alongside the road stood a line of new pylons carrying the electricity supply across the Rhône.

'The world's changing,' Thibon said. 'Look down there: the fields we sow by hand and plough with horses. They'll soon be ploughed by tractors. The contact with the land will be broken, the roots in the soil will wither. These homes where our workers have lived for generations, they'll be cottages for holidaymakers from the towns. I've seen it happen near Paris already.'

Simone looked at his profile as he was speaking. Although he was nearly as old as her father, she could see in him the same qualities that had attracted her in Pierre Letellier: the combination of deep learning, profound convictions and a sure, decisive strength that seemed drawn from the land itself. But whereas Pierre had left the country for the city, and she had watched his idealism slowly become the servant of a ruthless modern creed, Thibon seemed as independent and as rooted as one of his own vine trees. Although he was speaking of change, Simone wished that this time in Saint Marcel would never pass away.

●○●

Meinwen

The stranger's name was James Hudson. He was an American from Virginia, of Scottish and Irish extraction, and some English. And he was a shaman.

Meinwen was used to spaced-out hippies who claimed to be druids but who couldn't tell an oak tree from a telegraph pole, and who thought that a diet of magic mushrooms was the equivalent of hard-won spiritual insight. Theirs was the kind of superficial exoticism which wanted to borrow the lucrative magic word 'Celtic' to sell everything from samba music to samosas, but which studiously avoided any contact with real-live Celtic-speaking Celts. But James possessed none of the insubstantiality, none of the impermanence, none of the shallow, shifty self-dramatisation of the New Agers she had met before. Less than twelve months into his Welsh sojourn – he had come to study Celtic shamanism – he seemed as stable and as calm as the oak tree against which they were leaning.

Meinwen found herself asking question after question about shamanism. Was it a religion? Apparently, no; it was a set of practices for altering consciousness. Did it have a heaven? It seemed it didn't, not in the Christian sense, but it believed in the transmigration of souls. Was it old, or was it some modern cobbled-together hotch-potch like wicca? It was old, she learned. Very, very old indeed.

Thibon

'This landscape won't be lived and worked,' Thibon was saying. 'It won't be experienced and felt. It'll be viewed like a watercolour. Visited by motorists and picnickers from the cities. And when our roots have died, what will we be left with? What fruit will grow on the pylons of our modern world? What birds will sing on them? What sacrament will there be of man and nature then?'

Simone did not disagree. She thought for a moment.

'Sacraments. Do you believe in them?' she asked.

Thibon was getting used to Simone's elided and unsettling

dialectic. Initially he had found it bewildering, exhausting even. Now he was more familiar with it, he found it ever more invigorating. It was like fencing with a master: at first there seemed no pattern to discern, no way to counter the strokes. But on closer study, the artistry behind the subtlety could be discerned, and you could learn from it; painfully and slowly, but you could learn. He thought of the book of Proverbs: 'As iron sharpens iron, so one person sharpeneth another.' His mind had sharpened all right – it had had to – in the months since Simone had been staying with him. He knew he could afford to collect his thoughts a moment before replying.

'Oh yes, I believe in the sacraments,' he said. 'Bread and wine, earth, sunlight, beauty. They all embody God.'

'And the Church?'

'Another sacrament. Imperfect, material. But so's everything in this life.'

Simone turned to look at him.

'Gustav... can you take the Catholic sacrament without being a Catholic?'

Thibon was nonplussed, but he realised it was a serious question deserving of a serious answer.

'I'm not a priest. I don't know. But I will ask.'

Meinwen

James told Meinwen he had learned the Native American languages because he had become increasingly conscious of inhabiting a land which had been taken by force or by deceit from its original people. It had been as though the Indian names on his childhood landscape – Susquehanna, Rapahannock, Delaware – had been calling him to interpret them. He had responded, studying the languages in the only way that was possible, by living with the Native American communities, and slowly travelling the uneasy spectrum from mutual discomfort, through to painful encounter, to growing understanding and finally to deep identification. Further along the journey, many years and two languages later, he could understand the sense of dispossession, the hunger for wholeness and justice of all uprooted and displaced peoples. And he had been initiated into the dream quests, fastings, rituals and spiritual practices that had made him a shaman. Now he travelled 'where the wind leads', as he put it, campaigning, learning and, sometimes, teaching.

As the drumming and whistling went on in front of them, Meinwen found herself telling James of her frustrations; of her fear for what would happen to her own indigenous people and her own native culture, of her weariness at the seemingly hope-less struggle. She told him of the times she felt close to despair; to real, bottomless, paralysing despair. She had heard of the problems of alcoholism among the Native Americans, and for the first time she realised just how many of her nationalist friends seemed to be seeking in alcohol an internal haven from external pressures. In both cases, she could understand the hopelessness that sought oblivion in the bottle.

He listened; the wind stirred the oak tree's branches, rustling the leaves.

'Sometimes I just think it's hopeless,' she said. 'The more we seem to press our case, the more hostility we seem to get. It seems like they won't be happy until they've driven us out of our own country altogether.'

He nodded. His experience with the Native Americans had made this kind of narrative all too familiar, he said. The world over, majority cultures systematically defeated, dispossessed, demonised, and destroyed native societies. And then, when they were safely dead, and only then, they romanticised them.

Meinwen was telling James the things she could not tell anyone else; things she had scarcely admitted to herself. She found herself in that confessional mode that can sometimes be triggered by sudden intimacy with a sympathetic stranger one is unlikely to meet again. He let her talk, his silence drawing out her confidences.

'I can't give up. I've given my life to the campaign. But we're losing. Nothing we do seems to make any difference.'

'Have you told anyone how you feel?'

'No. No one. Not even Dewi.'

She looked over at where Dewi was talking with Mei and some other campaigners.

'Dewi's your boyfriend?' James asked.

'No... well... no. But we've been friends for years. He's my... closest friend.'

James smiled.

'So, wouldn't he understand, then?'

'I don't know. But telling him would seem like... a betrayal somehow.'

'A betrayal of what?'

'I'm not sure. Our past. Everything we've ever fought for.'

She thought a little more.

'And I suppose it'd feel like I'm betraying him personally. I don't want to hurt him. He's always been so faithful. It feels like... if I said I had doubts, then everything would fall apart. I couldn't bear that.'

James thought for a while. Then he said, with a kindly irony.

'So... it all depends on you...?'

Meinwen looked down.

'No. Of course not. But... I don't know... I suppose it does feel like everything depends on me. Sometimes. Most of the time, really.'

James said nothing, but simply kept his understanding half smile. Meinwen thought a little more.

'Dewi depends on me.'

'And you worry what he'd think of you?'

'I suppose so, yes. I don't want to disappoint him. It would be like breaking faith with him, with what we believe in.'

'It's a strange thing, faith,' said James. 'I was raised Catholic. Altar boy, *Ave Maria*, the rosary – everything. I used to think I had faith. I never really questioned it. Then I experienced doubt...'

He paused, as if detained by the memory. Meinwen was not sure if he planned to continue.

'And...?'

'And... that's when I found out what faith really means.'

For all that Meinwen found it so easy to talk to him, she was finding that he didn't seem to want to give her simple answers. It was as though he was guarding a secret he wasn't sure she would understand.

Meinwen had entered on the conversation expecting a discussion of campaigning tactics, a comparing of notes on the relative strength of Native American and Welsh cultures, and a comradely, confirmatory debate about the relative intransigence of the regimes they challenged. Instead, within this brief exchange, she had found herself in the dangerous territory of her unexpressed feelings and her deepest beliefs. Or were they beliefs? After this short talk with the American, she was wondering if she really believed them at all any more.

'I think I've lost my faith,' she said, and was immediately shocked at the truth. What James had meant by faith was not entirely clear to Meinwen, but she meant her faith in the ultimate victory of her cause. She looked at him, but he simply nodded, as if he had already known what she was going to say.

'Do you have faith now?' Meinwen asked.

'I'm American, remember? I believe in happy endings.' The half smile was back again.

Meinwen looked down. Welsh people didn't do happy endings, she thought. Dying young, being oppressed, drinking themselves into an early grave, they did that just fine; but winning, no, winning was for other people. She wished she had whatever it was James had got: that unhurried, trustful calm.

'Seriously, though,' she began again: 'How do you carry on? What do you tell yourself?'

James' half smile faded. She had asked him to be serious, and now he was: he pondered the question for what seemed like a long while. In front of them, the drumming from the protest seemed to be reaching some sort of a crescendo. Finally, James looked back up at Meinwen.

'Everything must change,' he said. 'That's the only way new life can come.'

Across the field, there was the sound of applause. The rally was breaking up. In a minute or so, the chance for further conversation would be over. Meinwen looked at James and asked simply: 'What should I do?'

James sat back against the tree. He was looking out beyond the demonstration, beyond the factory, and beyond the mountains into the clouds in the west. When he eventually spoke, there was something of that distance in his voice.

'*Bydd gall fel sarff, ddiniwed fel colomen,*' he said, then looked at Meinwen, the half smile back on his peaceful suntanned face.

She recognised the words from the epistles. 'Be wise as serpents, innocent as doves.'

Was that the answer, or just another question?

She was still pondering the significance of the words, when she saw Dewi and Mei and the others coming through the crowd towards them. She and James stood up, and went to meet them. Back to reality, she thought. There were a few introductions for politeness' sake, and then James excused himself, leaving the Welsh speakers to themselves. Meinwen watched him go until he was lost in the crowd of departing demonstrators. He had said little in response to her confidences, but what he had said seemed to have gone deep. It was just that she didn't know exactly what it meant.

His protest duties completed for the day, Mei was ready to celebrate. Any day of a demo was a high holiday for him, and had been ever since the heady days of the protest against the Investiture of the Prince of Wales at the end of the 1960s. His radicalism had its own reassuring traditions, as unchanging as those of any monarchy.

'Let's go back to that pub!' he said.

The crew walked off towards the town. Another protest – another sesh, thought Meinwen. Tonight we're going to party like it's 1969.

Perrin

Father Joseph-Marie Perrin looked thoughtful. He had not been a priest for long, but he wondered even if he had been in holy orders for a lifetime whether he would ever have had to consider such a strange request. Nothing in the seminary had prepared him for it. His friend Gustav Thibon was explaining the case to him as they walked through the cloisters of the Dominican convent in Marseilles. It was a warm summer morning, and the moths were fluttering among the white roses along the convent wall as they passed by.

'She wants to belong to the church, Joseph. She wants to take the sacraments, but she wants complete freedom of belief. She doesn't want to be bound by the church's creeds.'

They found a bench in the shade, and sat down. Thibon continued.

'She doesn't want orthodoxy to be a precondition of her belonging. She thinks the church's sacraments should be open to everyone, regardless of belief – or lack of belief.'

'She sounds a bit of a dilletante. Is she really serious?'

Thibon laughed.

'I've never met anyone more serious!'

He shook his head, then continued in earnest.

'You should know something else,' Joseph. 'I've watched her drawing nearer and nearer to the Christian faith. She listens to the mass. She reads the prayer book. But she has one major objection – the attitude of the church towards the Jewish people.'

'Well, you know my own views on that,' said Perrin. 'And for that matter, all the brothers here are the same. She needn't worry that she'll find any anti-semitism here.'

'It's not anti-semitism that worries her, it's *philo*-semitism.'

'But I thought you said she was Jewish?'

'She is.'

'What – she's... self-hating?'

'Not exactly. It's more complex than that. She's no great lover of her Jewish heritage, it's true. But it's more a question of theology than identity. She thinks the Old Testament is just a document of tribal hatred, and she thinks Christianity should repudiate it. She thinks the God of the Old Testament and the God of the New are opposed to one another.'

'But that's absurd. Does she know Our Lord was a Jew? Has she actually *read* the New Testament?'

'She's read it in the *Greek*, Joseph. She can *recite* most of it.'

Perrin frowned. He removed his glasses and began to clean them on his coarse white robe.

'Well, I'm sorry, but it sounds to me like intellect without understanding. I don't doubt what you say about her intellectual gifts, but are you sure she's not just some kind of crank?'

Thibon shook his head.

'I'm certain.'

He hesitated as though considering whether he should continue. Then, with an air of decision, he went on.

'I tell you, Joseph, there's a clear mysticism that shines out from her. I've never come across any other human being so familiar with religious mysteries. I've never felt the word "supernatural" to mean more, to seem more real, than when I'm with her.'

Perrin replaced his glasses and looked up with new interest from behind his thick lenses. There was a hint of a smile.

'She seems to have made... quite an impression on you...'

Thibon recognised the half-suggestion, but gave a slight shake of his head.

'It's not like that.'

Perrin's smile had not quite vanished as Thibon continued.

'One day, she asked me to take her to the church in Saint Marcel. It was a weekday. So I took her down with me, showed her in, and left her there while I went to pay some calls. I left her sitting in front of the reserved sacrament.

'When I came back a couple of hours later, she was still there. She hadn't moved at all. I've never seen such complete... attention. It was like she was opening herself up to the divine presence completely. Like she was allowing herself to be... irradiated by it.'

Perrin thought for a while.

'Very well,' he said. 'I warn you, I'm still sceptical, but now I'm intrigued as well. Please ask her to come and see me.'

Meinwen

In the aftermath of the Haverfordwest protest, Meinwen was asked to take part in a television discussion on the subject of the economy in rural Wales. Meinwen was aware that she knew about as much about economics as she did about astrophysics. Her only economic interests were who owned the local shops and whether the signage was bilingual; beyond that, questions of GDP and disposable income were largely meaningless to her. But she knew that as far as the programme-makers were concerned, she could be relied upon to turn up and to have something to say, which was what mattered.

This time, the interview was in an independent studio in Caernarfon, so Meinwen did not have to make the gruelling bus journey to Cardiff. The programme was a daytime one, and the slots were longer and the approach a bit more relaxed than for the prime-time current-affairs shows. In the green room, Meinwen found herself sitting next to the other part of the 'one-plus-two', Sir Anthony Thomas. He was doing the cross-word as usual.

'Here we are again,' he smiled.

'*Yma o hyd*,' she said. 'We're still here.' The words were the title of a nationalist anthem, expressing the irrepressible endurance of the Welsh people, and she had intended her use of them now as sarcasm. Sir Anthony seemed not to notice.

He put the newspaper aside, and laid his silver pen carefully on the half-finished puzzle. He had the gift of making easy conversation with anyone.

'I read your articles on Simone Weil,' he said, as Meinwen sat down.

'Did you?' Meinwen was surprised. The articles had been for a magazine whose readership, she had assumed, was entirely nationalist.

'Yes. I do read *Gair* occasionally. It's good for my Welsh. It has some interesting material now and again. Like your articles. I wanted to ask you something about them.'

'Go ahead.'

'Well, I was wondering: isn't Weil rather a strange role model for a Welsh nationalist? A conflicted figure, I've always thought. Didn't she rather hate herself, as a Jew and as a woman?'

'Maybe,' Meinwen replied, wondering what trap this old fox was preparing for her this time. But she was always ready to discuss Simone, so she went on, although cautiously.

'She was conflicted certainly. But you have to think about her experience as a Jewish woman subjected to pressure to assimilate. She had the kind of culture-shame many minorities have. It's common enough in Wales, after all. But she understands the importance of community so deeply. I wish more people took community seriously.'

She intended the last sentence as a barb. But again, it seemed not to have had any effect. Sir Anthony just nodded.

'Thank you,' he said thoughtfully. 'I can see what you mean.'

Meinwen knew she was on shaky ground. During his military career, Sir Anthony had spent a couple of years as a liaison officer between the British and French forces, and he had an interest in French history. He had even published articles on the politics of inter-war France, albeit in academic rather than political journals. She recalled reading one of his pieces not long ago while doing some research. If he wanted to, he could quote Simone in the original and make Meinwen look like an amateur, as she had only read Simone's work in English translation. She remembered how Sir Anthony had outflanked her in that radio interview about pacifism. Was he planning something like that again? What had this conversation just been? A kind of verbal reconnaissance before the big offensive? Probably. Sometimes Meinwen felt weary of living her life in a constant state of high security.

●○●

Perrin

A few days after the meeting with Thibon, Father Perrin was sitting on the same bench outside the convent chapel, this time with Simone.

'This is what troubles me,' she was saying 'the church can declare people anathema. Sinners, heretics. The anathema is nothing more than totalitarianism. I can't accept that anyone should be excluded from the sacraments like that. The sacraments should be available to everyone.'

'That's really not possible.'

'Why not? Why must you exclude anyone?'

'There has to be understanding. There has to be faith, otherwise the sacraments lose their meaning.'

'There has to be compassion, openness, too.'

'Yes, but, the laws of the church... you have to be baptised. You can't have the benefits without the beliefs... that relationship would just be false.'

Simone closed her eyes at the words. Then she looked up again, leaning forward slightly as she spoke.

'Not "false",' she said. 'That's hurtful. I think what you mean is "non-orthodox".'

'Well, yes,' said Perrin, taken aback. 'I suppose that is what I meant.' There was something almost desperate in Simone's frankness. Every minute was like a conversation on a gallows, climactic, fateful, with the vertiginous drop of error or dishonesty only moments, or inches, away. Simone was still speaking.

'Equating "false" and "non-orthodox" is confusing your terms, and that's incompatible with being perfectly intellectually honest. It can't possibly please Christ, as He is the Truth. I think this is really a serious imperfection in you.'

Perrin swallowed. No priest in a confessional could be as blunt as that. And yet, he could not deny that she was right in what she said. What's more, she was clearly speaking without rancour. He resisted the temptation to justify himself, and he let her continue.

'After all,' Simone was saying, 'why should you have any imperfection in you? It doesn't suit you in any way to be imperfect. It's like having a wrong note in a song. You see, this imperfection comes from you having attached yourself to the Church as if it were some kind of an earthly country. It's natural. It's understandable, but a fine thread – an infinitely fine thread – can hold a bird down just as much as a heavy iron chain can. You have to break it if you want to fly. Although...' she conceded a slight smile at last, 'I know that's frightening.'

Perrin took a deep breath. 'Yes,' he said. 'It is frightening to depend on God alone.'

He was glad he had allowed Simone to continue. However, while he could recognise the unsettling implications for himself of Simone's analysis, he nonetheless felt secure in God's mercy, and however beneficial for him might be her counsels of perfection, he knew that just now she needed him more than he needed her. He had to shift the focus of this conversation back to the object of her visit.

'Well, let us say your views are "non-orthodox",' he said. 'But that doesn't alter the fact that orthodoxy is still – for good or ill – something the Church requires before it can admit anyone to the sacraments.'

Simone was nodding, impatient to begin speaking again.

'Look, I don't want to shock you,' she said. 'I'd hate to do that. But I have to make this clear. I love God, Christ and the Catholic faith as much as anyone so inadequate can do. I love the saints – well, most of them, anyway – I love those Catholics I've met who seem to be truly spiritual. I love the liturgy, the hymns, the architecture, the ceremonies, all of it.

'But I haven't got the slightest love for the Church as an organisation. Not a bit. It seems to me that as a social structure it belongs to the Prince of this World. I couldn't possibly subscribe to it as an organisation.'

'Nothing in this world is perfect, Simone. You know that. I think you're setting impossible standards. At some point you simply have to trust that God will work despite the imperfections of human structures. You're clearly a very intelligent woman, but thought isn't everything. There's experience, ritual...'

Simone nodded her agreement.

'Yes, I know. I've experienced that: you can't reach the state of constant inner prayer unless you've worn out your will first by keeping rules.'

Perrin was encouraged: 'That's right. There's the beauty of nature, the blessing of music, of silent contemplation...'

Simone was enthusiastic now: 'Yes. Silence. Do you experience that as well? There's such a harmony there; more perfect than anything you experience from sound.'

'Er... yes. Yes, that's right.'

'But even the most beautiful silence in the world is like a noise if you compare it with the silence of God. Is that what you've felt too?'

Perrin nodded cautiously. He had felt what she described, but not with anything like the same urgency or intensity. He was beginning to realise just what Thibon had seen in this restless, troubled young woman.

In the background, the chapel bell began to toll, calling to mass. Perrin stood up. He and Simone walked towards the chapel.

'My child. You want so much to join the church. You are so isolated. Inside, I promise you, you would find peace. You have such a desire to do good. You could do great things for mankind. There's a Catholic circle which is always ready to welcome all who wish to become part of it.'

The enthusiasm faded from Simone's voice, and her brow furrowed.

'That's just the thing. I don't want to be adopted into a circle. I'm afraid of this feeling of Church patriotism. It acts as though the Church were a homeland. I'm afraid of it because I fear I might catch it. It would kill me. I can't bear the idea of separating myself from all the people who aren't fortunate enough to believe.'

A few congregants were beginning to cross the quadrangle on their way to the chapel. Only a few.

'I don't want to live my life among people who say "we"; I don't want to be part of an "us", I don't want to be "at home" in any human setting, of any kind.'

She paused for a moment, as if unsatisfied with her explanation, then went on.

'No, I'm expressing myself very badly. I'd like it very much. I'd find it delightful. But I don't feel it's permissible for me. I feel it's necessary – no, it's ordained – that I should be alone, a stranger, exiled from every human circle. No exceptions.'

They had stopped at the open door of the chapel. Through it, they could see the shining altar and could hear the preliminary organ music as the preparations for the service went ahead. All the *bragadoccio* and beauty of Catholic holiness; Perrin's natural home, Simone's unreachable ideal. They had no more words. It was an impasse.

They remained for a moment in the church porch, listening to the music. Over in the sanctuary, the acolytes were lighting the candles and preparing the elements of the eucharist. Amongst all the splendid externals, the rite really used such simple things: bread, wine, flowers, flame. The simplicity beyond complexity; the simplicity Perrin knew that Simone longed to experience beyond all the obstacles and mazes of her mind.

An elderly couple murmured a greeting as they walked past them on their way in to mass; two of the Catholics for whom this religion was part of their blood and bones; two who felt no impediment on their path to the miracle of the broken bread. They went into the chapel. Perrin blessed Simone and went inside himself. The heavy door closed behind him, leaving Simone outside.

Meinwen

The interview on the rural economy was halfway through, and had reached the question of the importance of community, when Sir Anthony, with the finesse which allowed him to manipulate social situations – even televised ones – to fit his own agenda, decided to depart from the role of passive answerer of questions and to turn interrogator himself.

'I have a question for Meinwen, if I may,' he said.

Here we go, thought Meinwen. At least Sir Anthony

would attack her more politely than John Sayle did. But if the rapier wasn't as messy a weapon as the battleaxe, it was still deadly. She recalled that bruising radio interview about militarism. She would have to have her wits about her if she wasn't to emerge from this one too looking like a novice. Bring it on.

'Tell me,' he said. 'On this question of community, you've quoted Simone Weil, the French philosopher, in your recent articles. Isn't she rather a strange role model for a Welsh nationalist? A conflicted figure, almost self-hating, I've always thought.'

It was the same question he'd asked her in the green room. Almost word for word. What was he up to?

'Maybe,' she replied. 'She was certainly a conflicted personality. But then, she was Jewish, and they were under pressure to assimilate, and that often causes what sociologists call culture-shame, a rejection of your own culture in favour of the majority one. That's one of our problems in Wales, so she's certainly worth studying with that in mind. And she's superb on the question of rootedness – the need to belong.'

A slightly fuller answer than she'd given in the green room, but essentially this was the same conversation. She felt she was in Groundhog Day. She waited for whatever attack was coming next. But Sir Anthony only nodded thoughtfully, and when he spoke it was with a note of respect.

'Yes, I see what you mean,' he said. 'Thank you.'

The interview continued, the presenter deftly picking up the thread of inspirational figures, and now asking Sir Anthony about what personalities had proved an inspiration for his own political thought.

Only when the programme was coming to an end did Meinwen realise what Sir Anthony had done – he had deliberately given her a simple question so she could look good at his expense.

Why? She couldn't imagine a reason, and she could only attribute it to some strange impulse of goodwill on his part towards her. Perhaps he was trying to make up for that radio interview.

After the sound engineer had unclipped her microphone, Meinwen thought she had better let Sir Anthony know she wasn't completely naive and graceless. It wouldn't hurt her to acknowledge what he'd done. She walked over to where he was fetching his overcoat from the coat-stand. He had used the only coathanger to maintain the charcoal grey garment's perfect shape.

'Thank you for that question,' she said.

He looked pleased, and turned towards her as he folded his coat neatly over his arm.

'Not at all,' he said. 'I was getting bored talking about house prices anyway. It's nice to discuss ideas for a change sometimes, isn't it?'

'I suppose so,' she said. She was trying to be polite, but, even now, the idea of having anything other than an argument with a Tory seemed to her like an unnatural act. Simply thanking him at all had exhausted her resources of cross-party cordiality.

'I often feel that in politics we do too much... point-scoring,' he went on. There was a hesitation in his voice, unusual for him. 'Sometimes... you can learn the most interesting things from people who have very different views from your own. I miss the chance for a proper discussion sometimes.'

Meinwen could agree in theory with what he said, but she had no actual experience of the kind of meeting of opposites which he was talking about. So she simply nodded. She could think of nothing else to say.

'Don't you ever feel a bit – how can I put it – isolated, sometimes? I know I do.'

Meinwen thought she understood. He was trying to explain why he'd been so severe with her in that radio interview. Trying to suggest it was pressure of work or something. OK, she thought, she could be conciliatory.

'Don't worry about it,' she said.

She wondered if there wasn't a trace of disappointment in his eyes as he accepted that the conversation had come to an end. She couldn't imagine why. He picked up his briefcase.

'Can I offer you a lift anywhere?' he asked.

'No thanks. Dewi's going to pick me up.'

'I see. Well... well, we must talk again sometime,' he said, as he smiled at her, and left.

●○●

Simone

Simone was working alone in the hayfield, raking the hay into piles ready to be stacked. It was a hot day, the hottest of the year so far, surely. She wiped the perspiration from her forehead, put down the rake and walked to the edge of the field. She picked a few berries from the hedge, filling her hand with them and eating as she walked. She stopped at the gate where it overlooked the valley, and then sat down, leaning against the rough, warm wood. She closed her eyes and rested for a moment, then she took out her notebook from her knapsack and began to write.

'I cannot imagine why God should need to love me, when I feel so clearly that even with human beings, any affection they show towards me can only be a mistake. But I can easily conceive that he could love that perspective of creation which it is only possible to see from the point which I occupy. But I have to withdraw so that God can make contact with the creatures chance has placed before my path and whom he loves. My presence there is tactless, as though I were coming between two lovers or between two friends. If only I knew how I could disappear, then there could be a perfect union of love between God and the earth which I tread, and the sea which I hear... May I disappear so that the things that I see may become perfectly beautiful from the very fact that they are no longer things that I see.

'I do not have the slightest wish that this created world should fade from my sight, simply that it should no longer be me personally to whom it shows itself. It cannot tell its secret to me. It is too high. If I am taken away, then creator and creature are free to exchange their secrets. To see a landscape as it is when I am not present... when I am in any place, I disturb the silence of heaven and earth by my breathing and the beating of my heart.'

She closed her eyes and drank in the silence of the high field. The warmth of the sun, the scent of the hay, the pleasant ache of rest after labour, the joy of present solitude sharpened by the anticipation of later companionship. She had never been happier. In all her years of searching, this was the closest she had ever been to contentment. The silence was like an embrace. The only kind of embrace she would ever permit herself.

Then she became aware of a noise. Footsteps. Heavy, hurrying footsteps. She opened her eyes. Thibon was hastening across the field towards her. She got up as he approached, brushing wisps of hay from her skirt. Thibon was red-faced and looked agitated. He stopped for a moment to get his breath back.

'Your parents have got places on a boat,' he said.

Simone closed her eyes and turned away. This meant the end of harvests, the end of watching sunsets after work in the fields, the end of conversations with Perrin and with Thibon.

'They've got a place for you as well,' Thibon was explaining. 'They won't go without you. I'm sorry, Simone. They're so afraid of the anti-Jewish laws. And they have reason to be. I simply won't be able to guarantee your safety here indefinitely. They're putting men more influential than me in the concentration camps.'

Feeling the tears spring to her eyes, Simone turned away, looking out across the valley. She wanted to take it in fully before it faded from her sight; she wanted to pack the scene into her memory to sustain her in the uncertain future. Thibon was still speaking.

'The steamer's leaving tomorrow from Marseilles. It should be in Morocco in a day or so. From there, you may be able to get to America. Your parents are already packing. You must go. I'm so sorry.'

Simone turned to him. She felt more compassion than grief. She realised she was more concerned at his distress than her own danger. She reached out to his arm, surprising herself with the involuntary gesture of comfort. As she touched him, he immediately embraced her. In the sudden, amazing proximity, she felt his strong arms constrain her body, though leaving her own arms free. Tentatively, she placed her hands on the warm, rough cloth of his jacket, and pressed, gently. She could feel his jerky breathing as he wept. They had never even shaken hands before. She knew this was the first and last time they would ever touch, and she knew that he knew that too.

'Simone. My Jewish friend.' His voice was hoarse. 'I have learned so much from you.'

Simone's voice was a whisper: 'And I from you.'

They remained in the embrace for a few moments more. Then Simone disengaged herself and reached into her knapsack.

'Here, take these.' She handed him her notebooks. 'Look after them for me. If you think you can use any of this in one of your own books, please feel free. I think these ideas will have better luck if they're joined with your name than with mine. I don't think my fortune in this world will ever be good.'

As Thibon received the books from her, Simone said simply. 'You are my closest friend.'

Thibon was too choked to do more than nod his reciprocation. Finally, he said.

'*Adieu*. Until we meet again, in this world or the next.'

Simone looked at him seriously.

'In the next world, there is no meeting again.'

She could see Thibon's regret that she could not relax her intellectual rigour even at this moment. She smiled.

'There'll be no need to meet,' she said. 'We'll all be one.'

He nodded. He could find nothing more to say. They were both in tears.

●○●

Meinwen

Meinwen was being chased across the hills by American jet fighters. Every time she tried to get up to run, another one would swoop down on her, its engine screaming, the sound filling the whole sky, an empire of decibels, a hegemony of noise, an illegal occupation of her whole consciousness. She'd never be able to make it back to Yr Hafan.

But she was in Yr Hafan. In bed. Light was coming in through the window. It was morning.

The jets were still screaming, though. She tried to collect her scattered thoughts.

No, it wasn't jets, it was something next door. Some kind of machinery.

She got up, rubbed the sleep from her eyes and went to the window. As her eyes adjusted to the sudden sunlight, she could see, at the base of Hermon's grey walls, Connor busy with some machine, working in a cloud of dust. God, couldn't these settlers leave well enough alone? They always had to strip paint from wood, chip plaster off walls, sand down the stonework until it was bare, always digging down to some supposed state of earlier simplicity, ignoring the troubling complexity around them.

She looked at the clock. It was only half past eight. On Saturday morning. Surely whatever he was doing could wait until a less ungodly hour. But then, she thought, as she pulled on her sweater and jeans, Connor probably didn't believe in godly hours. Goddess-ly hours perhaps. She pushed her bare feet into her hiking shoes, went out of the house and walked over towards Hermon, or Cloud Temple.

She walked up to Connor, and waited until the machine stopped for a moment before she spoke.

'Connor, can't this wait until a bit later in the day?'

Connor turned round, pulling the protective goggles from his eyes, and giving Meinwen a friendly smile.

'Hi, Manwen.' After knowing her for three months, he still hadn't bothered to learn how to pronounce her name properly.

But that wasn't Meinwen's main concern just now. As the dust cleared, she saw what Connor had been doing. He'd been using an angle grinder to remove the carved wording from the foundation stones at the base of the chapel. Where previously, the giants of the cause who had laboured and sacrificed to build Hermon had been commemorated in sandstone lettering, now there was only bare scraped stone. The cloud of witnesses had become a cloud of dust. She stared at the now wordless masonry.

'What have you done?!'

Connor straightened up. 'Oh, those old inscriptions,' he said. 'Bad vibes, you know? We needed a new start. I'm going to carve some symbols there instead.' It was clear he hadn't the faintest idea of the significance of his actions.

'But, those were the people who built this chapel!' Meinwen could hardly find the words. 'Those people have relatives still living round here. That was our history!'

'Yeah, but it's our house now, and, you know, a new start. A clean slate, like.'

Meinwen was numb. She couldn't begin to try to argue. She almost ran back to Yr Hafan.

She threw herself down on the sofa, and hugged her knees to her chest. Not even the words on the stones. They won't even leave the words on the stones. We're being scoured out of history while we're still alive. It's like a nightmare. Not even Yr Hafan was a haven any more. She had reached the end.

She thought of things she could say to Connor. The argument chased itself round her mind, trying to find the words that would make the noise stop, make things be as they were, stop them changing. The argument was in English, the words finding ever more familiar routes through her brain. Not even her mind was safe. English was pushing into it, colonising it cell by cell, possessing its neural pathways, Saxonising its synapses, supplanting, renaming, uprooting.

Outside, the angle grinder started up again, the sound cutting through the air, through the walls of Yr Hafan, through Meinwen's head. She put her hands over her ears and wept.

●○●

Simone

Simone stepped over the rubble and broken glass on the pavement. Usually, a day or so after an air-raid, paths were cleared through the debris so that pedestrians could pass. But this wreckage was too recent, the product of last night's German bombing attack on London. By now, in 1943, air raids were less common than during the early years of the war, but they still happened, and they still brought disruption and death.

Simone looked at the entrances of the office buildings she passed, searching for the number she wanted. She found it, the headquarters of the Free French forces. A large tricolour was hanging from the portico. She showed her identification card to the guard on the door, and was allowed in.

Inside, she was directed up the stairs and down a long corridor. At the end, another guard examined her papers before showing her into the office.

It was makeshift and cluttered, and had a furled tricolour flag standing in one corner. Sitting behind the untidy desk was an official in Free French uniform. Simone greeted him, and he introduced himself as Henri Closon, aide to General Charles de Gaulle. She handed him her letter of introduction and her *curriculum vitae*, and he motioned her to sit down.

As he read through the papers, she looked around her, finding a pleasing familiarity in the maps of France and the French language on the spines of the books. She tilted her head slightly to see what kind of library M'sieur Closon kept by him.

Military manuals, of course; a simple guide to English grammar; two biographies of Napoleon, one of which she knew was friendly to the self-proclaimed emperor, and the other critical; several histories of France; and the *Pensées* of Blaise Pascal. She looked at Closon with new interest.

He began reading out loud from the papers she had given him:

'Exceptional grades from the *Normale*. Third-highest in all France. Eight languages. A schoolteacher...'

He started to look puzzled.

'... in Le Puy, Auxerre, Roanne. Six months work in the... Renault factory. Three months at the Alsthom engineering plant. A writer for the *Worker's Voice*, the *Anarcho-Syndicalists' Journal*.'

He looked up frowning.

'You're an anarchist?'

'Anarcho-*syndicalist*. Or I used to be. I was in sympathy with them, anyway.'

'I... I see. You're not a member of any political group now?'

'No. I've never found an untainted cause,' she said simply. 'I hope I've found one now.'

Closon coughed slightly and reasserted his polite, official manner. He returned to the document, noticing the next item with some evident relief.

'Ah... I see you worked for the Resistance in Marseilles. Distributing literature. What kind of literature?'

'A magazine attacking fascism and racism, and the anti-Jewish laws.'

'You didn't get caught?'

'The police questioned me many times. But they only ever warned me and let me go.'

'You were lucky. How did you manage to get away from France?'

'Through Marseilles, then Morocco. And I was in New York for seven months trying to get permission to come here.'

'Very well. Now you're here, what can you do for us, Mademoiselle Weil?'

'I want to be a nurse.'

'A nurse? Well, we certainly need nurses in our hospitals. Especially ones who can speak French here in England.'

'No. Not in England.'

'What do you mean?'

'I mean a front-line nurse.'

'There's no such thing.'

'Not yet. But look. This is my plan.'

She pulled out a letter from her briefcase and handed it to him as she carried on with her explanation.

'A team of perhaps twenty young women. Dedicated, self-sacrificing. Trained in battlefield first-aid techniques. Ready to go to the thick of the fighting to help and comfort the wounded.'

Closon looked incredulous.

'And to be killed and wounded themselves! Do you know what the casualty rate is for front-line medics? It's higher than for the fighting soldiers!'

'Yes! That's the point. It would set an example of heroism, of sacrifice! Think of the effect it would have on morale: the example of young women, ready to lay down their lives to help others without thought of self. What could be more inspiring? We'd have a complete moral victory over the fascists!'

'Wait a minute...'

'Tacitus says the ancient Germans used to put young maidens in the front line of the battle, surrounded by young warriors to protect them, because of the effect it had on their fighting spirit.'

'But that was two thousand years ago!' Closon almost laughed.

'The principle is still the same,' Simone said.

'So,' he said, resorting to sarcasm, 'where do you think you would find twenty young women prepared for martyrdom?'

'Well, here's one to start with.'

Closon looked bewildered.

'I didn't see anything in your application about you having nursing training.'

'No. But I've thought of that. I've started on it today. I've bought a book!'

She gave him what she hoped was a disarming smile, pulled out a Field First Aid manual from her bag and displayed it as if it explained everything.

Closon had had enough.

'This is absurd! Do you expect me to go to de Gaulle and offer the services of an untrained schoolmistress for some kind of suicide mission just because you think it will raise morale?!'

'Just show him my plan. He's a man of vision. He'll understand.'

Closon tried to hold her gaze for a moment, then turned away.

In the brief silence that followed, they both found themselves looking at the flag of France where it leaned against the wall as if waiting to be picked up and carried into battle by some modern-day Jeanne d'Arc.

●○●

Meinwen

Meinwen walked into Caernarfon police station, and rang the bell on the stained formica counter. There was no answer. Granted, it was three o'clock in the morning, but weren't they supposed to work twenty-four hours? Where was a police officer when you needed one? She rang again.

She looked around the waiting room. Black plastic chairs with cigarette holes, foam spilling from splits in the covers. Linoleum tiles spotted with chewing gum. Blurred, photocopied posters for missing persons on the walls. 'Misspers' the police called them: Meinwen had been to police stations often enough to pick up some of the vocabulary. But it didn't look like she was going to find anyone to talk to tonight. She held her finger down on the bell.

After several minutes, a door in the room behind the counter creaked open.

'*Duw,* Meinwen!' It was Sergeant Dafydd Williams. Meinwen knew him well. He'd been the custody sergeant on several occasions when she'd been brought in after protests. He was a deacon in Seion chapel, where her father had been a member before he moved to Colwyn Bay.

The policeman's look changed quickly from one of surprise to one of concern. All their other dealings had been in daylight hours following well-publicised protests.

'Is everything all right, *bach*?' he asked.

'Not really,' Meinwen said. 'Everything's not all right at all. Will you please arrest me?'

'What for?'

'Vandalism... what do you call it? Criminal damage.'

'At this time of night? Posters again is it? Oh, come on Meinwen, can't you come back in the morning? We'll have more staff then. There's only me here tonight.'

'It's not posters.'

'Well, paint, whatever. Let's do it in the morning. If I take you in now, I'll have to check your cell every fifteen minutes to make sure you don't do away with yourself. It's the law. I'll be up and down all night like a flag, girl. Come back at nine when the morning shift are in. I'll arrest you then.'

'Dafydd, if you don't arrest me now, I'll go out and use this again.'

She put a claw hammer on the counter. Sergeant Williams stared at it. Members of the Movement didn't use claw hammers. He looked at her, suddenly serious.

'Meinwen, what have you done?'

'You'd better come and see,' she said.

She had smashed the window of every estate agent in Caernarfon. And not just cracked them, but smashed them until the plate glass carpeted the pavement. And she'd torn down the window displays and ripped up the photographs of houses for sale. She and Sergeant Williams looked at the damage. It was an impressive night's work and no mistake. The streetlights made the glass-strewn pavements shine like crystal.

She had not had another night of freedom since that moment. Sergeant Williams had reluctantly taken her into custody, and she had appeared before magistrates the next day. She refused legal representation, did not oppose the remanding in custody which the Crown Prosecutor requested, and was in a bail hostel awaiting her full trial before her fellow activists even knew she had been arrested. For the first time in twenty years of campaigning, she had acted alone, had told no one in advance, and had sought no support subsequently. So there had been none of the placards and groups of supporters, none of the press releases advertising the forthcoming court appearance, none of the usual publicity surrounding the jailing of a campaigner.

Her case was heard five weeks later. It was five weeks of unease and uncertainty for Meinwen's friends. But Meinwen was determined, single-minded, even fatalistic. When she appeared before the bench, she said she had not been acting in the name of the Movement, and that her action was a personal protest against the injustice of the housing market in rural

Wales, and the way indigenous communities were being displaced by wealthy incomers due to uncontrolled market forces. She would accept the sentence of the court, and, when released, she intended to do exactly the same thing again.

She got three months. Her string of previous convictions allowed that length of sentence, and the worryingly destructive nature of her protest had led the magistrates, who were not entirely unsympathetic to her aims, to decide that they needed to show that her actions on this occasion could not be condoned.

After she was taken from the court and the door of her cell closed, Meinwen felt a peace she had not experienced for years.

Closon

Closon knocked at General de Gaulle's office and went in. The general's room, in a converted mansion in Carlton Gardens near the Mall, was more spacious, and tidier, than his own, but it shared the same decoration of a French tricolour. The general, who was reading a letter, looked up as Closon came in.

'You called for me, General.'

De Gaulle handed Closon the letter he had just been reading. He looked at it. It was Simone's plan for front-line nurses.

'She's mad!' the general said.

Closon looked at the letter again. He could see why the general had come to his swift conclusion. In simple black and white, in the absence of Simone's passionate personal advocacy, the plan looked morbid and obsessive. De Gaulle continued.

'Why should she bother me with such nonsense? I thought you said she was a brilliant scholar.'

'She is,' said Closon, embarrassed. He felt the need to explain himself.

'I'm sorry, General,' he continued. 'She was so insistent that she wanted to do something for France. She's made a great effort to get to London at all. She made me promise I would show her plan to you. She's been to see me about it three times already. At least now, I can tell her I've shown it to you and that it's not possible to proceed with it.'

De Gaulle nodded.

'Fine.'

He turned to his other papers, but then looked up again.

'Wait a minute,' he said. 'I've thought of something. Perhaps she can be of some use after all. Although not as a nurse.'

He paused as he thought the matter through for a moment. Then he continued.

'Didn't you say she's an expert on all kinds of left-wing groups?'

'Yes, General. She was a member of many different ones.'

'Not my forté, the Left. But we've got all kinds of groups scrambling for influence for when we liberate France. They're already bombarding me with their manifestos. More than I have time or inclination to read.'

He indicated a tall pile of leaflets on his desk.

'But we can't afford to dismiss them. We'll need a broad base of support. It would be useful to get an inside view. Give her these wretched pamphlets, ask her to summarise them, to boil them down into the most useful parts from all of them, and to give me a brief article on... the rights and responsibilities of France after the war. That might be useful to me. It could help me to form a policy.'

Closon agreed.

'And it will keep her too busy to bother you with this nursing nonsense too,' There was the slightest hint of humour in the general's hooded eyes.

'That would certainly be a relief, Sir.'

He took the pile of leaflets and went out. De Gaulle, having defeated one army of material on his desk, turned his attention to the others.

●○●

Meinwen

Although Meinwen's case had not been an official Movement action, and although she had not allowed the Movement to hold any demonstrations at her court appearance, she had nonetheless received plenty of personal expressions of support. The fact that her action carried an unprecedented element of genuine economic sabotage as well as the usual symbolism, had not deterred most Movement members from feeling sympathy and respect for what she had done. Many had said privately that they wished they possessed her courage, and they regretted that even more effective action could not be taken against those who were asset-stripping Welsh communities. But all the same, no one copied her. They contented themselves with writing letters to the press in her defence and sending personal cards and letters to her in the women's prison in England where she was now incarcerated. Over the years, letter-writing to imprisoned comrades had become an accepted part of activist life and had developed its own conventions: the circumstances of the offence were taken for granted and rarely mentioned, while an effort was made to include positive news and gossip, preferably in detail, in order both to encourage the prisoner and to help fill their endless prison hours.

Mallwyd had written to her, comparing her action with that of Saunders Lewis, D.J. Williams and Lewis Valentine at Penyberth. His letter was crowded with proverbs and figures of speech; he seemed to feel a personal responsibility to keep even the most arthritic idioms in active, if painful, use. He assured her of his support and was certain that she too would become just as much of a symbol of Welsh freedom and of Christian pacifism as the Penyberth Three. Poor Mallwyd, Meinwen thought; Wales, Christianity and pacifism were his triune deity; a tattered, tired trinity. Mallwyd's letter went on to tell her that he was due to be a guest on the television current affairs programme *Under Fire* in a few weeks' time. He said he planned to use the occasion to accuse John Sayle of being racist towards Welsh speakers. Meinwen had to admire Mallwyd's unflagging zeal, the unfashionable faith he wore like a faded suit, which all but he could see was threadbare. She hoped she would still have as positive an outlook as him when she reached his age. But when she tried to imagine that age, she found she couldn't think beyond more than a few weeks into the future. Her horizons and her hopes seemed to be as confined as were her present circumstances.

Mei had written, offering to buy a round and have one hell of a sesh when she came out. He offered to come and fetch her in his car. Knowing the state of Mei's car, and how far away her prison was from Wales, that was also quite a declaration of faith, thought Meinwen, and was a proposal requiring no little trust on her part too. But then, faith was one thing that Mei, for all his failings, wasn't short of. In his letter, he had taken the opportunity to tell Meinwen about his latest campaign – an attack on a new website of a youth movement which was using slang Welsh, full of English words, in some misguided attempt to be relevant to young people while promoting sex education. Mei and his fellow campaigners wanted the website put into standard Welsh or else removed altogether for fear of it corrupting the language of the youth of Wales. It was all a deliberate conspiracy to destroy the Welsh language, he said. Meinwen wondered whether the computerless Mei even knew what a website was, and whether he really would prefer the youth of Wales to be infected with venereal diseases than with English vocabulary. A hypothetical question. There was only one answer to that. The language protest was in Mei's DNA. If there was a cyberspace equivalent of green paint, then Mei would be out there using it.

Dewi had written, of course, almost every day. He had been mystified and disturbed by Meinwen's actions to begin with, and was dismayed by her sudden departure from his life. But he was now her unquestioning supporter, and had moved into Yr Hafan to look after her home while she was away. He rather liked the didgeridoo, he told her, trying to raise a smile. Meinwen, however, hadn't smiled since the night she had decided that her old campaigning methods were a waste of time, and that more drastic direct action was needed; the night she had, for the first time in her life, truly despaired.

Arianrhod had written, on headed paper from the New York hotel where she was staying while filming. Her letter, while filled with amusing media gossip intended to provide Meinwen with some entertainment during her imprisonment, nonetheless managed to mention trips – imminent or recent – undertaken by Arianrhod to five different countries. Under the circumstances, Meinwen thought it rather tactless to have recounted such a travelogue to someone whose only journeys were confined to a small prison compound. But she was not angry. She would not want to be anywhere else. Except in a free Wales, of course. But that was one journey she knew now she would never make.

Bedwyr had written. Trying to cheer her up, no doubt, he had mentioned the success of various enterprises in Gwynedd which were supporting local business start-ups and locally-owned shops. The ventures all seemed to be represented by various acronyms beginning with '*Cy*', a combination of letters with almost kabbalistic significance for Welsh nationalists, forming, as they did, the first letters of the word *Cymru* as well as *cymuned*, the word for 'community'. Bedwyr as kabbalist. Now there was a thought.

Gethin had written. Of all of them, he alone seemed to sense why she had done what she'd done. She had not told anyone of the icy realisation of defeat which had filled her on the night she had taken the hammer from the shed and gone out on her nocturnal mission, but Gethin spoke of how despair was pernicious, how it sucked the joy and hope from life and left you only longing for the long sleep of death. He knew what it was like, he said, and he urged her not to yield to it; he had come through it and had found hope. Wales was more resilient than she thought, he said. It had been written off so often, but it always survived. The current challenge was population mobility, but even as people lost touch with their roots, they came to value the idea of rootedness all the more, choosing communities of belonging with a passion and commitment. He'd done that himself. Plenty of other people were already doing it and would do it in the future, incomers included – enough of them to safeguard the language. Gethin seemed to have rediscovered the innate optimism of his own English inheritance. Meinwen, with the dark current of centuries of defeat in her veins, felt that such a hope was not only unrealistic but irresponsible.

Her parents had written. When she had been jailed before, it had been easier for them. The acts for which she had been sent to jail on those occasions had been carried out with others, in the light of day, as part of a recognised campaign with a clear goal. This was different. But they were still her parents, and still supportive. Her father had asked if, when she was released, she would accompany him to a second-hand book fair in New York. The world's biggest. He would pay for her, as he felt he needed a travelling companion because he wasn't getting any younger. It would be the chance for them to have a break. 'Dadi, *bach*,' thought Meinwen affectionately, as she read through the transparent lies. Her father was perfectly well, and had no need of a travelling companion. He clearly thought she was cracking up, and the idea of the New York trip was to get her out of Wales for a kind of rest cure. He was never any good at lying. Did he think she couldn't see through that subterfuge? Did he think she was a child? Then she thought more softly, yes, of course, that's exactly what he thought.

Sir Anthony had written. That had really surprised her. The letter was carefully worded, but it said he was sorry at the situation in which she found herself, and it expressed the hope that they would soon meet again under different and happier circumstances. It was a personal note with the letterheading of Sir Anthony's home address rather than his political office; it hadn't even gone through his official franking machine, and was carrying an ordinary stamp. He'd been very careful not to allow the letter to go through anyone else's hands or to let it be identified as a communication from him in his official capacity. Not even the Tory's most inventive political enemy could have found in its wording the slightest hint of any endorsement of what she had done. But all the same, he was taking a risk in sending it, trusting that she would not embarrass him by making it known. And of course, she thought, he was quite right; he knew he could trust her. To her surprise, she found herself recognising that, whatever their political differences might be, she knew she could trust him too.

Even Alwyn Dyfed had written, with a handsome apology for his boorish behaviour on the night when she had asked for his signature. He told her he had sent a cheque for £2,000, the whole of his recent payment of development money for a new play called *League of Lucifer* – about rugby and devil-worship – to the Movement's campaign. Meinwen, aware that this sum represented many months' drinking money for Alwyn, knew just how much that had cost him. Two grand's worth of grace.

And John Sayle had written. In his column.

But Sayle had, of course, not written in support of Meinwen. The moment the court case was finished, and the contempt of court rules banning comment on cases which are *sub judice* became inactive, he had given her the full treatment.

'On November 9, 1938, a new word entered the world's vocabulary,' he had written. 'That was the night when Hitler's Nazi thugs smashed the windows of Jewish businesses, homes and properties all across Germany. It was the start of the persecutions that were to lead to the Holocaust. On that night, there was so much broken glass in the streets that they looked as if they were paved with crystal. So that night was given its beautiful-sounding, but unforgettably sinister name – *Kristallnacht.*

'It seems a long time ago and a long way away. Wales could never breed hatred like that, could it? Wrong. On June 13 this year, Wales had its very own *Kristallnacht* as a leading Welsh language campaigner turned the streets of Caernarfon into a window-shattered warzone. Mad Meinwen Jones attacked estate agents in order to stop them selling houses; houses Welsh people want to sell in order to put much-needed money in their own pockets. She wanted to deny the Welsh people the freedom to do what they like with their own property. But most of all, she wanted to deny the English the right to do what they like with their money, which, in this case, they want to use in order to buy a share of the beauty of Wales.

'A war has started in Wales. Meinwen Jones has warned that she and her fanatics will stop at nothing until they force their twisted vision of racial purity on Wales. It won't stop with estate agents. Next it will be newsagents selling English papers. Then every business owned by English people. Then the homes of peaceful English people themselves. On June 13, Meinwen Jones inaugurated the Final Solution to the English Problem in Wales. She and the crazed thugs who support her must not be allowed to win.'

Reading it, Meinwen was reminded of Yeats' words in 'The Second Coming': 'The best lack all convictions, while the worst / Are full of passionate intensity.' Would people believe that kind of thing? The letters columns in the local newspapers which Dewi dutifully sent her seemed to suggest that plenty of them did.

●○●

Simone

Simone sat at the table in her rented room in Holland Park, writing a letter to her parents. The room, in Simone's habitual style, was bare and comfortless. It had been considerably less bare and comfortless when she had moved in, but she had insisted that the landlady take away the carpet, the curtains and all the furniture except one chair and a table. Mystified, but grateful for the rent money, the landlady had agreed. Now, the room had the cell-like quality that alone felt appropriate to Simone. The window panes were taped to prevent them shattering in the event of an air raid. The bare floorboards were covered with Simone's books and papers.

'Dearest mother and father.' she wrote. 'I hope you are well. I am so glad to think that you are safe in New York... Please don't worry about me. I'm sorry to give you cause for anxiety by coming here, but I knew I had my contribution to make. If I had more than one life, I would have spent one of them with you. But I have only one life. If I had had to stay in America I think I would have died. Either that or I would have had to go and work with the blacks in the south. I simply couldn't stay in safety while France was suffering. It would have been morally impossible. One's native land never seems so beautiful as when it's under the heel of a conqueror, if there's any hope of seeing it again intact.

'Good news. I seem to be getting somewhere with my nurses plan. De Gaulle has asked me to write a report on the post-war government of France. If I do a good job, perhaps he'll approve my nurses scheme, or perhaps he'll give me some undercover work to do in France. I've been writing night and day and sending it to him by the chapter.'

Closon

Closon was sitting at his desk, reading the latest installment of Simone's work. For a summary, it was a bit long. At this rate it would be longer than all the pamphlets put together. But Closon would not have minded that. He was entranced.

'We have a terrible responsibility,' he read. 'It is nothing less than a question of refashioning the soul of the nation, and so strong is the temptation to do this by resorting to lies or half lies that it requires more than ordinary heroism to stay faithful to the truth...

'In order to do that, the concept of rootedness, of having a vital medium, is essential. In the same way as there are certain culture beds for certain microscopic creatures, and there are certain types of soil for certain plants, so there is a certain part of the soul in every person, and certain ways of thought and behaviour passed on from one person to another which can only exist in a nation, and which disappear when a country is destroyed...

'In making the definition of one's native country as a vital medium, we avoid the contradictions and the untruths which corrode the idea of a love of one's country. We eliminate hostility or xenophobia towards other nations, because, if our own particular vital medium is all-important, then the same thing must be true of other nations. Each one deserves the right to exist because it is life-giving...

'No human being should be deprived of what the Greeks named the *metaxu*, things seen as bridges between the temporal world and the timeless: those relative and mixed blessings, such as home, nation, traditions, culture, which provide warmth and nourishment for the soul and without which, unless one is a saint, a human life is impossible...

'Conquests are not of life, they are of death as soon as they take place. It is the distillations from the living past which we should jealously preserve, in all places, whether it be Paris or Tahiti, for there are not too many such places in the whole world...

'We have no other life, no other living sap, than the treasures which are preserved from the past and digested, assimilated and created anew by us. Of all the needs of the human soul, none is more essential than the need of the past...

'Once it is destroyed, the past never returns. The destruction of the past is perhaps the greatest of all crimes. Today, the preservation of what little of the past remains should be almost an obsession... we must end the terrible uprootedness which European colonial policy almost always produces. We must abstain, once we have the victory, from punishing the conquered enemy by uprooting him even more...

'Today, every Frenchman knows what he lacked the moment France fell. He knows it as well as he knows what he lacks when he is forced to go hungry. He knows that part of his soul will stick so closely to France that when France is removed it remains stuck to her, like skin sticks to a burning object.

'So it is self-evident that one owes an obligation to one's nation. It is not our sole obligation, and it does not require us to give everything always. But it does require us to give everything sometimes.'

Closon read on; the rest of his correspondence lay on his desk, untouched.

●○●

Dewi

Dewi sat at his laptop computer in Yr Hafan, writing. But for once it was not a letter to Meinwen, nor a press release or campaign leaflet. He was writing to John Sayle.

Like Meinwen, he had despaired of traditional campaigning methods; they only seemed to create more antagonism. Like Meinwen, he had decided for the first time in his life to act on his own account, without reference to anyone else.

He couldn't bear what Sayle was saying about Meinwen. He had known her for twenty years. She had never uttered an anti-English remark; she had campaigned for every progressive cause on the planet; she lived on virtually nothing and gave all her spare income away; she would die rather than think a racist thought. That sounded a bit ominous, he thought. But then, it was true, so he would say it.

He had decided to make a personal appeal to Sayle. He had marked his email 'Private and Confidential', and he was sending it to the email address which Sayle placed at the end of his articles, a convention the newspaper for which he wrote had adopted for all its named staff contributors. Dewi was going to appeal to Sayle's better nature. Assuming he had one.

He might be rabidly anti-Welsh, but he was still a human being. Dewi was going to ask him to consider that Meinwen was also a human being, and to give her a break, to try to understand why she was doing what she was doing. Was he trying to kill her by invoking all this hatred against her? Would he only be happy when Meinwen and the Welsh language were dead? Wasn't it time to halt the hatred?

He looked at the finished message, and combed it through once more for any errors of style or grammar. Was he doing the right thing in sending this? He wasn't sure. But he'd marked it as private, and said that it was not for publication. So it couldn't do any harm. What was the worst that could happen? Sayle would know how much he was hurting them, and he might get pleasure out of that and be encouraged to do it even more. But he could hardly do more harm than he was doing already, so what was there to lose? At least there was a chance that by doing this, Dewi might ease Meinwen's suffering, and if there was anything he could do to help her, then he would do it unhesitatingly.

He pressed 'Send'.

●○●

Simone

Simone was sitting up in her makeshift bed reading the latest smuggled note from her Resistance contacts in France. She was spending more and more time in bed. Even though it was summer, she felt permanently cold, and she seemed to have less and less energy. Perhaps it was the more northerly climate of England. Perhaps she had been working too hard. Perhaps it was the strain of exile or her frustration at not being able to take part in the struggle in France itself. She didn't know. Her physical incapacity seemed to mirror the decline in her morale.

It seemed as if the beast of totalitarianism was triumphing, and her own efforts to challenge it were unappreciated and futile. Yvette Bertillon and Pierre Letellier had disappeared soon after Paris was occupied; Léon Trotsky, in exile in Mexico, had been assassinated by a Soviet agent; his son, Léon Sédov, had already suffered the same fate in Paris, their respective cities of refuge having proved unable to protect them from the long reach of tyranny. Now, Simone's letter told her that Maria Skobtsova too had just been dragged from her Paris refuge by the SS and taken to Ravensbruck concentration camp for sheltering Jews. There was no one now to care for the wretches in 77, rue de Lourmal; no one to shelter them, feed them, clothe them, or to call on hidden love to pay for coal.

There was a knock on the door. Simone struggled out of bed, threw her cloak around her shoulders and went to answer it.

In the doorway was a tired-looking old man. He was out of breath after climbing the stairs.

'Mrs Evans?' he said, uncertainly.

'I'm sorry, no. She is in the apartment below.' Simone's

English, though heavily accented, was correct. She looked with concern at the man's dishevelled clothes and his unshaven face.

'Are you all right?'

'Yes. It's just that I've never been to this building before. You see, I was bombed out last night. Mrs Evans – she's my daughter's employer – has kindly offered to let me stay with her. I must have got the flat number wrong. I'm sorry to have disturbed you, miss.'

'That's all right.'

He turned to go. Simone was about to close the door, then suddenly she called to the old man. 'Wait.'

She went into her room, and picked up her ration book from the jumble of papers on her table. She ripped out more than half the coupons and gave them to the man.

'Here, take these.'

'I can't take all these, miss! You're not leaving yourself enough to keep a sparrow alive.'

'No, really, it is enough for me.' She smiled. 'I mean it, take them.'

The old man hesitated, but then took the ration coupons and put them in his top pocket. He raised his hat to Simone, thanked her, and went back down the stairs.

Meinwen

It was post day. Meinwen was getting more mail than most of the other prisoners in her prison, something which caused some resentment among her fellow inmates. The fact that the letters were in Welsh they regarded either with derision or with the deepest suspicion. So, rather than antagonise them, or attract unwanted attention by reading the letters where others could see, she waited until she had some privacy; a scarce enough commodity in jail. However, as she frequently skipped meals, the dinner period allowed her to have some time in her cell while the others were eating. As the door closed now behind her cellmate, Meinwen brought the sheaf of letters out from the magazine where she had concealed them, and began to read. Some were simple cards from wellwishers, most of whom she knew by name, but some of whom were strangers who had read of her actions in the press. All of them were supportive. There was nothing from Dewi today. That was unusual. There was one letter left. She didn't recognise the handwriting on the envelope. The brief covering letter was little help either. It was simply signed *'Cymraes'*, 'Welshwoman'. But its message was ominous. "I thought you should see this. Please don't think too badly of him. I'm sure he was only trying to help." Enclosed was a newspaper cutting. John Sayle's column.

She scanned the article through quickly. Then she read it again, more slowly. She could not believe it. But it was true.

Sayle had published, in full, the text of an email sent to him by Dewi imploring him to leave Meinwen alone. Sayle had entitled the article 'Don't Kill my Green Virgin', and had prefaced it by saying that two fanatical campaigners had finally admitted they were cracking under the strain of their misguided activities. But that was more or less all the comment Sayle had added. For once, he had been sparing in his own eloquence. The text of the letter itself did all the damage he could have wished, and needed no further help from him.

Meinwen felt the shame drench her like the cold spray from the prison showers. What in God's name had Dewi been thinking of? A month away from her company and he'd taken leave of his senses. They may as well forget their Property Act campaign now. They looked like a pair of second-rate soap stars conducting their affairs through the tabloids. She pictured all her friends reading that; her enemies; her parents. The thought was intolerable. She closed the paper. She never wanted to read it again. She never wanted to read anything again. She never wanted to eat anything again, or see anyone again, or do anything ever, ever again.

That night, lying in her bunk, Meinwen vaguely wondered why she felt no hunger despite having missed all her meals that day. The utter despair she felt at Dewi's stupidity and Sayle's cruelty seemed to have completely killed the little appetite she had. Could you die of losing faith, she wondered. By now, she wished she really could die. Her cause was doomed; her campaign had failed; Dewi had let her down and she had been publicly disgraced. Yes, death would be better than that.

Then it came to her. She could still win. And she could escape all the pain at the same time. The plan arrived fully-formed, with all the sense of completion of a revealed destiny.

She would announce that she was fasting to death unless a Property Act was passed.

She was so well-known that she would get nationwide publicity. People would know immediately that, coming from her, this was no idle threat. The issue of a Property Act would get straight onto the front pages. It was a proven tactic. When Gwynfor Evans had given notice of his intention to go on hunger strike unless a Welsh television channel was set up, the government had given in before he'd even had to miss a meal. The public sympathy for a young – or comparatively young – woman fasting herself to death for her cause would erase all Sayle's insults at a stroke. And what's more, she knew how it would work out. The government wouldn't give in to pressure straight away. Campaigns took time to gather impetus, and a change of policy would take months at least. Unlike Gwynfor, she wouldn't give them any period of grace. She would start the fast immediately. How long had she got left of her sentence? Two months. That would be plenty. By the time the government was getting ready to allow the subject into public debate, she would be out of it. Dead. Her supporters, with her example to inspire them, and with the moral power that would buy them, would make sure the act went ahead. She would win. And she would finally be at peace.

She climbed down from the bunk, found her writing paper, and began to compose a letter to the Welsh media. It would be her last will and testament. She had no possessions to leave. But her death would buy Wales its life. She began the letter with a quotation from Simone: 'Our existence is made up only of His waiting for us to accept not to exist. He is perpetually begging from us that existence which He gives us. He gives it to us in order to beg it back from us.

'We possess nothing in this world apart from the power to say "I". This is what we should deliver up to God, and this is what we should destroy.'

Closon

When his post arrived that morning, Closon had sorted it quickly, looking for the hoped-for package from Simone. When he found it, he left the rest of the letters unopened and took Simone's manuscript to the window to read with the help of the daylight.

'All Frenchmen have come to feel the true reality of France through the fact that they have been deprived of her,' he read. 'This poignant tenderness one feels for some beautiful, precious, fragile and perishable thing has a warmth about it which the sentiment of national glory altogether lacks. The vital current which provides the inspiration for this is perfectly pure, and is extraordinarily intense. Isn't a man easily able to perform acts of heroism to protect his children or his parents? And yet there is no vestige of grandeur attached to these.'

Simone

In Holland Park, Simone was putting her plan for the front-line nurses scheme into her knapsack. She reached for the first aid manual from the shelf, but had to pause as she was racked by a coughing fit. Presently, after it had subsided, she fetched down the book, packed it in the bag, and left the flat. At the bottom of the stairs she had to wait to regain her breath again before opening the door into the street. She pulled her cloak around her and went out, looking for the bus that would take her to the street where the Free French offices were. She had decided to make a personal appeal to General de Gaulle.

Closon

In his offices, Closon was still reading, facing away from his desk towards the window.

'The thought of weakness can kindle the fire of love in exactly the same way as can the thought of strength, but in the former case the flame is of a different order of purity altogether. The compassion one feels for fragility is always connected to love of real beauty, because we are painfully aware of the fact that the existence of the things of real beauty should be assured for ever, and is not.

'One can either love France for the grandeur which would seem to secure her prolonged existence in the world of time and space; or one can love her as something which, being temporal, can be subjected to destruction, and so is all the more precious. The true earthly blessings are bridges to the divine... if we are to respect foreign nations, we must not make our own country into an idol, but make it a stepping stone to God.'

De Gaulle opened the door without knocking. Closon, with his back to the door and lost in his reading, did not see him.

'Daydreaming, Closon?'

'No, General!' Closon turned round and came to attention. Taken by surprise, he spoke impromptu.

'Mademoiselle Weil... the study you asked her to write.'

De Gaulle looked blank.

'The young Jewish girl who wanted to be a front-line nurse.'

De Gaulle now registered recognition, although with the slightest curl of the lip, as though he would have liked to have been sarcastic but thought it in bad taste.

'The study you asked her to write on the duties of France after the war – she's been sending it to me by the chapter. I've just been reading it.'

'And?'

'And it's... breathtaking. The depth, the clarity of her vision of what a nation should be – its importance to the human soul. It makes these things...'

He looked around at the flag and the maps on the wall.

'Forgive me, Sir, it makes them look like children's toys.'

De Gaulle frowned, but Closon could see that his own conviction of Simone's extraordinary insight had made some impression on his leader. And he knew the general was too much the pragmatist to waste anything so potentially useful even if he did not fully appreciate it himself. De Gaulle thought for a moment and came quickly to a decision.

'So. If she can write so powerfully, let's make sure she's on our side. France will need to re-fashion its soul after this war. Ask this girl to come in. Tell her I'll meet with her personally.'

Closon nodded.

Simone

In the street outside, the bus pulled over to the kerb. Simone got out, and looked down the street to where the tricolour marked the Free French headquarters a block away. She set off in the direction of the building, but it suddenly seemed an inordinately long way off. It even seemed to be getting further away. The buildings around were changing their perspective too, swaying. Simone walked a little way forward, then another coughing fit racked her body. She took a few more paces, but then collapsed to the pavement. Passers-by clustered round her. She was at the entrance to the Free French building. Overhead, in her fading vision, the tricolour swayed in the breeze.

Meinwen

Meinwen sat at her desk re-reading her letter. In the morning, she could ask the duty officer to post it for her. She was fully aware that this would become a sacred text. This was her *Buchedd Garmon,* her 'Gettysburg Address,' her 'I have a dream' peroration. It had to be good. And it was. Meinwen knew her prose style was effective, and she knew this was a good example of it. The best work she'd ever done, perhaps. Certainly the last she'd ever do.

She felt a frisson of pride at the thought of how these words would be memorised, recited, turned into posters and postcards. Perhaps her face would appear on them as well, stylised like a kind of Welsh Che Guevara. Mei Guevara, perhaps. That would put one over on Arianrhod, albeit by drastic methods. Now she, not Arianrhod would be the poster girl. Her image could make an attractive range of merchandise. She should set up a franchise. Pity she couldn't benefit from it.

She felt a pang of guilt too. People would think she'd left this life reluctantly. They'd cry for her. People who'd never known her would mourn for her. And yet she was glad to be dying. She felt no regret at leaving Wales, or at leaving life, which was one and the same thing to her. If she lived she'd have to watch the language die, speaker by speaker, house by house, farm by farm, with every last opportunity to save it wilfully missed and missed again by those entrusted with governing Wales. She couldn't bear that. But if she died, the language might live. There was no argument really. She didn't even mind the fasting. For years she had found little or no pleasure in eating. This hunger-strike was only taking that to its logical conclusion, and, this time, finally, with the justification of a clinching moral imperative.

She put the letter on the bedside cabinet ready for posting. She thought she would lie down for a while. She kicked off her prison-issue shoes. As she did so, she remembered her hiking shoes, now in safe keeping in the prison lockers with the rest of her few personal belongings. Dadi had been right after all: they would last a lifetime.

●○●

The Doctor

The windows of the ward at Ashford Sanatorium were open, but the day was so windless that the white curtains hung straight and unmoving. The sunlight streaming through onto the polished wooden floors made oblique mirror-like rectangles, alternating with stark blocks of shadow. At the far end of the ward, where the windows opened on the rolling Kent countryside, there was a bed. In it was a dark-haired figure.

At the entrance to the ward, the doctor was discussing the case of the sanatorium's strange young French patient with the senior nurse. He frowned at the case notes, as he spoke in a lowered voice.

'Second stage tuberculosis. In both lungs.' He shook his head. 'How long has she been like this?'

'Probably months,' said the nurse. 'She's been neglecting the condition. If she even knew she had it. She's certainly been neglecting her food. We can't get her to eat anything. She's only thirty four. It's as if she's lost the will to live.'

The doctor looked past her at the figure in the bed.

'Let's hope not,' he said. 'And she's a professor of philosophy? I'm not sure that this is the best place for her in that case. Does she know it's mainly workers we treat here?'

'Yes, doctor. I told her that myself. But she just smiled and said that she couldn't think of a better place to be.'

'Hm. Well, wherever she is, she won't get better unless she takes some nourishment. There's no language difficulty, I take it?'

'No, doctor. She can speak English perfectly well.'

'All the same...' The doctor thought for a while.

'She's with the Free French, isn't she?' he said. 'I wonder if someone there can persuade her to co-operate with the treatment. I'll make some further inquiries.'

He handed back the case notes and left.

Simone

Simone, her eyes turned towards the open window, heard the nurse walking down towards the bed where she lay.

The nurse looked with concern at the untouched bowl of soup on Simone's tray. She sat down.

'Please, Miss Wile, try to eat something.'

Simone just smiled. The nurse tried to offer her some soup with a spoon, but Simone turned her head aside. The nurse gave up and took the tray away.

Simone continued to gaze out through the open window of the sanatorium. The apple trees in the garden outside reminded her of her parents' garden in Neufchateau, where she had sat that time with her soldier. Like then, it was now late August; the summer had reached its zenith and the year was balanced between increase and decay, as motionless as the still air. From now, there would be no more growth, no more freshness. But, just for this moment, there was perfection.

Meinwen

What would they all think of her? Meinwen was considering how her death would affect her friends. Mallwyd would make a saint of her, that was for sure. She'd be up there with Ann Griffiths and Mari Jones of Bala. She'd probably get a statue. A book for certain. Bedwyr, Arianrhod and Gethin? They'd acquire more gravitas, an air of sad destiny imparted by their long friendship with Meinwen the Martyr. That probably wouldn't do them any harm. Rather the contrary. Vicarious martyrdom: they'd get all the respect without having to die themselves. The best of both worlds.

What about her parents? She had been trying not to think of that. Her father would have to go to that second-hand book fair by himself. But she knew, that without his daughter to share his discoveries, he would never buy another book again. Neither would her mother keep any interest in the relationships of Meinwen's contemporaries. She would never take any interest in anything any more. Her attention would move from the births and marriages to the obituaries. Meinwen would be killing her parents too, just as surely as if they went on hunger-strike themselves. She closed her eyes at the thought. She couldn't allow herself to think of it. This was her life. She had to spend it as she saw best. Her parents had always taught her to follow her principles. That was what she was doing now. She could only hope they would understand.

And Dewi?

Dewi.

What would happen to him? He loved her; she knew that now. It was something she had pushed from her conscious-ness, something postponed to await a better day that never came. Now that there were no more days to come, she realised that what had motivated him to write to Sayle was love. She had refused to acknowledge that love, even to herself. But now the realisation came to her that she had really always known that he loved her. And as the extremity of her current situation dissolved her habitual mental defences, she admitted to herself that there was something else she had always known but could only now acknowledge: that she loved him.

She felt a piercing sense of protectiveness towards him, a feeling of responsibility she had never known before, and yet which felt more familiar, more true than her customary detach-ment. She'd seen already what her sudden absence had caused him to do. What if that absence was permanent? He'd never forgive himself. He'd never get over it. Did she have the right to do that? She couldn't bear the thought of the pain that would never leave his gentle eyes. Only now, when their relationship had no future, could she see how much she meant to him, and he to her.

She thought of how the darkness would soon close round her as one sense after another shut down through lack of nourishment. She recalled reading the story of the Maze prison hungerstrikers in the 1980s, and their slow descent into incapacity and death. That time would come in a few weeks. If she wished, she could guess the number of hours she had left before her heart stopped beating and the darkness swallowed her. And then...? There wouldn't be a then. There wouldn't be anything. She shivered at the overwhelming fact. Suddenly, she longed to feel Dewi's arms around her, to hold him, and be held.

●○●

The Chaplain

The door of the ward creaked open, and the visitor walked the slow length of the ward towards Simone's bed. She was lying without movement, still looking out of the window. A slight breeze had arisen and the curtains were blowing gently.

'Mademoiselle Weil?'

Simone turned her head at the sound of the French language. The visitor wore the uniform of a Catholic chaplain in the Free French forces, so he knew his purpose was evident. He sat down and took her hand. She did not protest.

'They told me you were here,' he said. 'Can I do anything for you?'

Simone smiled gently.

'I'm sorry, Father. I'm not of your faith.'

Her tone seemed to suggest more regret than recalcitrance, the chaplain thought. This was consistent with what he had been told.

He knew the rules of his church. But he was a battlefield chaplain. He knew that what happened in front-line fighting was messy and unpredictable and didn't fit the military manual; and he knew that what passed between a soul *in extremis* and one of God's ministers was no business of the central authorities. He'd absolved the foulest blasphemers, and anointed avowed atheists as they'd left this world. He'd prayed with dying German prisoners, the Latin words of contrition bridging the barriers of language even as compassion bridged those of enmity. God would understand. This sanatorium might not exactly be a battleground. But, God knew, this soul needed him.

'My daughter, your background does not matter. I've been told about your desire for baptism. In a case like this... we... we never know when our time may come. Can I offer you the blessed sacrament?'

Simone looked out of the window again. When she spoke, her voice was almost inaudible.

'Thank you. But it's not permissible for me. I desire it. But for that reason, I'm not fit to receive it. I can see his sacrament from a distance. That's all I can expect.'

It seemed as though, even with her existence reduced to little more than a whisper, anxiety and assurance were still at war within her.

But the chaplain could see that the time for arguments was over. He sat, holding Simone's hand, saying nothing. The wind stirred the curtains. Simone's eyes had closed. It looked as if she had forgotten he was there.

After a while, he decided she must be sleeping and that there was no more he could do, so he rose from his seat and started to release his hand, only to feel her fingers tighten on his.

'Please,' she said, without opening her eyes. 'When I was a little girl, I held a soldier's hand. I was just remembering it now.'

The chaplain sat down again. He took both her hands in his.

Simone's voice continued, speaking no longer to the priest, but to herself, as if continuing some interior dialogue. A dialogue that was now reaching a conclusion.

'I don't want this world to fade from my view at all,' she was saying. 'I just wish it didn't have to show itself to me personally any more. It can't tell me its secret – it's too high...'

The priest knew the power of words. He also knew when words were powerless. He stayed silent, holding Simone's hand. She was still speaking, her voice now quieter than ever.

'I have to disappear so it can be seen... Wherever I am, I disturb the silence by my breathing and... the beating of my heart.'

He looked at her pale fingers in his own. The hand was rather small and slightly misshapen. In his mind, he prayed for this strange girl, so far from home, so close to eternity.

He could not remember how long he had been sitting like that when he gradually realised that the hand he held had grown cold. He looked up at Simone. The anxiety had finally departed from her face. Only the tranquillity remained. She had gone.

It was late afternoon; the stark contrasts of white light and black shadow in the ward had disappeared, and the light that now slanted in through the tall windows had softened to gold. The priest slowly released his hand from Simone's and laid hers on her chest. He did the same with her other hand. Then he straightened up and made the sign of the cross.

Meinwen

It had been a long night. With the sleep of death only a few weeks away, Meinwen felt no desire to waste in slumber too many of the few hours left to her. She had lain awake for hours, with the memory of all the good things she was leaving behind running like a home movie on the screen of her mind.

Sunrise through her uncurtained window; sunset on the estuary below Bryn Aur. The scent of heather on the air when she stepped out of Yr Hafan in the morning, and in the evening, the sound of the wind under the door. The warm spring sun on her face; the rough wool of her frayed old jumper. The familiar solicitude in the voices of friends and family, and the unexpected friendliness of strangers. The minutiae of her neighbours' lives chronicled in the weekly paper; the serious, patient company of her books. Watching the street from a pavement café; watching the fields from the window of a bus. The thoughts prompted by every corner of the landscape she loved; the memories so intertwined that she no longer knew which were her own and which were other people's, their stories all interwoven into one web of belonging.

This dying business was going to be harder than she'd thought. She had anticipated the curtains falling gracefully, not this wrenching forced exile which was dragging her from her home like one of the villagers of Tryweryn; this destiny which was driving her from her hearth, destroying the building behind her while she watched, helpless. She wanted everything to stay the same: Hermon to stay open for ever; the Crew to stay together; the Movement to be always campaigning, and always winning; Wales to be the warm community that she knew from her childhood; Dewi to be always there.

She thought of all the occasions they had been together. Closer than comrades. Closer than brother and sister. As she contemplated her death, she found herself re-running their conversations, their years of companionable, unexploited proximity and easy, unexpressed intimacy, and she now revised those times with regretful hindsight: grieved by every word unspoken, pained by every touch foregone.

She slept at last, but restlessly. She saw the headlines telling of her sacrifice. She saw pictures of herself on posters and magazine covers, the respectful reproductions of her last, heartbreaking letter. It was too late to take anything back. The waters were rising and everything familiar to her was being drowned under a still lake, and she would never know anything else, ever again. She tried to think of her loved ones: her parents, Dewi. But their faces were blurred as though seen through water.

Yr Hafan was drowned, with all its posters, all its books and all its hopes. Hermon was drowned, with its polished seats and its musty hymnbooks. 'Save me, O Lord, for the waters have risen even unto my soul.' She tried to bring Jesus' face before her mind. Where was he now when she was, at last, following his example to the full? His face was blurred too. And Simone. Here was Meinwen following her path to immolation, and she felt no fire of inspiration, only a cold, damp, pervasive dread. In her mind, she saw that poster of Simone's face, with its enquiring look, its enigmatic half smile. It had no answers for her, only questions. All the prayers she had ever heard, all the hopes that had inspired her – they were all worthless. None of them were any comfort to her. They were just noise, like the monotonous drumming she had heard at the protest in Haverfordwest, when she had leaned back against the oak tree with James Hudson.

She could see the shaman's face clearly. More clearly than any of the previous swimming images. 'Everything must change,' he had said.

Everything must change.

The realisation hit Meinwen like a blow. Only now, when it was too late, did she understand what that phrase had meant.

It didn't mean she should accept her personal destruction fatalistically; neither did it mean the Movement's belief that circumstances could be forced to fit their ideology, against all the evidence; neither did it mean standing like a sandcastle, insisting that it would be the waves that would have to yield in the end. No, it meant recognising that mutability was inevitable; it meant riding the waves of transformation, working with the forces of change, channelling them to directions consistent with survival, and changing with them when necessary. Immutability could only result in death. Being flexible, adapting oneself, that was how to survive.

The water wasn't the enemy. The water meant survival. Nothing was so yielding, but at the same time nothing was so persistent, so penetrating, so inexorable as water. It could crush; it could caress; it could kill; it could cleanse. But it always remained water, keeping its own nature, insisting on its own way through good and ill. If she had only known this before. If she had her time again, she wouldn't use the tactics of the sand-castle, but the tactics of the water – giving here, gaining there; sometimes a droplet, sometimes a breaker; sometimes a still lake, sometimes a storm; sometimes pure, sometimes polluted, but always remaining itself, and always surviving. The thing was as essential as the instinct of life which had first dragged itself from liquid to land – evolve, adapt, but always, through every-thing, live.

It was as if the monochrome world of her interior life had suddenly turned technicolour. The places, the people were the same, but now, it was all far more complex, more nuanced, more beautiful, and far more real. The black-and-white verities vanished, and were now instantly, permanently obsolete. It was impossible now to imagine thinking that way again. At the same time, the way forward in the new landscape was preternaturally clear. No more stony-faced resistance; no more inflexible, brittle integrity; no more powerless purity. From now on, victory, not virtue would be her guiding principle. She would still be implacable where necessary. But only where necessary. Now, if it meant gaining ground, she would yield an argument; if it meant advancing the cause, she would retreat from a fixed posi-tion; if it meant frustrating an enemy, she would make them an ally; if it meant keeping the faith, she would challenge the most cherished beliefs of her oldest friend. If it meant survival, she would confront or confide, besmirch or befriend. And through it all, she would be more herself, and truer to the cause than she had ever been. No more obsessive plucking at her conscience's one-stringed harp. Now she knew the cause would be better served by a liberated life than a self-denying death.

But for her, the lesson had come too late. By now, all Wales knew of her determination to die. Talk about hindsight.

She woke up.

The cell. The ceiling. The lightbulb. How many times had she woken to that sight? Well, there wouldn't be many more.

She looked round. The door with the viewing hole. The window with the security mesh. The plain white bedside table.

With her letter to the media lying on it.

Unposted.

Meinwen sat up, her heart racing, and her hands tingling with excitement and relief. Of course, she had only been dreaming that she had already sent the letter – anticipating the effect it would have. Thank God she'd had that dream before letting the letter go. Thank God. She could still see James Hudson's profile in her mind. What was that other thing he had said to her? Yes. 'Be wise as serpents, innocent as doves'.

Now she understood. Now she knew what she had to do.

She reached for the letter, picked it up, and tore it in two.

●○●

Perrin

Father Perrin had just arrived back at his presbytery after mass when there was a knock at the door. It was Thibon. The landowner carried a thick bundle of yellow notebooks under his arm. Perrin motioned him through into the presbytery kitchen, where they sat down at the table. Like all the Dominicans' domestic quarters, the kitchen was sparsely furnished. Thibon placed the notebooks on the table.

'I was just praying for her soul,' Perrin said.

'I do the same,' said Thibon. 'And a great soul it was.'

Perrin looked at the notebooks.

'They're hers,' said Thibon. 'She left them with me.'

They were the unmistakeable yellow-covered volumes used in the *École Normale*. Perrin smiled as he recognised them.

'She never really stopped being a student, did she?' he said.

'No', said Thibon. 'But what a student. These notebooks: they're full of her diaries, thoughts, arguments, insights. I'm going to edit them for publication. I thought perhaps you'd like to help? There's an immense amount of material.'

'So I see,' said Perrin.

He picked up one of the volumes at random, recognising the tiny cramped writing of Simone's small hand. He read to himself for a few moments. Then he looked up.

'Of course I'll help,' he said. 'It's our duty to make her known to others. We had the privilege of knowing a saint.'

Thibon opened another of the notebooks.

'But she's not a saint our church would ever recognise,' said Thibon. 'There are things in these books... Listen to this.'

He quoted: '"Father, in the name of Christ, grant me this. That I may not be able to will any bodily movement, or even any attempt at movement, as though I were paralysed. That I may not be able to receive any sensation... That I may not be able to connect two thoughts in the slightest... Father in God's name, grant me all this in truth. Strip away my will, strip away my sensibility, my intelligence, even love if that is something that is part of me, not part of you."'

Perrin looked pained. Thibon read on.

'"May it all be devoured by God, transformed into the substance of Christ, and given as food to men whose body and soul are without every kind of nourishment. Father, since thou art the Good and I am nothing but mediocrity, tear this body and soul away from me to make them into things for your purpose, and let nothing still remain of me, forever, except this tearing itself, or else nothingness."'

'Poor Simone,' said Perrin. 'But I don't think you need worry God would ever grant that prayer. I think He's kinder than she suspected.'

'I suppose you're right. But I hope she was granted a peaceful passing.'

Perrin nodded his reassurance.

'One time she said to me she was a badly cut-off piece of God, but soon she would be united, and reattached. She's with her Maker.'

Perrin looked back at the notebook he was holding, and read

quietly: "'We only possess what we renounce; what we do not renounce escapes from us... God, who is nothing but love, has not created anything apart from love.'"

The two friends looked at the stack of notebooks, remembering.

●○●

Meinwen

Dewi was going to be Meinwen's first visitor. As soon as she had been sentenced, she had sent the necessary card to the Prison Service giving him the right to visit her. He had spent the following fortnight putting some kind of order on Meinwen's affairs, which had been abandoned by her in such a drastic fashion. He had also, of course, sent that disastrous email to Sayle. Now, with those tasks – the helpful and the unintentionally destructive – completed, he had made the long journey to Meinwen's place of incarceration.

Meinwen wanted to see him for a host of reasons. But the main one was so she could tell him she had forgiven him for that email. However unwise his action might have been, she understood why he had done it, and she needed to let him know that everything was all right. She had already written to him to tell him all that, but she had to say it face-to-face as well. He would need to see with his own eyes that their relationship was unimpaired. Poor Dewi must be feeling terrible. Strange that the prisoner should be feeling compassion for the visitor, but that's how things were this time. For the time being, other matters, such as how to revive the Property Act campaign, could wait.

She waited for him by the table in the visiting room. People were talking in pairs at some of the adjacent tables; in some cases, prison officers stood nearby watchfully. Meinwen felt as excited as if she was on a first date, and it was a long while, a very long while, since she'd felt like that. Having looked into the empty face of death, and not looked away, she now felt a strange, irrepressible vitality. Even the visiting room and its occupants looked beautiful. She felt as if she had been saved from the gallows. Her life was all before her. But first, she had to restore Dewi.

Meinwen saw him come in with the prison officer, who pointed at her table. Dewi came over and sat down. To Meinwen's surprise, he did not look as penitent or downcast as she had expected from his apologetic letter following the débâcle with Sayle's column. On the contrary, he looked as if he was hiding some secret excitement.

'It's OK,' he said, as he pulled a chair up to the table. 'We can speak Welsh. They said you weren't high security, so there's no need to monitor you.'

'Good.' Meinwen came straight to the point. 'Dewi, please don't worry about that email. I know why you wrote it, and I know you were only trying to help. I don't hold it against you for a single moment.'

Dewi looked down.

'Thank you, Meinwen,' he said. 'You're more generous than I deserve. Thank you for forgiving me.'

Confession, absolution. It was all in the past now.

He looked up at her.

'I've got something to show you,' he said.

He pulled a piece of paper from inside his jacket, and passed it across the table to Meinwen.

She read the words. It was a print-out of an email. A different email this time. One sent *to* Dewi not *by* him. It was only one paragraph, and it only took Meinwen a few seconds to read it and understand its significance. She closed her eyes.

'Thank you, God,' she said.

Six weeks later, the day came for Meinwen's release from jail. It was a busy day too. She was travelling back to Wales by train, and then she had been booked for an interview on *Wales on Wednesday* that evening. A 'one-plus-two'. They would be talking about the issue of affordable homes, and the far-reaching new measures introduced by the Assembly Government that day to address the problem.

Meinwen had been given a foretaste of the measures, as the programme makers had called her to read her a *Western Mail* preview story on the subject. It had said that the Assembly's Communities Committee was considering a new bill for a comprehensive package of measures. It was sponsored by the

Welsh Assembly Government and had the personal backing of Haydn Davies. No doubt in an effort to make it seem as different as possible from the Movement's 'Property Act', the administration had chosen to call the package the 'Community Housing Act'. It would apply to all parts of Wales, and had two main parts.

Firstly, there was an adaptation of a scheme already in operation in parts of England, in which councils could build houses for local people only, offering the homes for an affordable price on the condition that they were, in future, only sold on to local people, and for an affordable price again, in perpetuity. Substantial amounts of public money were being made available to make this possible.

The second element of the measure was to promote Common Land Trusts, where community groups, including local councils, could buy houses, freehold or leasehold, for social provision, letting them for affordable prices by taking the purchase price out of the deal. The trusts would then administer the properties in line with local community needs. Once again, the significance for Welsh-speaking communities was obvious. Again, this was not the Movement's 'Property Act' in name either, but, although its legal structure was different, it would be sure to have something like the same effect, namely affordable housing for local people. Crucially, it too was to be backed by a powerful and ongoing fund of public money, enabling the community groups to buy the land.

Taken together, they were everything the Movement could have wanted. The papers, ignoring the government's carefully-chosen form of words, were already calling the measures 'The Property Act'. Even given the continued tendency of many young people to migrate from the country, this would at least allow those who wanted to remain to have a viable future, and that would mean the language would have a viable future too.

Meinwen was delighted with this news. It seemed to coincide closely with the vision she had experienced in the prison, of turning the waters of history to the service of the language, making the forces of the modern world work in its favour. But as she hadn't had the chance to promote her ideas yet, she was mystified as to how the Movement's stalled campaign could have brought about this sweeping advance, and so suddenly. Her mind was filled with questions, but she would have to wait until she got back home before she could start getting the answers.

'Tea, coffee, soft drinks, snacks?'

It was a train steward with the trolley service making her way through her carriage. Out of long habit, Meinwen looked away.

'Have you got any cakes or biscuits?'

It was a middle-aged lady on the opposite side of the aisle. The trolley steward looked down for a quick inventory of her compact mobile store.

'Jamaican ginger cake. Highland oatcake biscuits. Fruit Shrewsbury.'

As the passenger made her choice, Meinwen thought about the connotations of those names. 'Jamaican' sounded congenial to her; it was anti-establishment, a bit radical, with a minority vibe. But wasn't there also a bitter little spice of empire in that connection too? 'Highland' felt homely, though; worthy, gritty and Celtic. 'Shrewsbury,' no way: English, and a border strong-hold of the Marcher lords at that; the place where Dafydd ap Gruffydd had been executed for rebellion in 1283. Meinwen felt the incoming tide of resentment. But then she suddenly felt the familiar flow of anger repelled by an unforeseen barrier of sheer distaste at her own exhausting ethics. God, even her food was political. She was sick of living like a character in a morality play.

'Can I get you anything?' the trolley steward was asking her.

'Yes, please,' Meinwen found herself saying. 'I'll have a cup of tea.'

'Anything else?' said the steward as she handed her the hot plastic cup.

Meinwen hesitated a moment. Then she said: 'Yes, please. A Fruit Shrewsbury.'

The steward handed her the packet, took her payment and moved on. Meinwen unwrapped the biscuit from its cellophane, and took a small bite. Not bad. Rather nice in fact.

She took a slightly larger bite, sipped her tea and sat back. The train rattled on towards Wales, towards the future, towards Dewi.

As Dewi and Meinwen signed in at reception in the television studios that evening, they found themselves standing next to Sir

Anthony Thomas. He was returning his identification card.

'Hello Meinwen,' he said, 'welcome back to the straight and narrow.'

His smile had a trace of mischief, but not of hostility. Meinwen simply gave him an ironic look.

'I'm glad to see you looking so well,' he went on. 'You've put on a bit of weight if I'm not mistaken – and if that isn't rather an ungallant thing to say of course. I always said our prison regime was too soft. You've obviously thrived on it.'

He seemed in unusually good spirits.

'Thank you,' said Meinwen. 'Leaving already?'

'Yes, I've been doing a radio interview about the new Property Act. The *proposed* new act, I should say.'

Meinwen thought of Sir Anthony's generosity to her on that television programme some months ago, and the letter she'd received in prison. But she didn't want him to think that one act of kindness, and a rather patronising one at that, meant that they were now friends. Even with the relief she now felt, she was long habituated to letting public affairs dictate private affections. So she said: 'You'll be opposing it, no doubt.' As she felt the instinctive sarcasm in her voice, she was annoyed with herself. He deserved better than that.

However, Sir Anthony seemed impervious to her apparent scepticism.

'Well, I don't know about opposing it,' he said. 'That would be a bit of an own-goal really, considering it was I who got it onto the agenda of the Communities Committee in the first place.'

Meinwen and Dewi stared at him. Sir Anthony continued conversationally, enjoying the advantage he had over them.

'Of course, Haydn Davies wasn't keen on allowing the bill onto the agenda at all. But when I told him that in that case we'd withdraw our support for his measure to increase Assembly Members' allowances, he had – how can I put it? – a change of heart.'

'You got it onto the agenda? But I thought you were *against* a Property Act.'

'I was. I certainly didn't like the idea of restricting people's right to sell the existing housing stock on the free market. And I certainly opposed your campaigning methods. But as for the broad aim of preserving the language in the community, I agreed with that. I assume you don't object to accomplishing the aims by different means.'

'I suppose not,' said Meinwen warily.

Sir Anthony went on: 'You wanted to get it on the agenda through civil disobedience. I used a bit of civility. You wanted to do it through sit-down protests, I did it through a sit-down meal. Haydn is quite an interesting chap when you get to know him. Good company. And full of goodwill towards the Welsh language too. You'd be surprised.'

He was right. Meinwen and Dewi were more than surprised. The Tory continued.

'He's very fond of fishing as well. There's a particularly good stretch of fishing on my parents' estate, and I've offered him the use of it during the recess. I doubt if he'll take me up on it – it mightn't play too well with his constituents – but I think he appreciated the offer all the same.'

Meinwen was trying to digest what she was hearing. She was too surprised to think of what to say.

Sir Anthony began to button up his coat, while he continued:

'And he's agreed to spend the day at the Denbigh and Flint Agricultural Show this summer, and I've arranged for him to meet a range of local organisations there. Carefully chosen ones, of course. After he's spent a bit of time in a Welsh-speaking rural area, I'm sure he'll be much better placed to speak in support of the bill in the Senedd. He's already convinced himself it was his idea.

'Oh, by the way, I'm trusting you to have the good sense not to mention this to anyone...' said Sir Anthony.

His listeners nodded.

Sir Anthony wasn't one to show his feelings, but his readiness to talk about this stroke of policy showed how pleased he was with his own acumen. He could not expect congratulations from Dewi and Meinwen, but it was clear that his own inner esteem sustained him. There was more than the usual brightness in his eye. He smiled at the two campaigners with a touch of complacency.

'But what did you get out of this?' asked Dewi. 'You just did this out of the goodness of your heart, did you?' Old habits died hard with Dewi too.

'Well you might be surprised that some politicians aren't

entirely untouched by a spirit of altruism, Dewi,' said Sir Anthony. 'Some of us do try to make a difference with our activities, you know. But since you ask, a committee chairmanship for me was part of the deal.'

'Which committee?'

'The Languages of Wales Committee. Or perhaps I should give it its new name: the Welsh Language Committee. It's reverting to its original brief. That was part of the deal, too. It's being announced tomorrow.'

'But what about – what's her name – Gloria Milde?'

'Ah, yes. Well, Ms Milde has been thanked for her excellent work on the committee and has been rewarded with a strong indication that she'll get the chairmanship of the External Relations Committee. It's coming vacant in a few months. It was felt it would... play more to her strengths. I don't think she was too disappointed. In fact, I think she rather relished it. It'll involve quite a bit of foreign travel.'

'So you're Mr Welsh Language now?'

'No, no, Dewi. I'm *Sir* Welsh Language.'

Dewi and Meinwen had to smile.

Sir Anthony picked up his briefcase.

'I must go.'

He straightened up and was about to leave.

Meinwen spoke without thinking.

'Thank you for the letter.'

Sir Anthony smiled, suddenly a little embarrassed.

'Not at all. I just thought... there but for the grace of God...!'

He moved quickly to the safer subject of politics, but, even as he did so, they both knew there was now a sense of shared enterprise in their conversation.

'You know,' he said. 'I do understand how you feel about the language. It's just that I think that these days it's better served by promotion than by protest. There was a time for protest when you were discriminated against, of course. But now those legal barriers have been removed, you need different tactics. Charm, not challenge.'

He stopped for a moment, struck by a sudden thought.

'Charm not challenge. That's rather good, isn't it? I think I'll use that in my first speech.'

Meinwen smiled. 'I'll look forward to hearing it. Especially with this news about the Property Act.'

Sir Anthony was clearly pleased. From Meinwen, even such brief approbation was high praise.

'It's called politics, Meinwen,' he said with an ironic smile. 'It's what I do. Try it sometime.'

He nodded his farewell and crossed the lobby to the exit.

Sometime she might, thought Meinwen, as the automatic door closed behind the departing politician. There was no doubt she had a lot to learn from his flexibility and pragmatism. That would fit with the vision she had experienced in jail. Yes, sometime she might well try it.

But not tonight.

Jayne

Jayne, who had just done Meinwen's make-up, thought her guest was even more uncommunicative than usual. But, for the first time ever, Meinwen hadn't objected to her putting on the cosmetics before the show. She had even consented to wear lipstick, which was a definite first. That was almost a cause for concern in itself. Poor thing, thought Jayne, her spirit's probably broken at last.

Meinwen left the chair without a word and went to sit in the green room where the show's other studio guest, John Sayle, was already waiting.

John Sayle

Sayle, never one for stillness or silence, looked at his watch impatiently. He was always more comfortable if he was talking. He looked at Meinwen, and looked away again. No point. He could bait her later once the cameras started rolling, when it would count for more. He was going to use his 'Taffyban' line tonight.

Meinwen didn't look as rough as he'd hoped she would after three months in jail, mind. That was a bit of a disappointment, especially after that email her fool of a boyfriend had sent. He really had hoped she would crack, especially when he'd published that message's contents. But fanaticism and obtuseness made for resilience, he supposed, and here she was back again like a bad penny. She was clearly a sight tougher than that idiot Dewi had thought.

No, there was no point in trying to talk to her. As usual, she was staring into the middle distance, taking no notice, lost, no doubt, in some private fantasy world of her own. She couldn't be bothered to make conversation. To her, non-Welsh speakers like him were unworthy of attention. The stuck-up cow.

He picked up a newspaper from the table in front of him. He flicked through it until he found his own column. He smiled to himself as he re-read it. If ever a columnist was on top of his game, it was him.

Jonathan Rees

The guests were seated behind the familiar *Wales on Wednesday* desk. The studio camera's red light was on. The floor manager began counting in, and Jonathan Rees began his opening piece to camera. The autocue began to roll

'Tonight on *Wales on Wednesday*, we're discussing housing. Things have moved on quite a bit since we last tackled this subject. The Property Act being advocated by language activists is now the subject of an Assembly committee investigation, albeit with some modifications, and seems likely to become law. And, since she was last on our programme, one of our panellists, the language campaigner Meinwen Jones, has spent three months as a guest of Her Majesty. Her fellow guest, the newspaper columnist John Sayle, has been one of her bitterest critics.'

There was a long piece of video tape tonight, which is why they could get away with just two studio guests. There'd only be about eight minutes or so left for a discussion after the film, so two panellists were plenty, especially two such as Meinwen and Sayle.

They sat there in silence as the images from the film flicked past on the monitors at the side of the set. For Sale signs. Estate agents' windows. Interviews with despondent would-be first-time buyers, aggrieved incomers, committed activists, fence-sitting bureaucrats, and finally a political analyst summarising what the

Communities Committee would be discussing, and a few graphics showing the proposal and the amount it would cost. As the film ended, Rees' autocue came on.

'Well, we've heard the issues,' he said. 'There's a problem. There's a proposal. But is it a solution?' He turned to the columnist: 'John Sayle. Is this the answer? *Is* there an answer?'

'No on both counts,' Sayle said. 'There isn't even a question. We need to see past the pious rhetoric of "communities" and "affordable housing". What's motivating this policy in Wales is racism – the sinister agenda which motivates people like my fellow panellist here.'

Rees was determined that Sayle wouldn't get an easy ride on this issue tonight. He had every right to question the panellists' viewpoints himself, within reason. He intended to exercise that right. 'But in all fairness,' he said, 'there are locals-only housing measures in existence in other parts of Britain. The Lake District for instance. And there's no language issue there. Why is it racist here in Wales?'

He could see the little curl of contempt come to Sayle's mouth as he got ready to answer. Poor Meinwen could look out now.

'It's precisely *because* of the language issue...' Sayle began.

But before the columnist could get into his stride, Meinwen interrupted. Her voice was clear and firm. 'Before we go any further, I have a question for John Sayle,' she said, turning to him.

If he was startled by this unwonted assertiveness, he didn't show it. Go on then, his eyes said. Just try it.

Without speaking, Meinwen just reached into her jacket pocket and pulled out three sheets of paper. She unfolded them and handed one to Rees and one to Sayle, keeping the third for herself.

Rees looked at the paper. Then he looked at John Sayle. Under the make-up, the columnist's face had gone pale.

'Do you recognise this piece of paper?' Meinwen said to Sayle.

He was staring at it. He recognised it all right.

'I'll read it to you,' said Meinwen pleasantly. 'It's addressed to Dewi Williams, the video librarian in the Welsh Broadcasting Records Centre. It says; "Hello Dewi. How's things? Look, I need a favour. Did you see that silly sod Mallwyd Price on *Under Fire* last night? I've been told he said something about my columns being racist. But I didn't catch the programme and I need a copy so I can make my response. If it's true, I'm really bloody annoyed about it. I saw Sohail Mohammed at a book launch this morning, and he said he'd been told about it. At least, I think that's what he said. Trying to understand him speaking English is almost as excruciating as trying to understand Mallwyd. Bloody cultural diversity. Send them all on elocution courses, I say, ragheads and sheepshaggers all! Anyway, if you can get me the tape I'd be grateful. I owe you one. Cheers, John.'"

She stopped. Everyone was looking at Sayle. There was a long pause.

Rees knew this programme was breaking all the rules, but he also knew it was fantastic television. Through his earpiece, his producer was urging him: 'Just let it run, Jonny. Let it run.' He had no intention of letting it do anything else. He was enjoying it far too much. He took a deep breath to make sure no trace of excitement would show in his voice when he spoke.

'This really was sent by you?' he asked Sayle. His air was that of a headteacher with a pupil who has done something unforgiveable. But the question was hardly necessary. Sayle's silence said everything. Rees didn't make it easier for Sayle by speaking himself. He let the silence extend a few more seconds, until the columnist was obliged to break it himself. 'Hold it, Jonny, hold it,' whispered the talkback.

'That email,' said Sayle at last, with his voice shaking. 'That email... was a private correspondence between friends. It's out of context. I can't understand how you could have had access to it. Dewi Williams would never have given it to you.'

'Dewi Williams of the records centre never got it,' said Meinwen. 'You sent it to Dewi Wiliams – one L – of the Movement by mistake. You'd corresponded with them both on email. Your email system will have kept a record of both addresses. And it would have offered you a choice of both when you typed "Dewi" in the address field. You sent this message to the wrong Dewi, the one with one L. One L of a mistake, you might say, Mr Sayle.'

Sayle had closed his eyes, no doubt reliving, for the first of what would become a million times, the oversight which had delivered him into Meinwen's hands. She was still speaking, with a chiding and deliberately patronising edge to her voice.

'You really should be more careful with new technology. And with what you say, too: "ragheads" and "sheepshaggers". Is that really what you think about ethnic and linguistic minorities in Wales?'

'In case any of the viewers don't know, Sohail Mohammed is the chairman of the Commission for Racial Equality in Wales,' said Rees, helpfully, in a matter-of-fact voice.

'And you call him a... "raghead",' said Meinwen. 'This is one of the worst examples of racism I've ever seen.'

'It's not racism,' said Sayle emptily, without looking up. 'It was banter. Jokes between old friends. It was just irony. I'm not a racist.'

'"Rag-heads". "Sheep-shagg-ers",' Meinwen read again slowly. 'Do your bosses at the newspaper know that you use your work computer to send hate mail like this?'

Sayle said nothing. Jonathan Rees stepped in. Time was up. 'Well, this has been a debate to remember,' he said, voice calm, eyes dancing. 'My thanks to the panellists, Meinwen Jones, and...' there was the slightest pause as if to suggest a change of category: 'John Sayle'.

Meinwen smiled across at Sayle brightly as she took off her radio-mic. 'Cheer up, John,' she said. 'It might never happen.'

Sayle was just staring at the piece of paper in his hand.

'Except, of course, in your case, it has.' She got up, and walked off the set.

A zone of embarrassment spread around Sayle as though he had fouled himself. Rees moved away from him without saying a word. Even the technicians hesitated to approach him to remove his radio-mic. He'd become untouchable. He sat there, unmoving in the gathering darkness, as the studio lights were switched off one by one.

Jonathan Rees

Jonathan Rees caught up with Meinwen in the corridor. For once, he thought, just for once, he'd express his own opinion, his delight at what she'd done. 'Meinwen,' he said, 'that was...' Then he hesitated – what if she repeated his comments? She'd shown how ruthless she could be. He couldn't risk compromising his impartiality. 'That was...' he searched for the appropriate neutral word.

'Don't worry, Jonathan,' said Meinwen, and put a hand on his arm. She looked at him as if they were comrades of old. 'There's no need to risk saying it. I know what you want to say: "That was bloody marvellous".'

Rees looked at her with relief. She'd understood him. She knew. She gave him a moment more of that you're-one-of-us look, and then she turned and walked down the corridor. Rees smiled as he watched her go.

Meinwen

Meinwen knew Sayle wasn't a racist in the sense she'd portrayed him. She knew that what had passed in that email was, as he'd said, merely banter between old friends playing ironically with the language of racism. But she wasn't going to let that stop her exploiting to the full the way those words looked in black and white. Copies of the email had been posted that morning, with accompanying covering letters, to the Commission for Racial Equality, to the Press Complaints Commission, to Sayle's employers, to every newspaper, magazine and broadcasting station in Wales, and to every Welsh Assembly Member and Member of Parliament. And a friendly solicitor had sent the letter to South Wales Police asking them to look into the circumstances as a possible case of incitement to racial hatred. That would complete the destructive work of the television programme.

What had Sayle once said? 'All's fair in love and politics.' Well, she thought, she'd learned something about politics, now. She'd learned not just how to fight, but how to win. Not to fight and die, but to fight and live. That was a stronger instinct. Victory was always the best answer. She had Sayle to thank for that lesson. Sayle who was now defeated – defeated completely, and for good.

Meinwen felt as if she had left a former version of herself behind her in that studio, a virginal, fastidious self. It was like having sex for the first time: the sky hadn't fallen, but the world was now a different place, and instead of the expected feeling of guilt, there was only a tingle of remembered pleasure, and of freedom. She was no longer the green virgin. She thought of Simone. She would never have done anything like that. But once again, to her surprise, Meinwen felt no guilt; the picture of Simone in her mind now seemed less like an unblinking and searching mirror-image of her own self, and more of a silent icon of another person from another age; something to admire in its austere purity, certainly, but no longer anything to emulate. Their paths, so long convergent, were now growing further apart each day.

Meinwen knew she still had a lot of learning to do, and a lot of unlearning; it would take time to find the point of balance in her new life. But she knew she would find it. In that vision in her prison cell everything had changed. As she walked on down the corridor, the words of James the shaman came back to her: 'Be wise as serpents, innocent as doves.' It was a paradox as strange as any which had inspired Simone, and as real. She carried the truth of it inside her like a secret power.

She knew now that she could survive, and so could her culture. Sometimes it might take agreement, sometimes it might take aggression; sometimes diplomacy, sometimes daring; sometimes rashness, sometimes restraint. But whatever it took, she would do it, and through engagement, now, not isolation. She didn't think she'd be living in Yr Hafan any more. It was time to come down the mountain.

Dewi

Dewi was waiting for her in reception.

He embraced her. They had never embraced. Meinwen's dislike of physical contact had prevented that. Now, as they did so, he was amazed at the thinness of her body, amazed too at the rush of tenderness he felt for her. She hugged him back, as if, now she'd got him, she wouldn't let him go. He pulled back to look at her; still she didn't pull away.

'That was fantastic, Meinwen,' he said. '*You're* fantastic.'

There. He'd said it. She smiled back at him. The fact that she still held him meant more than any words either of them could say.

Her hand slipped into his as they walked to the taxi.

'How shall we celebrate?' asked Dewi, as the taxi drove down Cathedral Road towards town. Outside, the evening was clear and dry.

Meinwen looked up from where she was resting against his shoulder.

'I know exactly what I want to do to start,' she said. 'Take me to Rhyddid, and buy me a meal.'

She smiled at his surprise.

'And then,' she went on, with a new note of intimacy in her voice. 'Then... we can talk about what we can do... afterwards.'

Something big had changed inside Meinwen. That was clear. But there was something different about her appearance, too. Her skin had lost its pallour, and her lips were glossy.

'Meinwen,' he said suddenly. 'You're still wearing your make-up!'

'Am I?' She put her hand to her mouth, shocked. In the excitement following the show, she had forgotten to wash her face.

Meinwen slowly brought her hand down from her lips, and was now staring at a tiny smear of blood-red cosmetic on her pale fingertip.

Then, without looking up, she asked, with a nervousness Dewi had never heard in her voice before.

'Does it suit me?'

'Yes,' he said, and bent his head to kiss her.

The taxi stopped outside Rhyddid/Freedom. Dewi paid the driver, and, mindful of the need to reclaim the travelling expenses, asked him for a receipt.

'Welsh speakers aren't you?' the driver said as he reached for his pen. He was a burly man in his fifties, his hair a rough silver stubble.

Dewi felt Meinwen's hand tense slightly. The driver continued; his Cardiff accent was as broad as the river Taff.

'My grandchildren go to the Welsh school in Canton,' he said. 'Bloody marvellous. Best thing that could have happened to them. I never had the chance to learn Welsh, I didn't. But the kids, they've got it for life now. Bloody marvellous.'

He was taking a little more time than seemed necessary to make out the receipt. Dewi and Meinwen smiled at him, as he finally handed the piece of card to them.

As the taxi drove away, and they turned towards the entrance of the club, Dewi looked at the hand-written message on the receipt in his hand. To the record of the date and the price, the driver had added one other line.

'*Diolch yn fawr,*' it said. Thank you very much.

● ○ ●

Pierre

The black limousine turned off the new bypass on to the main road into the town. The road was lined with trees whose leaves were bare in the cold air of late February. The car slowed as the driver checked the street names as he went past. Finding the one he was seeking, he turned in, but carefully, because the car was a left-hand drive model, designed for use on the continent, not on British roads. The street sign read: 'Simone Weil Avenue'.

In the rear seat of the car sat Pierre Letellier. It was a cold morning, and even with the heating of the limousine turned up, he had kept on his overcoat over his dark suit. At the age of ninety six, he felt the cold. He looked out thoughtfully at the passing scenes behind the slightly tinted windows of the car. There were estates of new houses with those half-timbered decorations of which the English seemed so fond. It looked like quite a prosperous area, he thought, with a faint ironic smile. The comfortable bourgeoisie. The car approached a set of wrought iron gates with the sign 'Kent County Council: Ashford New Cemetery'.

'This must be it, M'sieur Letellier,' said the driver.

The car stopped at the parking area just inside the gates, and the driver got out and helped Pierre from the seat. Once on his feet, he stood erect, fastened his overcoat, and walked slowly, but unaided, towards the path leading to the graves. The driver stayed by the car to allow his charge some time alone with his thoughts.

A man in council overalls was putting some dead flowers into a bin by the entrance. The caretaker. He came over to Pierre to ask if he needed any help. He nodded as Pierre explained what he was looking for.

'Yes, she's here,' the man said, and pointed towards a row of trees on the skyline. 'At the top, just between the Catholic section and the Jewish section.'

Pierre thanked him and walked away up the path.

Soon, he found the Jewish burials: the carved Stars of David, the menorahs, the tablets of the Law; the names – Abraham, Cohen, Levy. Then he found the Catholic section – Maguire, Donovan, Costello – and their carvings of the Sacred Heart, the Virgin Mary. Where else would she lie, he thought, except forever on the border of those two faiths?

He stopped at a single stone, set flat into the ground. The inscription was simple: *'Simone Weil, 3 fevrier 1909 – 24 août 1943'*. It was neatly kept. A few ghost-like, transparent leaves, relics of the winter whose chill was still in the air, lay on the plain grey surface. They were so attenuated that air and light could flow through them almost unimpeded.

'So you found her then, Sir?' It was the caretaker, who had walked up to join him.

He followed Pierre's gaze to the stone, and read aloud: 'Simon Weel.'

'She always pronounced it "Simone Weil,"' said Pierre quietly.

The caretaker looked at him with new interest, and no little surprise. He glanced at the dates on the gravestone and back at his visitor.

'Did you know her, then, Sir?'

'Oh, yes,' he said. 'I knew Simone Weil.'

He thought for a moment, then added.

'At least, I thought I knew her. But there was so much I did not know.'

'Well, she's our celebrity here, I know that much,' said the caretaker. 'She gets lots of visitors. Students, loads of them. And priests. Nuns. Jewish people too, sometimes. But, do you know, she never seems to get any flowers.'

'Ah,' said Pierre, with a slight smile. 'If you had known Simone, you would understand. Flowers would not be...'

He paused while he searched for the right English word.

'... permissible.'

He looked up from the gravestone at the trees swaying in the breeze overhead. It was no longer winter; it was not yet spring. The branches of the trees lay bare, without buds, in the cold air full of sunshine.

Thanks and Acknowledgements

The idea for this novel was conceived when I was writing a volume of literary criticism and cultural theory based on my doctoral work in the Welsh department of the University of Wales, Cardiff, which included a study of Simone Weil. I was struck by the way Weil's remarkable life story would lend itself to a creative narrative treatment. Therefore, a few years later, I began a novelisation, combining her story with that of a fictional present-day activist, so that issues of conscience and political engagement could be explored in a contemporary context. That book first appeared in Welsh as *Rhaid i Bopeth Newid* (Gomer, Llandysul, 2004) and was longlisted for that year's Book of the Year prize in Wales. This English version has been substantially revised and expanded, and is nearly twice the length of the original.

I have drawn on a host of different articles and publications, and I note here some of those which will be most useful to anyone who wants to learn more about Weil. I am happy to record my debt to the following studies and collections, in particular the excellent *Utopian Pessimist: the Life and Thought of Simone Weil*, by the historian of Marxism, David McLellan (Macmillan, London, 1989); it is by far the most readable one-volume study. Among the other important biographical studies on which I have drawn are: *Simone Weil: Portrait of a Self-Exiled Jew*, by Thomas Nevin (University of North Carolina Press, 1991); *Three Outsiders: Pascal, Kierkegaard, Simone Weil*, by Diogenes Allen, (Cowley, Cambridge, Massachussetts, 1983) and *Simone Weil: A Life*, by Simone Petrement, (Pantheon, New York, 1976), a friend and contemporary of Weil. For readers of Welsh, my own *Sefyll yn y Bwlch* (University of Wales Press, Cardiff, 1999), contains an extended study of Weil. Among the best-known collections of

Weil's own writings are: *Gravity and Grace, (La Pesanteur et la Grace)* edited by her friend Gustav Thibon; *Waiting for God (L'Attente de Dieu)*, edited by her friend Father Perrin, and *The Need for Roots (L'Enracinement)*, to which T.S. Eliot contributed a notable foreword. It is from those translations that the passages of this book which represent Weil's own writings have been adapted; in those cases, I have tried to keep close to Weil's own particular voice. In the collections mentioned above, as in this novel, emphasis is placed on Weil's relationship to Catholicism, but it should be noted that this is only one selective way of reading her life and thought, and that other editors have provided vastly different interpretations.

The book is based on Weil's life story, and nearly all the major characters are based on real people, although telescoping, simplification and compositing have been necessary in both narrative and characterisation. The reader is referred to the scholarly studies mentioned above for authoritative detail. In the story of Meinwen Jones, all contemporary characters and situations are imaginary, and any resemblance to real people is accidental.

I would like to thank my editor at Gomer, Bethan Mair, and my three successive editors at Seren: Will Atkins, Cary Archard and Penny Thomas, for their diligence and guidance. I am grateful also to Mark Woods for suggesting the idea of the novelisation. Ion Thomas and Owen Martell provided valuable insights while reading the Welsh version in draft form, and I am very grateful to them. My thanks also go to the many readers of the published Welsh version who provided their comments and thoughts. Much of the writing of this book was carried out with the aid of a Writer's Bursary from the Academi, the Welsh National Literature Promotion Agency, and I am glad to record my gratitude to the Academi for the grant and to my employers, BBC Wales, for allowing me the time off work. My grateful thanks also to Matt Thomas for conducting a special photo shoot in Paris to obtain the cover photograph.

Finally, I thank my wife Sally and my daughters Haf and Alaw for their patience, support and love. *Ceir llawer ffordd i'r nefoedd. Chi yw fy ffordd i.*